VANITY BLADE

DIVERSIONBOOKS

Also by Samantha Harte

Cactus Heart
Timberhill
The Snows of Craggmoor
Kiss of Gold
Hurricane Sweep
Sweet Whispers
Autumn Blaze
Summersea
Angel

Diversion Books
A Division of Diversion Publishing Corp.
443 Park Avenue South, Suite 1008
New York, New York 10016
www.DiversionBooks.com

For more information, email info@diversionbooks.com

First Diversion Books edition March 2015.
Print ISBN: 978-1-68230-091-6
eBook ISBN: 978-1-62681-660-2

Prologue

1845

From dark, low clouds, silvery bits of snow sifted onto the freezing ruts of the deserted wagon track. Hushed, and growing colder, the night shivered with the promise of winter descending from the jagged Sierra Nevada Mountains to the east.

From the bank of the rushing Sacramento River where a shallow-draft keelboat lay rotting, the lonely twisting track climbed through jumbled boulders and scattered pines to a roughhewn traders' camp called Tenderfoot, in the California Territory.

Huddled in hollows and perched on promontories, dozens of haphazard shacks and weather-darkened tents stood tensed, as if listening. From the two front windows of a larger log cabin lanternlight spilled, casting crooked yellow squares across the mud.

Over the door, a sign sliced from a pine trunk hung from a twist of rusted wire. BROKKEN ROCK SALOON had been lettered in white some years before, and RED-EYE JACK WHISKEY SOLD HERE! had been etched into the sign's edge.

Six bearded men in bedraggled fur-lined coats jostled one another as they tried to get through the narrow doorway. Snow settled on their battered sugar-loaf hats, and a rousing cheer from the saloon broke the silence.

As a wheezing concertina began squawking a lively German drinking song, the floor planks shuddered. Feet began to pound and stomp. A crowd of bright-eyed men outside cursed as they shoved and pushed their way into the already packed cabin. After a brief pause, a young woman's voice sang out high and clear.

"Give me plenty of cheer, boys! Give me all ya got! Heaven's mighty far, boys! But hell is nice and hot!" With a raucous chuckle, she stamped her heels.

Up the track, the plank doors to three ramshackle, drafty cribs fell open. The patrons stumbled out, tucking shirttails into baggy-kneed britches and hopping into mud-crusted boots.

In a nearby rain-stained tent the shaggy heads of four gents playing poker jerked up. Seconds later, the frayed cards drifted to the rumpled gray blanket on the ground, and the players departed.

Men from nearly every shack hurried through the freezing darkness to get to the Brokken Rock, only to find a line out the door.

Inside, there wasn't even room enough to spit. On the far wall, the plank-and-beer-barrel bar closed for the show. A bartender in a stiff derby hat and red sleeve garters settled back with a sigh. He rubbed his blue eyes, which ran constantly from Pearlman's Royal Stogie smoke, and chuckled as he thought of how much cash the little lady brought in.

Every man in the place watched the petite young woman strut and prance around the black potbellied stove. When she circled near them, they drew back, holding their breath, but once she swirled by, they edged forward again, their bodies heavy with yearning.

The thick heels of her red high-button shoes clattered on the whipsawed floor planks. She held her yellow satinet skirts high to reveal generous red petticoat ruffles and dark-patterned stockings on her shapely legs.

With a saucy wink and a mischievous glint in her eye, she tossed back her long tangle of dark gold hair, which still bore crimping marks. Her soft cheeks were rouged almost the same color as her gaudy petticoats, and her scarlet lips glistened when she licked them.

As she twirled, she lost awareness of the traders, trappers, and mountain men. She danced with abandon, thinking only of her body, her beautiful hair falling across her face, and her heart beating with excitement. She was young! She knew she was very pretty, and each time she circled the saloon the men whispered her name as if to a lover. Vanity. Vanity! *Vanity!*

She loved the sound of her chosen name. She wanted to dance forever! "Give me plenty of cheer!" she shouted, gasping for breath. Then she strutted, tossing her skirts so that her legs showed to the tops of her lacy garters where the plump, pale flesh of her thighs beckoned. "Give me all ya got!"

With a squeal, she bent forward, flipping her skirts up to expose rows of red ruffles sewn to her short, snug under-drawers. She could feel the men's eyes burning into the backs of her legs.

A frenzied whoop filled the saloon. The men clapped, tossed their hats, and choked on their cheers as plugs of tobacco dislodged from inside their cheeks. Coughing and guffawing and shouting her name, they wiped their mouths with their sleeves and threw heavy gold coins at her feet.

Vanity straightened, and her skirts settled about her once again. A wave of discomfort rippled through her, and puzzlement tensed her flushed young face.

Noticing the expression on her face, the men surged forward, crowding her dangerously close to the glowing potbelly.

But the odd, deep tensing of her muscles eased, and Vanity resumed her bawdy song, skipping among the coins like a wood nymph. "…but hell is nice and hot!" she sang, delighted with the effect her words had on the men.

The coins on the floor caused her to skid and laugh. The claret-faced German gentleman squeezing and yanking the melody from the silver-trimmed mahogany concertina frowned as Vanity slipped again and again. Her eyes were brighter than usual, her dancing heavier and surprisingly awkward.

She had to keep going, she thought. To dance and sing for these men who loved her was all she wanted! Though she longed to lie down, she forced herself on.

The bartender wiped his big white hands on his stained apron and made his way from behind the bar. Shouldering aside the transfixed men in his way, he caught Vanity's arm and steadied her. "Feeling all right, Vanity, dear?" His eyes went over her with tender concern.

She sagged against him, startled by the trembling she felt. Suddenly this was not the strong body she'd always had. Still, she felt wildly reckless this night, as if time had run out, as if her sins had at last caught up with her.

"I'm fine, Doby, truly!" she panted as she pecked his stubbled cheek and swung away. "Give me hugs and kisses, boys! Give me all ya got!" She threw out her bare arms to the men, her men!

The frowning bartender signaled to someone on the sidelines. A tall woman who called herself Belle and who was wearing a dangerously tight purple and green low-necked gown, edged her gargantuan bosom into the crowd. "Give a girl room," she said in a low, suggestive voice, insinuating herself into the group of tightly packed men, giving some an inviting eye and others a scornful glance.

As Belle watched Vanity slow her stomping around the stifling saloon, her mouth worked with worry. Finally she took her head as if she could stand no more. She pushed two scrawny drifters from her path and caught Vanity as she swirled, grimaced again, then stumbled.

"You done enough fer tonight," Belle whispered, gripping Vanity's shoulders with her big hands.

Afraid to stop dancing, Vanity felt driven to sing every tune she'd ever known. "I can make it," she gasped, patting Belle's arm. Then, flinging her pale arms high, she thrust her own partially exposed, ripe charms at the men. "I'll take my pleasure now, boys! Let the pious rot!"

The resulting cheer shook Brokken Rock's precious window glass. Coins clinked and spun at Vanity's feet. She scooped up handfuls and gleefully dropped them into her bodice. They felt cold against her burning skin.

Then, briefly, her dark eyes tightened with discomfort. A wave of dull pain ran along her back, and she moaned, letting a handful of coins clatter to the floor. She couldn't go on. If she straightened, she'd break in two!

Her hands suddenly trembled and she clutched at her thick waistline. Not now, she thought! She wanted to wait forever if she could.

Belle caught Vanity as she crumpled to the floor. "I'll help you up to yer shack, honey," she whispered, lifting the young woman from her sea of gold coins.

Seized by pain, Vanity grabbed Belle's thick arm. "Please...wait! I'm all right!" She began to pant. "Let me lie down a minute in the back room. I can do my next number..."

Belle gave the bartender a look that conveyed her alarm. "Make her stop, Doby!"

"That's all for now, boys!" the bartender shouted, returning to his square green bottles and wooden kegs. He thrust shot glasses onto the plank in handfuls of six. "Bar's open. One drink on the house!"

As the men surged toward the bar, Otto Meyer stopped torturing his concertina. Belle, supporting the staggering Vanity with one arm, beat on the door of the back room with her fist. "Hurry it up in there, Gardenia! Ya ain't entertaining no big spender, I'd be willin' to bet!"

Moments later a chunky blonde in a black gown with pink ruffles flung the door wide open. Gardenia, a sultry woman of indeterminate age, glared at Belle as she straightened her gown's plunging neckline. "You got nerve—" But when she saw Vanity, Gardenia forgot what she'd been about to say. Laying her perfumed hand on Vanity's flushed cheek, she looked down at the girl's high, taut belly. "You got pains, sugar?"

Vanity shook her head. "I need my money! I'm fine, really. I've got just a little...ache in my back. I didn't think it'd hurt to go on dancing."

"I'll get your money, sugar," Gardenia said, smiling enviously at the gold litter around the stove.

Some of the men had left, but the floor still groaned as the remaining patrons jockeyed for position at the bar. A crisp breath of cold air laced with tiny white flakes drifted in when the front door was kicked shut. Dust from the low, bark-covered pine rafters sifted onto everyone's head.

Belle tapped a finger on Gardenia's rosy cheek. "See to it Vanity gets *all* the coin comin' to her."

Gardenia made a face and a vulgar motion with her hand. "You think you're so special...I got more men than you can count! See if it fits, *sugar!*"

"Same to ya, black-hearted mivvy!" But Belle's insult lacked malice as she assisted Vanity into the barren back room and slammed the door. "At least *I* can count. Set yourself down, honey. You make me tired to look at you."

Vanity settled herself gingerly on the rumpled brass bed. The ravaged satin pillows behind her bore traces of rouge. The room had no window, only a second narrow door that opened onto an alley.

"Is it time?" Belle asked, pushing back her masses of naturally curly black hair. She made a huge shadow in the flickering light. Outside, the wind stirred in the pines and whistled through chinks in the logs.

Vanity's stomach knotted with fear. "I don't see how it can be. I only feel a kind of...fullness. Maybe I should go to the privy." Then she doubled over and groaned.

A serious contraction seized her belly. She clamped her chilled hands tightly between her legs. The nearest doctor lived in Yerba Buena! There was no time to fetch him.

"Great snakes, Vanity! Don't go to the privy at a time like this!" Belle shook her head. "That baby of yours could fall out!"

Vanity laughed, though her flushed face reflected fear. Then she shook her head at her own foolishness.

Belle was about to say something more, but Vanity put up her hand. Just when she thought she could rise from the bed, another contraction made her arch her back. Then she collapsed. "Have a look under my skirts, Belle! I've wet my drawers!" There was a warm puddle near her feet. She felt Belle parting her knees. "I'm so weak. I've had this backache since morning—it's getting worse!"

"You ain't got the brains God gave a jackass," Belle muttered, pushing Vanity's skirts back over her knees.

Vanity felt smothered by red satinet.

Belle pulled off Vanity's cotton drawers. "Dancing at a time like this—Holy be-Jeezus! Sit tight, Vanity! It's comin' right now!"

"I couldn't get up if I wanted to!" Vanity laughed, then rubbed a tear from her eye. Another contraction gripped her. She threw back her head, eyes wide, her hands grabbing fistfuls of lacy coverlet. "I don't want to die, Belle!"

"Hush, gull-darn it! Scoot back. I need room to work. Ain't nothin' going to happen to you, honey. Not with ol' Belle takin' care of you. I been around, I have, and I've birthed a few babies in my time. You can't work in my line long without seein' a few. You just see to it you don't take up my line of work. Next thing you know, some real fine upstandin' gent's goin' to walk into this God-forsaken pile of logs and marry you up quick!"

"I came here to get away from men like that," Vanity said, panting. The pressure was intense now, driving her to pull up her knees and strain until she couldn't breathe. "Bell-l-le, it's so big!"

She longed for it to end, prayed to be forgiven for her foolishness. She didn't want the marrying kind of man to find her in this place! She'd already tangled with that kind, and he'd proved to be the fathering kind. She'd learned too late that he'd already done marrying and fathering long before he met her.

She grabbed at her thighs, her mouth stretched wide, her body working with all its strength to deliver the child. Her thoughts became a jumble then, and everything was blotted out. Her only awareness was of a birthing she couldn't stop.

"Almost out!" Belle whispered.

Vanity fought, holding back her screams. She knew nothing but the intense fullness between her legs, the blazing need to free and be freed. Stretched to the limit, oblivious to anything but the bright hot birth canal filled with her child, she finally gave out with one shuddering, gut-deep groan.

As if blessed and forgiven, the pressure eased. A tingling gush of strength flooded her body.

"Holy mule shit! What a beauty! Look at this little honey!" Belle crowed.

A tiny indignant wail erupted from beyond Vanity's red ruffles.

"To be born in a saloon..." Vanity wept, forcing away her sorrow, then rejoicing in astonishment to hear the high, clear voice of her child. This child had never been real to her, not in all these months. What a wonder to think a living creature had come from a few innocent nights of stolen love!

"It's one helluva girl!" Belle announced, lifting a squirming rosy infant high for Vanity to see.

Vanity reached out, her arms suddenly aching to embrace her child.

"Don't take her yet. She'll stain yer dress. Let me wipe her off a bit first. Lay back, for Chrissake! You've just had a baby! I still got to cast off her moorings…" Belle looked around frantically. "Shoot! You'll have to hold her after all, honey. I got to get a knife or something. Careful! She's slippery as a happy man!"

Vanity took her solid little daughter into her arms and laughed. Belle thundered out, shouting that she needed a knife, any kind of blasted knife.

Gazing into the face of her daughter, Vanity's eyes filled with happy tears. They were alive, both of them! Her heart felt near to bursting with pride. "Oh, my darling! If only your foolish ol' grandpa could see you now. Wouldn't he be sorry he ever threw us out? Wouldn't he be sorry he called you that awful name?"

Belle returned with a big Bowie knife. She paused when she heard Vanity whispering to the baby, her expression saying clearly that she'd known all along that Vanity wasn't married.

Behind her, Gardenia burst in holding a knotted bandanna sack heavy with coin. Her eyes went round with disbelief. "You didn't scream once!" she exclaimed, setting the bundle on the bed beside Vanity. She looked a bit disappointed.

Vanity suddenly felt weary. She plucked a handful of the coins from her bodice, then sank back on the pillows. She wanted to weep for both joy and sorrow—joy in the birth of her daughter, sorrow because, except for these few friends, she was so very alone.

"What did our babe's grandpappy call this little treasure?" Belle asked gruffly, her eyes sly as she tied the cord with a ragged piece of green ribbon torn from her garter. With the big Bowie she cut the baby free. "I'll teach the old pecker a lesson! You just tell me where to find him. Leavin' you to this kind of place in your fix…"

Vanity shook her head. "It doesn't matter. I'm here because I want to be. Promise never to ask where I came from because that part of my life is over. Never speak of my past to my baby. This is our home now, for as long as it takes to earn enough for a new start back east."

"Your family oughtn't to have thrown you out," Belle said, curiosity rampant on her wide face.

Vanity shook her head again. "What's done is done."

While Belle slipped a clean piece of towelling around the baby, Vanity tended to her personal needs. Then, though her strength was ebbing, she cradled her daughter close to her swollen, aching breasts. "Bring me the wash basin, please."

"Going to wash her already, in this cold?" Belle gasped. "Great snakes! You're one bold and reckless girl! You come to this God-forsaken sinkhole and won't say who you really are or where you're really from. Then you go dancin' like you was born to it, and pregnant, no less. Dad blast it, you're one puzzle of a female!"

Vanity didn't reply. Me and my reckless, trusting heart, she thought. It pained her to think of all she had sacrificed for this child. She dipped her fingertips into the cold river water. "I christen thee Mary Louise Mackenzie," she said solemnly and hoped her personal blessing would be enough. There were no preachers for a hundred miles.

"Is that your real name? Mackenzie?" Belle was cooing to the baby but eyed the mysterious young girl who had arrived in the camp six months before and in all that time had given not a single clue to her true identity.

Vanity looked into the alert brown eyes of her newborn daughter. "Mackenzie," she murmured. "Not...'bastard.'"

1850

To honor California's admittance into the Union, the hastily built raw-pine warehouses along Tenderfoot Landing on the Sacramento River had been draped with red, white, and blue bunting. Since the birth of the boom camp's first and only child, the place had changed beyond recognition.

Where once there had been wooded hills that sloped to the river's edge, there was now a wasteland of mud and jagged pine stumps. When gold was discovered on Sutter's land upstream on the American River, prospectors had descended on the area by the thousands. Hourly, small steamboats paused at the landing, disgorging customers for the dozens of crude saloons that now stood cheek by jowl along what was once a forlorn wagon track.

Crude shack after shack, sagging gambling tents, and false-fronted stores crowded the meandering muddy paths that served as streets for the heavy wagon and foot traffic.

The camp had grown so large it now spilled in all its rustic chaos right onto the banks of the river. Tenderfoot boasted its own bank and theater, plus a dignified hotel of two floors called the Pacific Congress American, a name rather more pretentious than a leaning pine shack merited.

The steep hillsides had been quickly denuded of pines to build prospectors' shanties and much-needed stores. Now the town had a biting smell of pitch and whiskey about it. The land was scarred and pitted from the diggings of a thousand gold-hungry fiends.

As the little steamboat *Sacramento Sal* eased bow first against the muddy landing, dozens of men crowded around to help off-load desperately needed cargo—shovels, boots, and red-eye whiskey. Impatient passengers spilled down the broad stageplank, lured by tales of gold hidden in placer stream beds. But first they'd crowd into the most renowned saloon in the valley, Broken Rock. (This time the sign painter could spell.) The queen of the boom camps, beautiful, mysterious Vanity, sang and danced there, sometimes six times a night!

As the greenhorn passengers disembarked that day, a tall handsome one separated himself from the rest and sauntered into the muddy roadway. Pausing to light a slim cigar, he noted the stumps in the streets and the branchless pine trunks punctuating the muddy fields.

He had seen every boom camp northwest of Sacramento. This one looked no different. No cottages stood tucked along the outskirts of town, which was to say that civilization, law, and decent women hadn't yet arrived. Save for a few gaudy skirts visible in the distance where a house of convenience stood, he saw few women. Judging by the number of whiskerless faces he saw milling around in search of entertainment, enough innocents filled this camp to make it worthy of his attention.

Fingering a pair of reliable dice in his trouser pocket, he caught a flash of red calico atop a pile of crates. A closer look revealed a child wearing a smudged smock and long apron pitching pebbles into the river.

He exhaled a long stream of tobacco smoke as he approached her. The child immediately drew her scuffed knees to her chin, exposing ruffled red drawers. He chuckled. She was the filthiest, most adorable heathen he'd ever seen.

He stopped directly in front of her, then wondered if she'd dart away. "Good afternoon, my bright-eyed little lady. What's a tyke like you doing in a place like Tenderfoot?" He swept off his derby and bowed. In ten or fifteen years she'd be a caution!

Five-year-old Mary Louise looked up into the man's grinning face. He had a long, neatly drooping moustache and rosy cheeks. Here was someone large who was smiling and who didn't smell bad!

"I don't talk to strangers!" she chirped, thrilled to be so very wicked and doing exactly that.

He laughed. "I see. Do you live here?"

She nodded, feeling long tendrils of her glossy chestnut hair caress her neck. She wondered if he'd give her a penny.

Most men liked to give her something the moment they set eyes on her. Nearly every day she made her rounds of the shacks to collect her pennies, saying how-do to all the regulars. She calculated she was very nearly as rich as her mama!

The few "ladies" in town, however, didn't give out pennies. Mary wasn't to talk to them in any case, though she did. Those ladies gave out gold dollars and said, "Here's hoping you stay out of my shoes, cutie."

"Would your papa mind me giving you a piggyback up the road?" the stranger asked, straightening and looking around. At once his gaze returned to Mary's darling upturned face. What a beautiful child in such a crude camp!

"What's a papa?" Mary Louise asked as the man's big hands slipped beneath her armpits and lifted her high over his head. She settled happily astride his shoulders, her bare legs smudging the fine Merino wool of his frock coat with mud. She laced her dirty fingers into his shiny long brown hair.

"Come, come. You don't expect me to believe a little lady as cute and smart-looking as you never heard the word *papa*." He strolled beyond the warehouses, puffing on his cheroot. "Though I suppose it's possible that if you didn't have…that is to say, if everyone around here knew you didn't…" He cleared his throat. "My dear, a papa is a man. A mama is a woman. I should imagine you have a mama."

"Yes'ir!" she said, happily thumping her heels against his chest. She hadn't had this much attention since the last time her mama held off an unwelcome caller with her Colt pistol. "I sure do got a mama!"

"Well, a mama sews up a little lady's dresses. A papa generally works every day to buy a little lady her shoes." He tickled her naked feet. "You, my dear, have no shoes on your tiny toes today."

"I got shoes!" Mary Louise protested. "I just don't get to wear them!"

"Is your mama pretty?"

"Prettiest in Tenderfoot!" She felt like a princess as her stranger strode up the winding, rutted road into the heart of the camp. They were passing saloons boasting pianos and gambling tents where hawkers were attempting to lure miners inside in hopes of separating them from their heavy pokes of gold.

"Well, missy, by the stares I'm getting, I suspect folks wonder what I am to you. Frankly, I hadn't intended any entanglements on this journey. So, I believe I'll take my leave of your precious company before someone attributes your paternity to me. Do you understand what I'm saying, little lady?"

She was annoyed with herself because she didn't. "You talk too fancy," Mary said as he swung her down onto a boardwalk in front of a store and looked swiftly about.

He backed away with a tip of his derby. "I must say, though, you're the prettiest little girl I've ever seen in my long and distant travels. Where might I find your mama, if I had a mind to look her up?" He looked only a bit nervous as he calculated the first saloon he'd work that evening. Then he winked at Mary. "If she's anything like you, she'll be the prettiest thing west of the Rockies!"

Mary pointed toward the Broken Rock Saloon, then squealed and dashed away. At a safe distance, she turned to watch as her handsome stranger disappeared into the dense crowd of prospectors and other folk streaming through the muddy spaces between the buildings.

He'd taken his leave mighty quick, she thought, and stuck out her lower lip. She didn't know what she was feeling, only that he was wonderful and she wanted him, or someone like him, to smile down at her always with that sparkle in his eyes and to say all those nice things to her.

Darting between the store and a supply shed, she scrambled up the narrow muddy path leading to her mother's sheltered cabin overlooking the rooftops of Tenderfoot.

"Gimme plenny o' cheer, boys. Gimme all ya got," she sang aloud to herself. She stopped to pick a wildflower for her mother.

Behind her, several pistol shots rang out in celebration. Shrieking with excitement, Mary raced to a promontory and clapped her hands. "Hang 'em high, boys! Hang 'em high!"

She was within sight of her mother now and heard her mother's soft insistent voice calling. "Mary Louise! Stay clear of that ledge! Come up here this minute! Did you bring our supper tray?"

Mary turned and waved to her beautiful mother standing on the sagging porch of their log cabin a hundred yards up the wash. Then she ran to her mother, calling, "Mama! Mama! Where's my papa at?"

Mary knew perfectly well what the words *papa, pa, paw, pappy*, and *father* meant. It meant people got red-faced and shut their mouths. Those were powerful words, better than *danged, shoot,* and just plain *hell*. Until this day, however, she hadn't guessed it meant a person. Suddenly it was as plain as anything that she ought to have one.

Vanity Mackenzie scowled at her daughter, then tugged at Mary's dirty smock and shook her head. "Did you forget to bring our supper tray again? Mary Louise Mackenzie, what am I going to do about you? We'd go hungry if I didn't keep after you! Where were you dawdling this time? Not begging for pennies again, I hope. Were you at the riverfront, then? Mary Louise, look me in the eye! Haven't I told you never ever to go there! You could fall in and drown!" Vanity looked as if she was considering putting clean clothes on Mary and finally decided against making the effort.

Mary squirmed impatiently with her news. Her mama was so full of rules! Mary didn't care a whit for any of them. Well, not too much anyway. Mary was free, adored by every person who had ever seen her. She belonged to the whole town of Tenderfoot, to the whole world! She did not belong entirely to a mama whose only word was "No!"

Lifting her pointed chin, Mary looked at her mother squarely. Her heart pounded, and her voice came out breathy and strong. "I let him carry me," she said, as her mother's dark eyes widened.

Vanity straightened, her expression one of alarm.

"He talked real pretty!" Mary said, thrilled to see how she could make her mother snap to attention.

Vanity snorted and marched back into the cabin. "I don't know what I'm going to do about you! You are as willful a little wretch as I have ever known! One day you'll give me gray hairs!"

Mary's spine tingled. She followed her mother into the cabin. Her mama was wearing shiny red ruffled petticoats that to Mary looked as beautiful as gold dust did to crazed miners. On top, her mama was laced tightly into her boned white corset so that her puppies squeezed up ripe and round. Mary Louise hooked her grimy fingers under her own rib cage and pretended she had breasts as big as her mother's pretty ones.

"I hope you remembered to give Wong Soo yesterday's tray," her mother said, reminding Mary why she'd been allowed to go down the trail in the first place. Vanity frowned into a bit of broken looking glass nailed to the far wall and rubbed rouging powder onto her cheeks. She caught Mary's rapt expression reflected in the glass and paused. "If you're hungry, we'll have to get supper at the store. I don't like paying three dollars for an egg, I can tell you." She turned, and at the sight of Mary, her dark eyes warmed. A person couldn't help it. "Come here, you minx. How do you get so dirty? Let's take these muddy things off. You're supposed to be growing up something of a lady."

Mary threw herself into her mother's soft warm arms and hugged her. Her mother smelled of rouge and dusting powder and…Mary suspected she sipped red-eye but wasn't supposed to notice. She savored the feel of her mother's strong hands on her back. Her mother was wonderful, beautiful, the most adored woman in all of Tenderfoot—in all of California, some claimed!

Secretly, Mary liked to think that she herself was most beautiful and adored, but for the moment she was content to share the praise. It was a proud thing to be the daughter of Tenderfoot's queen.

Firecrackers began to pop in the distance. Mary squirmed to go out onto the porch. It wasn't every day they became a state, whatever that was.

"Not so fast," Vanity said with a chuckle. "I have a surprise for you. Tonight we sing together! Now, don't move an inch. You're going to take a bath whether you want one or not."

Mary danced around in a circle. "Gimme plenny o' cheer, boys—"

"Not that song!" Her mother laughed, her cheeks going pink. "You are supposed to be a little lady!"

While Vanity dragged a wooden tub into the middle of the cabin, Mary went on humming the bawdy song, trying to provoke her mother. Vanity helped her daughter undress, relishing the feel of her child's silky skin. She brushed Mary's long chestnut tangles, her eyes shining with wonder the way those of everyone did who looked at her daughter. Mary was more than just pretty, more than beautiful.

Mary was free from all care, free of most restraints, particularly those of the rigid society Vanity had escaped. How very lucky she was, Vanity thought, helping Mary into the tub and then dousing her with the carefully warmed water. As she soaped the perfect pink body, her heart caught to think what this squirming, headstrong bit of beauty had cost her. But she knew she would gladly pay it all over again one hundredfold to have this wonderful child.

Mary was preoccupied with her own thoughts of firecrackers and the forgotten supper tray. Then her charming stranger smiled his way back into her memory and the warm bay rum fragrance of him was as real as her mother's gentle hands. "Mama? Mama! Where's my papa at?"

Vanity went rigid. A crease showed between her brows. She swallowed hard and went on rinsing Mary, who was puzzled by the effect her forbidden word had on her mother.

"Sit down so I can soap your head. Eyes closed. No peeking."

Mary sank into the water, and her mother scrubbed vigorously at her scalp to get at all the sand. How such a beautiful child could get so much sand in her hair…Vanity hoped her daughter would soon forget her question.

"Someday," Vanity said in a storytelling tone, "you'll wear the best clothes money can buy. You'll have perfect corkscrew curls all the way down your back and great big hair bows of real satin in every color. You'll have a jolly lady cooking you tea cakes for every meal. You'll have a hired girl to iron every one of your hundred ruffled dresses…all made in Paris, France.

"You'll have a maid just to take care of your upstairs, and another maid just to dust the whatnots sitting around your downstairs. You'll have a tall man in a fancy suit to hold open your front door. There will be another man to help you get into your fine, black carriage. And you'll go to an exclusive school for petite June fillies—that's 'little ladies' in French, you remember—where you'll learn to dance a cotillion. Your French dancing instructor will teach you to curtsy like royalty. Not a person alive will fault you!"

Vanity poured rinse water over Mary Louise's head until all the mud, sand, and soap sloshed around the child's ankles.

That "someday" talk was wearing mighty thin, Mary thought. She wanted those fine things now! "I want a papa! Papas buy shoes," Mary said, her dark eyes snapping as she watched her mother flinch.

"You fill your shoes with mud!" Vanity's cheeks went fiery red, and her hands began to shake. She spoke softly. "Tell me, minx, who's been asking you questions?"

"My charming stranger," Mary Louise said. "He got off the *Sacramento Sal* today and gave me a piggyback up the hill. Where's my papa at?"

"Don't move from this spot. I forgot the towel. If you get dirty again, I won't let you sing with me tonight. Someday I'll buy you the best shoes in the world. I've got more than five years' worth of gold saved for you, and I've got a sight of it left even if the prices around here are sky-high. Don't you forget that one of these days when I feel ready we're going to ride out of here all the way to the ocean on the *Sacramento Sal* like ladies, and…and some other people I won't mention can just go to—Piggyback! I told you not to talk to strangers!"

"I didn't," Mary said, shivering as her mother rubbed her with a scratchy towel.

Vanity helped her into her underdrawers and then pulled a miniature red gown over her head. It had rows of gold tinsel fringe around the neckline. Mary loved it. They had stitched it from one of Vanity's old ones. "Don't make up stories, Mary Louise," her mother said. "Who did you talk to?"

Mary ducked her head. "He talked to me first."

"Same thing! No talking to strangers! *Especially* the ones who talk first!"

"What about my papa?"

Vanity hooked Mary's dress with irritated little jerks. Mary twisted around, startled to see tears in her mother's beautiful eyes. Frightened, she stopped squirming.

"You want to know about papas? I'll tell you. A papa made you in my belly. You grew right here inside me like the kittens in Bart Tooley's cat. A papa put you there. And papas are supposed to be tall and handsome and very rich, but sometimes they're not. Sometimes they don't even tell the truth! You do as I tell you, Mary Louise Mackenzie, and you'll never have to worry about that. Someday you'll find yourself a grand gentleman to fall in love with you. You'll wear a beautiful white gown and get married in a church, and then afterward he'll put beautiful little girls and darling little boys in your belly. But not for a very long time yet. Not until you're eighteen, at least, and I say he's a gentleman worthy of you."

"I want my papa now! Where's he at?"

"You can't have your papa. He's...not here."

"Do papas cost a lot? Like shoes? Buy me one."

"If you're good I'll let you put on your red dancing slippers right now, but then you can't go outside. We're going to be a sensation tonight! You and me will make so much money—" She stopped and frowned. "Buy you one! Mary Louise, just hush! This place is turning you into a heathen!"

"Do I really have a papa?"

"Don't be silly. Of course you do."

"What's his name?"

Vanity flounced to the corner of the cabin where her special dresses hung. She paused and bit her knuckle, then glanced back at Mary, wishing she had better prepared herself for this kind of conversation.

Vanity's face brightened. She struck a stage pose. Her voice became animated as if she was telling another of her many stories. "Your papa's name was Maxxmillon Blade! He was the all-time greatest riverboat gambler on the Mississippi! He was seven feet tall, with long, waving black hair and a long black moustache. He had eyes blue as the sky. He always wore a midnight-black frock coat and a diamond stickpin as big as your eye in his neck cloth!"

Mary squealed. For the moment it didn't matter if this story was true. "Can he come for my birthday?"

"No, you goose! He lives two thousand miles away on a boat ten times bigger than the *Sacramento Sal*. Now, don't tell anybody this. He's our secret. It's time to sing songs for me. Before you become a proper young lady you have to help us get stinking rich!"

Mary stepped onto the gritty floor and let her mother put on the tiny gilded dancing slippers that Otto had had custom-made for her in San Francisco. But Mary wasn't thinking of her shoes. She was wondering if her papa had put her into her mama's belly, then how come he went off and left her? She was really more her papa's daughter than her mama's. She was only on loan!

Mary gazed into her mama's distracted face. Her papa wouldn't insist that she act like a lady. He wouldn't say she couldn't cuss or accept pennies from men. He would never expect her to take a bath. Mary Louise Mackenzie's papa would never think to say no!

Broken Rock Saloon had been moved from the sagging, low-ceilinged log cabin where Vanity made her debut before a collection of drunken traders and trappers to a new two-story pine structure where two hundred prospectors at a time could now pelt her with coins and gold nuggets.

The new Broken Rock had a spacious main room sporting a stage with genuine maroon-plush curtains. Upstairs, rooms with brass beds could accommodate six customers at a time. Broken Rock employed the choicest cuts of female flesh east of the Sierras, or so Doby Gartell whispered as he served the new boys at the bar.

In six years Vanity Mackenzie had never gone into the back room or climbed the fine new staircase in any official capacity. But after hours, when the nights were long and cold, and her heart grew disappointed and sore over the life she had chosen, she welcomed an occasional friend at her cabin—only, that was, if Mary was fast asleep.

In recent years, Vanity had welcomed far fewer friends to the warmth of her bed, finding that the thrill of the forbidden had lost its edge. She was tired of finding herself alone in the morning.

Now Vanity stood in the wings, waiting for her first show to begin. The darkness outside held a chill that was no longer exhilarating. The smell of the men no longer reminded her that she was among the wild and wicked. The night was just cold, and she was merely among the dirty and greedy.

Tonight, however, Mary was to dance with her. Somehow that promised to change things. Her dancing would be carefree and harmlessly bawdy. Her songs would seem daring and naughty once more. Vanity yearned for the satisfaction she had once gotten from entertaining, for now it seemed rather pointless, and if she had given up her parents and respectability for something pointless, that meant she had wasted six years of her life.

Firecrackers were still going off around the boom camp. In saloons up and down the line there was the same tin-horn music, the same throaty men's laughter. Vanity was sick of men. Yet she yearned for one now, just one, one special one to take away the ache and the fears that came in the night after Mary was asleep.

When Vanity heard Otto's office clock strike eleven, she threw back her head. Her worries retreated to a private corner of her mind. Things would turn out differently for Mary, she hoped. Her beautiful daughter wouldn't find herself too disheartened to move on. Someday Mary would be a lady.

Then the rouged and ruffled Vanity Mackenzie, queen of the camp, strutted across Broken Rock's small stage, her face lit by a smile, her eyes snapping with fire. Along the stage's rim flickered small candles set in tin cans cut to resemble footlights. As Vanity moved past them, the flames danced.

"Statehood!" Vanity suddenly shouted. She threw up her dimpled arms. "To honor the new state of California, I introduce to you Mary Mackenzie, Princess of the Gold Rush!"

Waiting in the wings with her Uncle Otto, Mary Louise heard her cue. Like her mama, she threw back her head. Her chestnut ringlets spread in a busy halo around her darling face. She grinned to show all her tiny pearly teeth—even the front one that was already loose. With the confidence of a supremely self-possessed little girl, she pranced onto the stage. In her imagination she'd done it a thousand times.

Through the flickering glare, Mary saw dark heads silhouetted against a haze of Queenet cigar smoke. A few bearded faces were distinct in the front row. She could hear the continuous click of the wheel of fortune, the drone of a faro dealer's voice, and the rattle of poker chips.

Already coins and small leather pokes of gold clanged and thumped onto the stage. Mary lifted her shining face and was met with wave after wave of rousing huzzahs.

When the noise died down, Otto Meyer began to play a song on his concertina. Nothing was quite so right for dancing as Otto's concertina, Mary's mother always said. Vanity clapped while smiling proudly at the miniature of herself.

With a flourish and a leap, Mary jumped into place. She flung up her slim white arms. The gold fringe on her dress shook. "Statehood!" she shrieked, swinging into a chirping rendition of "Yankee Doodle."

Immediately the crowd was cheering, drowning out the concertina. Mary's golden voice rang high and clear. She pranced and strutted, shaking her fringe, winking, and tapping her tiny gilded shoes as her mama had taught her. When she finished her first song, the rain of coins along the simulated footlights made her squeal with delight. Every coin, Mama said, meant another cake, another pretty hair bow, another day at her special school.

Mary sang four songs before the stage floor was so littered she could no longer stamp her feet. She ended her first performance with a curtsy and blew kisses before she ran offstage.

Before she was whisked home by a bouncer charged with her safety, Mary heard patrons clamoring for drinks at the long carved mahogany bar shipped up especially from Sacramento. Then she saw her handsome stranger waiting by the rear door. "Did you see me? Wasn't it fun?" she hollered.

Her mother dashed back and hugged her. "You were wonderful! Do it just the same way tomorrow night. Off to bed with you now." She handed Mary to the bouncer with a kiss. "See that she locks the door, Henry." Then Vanity's eyes fell on the smiling stranger from the riverboat. Her ruby lips curved into a smile. Mary didn't know whether to be happy or furious.

At dawn the next morning Mary awoke to whispers and saw her mother standing at the open cabin door kissing her tall stranger! They looked wonderful standing close like that, her mother's upturned face, the curve of her back held possessively by a big hand. He was bent over her, his hair shifting in the breeze. His lips moved down to cover her mother's.

Mary's heart twisted with something she didn't understand or welcome. He had belonged to her first! All the next day she was sullen. But soon enough her jealousy subsided because the handsome, charming stranger stayed for three months.

They were happy months. Mary never heard her mama laugh so much. She had never before been invited to watch her mama perform, though often enough she'd sneaked down to peek through the Broken Rock's windows.

Now she was allowed to watch from Mr. Charming's broad shoulders as her mama danced with abandon.

The stranger who called himself Smiling Ace Malone squired Mary and her mother up and down the river on the *Sacramento Sal*, treating them to expensive dinners when he was flush, and letting Vanity pay when he wasn't, which was often, since he played some of the slickest gamblers ever to find their way to the goldfields of California.

At night Mary lay awake with the warm, tingling feeling that having a man in the cabin gave her. She didn't mind sleeping on the floor on a pile of worn quilts so long as "he" was there each morning, groaning that he'd drunk too much of Doby's bad whiskey and stayed up too late playing tops and bottoms with her mama.

Mary soon realized tops and bottoms was a game she wasn't to mention, like all the games she'd inadvertently witnessed when she spied at the cribs along the line.

Secretly, Mary believed Smiling Ace Malone was her papa, and she worked ceaselessly at stealing his attention with calculated bursts of coquetry and charm.

Her rebellion and jealousy dimmed whenever her mama spoke in a reverent tune of having found "him" at last. Mary took that to mean that her mama had somehow lost her papa and that he'd finally found his way back. Mary couldn't stay angry or remain selfish when her mama was so obviously happy with him.

But winter returned and snow threatened. Many prospectors left for the valleys, and the gaming tables turned less of a profit. One night Mary's mama and Smiling Ace were late coming back to the cabin. Mary lay awake worrying.

When Vanity slipped inside the cabin near dawn, she was alone. Thinking Mary to be asleep, she collapsed on the bed she'd shared with Smiling Ace and wept until the pillow was soaked with her tears.

Her crying went on for days.

Doby put the word out to his bartender friends in camps along the river, but Ace Malone had gone to seek his fortune where the wind and snow didn't sift so freely through the chinks in cabin walls. He was off to a place where a beautiful woman wouldn't lure him into something he'd always managed to avoid.

For him, Vanity Mackenzie's love had been a summer frolic. She'd been a warm, willing body to sleep beside, and a pleasure to behold, most assuredly, but nothing more.

In years to come Mary would look back on those three months and half wish they had never been.

Eventually her mother stopped crying. She resumed dancing and singing three shows a night. Though she was never quite the same, and tended to sip red-eye at night when she thought Mary wasn't looking, Vanity would sometimes break off in the middle of a sentence and muse, "But didn't he have the most wonderful way of saying things?"

Some months passed before Mary found the courage to ask, "Was he my papa?"

Vanity's steady smile disappeared. "Once and for all, he was not. I would've told you if he was. He was…a friend. But he could have been your papa for all he's stuck by me."

In the spring her mama became ill and couldn't dance. They stayed together in the cabin, Vanity in bed and Mary her nursemaid. It was a strained time, half fun and half frightening.

One night Mary was whisked off to sleep in the back of Wong Soo's restaurant. No one would tell her why. In the morning she was allowed to return home and found her mother lying in bed looking even more gaunt than before.

For a time her mother cried at the least little thing. Mary learned to amuse herself riding a burro, throwing Otto's jackknife, and cursing a blue streak in German and Spanish. She explored the town to the last corner and made it her own.

But in time Mary's mother recovered and sewed herself a new gown of genuine silk, lead-gray and pink. Once again she danced her gay dances.

That year Mary's mama stopped talking about going east. Dreams for Mary's schooling got pushed into the future. Mary danced one show a night with her mama, and together they gathered the coins thrown at their feet, paying half, as always, to Doby.

On Sunday mornings Mary and her mother climbed the hill behind their cabin for a picnic. While Mary played with Vanity's new feathered bonnet, Vanity buried her week's take beneath a wind-twisted pine high on the ridge.

1858

The placer and quartz gold found around Tenderfoot were pretty well played out by the time Mary Louise Mackenzie turned thirteen. The women and gamblers had moved on to other, newer camps up and down the Sacramento Valley. Storekeepers sent for their wives and built cottages from the tumbledown shacks. For a time Tenderfoot looked as if it would settle into something of a real town, with permanent residents and a semblance of peace.

But with most saloons closed and prospectors gone, the place turned strangely quiet. Weeds grew again on the muddy ravaged hillsides, until the grasses were deep and green, and the abandoned cabins looked as if they had been swallowed by neglect.

The Broken Rock remained, sagging slightly. Only the whiskey-stained poker tables were left now, and Doby finally sold three of the upstairs brass beds.

The mirror behind his rows of whiskey and gin bottles had been painted with a scantily draped plump lady, but it was cracked and had a bullet hole in the upper right corner. Doby had no intention of replacing it. He liked Tenderfoot's new serenity and saw himself tending bar until he fell over dead from drinking his own rotgut.

His choice cuts worked less now. Gardenia stitched shirts in her spare time. Belle liked to cook. They were an odd family, cross and salty, but family nonetheless.

Now when Vanity Mackenzie pranced across the narrow stage, the rain of coins from the aging customers was a token gesture. Her pleasure in her work was gone and her friends could see it. The strangers who came upriver to watch her one nightly show saw that her vitality had been sapped, just as the gold had been stripped from the surrounding hills.

Deep in her heart, Vanity knew little hope remained for an entertainer who was thirty years old and looked it. She had come to Tenderfoot to escape her world. She'd lost her hope when Ace Malone had left. Tenderfoot would do now because it was worn and broken like an old shoe, comforting because so much had been shared and lost with the other residents.

What she would do about Mary Louise, however, she couldn't guess. She had had such dreams for her daughter...such good intentions.

To Mary's way of thinking, the answer was obvious. "It's time I joined you in the midnight show!" Mary followed her mother from one corner of the cabin to another, night after night after night. "I'm thirteen, a woman grown. I've known your songs for years. I don't forget the words like you."

Mary had her own brief show now, at seven, before the locals had had too much whiskey. To dance for them was like performing for a gathering of doting uncles, all of whom knew her routines by heart and would have applauded regardless of what she did.

Mary liked performing, but she didn't bring to it the passion her mother had. With no new dances or songs to try, and few new patrons to impress, her performances were just plain boring.

She wanted life to take on the brilliance she remembered from her happy childhood, to seize the world as her mother had.

Always at the mention of the midnight show, Vanity whirled on her daughter. "I'm telling you for the last time, you know where the midnight show leads! Some old goat is sure to—" She would cover her eyes with a trembling hand. Why couldn't Mary go on being a beautiful child forever!

For Vanity the days were so long now, the nights oblivion. She found no satisfaction in anything except drilling her daughter in manners recalled from her own girlhood. Mary, however, was not a willing pupil. She had been indulged too long.

Mary was at the gangly stage now, but the promise of an alluring woman's body was there. Her cherubic face framed with chestnut curls developed a mature curve and was frighteningly beautiful.

Mary sensed her mother's fear. As a child, she had been so free, though part of her freedom had been with Josh Harbro, a lad who had come to the camp with his father more than a year ago. Josh had teased and taunted with promises to show her his if she'd show him hers first.

The passions kindled by that loveplay had surprised Mary, who had long suppressed her desire to play tops and bottoms. Then, thankfully, Josh and his pa moved on. Mary had realized, however, that womanhood was rapidly approaching. She wanted to dance the midnight show, but had no intention of giving herself to anyone.

"You love singing for the men," Mary persisted. "I do, too! You write wonderful songs!"

"I will never let you sing the midnight show! You're different... better. I don't sing songs you know at the midnight show. I sing... midnight songs."

"I'll learn them!"

"No, you won't! Don't pester me, baby. Do your chores and let me nap. I'm tired."

After her mother climbed into bed, Mary flounced onto the porch and sat, knees beneath her chin, her mind churning. She was worried. If only "he" hadn't gone away, Mary thought, harboring a burning hate for Smiling Ace Malone.

Mary knew now about Ace's baby who had died shortly after birth. She had gone up to the graveyard once to see the tiny marker carved into the shape of a kneeling lamb.

What was all that money buried under that tree for if she wasn't going away to school? Couldn't they use it for clothes or a bigger cabin?

Mary pitched stones onto the roof of an abandoned shack down the hill. She felt Tenderfoot dying. If it took midnight songs from a thirteen-year-old virgin to breathe life back into it, then that's what it would take!

Now when Mary made her daily rounds, saying how-do and refusing pennies, she heard the girls on the line say she was meant for nothing better than Vanity. Some thought that her mama held herself too high as it was.

Their talk made her impatient and angry. She wasn't as pretty as her mama, not in this awkward stage of arms and legs that were too long and brown eyes that appeared too large for her face, even if they did see the world for what it was. She knew Tenderfoot was a low place. In other places gambling wasn't acceptable, ladies of the line were snubbed, trains ran on iron tracks, and buildings stood higher than those in Sacramento.

Her memories of Sacramento and "him" had dimmed. She burned to go, to see, to do...yet she didn't think of leaving her mama. She just wanted to be a part of the midnight show.

Mary considered going down to the river to watch the boats pass by. She knew every river pilot. All the riverboat chefs gave her treats. She no longer watched for the *Sacramento Sal*. That old wreck sank when she was seven.

Mary was still sitting on the porch, twisting her long chestnut waves into knots, when her mother came out at dusk. She wore a frayed yellow satin dress with faded red petticoats.

"Did you find supper?" Vanity yawned.

"I want to sing at the midnight show."

Vanity sighed. "Aren't you the stubborn one. Well, my darling girl, I was once willful and stubborn. You see where it got me."

Mary couldn't imagine her mother as anything but a woman who always said no.

"Give Mother a kiss. Find some supper. You're too skinny."

Mary stood and tossed her shaggy mane. "I'm not! I'm getting nice big puppies!" She hooked her fingers beneath her rib cage and drew a deep breath.

They both laughed at her childish gesture, but Mary was indeed ripening. Beneath her smock her nipples were swollen and pink, her breasts softly rounded. Her hips flared, and her thighs had grown long and sleek. Vanity searched her daughter's shining face and feared for her future.

"Behave yourself. Get to bed early. And keep the pistol near at hand. Mind me, now," her mother whispered, giving her a gentle kiss on the forehead.

Otto's wagon struggled up the muddy track to give Vanity a ride down to the Broken Rock. This courtesy supposedly spared her kid shoes, but Mary knew that sometimes her mother was in no condition to walk across their cabin, much less follow a rutted track down a mountainside at dusk.

Otto bellowed his usual hello and then carried Vanity to the wagon. When they had gone, Mary went inside and scowled at her mother's gowns. Each night she wriggled into one and strutted around singing "Give Me Cheer," while down the hill her mother did the same, albeit with less enthusiasm. Mary imagined men grinning up at her on the stage. She flounced her skirts and shook her chest. When a tall, dark-haired stranger with an armload of flowers appeared in her imagination, she went to the bed and slid her mother's Colt pistol from its hiding place inside the oiled cloth.

"Get out of my way, you varmint!" she threatened, brandishing the pistol at the imaginary man. "You're not going to break my heart again, no sir!"

She could hear eager shouts from the few remaining saloons, then a volley of pistol shots. None of the rattling pianos faltered.

Shaking, Mary replaced the pistol beneath the bed and hastily returned her mother's dress to its hook. She had thought the rowdy nights were over. She remembered them well from when she was eight and nine and ten, but now hearing shots no longer thrilled her. She knew too well the straggling processions up to the graveyard.

She moved out onto the porch and looked across the rooftops. The tents on the fringes of town glowed from the lanternlight inside. Some of the shacks had windows that were bright yellow with light. Silvery flakes of snow drifted down, settling on the muddy ruts.

She had just crawled into bed when Otto's wagon rattled up the hill, hell-bent for leather. Leaping from bed and running onto the porch,

Mary saw the unmistakable buxom silhouette of Auntie Belle driving the draft mule with a whip.

Her heart in her throat, Mary leaned over the edge of the porch. "What's happened?"

Belle reined in and jumped down heavily from the wagon. She slogged through the mud, almost losing one of her gold shoes. "I thought you'd be sleeping," Belle said, not attempting to hoist herself onto the porch, but panting and looking sick.

"You're getting your skirts muddy!" Mary exclaimed. For a woman of the line to dirty a precious gown…

Belle staunched a sudden flow of tears with a handful of her long gray hair. "Mary, honey…I don't know how to say this easy. Some jackassed drunk was losing money bad at the Rock tonight. He pulled his pistols, two of 'em…" She faltered, choking back a sob. "Your ma's been shot. He got Otto in the shoulder and shot two drifters dead where they stood."

In the darkness, Mary blinked. Hysterical laughter bubbled in her chest. Shot? Impossible!

"We'll have the funeral in the morning." Belle was crying now and carried on for some time before looking up at Mary's stricken, dry-eyed face. "Sweet Jesus! You ain't lost your mind, have you, honey?"

"Mama's dead?" Mary thought Belle had been talking about a funeral for the drifters.

Belle nodded. "What are we to do about you, Mary? I ain't never got your ma to confess to kin anywhere, excepting your grandpappy, who called you a—We got no idea where he's at. Close as I can figure, you're an orphan. Lord knows a woman like me can't take you in. It wouldn't be right. I suppose there's an orphanage in Sacramento or San Francisco. You can't stay here. I always said you ought to have schooling."

"She's put-her-in-the-ground-forever dead?" Mary screeched.

Belle hefted herself onto the porch and then went into the cabin. Indignant, Mary watched her look through her mother's gowns.

"What're you doing?" Mary whispered.

"She liked this one. Don't you think she'd look nice laid out in it?" Belle's strength failed, and she sagged against the wall.

A shudder of disbelief went through Mary as she pictured a pine box and her mother inside.

"Damned fool drunk…Your ma didn't feel a thing. She was my best friend," Belle said softly, taking the gown and smoothing its creases. "Thirteen years and never once did she say an unkind word to me. She was one helluva lady."

The black gown she fingered was covered with jet beads, a gown ordered from Sacramento for a special evening on the riverboat with "him."

Belle heaved a ragged sigh. "Get yer coat. I don't want you staying here alone tonight."

Mary wrapped her arms around herself, shivering with the fear that her desire for change had somehow brought about this tragedy. "No," she whispered.

Belle looked weary and sad. "But, honey…"

"If Mama's dead, I'm packing. I'll find my papa." She felt as if the muddy earth of her world was sinking from beneath her feet. She would clutch at anything to keep from sinking, too.

Belle chuckled, wagging her head. "You ain't—"

Mary threw back her hair. "Before I leave this cabin I want you to send somebody up here with a trunk. I'm taking all Mama's things. I'm going on a riverboat to Sacramento. Then I'm going on a stagecoach, and a train if I can find one!"

Mary's heart was bursting with grief, but if she knew one thing in that moment before her mother's death was truly real, it was that her mother would want her to go back east before she became trapped here singing the midnight show. Tears came then in a chest-squeezing wave of heartache.

"A skinny little thing like you, traveling alone?" Dabbing her eyes, Belle laughed harshly. "Ain't you the wonder! Just like your mama." She went outside and heaved herself up onto the wagon.

The moment Belle was out of sight, Mary threw on her coat. With snow falling gently from the dark sky, she hiked up the hill to the spot where she and her mother had picnicked, and dug up three small ironbound chests.

By dawn, Mary had dressed and tidied the cabin. Otto, his massive arm in a sling, arrived with a trunk. They packed her mother's gowns and stripped the cabin.

Otto carried the chests to the bank, having no idea that Vanity had saved so much. The twenty-dollar gold eagles were converted into United States greenback dollar bills of denominations large enough to strike a look of amazement on the banker's bearded face.

When thirteen-year-old Mary Louise Mackenzie, head high, marched out of the bank that day, she was one of the richest people in Tenderfoot.

An hour later she stood at her mother's graveside, staring down into the raw hole. She hadn't been allowed to see her mother dead. She would remember her as she had looked for so many years—young and pretty, brilliantly dressed, and winking as she smiled at all the men who worshipped her.

But the sight of the yawning hole and the yellow pine coffin shredded Mary's resolve. When she moved in close, no one suspected that she was thinking of sinking down into the hole with her mother. Being beautiful, adored, and spoiled did nothing to ease Mary's overwhelming grief.

After solemn words were read from the only Good Book in the camp, Otto and Doby peeled Mary's numbed fingers from the edge of the coffin and guided her off where she wouldn't hear the clods of dirt hitting the pine box.

They spent the day talking of Sacramento, and how Mary would enjoy being with children her own age at the orphanage. Belle talked as if learning to read and count would far surpass the joy of singing and dancing onstage.

They were well-intentioned but their words fell on deaf ears. Mary knew her need for playmates had passed. She had no intention of going to any orphanage, which she imagined as a sort of saloon for children.

A week after Vanity Mackenzie was laid to rest, Mary Louise gathered her aching heart, bulging reticule, and battered trunk, and docilely boarded a riverboat bound for Sacramento. Someone charged with taking her to the nearest home for orphans was to meet her. She vowed to elude this unsuspecting person.

Mary waved good-bye to the only home she had ever known, to the friends she had thought of as family. Silently, she promised them all, *I will make you proud, cross my heart.*

One

1859

The deserted landing at Crystal Point, Missouri, shimmered in the silent dawn. The muddy Mississippi River curved around wooded hills like a sleepy lover, its broad surface reflecting the rising sun's brilliant gold.

Though Crystal Point wasn't so large as St. Louis downriver, it was an important stop for the local mills. Like laying hens, small white clapboard houses roosted atop the bluff on the river's Missouri side, looking down on clustered brick buildings along unpaved streets still swimming with mud from a recent spring rise.

Without warning, a battered stern-wheeler at the wooden wharf split the quiet with a whoop from its steam whistle. Bare-chested deck hands of all colors heaved up the wide stageplank at the bow.

With its gracefully curved boiler deck laden with bulky crates and a full thirty cords of wood, the broad white boat eased out and began paddling its frothy way upriver, headed for Hannibal and farming centers to the far north.

Soon the black smoke left behind by powerful smokestacks dissipated, leaving the air sweet with the fragrance of new grass. Townsfolk stirred from houses to stores. Another crisp spring day had begun.

Sitting on a stack of spattered crates, a brightly dressed creature recrossed her long dark-stockinged legs and sighed. With her defiant chin resting in her hand, the girl glowered down the broad, undulating brown ribbon of water.

Not far from her mud-caked high-button shoes the water licked the pebbled bank. An odor of decaying catfish wafted around her, but with the exception of the lingering dawn chill, this land was comfortingly similar to California. The lands she had traveled since the fall before had been frightening and alien.

Upriver, a hulking side-wheeler appeared, splashing steadily around the point. Sending a spine-tingling echo up and down the river, it eased toward the dock, reversed its paddle wheels, and churned to a stop. A deck hand lowered the stageplank against the wharf.

Mary Louise stood up and squinted through the soft morning haze, wondering if this was the boat she waited for. Those she'd questioned said Maxxmillon Blade's floating gambling palace would likely come from the south. Then they looked down at her as if she were asking after the devil.

She couldn't have read the boat's name, even if it had been the *Natchez Trace*. She had only recently mastered twenty pages in her reading primer, so she could scarcely remember four-letter words, much less a riverboat named after a famous Indian trail.

Annoyed, Mary dropped back down, pouted, then cursed herself nine ways to Sunday because she couldn't read worth shoe nails and would be danged if she'd ask again! She crossed her legs and fussed with her ruffled red satin petticoat. Her shoes had been ruined by months of travel, but they'd been her mama's old ones and too big besides, so she didn't trouble herself over them.

What did trouble her was a niggling notion that she had lost her favored place in the world. In the past months she'd passed through an astonishingly vast land, herself an insignificant, bothersome speck.

No longer was she the adored darling of a boom camp. She was a stranger, a queer little bird to be smirked at.

With her jaw set, she plunked her chin into her hand again and glared. Mr. Maxxmillon Blade had just better come along soon before she lost her patience. Well-meaning folks were forever asking her who and what she was. If one more son of a snake asked where she'd dug up her dress, she'd spit nails!

She'd taken great pains to alter her mama's gown. She smoothed the kelly-green satin and adjusted the gaping neckline as best she could. Her mama had not taught her enough about the art of sewing.

Regardless, Mary simply didn't have the puppies to fill a bodice... yet. Certainly, her mother's boned corset did nothing for her since she was lean as a post. And her lamentable stockings had more holes than she possessed the patience to mend. Whose dad-blamed fool idea was this to come so far just to...

She froze when she heard footsteps.

"Bless my soul! If you aren't the most unusual white female girl I have ever laid eyes on." The voice came from the direction of the side-wheeler being off-loaded into the mud and weeds.

He was a compact, muscular youth with satiny skin the color of a fine tobacco, and he was wearing a loose, hip-length white shirt of some very fine fabric indeed, except that it looked long overdue for a rag bin. His britches were gray cotton homespun, frayed at the bottom and skintight. They fell well above his ankles.

He was barefoot and bareheaded. On his broad shoulder he balanced a small ornate traveling chest of tooled brown leather bound in sun-catching brass.

She leaped to her feet and gave him a theatrical bow. "How-do! I'm mighty glad to have somebody to talk to!"

He approached with caution, but she saw his brown eyes dance over her getup.

"Can you tell me the name of that riverboat?" she asked.

"*Brunswick Queen*, missy. Can't you read?"

With her chin out, she waved her primer at him. "I'm learning, but it's harder than hell to learn without somebody telling me the words first."

The tawny-skinned youth gaped at her shining face with the kind of wonder she had enjoyed since babyhood, but like everyone else she'd met since leaving Sacramento, his keen brown eyes crinkled with disbelief at her gown.

Nevertheless, she felt safe demanding an explanation. "I'll thank you not to gawk!" Unease washed over her. "How come folks keep staring at me?" She balled her fists, ready to slug him.

He laughed and then coughed. Rubbing his nose as if looking for the exact words, he shifted the traveling chest to his other shoulder and glanced around quickly. "You're asking honest-like?" He looked as if he couldn't believe she didn't know why. What was more, he couldn't believe she was asking his opinion. He wasn't sure which was the more remarkable.

"I'd be obliged if somebody would tell me why I've come two thousand miles to find folks staring and snickering like I've got mud on my face. I've washed. Mama taught me cleanliness is next to godliness." Whatever that really meant, the words usually had an effect on people who stared at her.

"Two thousand..." He stepped closer, electrified with curiosity. He had a gentle, voluptuous mouth, but his eyes were skeptical.

Standing on the crates, Mary swaggered in a happy circle. It was like a stage. "Aren't you going to set down that chest? It looks heavy."

He glanced around again to see if anyone was watching. His brown eyes had a penetrating quality that made her think he knew too much. "If I set it down, my boss man'll have my ears. Are you some kind of fancy lady? You don't look near old enough."

Mary leaped down in a flash of red petticoats and gave him a warning poke. "Don't start in calling me names!"

He backed away, wide-eyed with alarm.

She flounced after him and shoved. "Don't start with me!"

"Sweet Miss Susie's pearls! I'm not calling nobody nothing! Please, don't shout like that, missy! I'll get strung up quicker than lightning. You said you was asking honest-like, and so I asks, honest-like, if you was... Settle down, missy! You can't go around in red and green satin like some Natchez floozy and not draw an eye or two. Sweet Susie! When am I going to learn to mind my own business! Good morning to you!" He spun on his bare heel and marched away.

She hadn't expected his reaction. She hated the way his eyes danced from side to side, as if he really did expect to get strung up on her account. She shook her fists. "I'm sorry!" she called.

But he kept moving, giving her a backward look that said she was as dangerous as blasting powder.

"Don't go! Please!" she called, dashing after him and grabbing his arm. No one had ever walked away from her before. "I really am sorry! I don't have manners at all."

"You haven't told me nothing I hadn't figured out already for myself!" he said, slowing. He eased away from her touch.

"Please, stay and talk to me for just a minute more. I don't know a soul here. All I can do is wait day after day for the *Natchez Trace*. You don't happen to know when it'll get here, do you?"

"No, I don't, and if you're getting on it, I hope I'm a-staying behind," he snapped. He would never trust a white woman.

She didn't understand his anger and was alarmed that he was not charmed out of his socks by her beauty. Maybe it was because he had no socks. "I said I was sorry!"

He finally stopped and heaved a sigh. "I must be a fool," he muttered, turning. He sniffed a bit, but she saw him fight a smile. He couldn't help himself. He liked her.

"I'd tag along and talk awhile, but I've got to stay near my trunk," Mary said, sidling back toward the crates. "All I have in the world is in it. If you hear about that riverboat, will you tell me? Folks I've been asking think I've got no true business with it, but I'm staying put till it gets here. You can bet on that!"

"You got no place to go, missy?" he asked, his eyes growing soft and concerned. "Sweet Susie."

She shook her head. "I been taking my meals over there," she said, pointing toward the town's muddy main street where there was a restaurant. "I'm waiting for my papa. He owns the riverboat!" She gave him a prideful smile.

He shifted the chest again, his expression skeptical. "If I hear about it, and I ain't a hundred miles off somewhere, I'll likely let you know. But you watch yourself sitting in plain sight like...like that. I'm surprised you haven't been hauled off for wearing that getup in broad daylight. Don't you know what you look like?"

She looked pretty like her mama and as bright and sassy as Belle, she thought. But her throat thickened. This was the new bewildering world where ladies didn't dress in gaudy colors. "I'm wearing the best I got!"

"Well, missy, my boss man don't take lightly to idle folks, so I got to go. He'll be along any minute. You got any money?"

She clutched at her reticule, which still bulged with greenbacks and her mama's old pistol. "Why you asking?"

"You ought to buy something more fitting to a nice young lady. Look out for yourself, hear? These docks ain't no place safe after dark."

Mary knew that only too well. She'd waited nearly two weeks, and in that time she'd seen plenty that was reminiscent of Tenderfoot's rowdiest days.

Hurt that he couldn't stay, she settled once again on the crates. "Will you come back when you're done with your chores?"

"Missy, I'm never done, but I'll try." He scratched his head.

"Are you somebody's servant?" she called, watching him glance nervously at the boat. Travelers turned to stare at her now, just as everyone had been doing for days.

"Missy, I belong to my boss man. If he says I got to work till I drop, then I'll do it. But don't fret. We'll be around a night or two. I may have time to talk. I want to know where a girl like you comes from."

"California!" she said, her spirits lifting at the mention of home. "That's gold country, in case you didn't know. What's your name?"

"Quarter Dollar." He grinned. He gave a salute and started away toward several hump-backed trunks.

"That's no kind of name!"

"It is when that's all you're worth to the boss man!"

• • •

She watched him wait a good ten minutes beside the trunks. A slave, she thought with a shudder of curiosity and horror. He was scarcely dark enough to be taken for a black man. In the slaveless wilds of California she had gathered from general talk that slaves were mule-like people, but he was just like anybody else.

Then a young gentleman wearing a buff-colored frock coat and snugly tapered trousers sauntered down the wide stageplank. He wore a cream-colored hat with a narrow flat brim and a flat top, nothing like Doby's and Otto's stiff black derbys. Everyone in the states dressed so different. She was beyond understanding how folks could dress in such sober colors.

The elegant gentleman had clipped side-whiskers, a jutting jaw, and wavy black hair. His short moustache curved in a thin dark line along the edge of his upper lip. She guessed at once that he was a gambler. She knew his stripe and turned up her nose. The memory of Smiling Ace Malone made her clench her teeth and narrow her eyes. He'd been a gambler of the worst sort! If she ever saw him again, she'd break his dad-blasted nose!

Maxxmillon Blade was a gambler, too, but that didn't trouble her because a man who owned a riverboat wasn't in the same class as that no-account bastard Ace Malone.

Quarter Dollar's boss man flicked his gloved hand toward the humpbacked trunks. Quarter nodded, almost bowing. After taking a second one up onto his shoulder, he staggered along at a respectful distance. The white gent ambled into town like visiting royalty.

Boss man, Mary thought, eyes flinty. She'd never take to the likes of him!

Pacing to work off her impatience, Mary thought of the trip that had brought her to this town alongside the mighty brown river.

She'd arrived in Sacramento knowing someone waited to take her to an orphanage. She'd exited the boat in a clutch of disgruntled prospectors, then had hidden on the crowded docks until nightfall, when she hired a Chinese to tote her trunk to the stage office.

Her reticule tightly in hand, she'd taken a four-seater Concord stagecoach south on the Butterfield mail route to Los Angeles and on to Fort Yuma. She'd been lucky to be traveling in winter. The temperature was bearable.

At times they were detained at missions, awaiting a clear way past Apaches and Comanches. For a time, no one questioned her right to travel alone. She repeated as often as necessary that she was on her way

35

to meet her father, implying he was expecting her.

The mission priests had asked after her religious education. Learning she had none and could neither read nor write, they set to work at once introducing her to a bewildering constellation of thou-shalt-nots that she made a point to ignore. Any decent person already lived by such laws. It came naturally, her mama had always said.

By the time Mary reached Fort Bliss she could recite several pages from her new primer. She survived southern New Mexico Territory's wilds by memorizing. Everyone who listened thought she was actually reading. Only now did she realize how useful reading might prove.

They had gone on to Fort Chadbourne, Fort Belknap, and Fort Smith in Texas, until they finally reached a part of the country she recognized as real country and no longer scrubby desert.

Those men who took it upon themselves to watch over her would have taken her on up the Mississippi and Missouri and back around to California by way of the Nebraska Territory, probably. But she had declared her father would have them hanged and horsewhipped for kidnapping if they didn't leave her off.

She had come two thousand, four hundred miles by coach and paddle-wheeler, and she'd worn the green satin most of the way, with an occasional change into a slightly more subdued but equally improper gray-and-red-striped silk.

She had yet to see a properly dressed girl her own age. Young ladies didn't tend to ride dusty mail coaches, or travel open-deck passage on no-account riverboats.

She'd seen priests, soldiers, Indians of a dozen tribes, traders, cowboys, and ranchers, as well as pioneer folk looking no different from a cross between a trapper and a Comanche. She'd seen fancy ladies aplenty, and felt no particular kinship with them, though she did feel at home among them.

Since waiting at Crystal Point, she'd hidden herself when anyone resembling a pious matron had appeared. She knew well-meaning ladies in gray, brown, or black had "orphanage" branded in their brains. She'd even met a few who might've hired her to tend children for a few pennies a week!

She hadn't come this far to fall prey to some stranger bent on taming and reforming her. She prided herself on being wild. She was California's gold rush princess, bound to find her papa, and find him she would.

Two

Returning from a hastily eaten lunch, Mary noticed a curious assemblage gathering on the grassy riverbank several hundred yards up from the wharf.

A number of gentlemen in dark suits and tall hats stood among the somber gowns of married ladies whose fringed lace-work shawls fluttered in the afternoon breeze.

Mary saw several children dashing along the edge of the group. This would be her chance to see how young people were properly dressed! She didn't want to greet her distinguished father looking like a little harlot.

Making sure her trunk was covered by a mud-encrusted tarp, she moved quickly alongside a deserted brick warehouse, climbed a woodpile some hundred cords long, then strolled along the grassy bank to a secluded place where she could hear a brimstone sermon being preached by a man perspiring in God's name.

Wearing heavy black wool, he resembled the priests of New Mexico Territory, but they had been Spanish, with cultured voices that were soft and mellow. This man had a handsome white face. He shouted his message with the fervor of a starving barker standing outside a deserted gambling tent.

She moved close to some sturdy oaks to hide her gaudy dress. Everyone was so engrossed in what the preacher was spouting, Mary went unnoticed.

The preacher stood on a white-painted wooden platform. Beside him sat a blank-eyed, dour little woman in dove-gray. She wore a lovely bonnet, ruffled in front with long ribbons on either side of her head. They fluttered in the breeze, tickling her nose and cheeks. She raised a gloved hand now and again to keep them from her eyes.

Beside her was a girl of ten or eleven, wearing a matching gray dress and cape with a simple straw bonnet and ribbons. Her skirt was short enough to show a bit of lacy bloomers and black stockings above high-button shoes. Mary thought the child looked charming, but felt the style was too babyish for herself.

Then Mary noticed the youth seated on the far side of the preacher. He was visible only when the man stepped back and bowed his head before flinging wide his arms for another diatribe against sin. The man's voice was little more than a distant drone to Mary as she strained to catch another glimpse of the young man sitting so erect on the platform.

He wore no hat. His pale hair glinted like silver in the afternoon sun. He wore a severe black frock coat and trousers like his father— the preacher had that same startlingly pale hair. The young man wasn't listening; she could tell that with certainty. She longed to get closer so that she could see him.

The sun felt warm on her head, pouring from the sky like watery gold. The air shimmered with the yellow light, blurring the sun-dappled green of the trees. The river slipping by seemed suddenly loud and insistent. The grassy field with its heady fragrance beckoned to her.

"Brothers and sisters, I am here to save you! Open your hearts…"

Transfixed, Mary edged forward. The group closed in around the platform. Women nodded now, dabbing at their eyes, wringing their hands. Children were gathered in and hushed. Everyone murmured "A-men."

The tow-headed young man seated on the platform turned his head and looked straight at Mary. Her breath caught in her chest. Had he noticed the flash of her skirts? Oh, what would he think!

She clutched at her neckline, then caught her billowing skirts so they wouldn't flash so brightly against the freshness of the meadow grass.

Heart pounding, she wondered why she should react in such a way to this particular young man. He might be mean-hearted and laugh at her dress and her ignorance.

"Brothers and sisters, I beg of you to cast the sin out of your hearts. Come with me to the river!" the preacher shouted. "And to show you what a wonder redemption can be, and what a difference it can make in your life, my own son will testify…" He turned toward his son, hand outstretched.

But the son was staring at Mary.

Mary had heard brimstone sermons in Tenderfoot. Those words could make grown men cry and fall on their knees. But she was no sinner. She didn't lie or steal. She loved people and animals, and respected her mother.

The preacher's son was still staring at her, his blue eyes boring into hers even at that distance. What was he thinking?

She ducked behind a tree, cringing there until she had to draw a breath. Her chest felt crushed, her cheeks hot. If she could only turn into that beautifully dressed, proper young lady her mother had always dreamed about...

Peeking, she saw the youth on his feet. He stood several inches taller than his father, his handsome face rigid, his silvery-blond head back. He looked angry as he scanned the congregation. His gaze seared them. They expected him to rain brimstone on their heads like his father.

But he said nothing.

Then Mary saw him shake his head sharply and turn from his father. He leaped to the ground and struck off for the side of the open meadow where Mary hid behind a tree.

After a strained silence, the preacher's voice rang out again. Mary heard nothing as she watched the blond youth walk toward her. She couldn't move!

Her heart stood in her throat. Her pulse raced. Though she was not yet fourteen, she knew he was the one. In his rebellious stride, in the lithe strength of his lean young body, in the predatory, sensuous, challenging flash of his hooded blue eyes she recognized his power over her.

If only she were older! If only she had a similar power over him. But she was a child, foolishly, ignorantly dressed. She had no hope...

She was terrified he would demand that she take herself away, but he stopped, tore his blazing eyes from hers, and turned back to watch his father.

Mary's breath came in gasps. What a remarkable face! What dazzling hair! And his eyes!

A few ladies had turned to watch him, their faces shocked, disapproving. When they saw Mary, their heads went together. A rustle of whispers tore through that side of the crowd. Mary watched, the hair on the back of her neck standing straight, as the congregation stole glances at her.

"I don't care what they're saying," Mary whispered in a small, hurt, but defiant voice. "I'm wearing the best I got. I'm no floozy!"

She looked up. The young man's dark blue eyes were fastened on her. He was no more than seventeen or eighteen. His hair shined hypnotically in the sunlight. His face was oddly molded, with high arrogant cheekbones and defiant sultry hollows beneath. A low straight brow cut sharply across the tops of his eyes. Some might have thought he scowled, but the expression was perhaps more a disguise for his secret amusement, his self-imposed reserve.

He had a mouth that dared her to come closer and speak to him.

When she didn't, he moved two steps closer. "I noticed you," he said in a delightfully deep voice. "Do you live around here?"

"I'm waiting for my papa to come upriver on the *Natchez Trace*." Her voice was little better than a self-conscious squeak. Then she laughed and gave a little curtsy. She felt weak and silly. This was the finest stranger she'd ever spoken to! "How-do, sir!" Her face flooded with color. What exquisite torture to be aware of herself this way!

His eyes softened, and a smile played about his mouth. He got that same wonderstruck look on his handsome face that she always found so reassuring. He found her pretty, she knew, and it buoyed her courage.

"Are you from around here?" she asked coyly. If he was, she'd never take her leave of the place. All she wanted was to draw a smile from that face.

"We're from Ohio. Pa's preaching at every landing, baptizing when he gets the chance." His eyes turned toward the muddy water nearby. "We've been at this two weeks. I'm weary of it. I've got schooling to finish! I'm going to sea as soon as I'm graduated. I can't hope for a commission in the war if I don't graduate!"

She'd heard talk, talk, talk about a war coming, but had shrugged it off. She envisioned war as something of a feud over claims.

"Where are you from?" he asked finally.

"California," she said, raising her brows and grinning. "Gold country!"

His eyes lit up. He gave her a nod she took as a token of respect. "And you're a...a..." His half smile dimmed as his neck reddened. He looked down and away as if regretting his words.

"I entertain," Mary said with a proud, belligerent smile. She knew what he suspected. "I sing and dance—at least I did until...my mama died. I've been on the stage since I was five."

"An actress, then," he said, jamming both hands into his trouser pockets. "You'll excuse me for what I was thinking."

She blushed. "Not an actress, exactly. Just a singer of...songs." It didn't sound like much so far from Broken Rock and the memories of her proudest days onstage. "I've never known any other life," she said softly, hoping he didn't mistake her modesty for shame. "And I don't have any other clothes, though I expect I'd better get some 'fore I meet my papa! Before he even says how-do, he's liable to take a strap to me for looking the way I do."

Studying her face, he looked as though he needed all his wits to remember she was only a half-grown child. "I expect my pa will take a strap to me tonight for embarrassing him this way," he muttered, though he didn't look terribly troubled. "I don't hold to testifying, not after what he's done."

"You're a mite big for strapping anyhow," Mary said, reddening. She began to giggle.

A smile twitched at the corners of his mouth.

"How come you didn't want to talk to the folks?" she asked, seeing the preacher grow distracted as he watched them from the corner of his eye. The poor man looked pretty worried about his son standing beside a chestnut-haired temptress in green satin.

"Pa knows I won't be a preacher." He drew a white-knuckled fist from his pocket. "I'm going to be a naval officer!"

She saw the set of his jaw, the conviction in him, and was proud of him.

Turning, he tore up a fistful of grass and wadded it. "My pa's no traveling preacher. Our home's in Cold Crossing." He sniffed. "For years I fought every rough-and-tumble grub who called me names. I made folks take me for what I was, but now we have to travel to give all the new talk time to die down."

Intrigued, Mary inched closer. "Talk?"

He met her eyes and then glanced over his shoulder at his father, who was drawing the meeting to a hasty, awkward close. "Pa seems to find it necessary to give private...sermons...to the prettier members of his congregation. I found out about one a few years back..." He shook his head. "I never said anything, but...I don't hold to a man saying one thing and doing something else again, especially if he's jumping down my throat night and day for that very thing. I can tell you, he's given me enough cold dunks in the river back home to freeze up a—" He broke off. "The whole town knows about Pa's latest 'sermonizing.' It's nearly killed my ma. We don't know yet if we're going back."

Mary was struck speechless to think a preacher man would get himself caught up in scandal. She disliked him immediately.

Suddenly her tow-haired Mr. Charming, gazing so intently at her, finally did break into a grin that brightened his face. Mary's heart leaped with excitement. He was about to say something wonderful, she was sure, but then his head jerked up. "Judas! Here he comes with Ma and Rowena. Don't run off. I want you to meet my family."

Her heart thrilled. "I won't, no, sir!" Mary said emphatically, raking back her long tangles and straightening her bodice.

"Ah, there you are, John Travis. I thought perhaps you went back to the hotel. Weren't you a bit abrupt in your exit, son?" The preacher strode toward the broad oak where Mary stood, his eyes locked on hers.

The preacher cupped his wife's elbow as she picked her way across the uneven meadow. Behind them trailed the little girl, her dark blue eyes huge. The woman looked frail and bleached, and her eyes were damp.

At the sight of his mother's distress, Mary's stranger scowled. He plunged his hands into his pockets again.

"John Travis, be so good as to introduce us to this interesting young...lady." The preacher's expression conveyed his assumption that John Travis and Mary had secretly met before and conspired to meet here.

"I don't know her, Pa."

"How-do, sir!" Mary said, thinking this the proper time to extend her smudged hand. "I'm Mary Louise Mackenzie! Proud to meet you!"

With a look of consternation, the preacher regarded her ungloved hand. Realizing she expected him to shake hands like a man, he did so, bowing stiffly, as if willing to show respect to even the lowliest of God's creatures.

"My dear young lady, how very pleased I am to make your acquaintance," he said, memorizing her from windblown head to muddy shoe toe. He had one sad, bleak eye, as if the world greatly distressed him, and one eye blazing with alarm, as if he considered it his duty alone to save that distressing world from everlasting damnation.

But as Mary peered into his drooping face, marked by weary bags beneath those strangely conflicting eyes, she thought she detected a deep sorrow. What a cheerless man he must be to live with, she thought.

"Mackenzie...Irish, I believe. Irish Catholic," he said.

His wife recoiled slightly.

Mary stiffened. "Folks tell me that's how my name sounds. If it does, you and everybody must be right. I don't have a notion where my name came from. Such things don't trouble folks where I come from. We take each other as we are."

Taken aback by her honesty, the preacher squinted at her and then turned his attention to his son. He drew in his breath, disapproval visibly settling in his eyes, but his intended words were cut short.

Mary's young man interrupted, as if deliberately keeping his father from saying anything more. "This is my father, Theophilus Holloway. And my mother, Submit...and my little sister, Rowena. I'm called Trance."

All were nodding as if very happy to meet, but then Preacher Holloway frowned again. "I should think the young lady would find your given name more to her liking. John Travis..."

"Oh, I think Trance is a perfect name for him!" Mary said, unable to understand why she found this encounter so exciting. "I'm waiting for my papa…" She went on to explain how she'd come to be in Crystal Point, including some colorful highlights of her trip through New Mexico Territory and the state of Texas. In moments, she had Trance's mother gasping for breath and Rowena pop-eyed with disbelief.

"That's a fine story, young lady," Preacher Holloway said, as if bored, "but if you'll excuse us now, we must make arrangements for the next leg of our journey. I wish you luck finding your…uh…father." His expression iced over. "Submit, dear, come along now. It's getting late. John Travis, would you please bid your…young…acquaintance good day now? I wish to discuss today's meeting with you—in private, if you please." He moved away, talking as if he thought John Travis—Trance— was right behind him. "Of course, I'm sorry we weren't able to have a baptism this afternoon. I found your behavior most bewildering, so much so that…" He paused, realizing Trance had not followed. When he turned back to see Trance still staring at Mary, a look of pain crossed his face.

For several seconds, Trance didn't move. Then, as if just becoming aware that he was expected to take his leave of Mary, he said to his father, "Don't ask me to testify again, Pa. I can't do it anymore."

The words seemed to bow the preacher's shoulders.

Trance noticed his mother's face and tightened his lips, forcing himself not to say another word. Mary watched his expression return to impassive lines and knew he was now lost to the freedom and joy she had so briefly brought him.

Trance shrugged. Turning, he followed his parents and sister, his body alive and quick with restrained power.

Preacher Holloway smiled ingratiatingly. "John Travis, do bid a proper…good-bye…to your young…" He was interrupted by his wife's insistent whisper, which Mary could not catch. Preacher Holloway reacted by rearing, as if his wife had uttered a curse.

As if aware that she was provoking her husband, Mrs. Holloway pressed on. "But, Theo, she looks like such a helpless little waif in those tawdry trappings. She may need our help!"

Alarm spread through Mary. She'd forgotten that well-intentioned ladies thought her incapable of looking after herself, even though she had traveled over two thousand miles, most of them through hostile Indian country.

Trance paused, letting his parents and sister go ahead. He turned back, his voice soft. "I'm glad I met you," he said, his eyes searching her face. "How old are you?"

She was tempted to lie. "Thirteen," she said finally.

"You look older." A soft smile spread across his lips. "You're the prettiest girl I ever met. I'll think about you."

She dashed across the space separating them, her thoughts wild. He couldn't leave, not yet! "Give me a token...to remember you by!" She pulled gently at his coat sleeve.

He looked bewildered. "I don't have anything." He drew two handfuls of odds and ends from his trouser pockets—coins, bits of paper, a jackknife.

"This! Please, this!" she said, snatching the knife. She pulled it open with her thumbnail and expertly threw it at the broad oak. Its tip lodged in the bark and quivered like Mary's heart. "Otto taught me to do that when I was only six. You won't forget me?" she asked, grinning up at him.

"I don't expect I'll be able to," he said, gazing deeply into her eyes as if trying to imagine the young woman she would soon become.

On tiptoes she sprang, brushing his startled smile with her lips, and then she dashed to retrieve the knife. She darted away, clambered over the woodpile, and returned to her perch near the dock. She was too embarrassed to look back.

Trance, she thought, pondering the knife she had all but stolen from him. He had looked entranced when she first saw him seated on the platform, staring straight ahead, lost in his private thoughts. She could almost imagine those private thoughts, and now she would be a part of them!

She saw the preacher and his family that evening when she ventured into town to eat supper. The preacher's wife deftly guided her family to the opposite side of the street. Mary was bitterly insulted.

After dinner, Mary stopped again at the shipping office to ask after the *Natchez Trace*. She was storming away when she heard someone hissing at her from the shadows beyond the building.

"Great snakes, Quarter Dollar! You scared me! How-do!" she said, shaking her head. "I don't know as a person could ever get used to calling you such a name. Don't you have a real one?"

He shrugged with amusement and shook his head as if it wasn't important. "Had your supper, missy?"

44

"I have, and it wasn't half bad. Are you really a slave? Why didn't you say so right off? It doesn't seem right. Can't you do anything about it?"

"I ain't up to changing the color of the sky this evening, missy. I just heard that riverboat you was asking about is due in tomorrow afternoon. It's no regular riverboat for hauling goods and such like. No'm, it's a gambling boat!"

"Didn't I tell you my papa's the greatest riverboat gambler in the world!" She gave a whoop of delight.

She could almost picture the boat splashing up to the wharf. She'd imagined a thousand times how she'd march up the stageplank and unhesitatingly announce herself. Now that the hour was finally upon her, she felt uneasy and shy.

"I'm nervous as a claim jumper. If I just had one decent dress…" She looked down at herself and felt truly tawdry for the first time in her life.

"You might buy one," he said.

"Hadn't thought of that."

He drew her along the street, reading off the signs of establishments until they came to a shop with ladies' ready-to-wear displayed in the bay window. "Buy something here come morning."

Mary shook her head. "I won't go in if there's a lady inside." She told him of her encounters with well-meaning matrons. By and by they came to the sheltered spot behind the hotel where she'd been sleeping.

Quarter Dollar hunkered down beside her and listened intently as she described Trance Holloway, nodding and grinning at all the right parts, and then saying, "Sounds like a fine young gentleman to me. Mighty fine!"

"You know almost all there is to know about me now," she said after a time. "Where are you from?"

"Me and my boss man, we're from down south Louisiana way. I was born on a plantation. My boss man's father is a cane planter. You ever hear that expression, 'sold down the river'? That's where I was born at. There's not a place where I can go where the work's harder. So I reckon I'll stay on with my boss man till that lawyer from Illinois gets himself elected President. I hear tell he's a powerful Abolitionist. Another year or two, the whole South just might tear itself away from…" He chuckled. "I can see you aren't interested in war talk."

"I'm more interested in hearing about you and your family." She couldn't imagine what a cane plantation looked like and still wondered why Quarter Dollar didn't just take his leave of the place.

He was quiet a moment. "I got no family to speak of. There's no such thing for a slave. I got a mama, though." He smiled sadly. Abruptly he rose, his expression suddenly dark, as if he was remembering something important. "I can't dawdle any more with you, missy, but it's been nice talking to you. Likely, I'll see you tomorrow. Boss man's thinking of going on the *Natchez Trace*. I'd be obliged, though, if you didn't say how-do to me then. Boss man might figure out I was here with you tonight. He might take it in his head that…You understand, I hope. If you don't, you got no business traveling by yourself."

She frowned at the fear in his voice. "Take care of yourself, Quarter," she whispered, gathering her skirts and shawl tightly around herself for the long night ahead.

He disappeared into the shadows. She was sorry when he had gone and felt a stab of loneliness.

At dawn a stray dog woke her up. She skipped breakfast, too excited about the arrival of her papa's steamboat to eat.

Not liking the looks of the ladies going in and out of the dress shop, she decided her papa would have to take her dressed as she was.

Less than an hour later a long sleek white side-wheeler splashed into view from the south. The *Natchez Trace* was a pretty boat with two white-railed decks and twin black smokestacks with fluted tops. An American flag snapped from the jack staff.

The boiler deck was surprisingly empty of people. Only deck hands and a few elegantly dressed passengers stood at the stern.

Mary's heart leaped as the boat drifted close in and tied up. She found herself rooted to her perch on the crates, too terrified to approach. Never before had she been afraid to do anything. The feeling rankled, but still she didn't move.

Not until the last passengers started toward town did she notice a silver-haired gentleman in red suspenders and shirtsleeves emerge out of the upper deck. Making his way down to the boiler deck, he situated himself on the far side of the boat on a Windsor chair.

Mary's courage was renewed, he looked approachable. Perhaps he'd introduce her to her papa! She eased herself off the crates, dusted off her skirt, and pushed her long hair behind her ears. Then, as if on a Sunday stroll, she sashayed toward the stageplank.

She found the gentleman impaling a writhing brown night crawler onto the hook of his fishing pole. He was humming, glancing up at the broad brown river at intervals, squinting at the yellow sun glancing off the sluggish water.

At her approach, he raised his white head. He had the finest, sleekest hair of any old gentleman she'd ever seen. His beard was immaculate down to the last curved inch-long whisker. He was just a bit stout, with the wonderful aroma of fine Cuban tobacco and bay rum shaving soap about him.

He cocked an eyebrow, then flung the line over the white railing. "Mighty fine day," he said in a strangely accented deep voice. "Uh-huh, mightly fine, indeed. Myself, I'm goin' to catch a mess of catfish for my supper. Look yonder there. See the catfish fighting to catch hold of my hook? Once upon a time I caught myself a catfish a full five feet long!" He nodded, tipping his chair back. His eyes closed and he smiled to himself. "'Course, I was only three feet long at the time."

Three

Trance followed his parents along the hall to their hotel suite. At his side, Rowena snickered and gave him the eye, trying to imitate the wide-eyed expression of that nymph from California. Trance ignored his sister and was kicked in the shins for his trouble.

Ahead, his father stopped and stared with disbelief at his wife. "Why must we leave so soon? My work isn't done. So many were eager to be baptized. If John Travis hadn't—"

At the mention of his name, Trance tensed and looked to his mother, so small and seemingly meek. She reared up like a cobra to glare at her husband.

"You know perfectly well!" she hissed, glancing back at Trance with the same expression she'd been giving her husband since a certain pretty young woman in Cold Crossing made a seemingly innocent remark about a certain late-night visit from the good preacher. "It's in his blood just as surely as it's in yours. I won't have it! We're going on the next boat. I don't care if it's a barge bound for China!"

Trance gathered his resolve and approached his parents. "Pa, it might be best if we did move along. You remember Lester Catz? I saw him this afternoon coming out of a beer hall."

His father's lips tightened. A no-account such as Lester was of no consequence except that the man might go home and say he'd seen the wayward preacher. Tongues might continue wagging.

Trance couldn't see that it was so important, really. They'd have to face their neighbors again someday. It was distressing, however, for his mother to be reminded of home when her humiliation was still raw.

His father turned away. "Perhaps it is best we move on at the first opportunity, but surely I can conduct one last meeting this afternoon. We could leave tomorrow. I doubt we could get cabins on the *Brunswick Queen* this late. She's likely to be gone soon in any case."

"I would like to be gone from here in any case," Submit muttered, her voice bitter.

Theo's shoulders sagged. "We cannot spend the rest of our lives fleeing. Someday we must go home!"

Submit raised her eyebrows, her downturned mouth eloquent with hurt pride. "We can book passage on that other boat if John Travis will hurry and secure us two cabins right away."

The opportunity to see the girl in the green dress loomed in Trance's mind. "I'll go right now, Mother," he said, almost too eagerly.

His father cleared his throat. "Out of the question, Submit! I realize you're not aware of such things, but that particular boat is a gambling boat, a veritable den of iniquity! It's likely to have aboard a variety of low persons and loose women."

Submit regarded her husband coldly. "That should suit our purposes quite nicely." They moved into their suite, where Trance couldn't hear his father's strangled retort.

Would his mother never relent? Trance wondered. He didn't intend to forgive his father's adultery, but he felt angry that his mother treated him as if *he* were equally guilty. He'd done nothing!

In no time, he was out of the hotel and at the wharf. Instantly, his concern for his parents receded, replaced by his memory of beguiling brown eyes and cascading chestnut curls.

The *Natchez Trace* would remain one more night before returning south, he'd been told, because of ice upriver.

Trance felt conspicuous marching toward the boat. A young black man about Trance's age dashed by, grazing Trance's shoulder. "Excuse me, sir!" he called, turning and bowing slightly.

"No harm done," Trance said, curious as to why the black was in such a rush to board the riverboat. "Have you seen a girl in green satin hereabouts?" Trance called, blushing at the mention of her.

The young black's attractive features folded into a knowing grin. "Indeed, I have, sir! She's a-fishing with a white gentleman t'other side of this boat."

Trance tipped his cap and mounted the wide stageplank. "I'm Trance Holloway," he said, offering his hand.

"Honored, sir! The name's Quarter Dollar. Don't pay no mind to Miss Mary's peculiarities, sir. She thinks she knows everything, but she don't know the half. Mighty nice to meet you. Mighty nice!"

Trance watched Quarter Dollar lope up the boat's wide stairs to the main deck. Threading his way around a surprising amount of cargo, considering this was supposed to be an iniquitous gambling boat, he found the object of his fantasies perched on the railing alongside an aging gent with silver hair.

She was swinging her dark-stockinged legs back and forth, and most of her red ruffled petticoat showed. The wind teased her chestnut curls, and when she laughed his heart swelled.

From the girl's easy chatter, Trance gathered she wasn't aware she was talking with a gentleman of some station. Trance recognized the expensive roll of the man's Cuban cigar and the expert cut of his wool trousers.

At the sound of Trance's footsteps on the deck, she turned. Blushing, she tried to cover her petticoats. "How-do!" she said, swinging around and hopping down before Trance. She looked back at the amused gentleman. "Thanks ever so much for letting me fish with you."

"Afternoon," Trance said, tipping his cap, unsure how to address her.

"Did your pa give you the strap for talking to me yesterday?" she whispered. They edged away from the gentleman whose merry eyes looked on knowingly. "Let's walk!" she said, tugging Trance's coat sleeve and propelling him toward the stageplank.

They looked up to see Quarter Dollar's boss man bearing down on them. He wore an immaculate black frock coat and ruffle-breasted silk shirt. Halfway up the stageplank he shoved Mary aside and collided with Trance.

Trance and the gambler were nearly the same height. With his lip curled in mocking amusement, the gambler surveyed Trance. Then he turned his attention to Mary. For an instant he was taken aback. Then his eyes swept over her undeveloped figure and his eyebrows lifted as if wondering who would take notice of such a child.

The gambler dusted his sleeves and tugged at them. "I believe you owe me an apology, sir, for crashing into me," he said to Trance. His attempt to disguise his thick Southern drawl was unsuccessful.

Trance bristled but said nothing.

"I realize you must be in a hurry to enjoy that for which you have paid," the gambler went on. "I reckon it must've been a tiny sum, though, for such a young honey of a chit, but that doesn't give you the right to shove your betters." His thin dark moustache twitched just above his smirk.

Trance summoned all his strength to control himself. He knew this sort only too well. He'd been fighting them since he was in knee britches. Only recently had he learned such men weren't worth his blood. With supreme control, Trance edged aside just enough to let the arrogant

Southerner pass.

But Mary wasn't about to let him off so easily. "You three-legged jackass! Just who are you calling names? No-good drunken shallow pate! I know your kind. You're nothing but a highfalutin, fancy-talking poker. Get out of our way! You're not fit to be around decent folk!"

Trance seized her shoulders and shook her a bit. "Come on, before he has you arrested for public blaspheming!" A grin stretched his face.

"I'll be damned if I'll stand by while he calls me fancy names!" she said, giving the speechless gentleman an unexpected shove.

Reeling backward, he fell off the stageplank into the shallow mud between the boat and the dock.

Mary roared with delight as Trance dragged her away toward the meadow. "Call me names, will you! Gull-danged son of a snake!"

"Where did you learn to cuss like that?" Trance asked, laughing as they skirted the cords of wood and turned to watch the gambler struggle out of the river.

She looked up at Trance, basking in triumph. "I told you. California! If a body can't cuss his way around Tenderfoot—that's where I was born—then he isn't fit to walk the streets. I guess I showed that fancy Dan just who his betters were!"

"Have you found your father?" Trance asked, still grinning in admiration.

She made a face, then shook her head.

Trance smiled down at her. "Any man would be proud to claim you as his daughter. If he isn't, you just cuss at him awhile and he'll come around."

She shivered happily. Then she turned to look back at the riverboat. "I have to get up the gumption to meet him soon. They leave tomorrow morning at eight-fifteen." She swallowed. "You know, if he doesn't take to me, I think I will cuss him out! Leaving my ma to live out her life in Tenderfoot...I'll have a heap of things to say!"

In the fringed and varnished elegance of the captain's quarters on the Texas deck of the *Natchez Trace*, Maxxmillon Blade poured another short brandy. "Umm-um, Sharona, don't you worry your lovely head. I'll watch that rake all the long night. Indeed, I will," he said in an unhurried French Creole accent to the naked, raven-haired woman languishing in his massive brass bed.

She stretched, combing her slim white fingers through long black waves. Rising from the bed like Venus from the sea, Sharona Doherty crossed to the ornately carved mahogany wardrobe. "I didn't like the looks of that cad, not from the moment he set foot on board. He's trouble, sure. Ring for Lubie, please, darlin'. I'll hurry myself and dress. You won't be letting him win too much tonight, will you, Maxx, darlin'?"

Grinning, Maxx turned, tugging his tailored black cutaway over his lordly paunch. "My lovely, don't think I'm not aware of why that scoundrel bothers you so. Myself, I saw him thirsting after you, but I won't call him out, no. I know you love only me." When he spoke this way to Sharona his accent grew especially thick.

Mollified, Sharona lingered, observing her tall shapely body in the looking glass. Though almost thirty-nine, she liked reminding Maxx of her svelte figure. "And what of that pint-sized floozy you were fishing with this afternoon? Did you shoo her off?"

His brown eyes swept over her appreciatively. "My charming companion dashed off with some wonderstruck lad in a gray schoolboy's hat. Too old for her, I said to myself. Umm-um, they do start young, they do!"

Maxx grinned as Sharona donned her long apricot-silk dressing gown. What a minx that child had been! Coy and pretty as a new boat, spanking fresh from the western mountains…She'd told him about her childhood in a place called Tenderfoot in California and about her trip to locate her father.

How strange it was, Maxx thought, pushing a diamond breastpin into his cravat and sticking a geranium in his lapel, what an overpowering urge to protect her had come over him. He took a tiny gold knife from his pocket and pared his nails. Then he adjusted the spring-activated derringer pistol with the inlaid French silver hidden in his sleeve. His black cat, Napoleon, sprang from his place on the sill and rubbed Maxx's ankles.

Now Sharona, she needed no protection, though she would hotly deny the fact. No, she hissed and bit with the best. But that whisper-thin beauty from California—he'd wanted to draw her onto his lap and tell her stories!

Chuckling, Maxx brushed his silver hair and smoothed his beard. For some reason he had the very unpleasant feeling that Mary Mackenzie sought the loathsome Southern gambler who had booked passage aboard the *Natchez Trace* only hours before.

Distracted, he almost went out without giving his lovely Sharona a kiss. She felt sleek and warm beneath his big manicured hands. Snuggling against him, she gazed up into his face.

"Myself, I think you have me bewitched, my lovely," he said, knowing how she adored his love talk. "I'm twined about your pinkie finger. You give me much pleasure, you do."

Her eyes softened. What a strangely insecure creature she was for such a beautiful grown woman, he thought. He couldn't fathom her fear that he might find another to warm his bed. At this late date he was far too set in his comfortable ways to take up the search again.

"It's worrying you, he is," Sharona said, fussing with his cravat. Then she tugged his beard and pursed her lips.

He kissed her long and hard. Warmed by her eagerness, he was foolish enough to think she truly loved him and not his wealth.

Patting her soft fanny, he started out then. "Not in the least, my lovely."

She had the distressing impression that because he'd recently had his sixtieth birthday he now feared any young buck professing a passing knowledge of cards.

She must think him in his dotage, he thought, watching her turn toward the dressing table to brush out her long hair. She'd had a painfully hard childhood, he knew, though in their eight years together he'd refrained from questioning her about it too closely.

She seemed to think that if she didn't look after him like a seductive beautiful nanny, he'd fritter away his life's savings in one hand of poker. She didn't know the number of banks he kept solvent with his years of accumulated winnings. He couldn't support such a lavish riverboat or life-style on the paltry sums freight brought! He played to win, and win he did, from fools and brigands alike.

Leaving her to her toilette, Maxx sauntered from his quarters as he did at that hour each evening to greet his guests and passengers in the grand saloon. His was an easy, leisurely life, warmed by the finest wines, the best cigars, the tastiest foods, and the companionship of a woman he liked above all others.

He did not think, however, that he loved Sharona. He believed himself a generous, loving man, but love was a strong word for any sort of relationship with a woman as clinging and clever as Sharona, loyal as she appeared to be.

Making his entrance into the riverboat's glittering dining room, Maxx often thought, as he did now, of how far he'd come since his own poor childhood. His father, Esteban, had been a fur trapper. Maxx had no idea of his true surname. Blade had been Esteban's nickname, an appellation he had received because of his deadly skill with a knife. He was rumored to have killed a good many men with it, and had subdued a good many women as well.

One such innocent had been Maxx's mother, Marie, a chambermaid. Maxx had never known his father, though he had feared, hated—and longed for—him. He grew up under the influence of his mother's brother. He spent his early years thieving on the streets of New Orleans, which propelled him naturally into a life of gambling. Some of his youth was spent exploring the east and France, where his skill with cards and his wealth grew.

Maxx took his customary place at the captain's table. There he observed his passengers for the evening while enjoying the company of Sharona, his indispensable, keen-eyed hostess.

His first love, he supposed, was the river and this life of idle luxury. There, he was master of all, benevolent, respected, a powerful, admired gentleman spawned in a waterfront hotel and raised as a window-sash thief.

Maxx's personal servant, Jim Hickory, appeared at his side to uncork the evening's champagne. Jim was a good and loyal friend, one of the darkest-skinned blacks Maxx had ever seen and considered a man of distinction in his own right on the river.

Free, Jim was paid wages better than most white men. As a consequence, he felt himself entitled to a wife and family at both ends of the river.

Maxx nodded and sipped the champagne as Sharona made her entrance into the dining room.

She was, Maxx had to admit, a most pleasant and stimulating woman with whom to live. She didn't fuss unduly over her appearance but seemed beautifully groomed with no effort. Her raven hair showed only a hint of gray on one side, and her creamy Irish skin was still freckled like a girl's.

She wasn't catty like some women he'd known. So long as he bedded her with some regularity, she considered her position with him secure. She wasn't given to swooning or swearing. For that he was grateful. He had little patience with either, and, for that matter, he felt he had little time left to trouble himself with a woman who might badger him.

Sharona did not know—no one but a priest in Natchez did—that Maxx had had a mild heart attack four years before. Reminded he wasn't supposed to drink so much, he set the champagne aside. He fingered the large copper penny in his vest pocket. It was blessed by that Natchez priest, a comfort to a man unwilling to die.

Sharona's smile distracted him now. She pointed out the more interesting passengers. She was particularly amused by the family of four huddled like lambs in a wolves' den in a far corner. Soon Maxx lighted his Havana and puffed contentedly.

"They were desperate for passage," she whispered, smirking behind her fan.

Maxx let her direct his attention to the so-called Southern gentleman at a nearby table, and finally to other travelers and perennial salesmen en route to greener pastures. He did not expect the evening to be in any way remarkable.

They had just finished an after-dinner cordial when a flurry of excitement came from the vaulted room's doorway. Maxx had been watching the rebel gambler charm a bevy of ladies of reasonable quality whom Maxx employed to brighten the decor of his gaming parlor.

Sharona tapped his sleeve with her fan. "That ragged creature's trying to get a handout. I'll take her to the galley and see she's fed. Shall I give her a few dollars, too?"

"That's my fishing crony," Maxx said, crossing his ankles beneath the table as he leaned back and watched the adorable girl gain admittance to his gilded, plush dining room. "Sharona, my lovely, ask if she cares to join us for jambalaya. What you might offer her later is one of Lubie's castoffs. My small friend could stand to look something less of a *putain.*"

Sharona rose, her face pinched with disapproval. "If you insist, I'll ask her to join us. If she isn't a whore now, she'll soon learn the trade. It's asking for trouble, she is."

Sharona's décolletage accentuated the tops of her pale breasts and soft, bare arms. Maxx licked his lips, chuckling as she dipped and swayed her hoop-skirted way between the linen-draped tables. She passed the stiff-necked preacher and his family, greeting them and laughing when she was rebuffed.

The blond lad stared openly at the sprite in green satin standing in the doorway, paying no heed whatsoever to his father's whispered reprimands.

Sharona spoke briefly to the girl. Then, as she turned to convey her disapproval to Maxx, he saw she looked jealous. Surely she wouldn't begrudge him an amusing meal with the urchin from California. He did want to protect the girl should she discover that *boque*-rebel gambler in red-trimmed ruffles was her father. He could only imagine what such a man as that Southern rakehell would say if she announced herself his child.

She crept toward Maxx now, her beautiful brown eyes alight. She was, by far, the most beguiling little darling Maxx had ever seen. Now she stared at him, eyes and mouth wide, her face scarlet. Then her expression changed to one of disbelief.

"You're Maxxmillon Blade?" The huge chocolate eyes raked him from silvery head to patent black toe.

Maxx stood and bowed. His heart swelled, though he could not have said why. "My humblest pleasure at making your acquaintance, miss," he drawled, taking her hand and kissing the rough knuckles. She smelled of mud. She must have bathed in the river before coming aboard.

She blinked and stuttered, "I-I came all this way to find my p-papa, and here you…and me were talking and fishing like…like…Mr. Blade, how-dee-do, sir! I've come to find you! I'm Vanity Blade, your daughter!"

Sharona's face went white as marble.

Maxx gaped for several stunned seconds. Then he drew back his head with a roar of laughter. "My dear, dear child! Here you go. Sit with me. Can you tell me how on this good earth you can possibly think I sired your incredible beauty?"

Four

Mary stared at the gentleman wearing the distinguished swallowtail cutaway evening coat with black satin lapels. "You're not seven feet tall!"

Disappointed, she looked closely at this man calling himself Maxxmillon Blade. She'd thought his hair would be black, as her mother had said. His eyes were merry and cunning. He had a big straight nose and a smiling mouth.

"You don't look like any gambler I ever seen in my life!" she added, feeling more than a bit miffed. "Not with a fishing pole in your hand!"

Maxx chuckled. "For true! Didn't you tell me your name was Mary Mackenzie and that you were from California?"

"Mary is the name my mama gave me. Mackenzie was her name. You're my papa, so that makes my real name Blade. Since I'm an entertainer—have been since I was five—I've got a right to call myself whatever pleases me! That makes me Vanity. Are you really Maxxmillon Blade, the greatest riverboat gambler on the Mississippi?" She cocked her head.

"I am Maxxmillon Blade, for true. About the rest, I cannot humbly say. Umm-um, no, I can't, indeed." He waved for the waiter to bring Mary—Vanity Blade—a deep china soup plate of fragrant jambalaya. In moments she was eating with abandon and watching him between bites.

Sharona seated herself next to Maxx and nudged him. Her expression was openly disapproving. "I wouldn't be indulging her fantasies, darlin'."

Between mouthfuls of the most delicious concoction she'd ever eaten, Vanity told the fine-looking gentleman how she had learned he was her father. He listened with interest, nodding and chuckling at the high points until she was certain he was convinced.

"But my dear little catfish, I am most sorry to tell you I've never been to California. I've never had the pleasure of meeting your imaginative mother," Maxx said gently.

"She didn't come from California!" Vanity said impatiently. "She met you here. She knew all about riverboats and told me about the ones here. She said her own pa had a boat, but that's all she ever did say. My grandpa disowned her, but that doesn't matter now because Mama's... dead..." She faltered before forcing herself to go on brightly: "And here I am to stay!"

The beautiful raven-haired lady sitting beside her papa gasped. She was wearing a black-and-red foulard silk gown that would have made Vanity's mama cry for wanting it. It was all ruffled and finely sewn, and she smelled just like a flower.

Vanity disliked Sharona immediately. The woman got that "orphanage" look in her eye, and now she had something else written on her face, too. Miss Vanity Blade recognized it as plain jealousy!

Sharona slipped her hand possessively into the crook of Maxx's arm. "Tell the child she can't possibly stay, Maxx, darlin'. A riverboat of this kind is no place for her!" Sharona turned to Vanity. "Sweetling, you must be accepting the fact that your mother didn't care to tell you who your real father was. She probably didn't even kn—"

Quickly, Maxx covered Sharona's hand with his and squeezed it hard. Startled, Sharona said nothing more for several moments but looked at Maxx with disbelief.

"It isn't possible, is it, Maxx?" Sharona whispered finally.

"Anything is possible," Maxx said, looking as if he was trying to control his amusement. He returned his attention to a wide-eyed Vanity.

Vanity was frightened. She heard nothing he said, but she knew that he didn't want to claim her.

"Much as I want to, I cannot seem to recall ever having met a woman thirteen years ago who might've been your dear mama," he said. "If I had, I would've remembered. For true, I surely would have. She would have been as beautiful as you are now."

Vanity's fears abated somewhat. He was smiling at her in that wonderstruck, loving way that assured her she was at least acceptable for appearance's sake. But she had never dreamed he would claim he had never even met her mother.

He went on kindly. "Most unfortunately, I am old enough to be your grandpa. I caught that five-foot catfish many a year ago. That's the truth. This boat is no home for you, little catfish. I'm in no position to offer you my hospitality, much as I'd like to."

"But I mean to stay!" Vanity cried, standing, her meal unfinished. "I'll earn my way. Just let me show you! I know all my mama's songs. I was born in the back of a saloon, after all! I've never had a life away from gaming tables, gamblers, and gamblers' floozies." She looked directly at Sharona, daring the woman to contradict her.

Sharona was speechless; her cheeks reddened as her eyes narrowed. "Perhaps children can be running free in the wild west, darlin', but here in civilization a thousand laws will be saying a girl under the age of consent cannot stay under the same roof with—"

Maxx silenced Sharona again. He pursed his lips as if calculating possibilities.

"Myself, I am charmed by the idea of you entertaining us. You might give us a song or two." He appeared eager to do whatever might restore the girl's radiant smile.

Ceremoniously, he rose and offered his elbow. With a beaming smile and the grace of a seasoned, if shabby, entertainer, Vanity hooked her slim hand around his arm and let him lead her through the doors opposite the dining room's entrance.

Though she found the gaming parlor filled with familiar green-felt-covered tables, wheels of fortune, and fancy ladies, the decor took her breath away.

Whatever was not covered in maroon velvet was gilded. The black background carpet displayed huge limp flowers in reds and golds. Maxx's dealers were all in place, and a number of patrons were already playing poker at secluded corner tables.

At the head of the room, on a small raised stage, a black gentleman played softly on a piano. A half dozen more young black men in matching trousers and vests sat about with banjos, awaiting the time for the evening's entertainment.

Vanity jumped for joy to see the stage. Ignoring Sharona's discouraging frown, she dragged Maxx to the head table and made him sit. "Let me show you how much money I can bring in on one night!"

Grinning, Maxx nodded. "Carry on, little catfish!" He fished in his breast pocket for a gold cigar case, selected a Havana, and busied himself lighting it.

Vanity dashed onto the stage. She whispered to the piano player, who nodded. His fellow musicians snapped to attention.

Preacher and Mrs. Holloway had ventured in through the gaming parlor door, though they motioned their children not to enter under any circumstances.

The piano player rose from his round stool and approached the edge of the lamp-lit stage. Vanity stood to the side, puffed up with excitement, her face shining, her bright green dress suddenly looking less shabby.

The arrogant gambler strutted his way into the gaming parlor, bowing to the preacher with a smirk. Rowena Holloway darted in and hid behind a potted fern. Trance kept his place in the doorway, watching, and then grinned when Vanity waved her fingers to him and gave a wriggle of delight.

The piano player spread his arms for quiet. "Ladies and gentlemen!" he said in a resonant voice. "May I introduce Miss Mar—"

He was loudly shushed. Mary dashed to his side, whispered loudly in his ear, then returned to her place at the side.

"I have the pleasure of introducing Miss Vanity Blade, late of the great golden state of California!"

He stepped aside, arm outstretched, then seated himself at the piano, his long dark fingers moving up and down the keys until a familiar melody emerged.

Vanity strutted onto the center of the stage, her head back and her chin high. She clutched her skirts in one small white hand, and swished them back and forth as her mud-stained shoes thudded across the stage.

Her ears rang with terror. The banjos were nothing like Otto's concertina! The tempo was much faster than she was used to. The room wasn't crammed with bearded, half-soused miners. It was nearly empty, and the faces turned toward her were not doting.

Only Maxxmillon Blade smiled, and he looked so terribly indulgent she wondered if she was any sort of entertainer at all. Maybe folks here weren't charmed by a few coy songs and a cute young face!

Nonetheless, she tossed her head, sending her long tangled curls swirling about her face. She made a smile so big her lips stretched. Then she burst into song. "Kiss me, William! Kiss me fast! Kiss me 'fore our chance is past. Kiss me, William! Kiss me quick! Kiss-s-s me-e-e…every night and every morning!"

She heard a ripple of laughter and saw the room was beginning to fill. She flounced her skirts and whirled about the stage, hoping to lose herself to the thrill of performing.

But her heart pounded and her stomach was knotted worse than the night before, when she had sat hunched on the crates watching the intimidating riverboat's glittering windows.

In the middle of the stage, she flung up her arms, wishing she had puppies to wriggle. That had made miners throw coins. So far, however, not a coin had landed at her feet. "Kiss me, William! Kiss me long. Sing me your sweet evening song. Kiss me, William! Kiss me now! Kiss-s-s me-e-e…every night and every morning!"

The song might have gone on through a dozen verses, each more suggestive than the last, but Vanity sensed it wasn't charming them. She ended close to the piano player and whispered the name of another popular tune.

Nodding, he expertly changed the key of the last song to the key of the next. The banjo players grinned, charmed by Vanity, even if no one else was.

"Alice Mae, your time's a-coming. Don't cry your tears while I'm away. Dear Alice Mae, your time's a-coming. You'll be my bride some summer's day."

She sensed even less response as she completed that song. It had always brought the miners to tears, and the coins had rained as if from the sky. Still not a one had sailed through the air to land encouragingly on the *Natchez Trace*'s stage.

Finally she danced into a frenzy and stopped, not knowing the real title of her mother's infamous tune. Hoping the musicians would be able to take it up once she began singing, Vanity fixed her audience with her most seductive look. She shook her hair and then seized her skirts, flinging them about her slim legs in a flurry of rustling fabric.

"Give me plenty of cheer, boys! Give me all ya got! Heaven's mighty far, boys, but hell is nice and hot!"

Laughter brightened most of the faces in the gaming parlor. The banjos picked up her tempo and tune, filling her with courage.

"Give me hugs and kisses, boys! Give me all ya got." She had them at last, she thought! She was sure of it! She flung her skirts about, knowing from experience that she couldn't show her drawers to any crowd, being a child, but in desperation she very nearly did. She heard Maxx laughing out loud. She clattered her heels and shook her shoulders, whirling around the stage. "I'll take my pleasure now, boys! Let the pious rot!"

Nearly everyone stood, laughing and clapping. Still, no coins rained at her feet. She was wounded to think they wouldn't pay her for the best performance she'd ever given, but at least Maxx was smiling up at her with the loving eyes of a father.

She made her curtsies, then clattered down to him. Throwing herself into his waiting arms, she squealed, "Didn't I tell you I'd bring them in? Your parlor's almost full!"

"Your mother taught you to perform like that?" he asked, smoothing back her hair.

"She sure did! I know dozens more songs, all by heart! I can sing all night if you want!"

Her excitement was dampened as the arrogant gambler she'd cussed out that afternoon made his way across the parlor and bowed elegantly before her.

"May I present myself? I am Jules Pearson, Esquire, of Louisiana. What a charming display, Miss Blade," he said, looking as if he did not care to remind her that she had called him a very vulgar name only hours before and pushed him in the river. Mr. Jules Pearson, Esquire, regarded Maxx with admiration. "Let me say, sir, you have a most charming daughter. If I had known of your delightful entertainment, I would surely have booked passage sooner. May I sing your daughter's praises to my friends?"

Vanity scowled up at him. "You washed the river mud out of your hair, I see."

"I beg your pardon?" he said, blinking.

Maxx looked startled at her outburst. Sharona just shook her head, as if such uncouth behavior was to be expected from a heathen child.

Vanity couldn't believe such a rude man would ignore the fact that she'd humiliated him. She must have put him in his place but good. She puffed with pride. "Next time you insult me and my friends, you'll think twice, I bet!"

"Did I do that? I must've been drunk. I fear I have all the vices of a gentleman. My dear young lady, I most humbly beg your forgiveness. I shall not rest until you tell me that I have it." He bowed over her hand.

Vanity reeled with triumph.

Sharona shook Maxx's arm. "You can't be thinking of letting her stay! There are laws, I'm sure! If anyone would be pointing that out, it'd be that black coat headed toward us."

Maxx turned his smile toward the man of the cloth being led forward most reluctantly by his wife. "For true. Let me handle the preacher," Maxx said. "Good evening, parson. I trust you enjoyed our little show."

"Sir, might I speak with you privately?" The preacher glanced at Jules Pearson with a visible shudder. His eyes drank in Sharona's lovely face and figure. Then he scowled down at Vanity.

"This is Preacher Holloway," Vanity said sullenly to her papa.

"If you will pardon us, Mr. Pearson," Maxx said, steering the preacher off to the side.

Mrs. Holloway looked down at Vanity. "My dear, dear child…" She gathered her strength. "You must promise me to never sing that wicked song again!"

Vanity swallowed and stepped back. "W-well, maybe I won't…for a while," she said, realizing what she and her mother had been promising with the song's words for all those years.

Hadn't she told Trance she was no floozy? What was she doing singing a floozy's songs? Had her mother been—No! Vanity tossed back her hair. No!

Then she saw the preacher talking earnestly with Maxx. Her heart began to pound. Without a word, she went to Maxx and grabbed his arm, holding on with the desperation of a child poised on the brink of becoming a ward of the state of Missouri.

Maxx patted her hand. "Ah, my little catfish. Myself, I was just telling this good parson it's just possible you are my own flesh and blood. I couldn't let him take you away to a home for wayward girls, in any case. So good of you to express your heartfelt concern, parson," Maxx said, his words more solicitous than the flinty look in his blue eyes. "But I don't think this little vixen is after my money. For true, she is not."

Indeed not! Vanity thought with indignation. She was about to announce she had a fortune in her own right, but Maxx gently quieted her.

The parson tipped his hat, retreated with pious dignity, and dragged his wife out of the room.

Vanity hung on Maxx's arm. "Does that mean I can stay?"

He cleared his throat. Gazing down at her with a mixture of disquiet, love, and admiration in his eyes, he said, "I still don't think I'm your papa. Nothing would give me greater honor than to claim you, but to do so would be wrong. Wrong indeed. Still, I can't let them take you away to a bleak ol' place, not when we've only just met. Let's cogitate on the possibilities a spell, and see if we can't find something to do with you that sits well with us both."

She was bewildered.

The corners of his mouth twitched. "I still don't think I can keep you here with me, not that I wouldn't want to—Don't pout up your pretty face like that, catfish. You can stay a night or two while we consider things."

Vanity knew he was just stringing her on. He was her papa! "How come you went off and left my mama?" she blurted out.

Startled, he smiled, his eyes strangely sad. "We do heaps of foolish things, catfish. For true. For true. We spread ourselves all over creation, not wanting to settle down any ol' place, just wanting our freedom. But then comes the gray day when all we've got is freedom, and the time for wives and children is long past. Uh-huh, it surely is past for me. That's why I can't promise to keep you, no. But I know men all up and down this river hereabouts. They can tell me where we'll find you a place."

Her heart soared. In no time she'd be rooted so deeply in his lonely old heart he'd never let her go.

She seized his lapels until he bent down and drew her tightly to him. She could feel his big hands spread across her slim shoulder blades. "Papa!" she whispered in his ear. "Papa! Papa!"

He patted her gently and then drew away, straightening and pulling out a big silk handkerchief to mop his eyes.

Winking, he showed her the magnificently embellished MB embroidered in white silk in one corner of his handkerchief. "Done by real nuns while praying," he said with a chuckle. "What would you say to a few new dresses and a pair of shoes made of Italian kid?"

The next morning promptly at eight-fifteen, the *Natchez Trace* splashed away from Crystal Point, heading downriver.

Still in their respective cabins were Preacher Holloway and Mrs. Holloway. Still asleep in the captain's quarters were Sharona and Maxx. Vanity had slept with Sharona's maid, Lubie, in a cabin just below and had gratefully accepted the loan of one of the young woman's afternoon dresses.

What Jules Pearson had done after making his courtly exit from the gaming parlor at three in the morning, no one was sure. The remainder of the passengers spent a quiet night.

The only ones who saw the wooded riverbank recede, and heard the rhythmic thrashing of the paddle wheel in the muddy water, were the deck hands and three passengers.

Rowena Holloway had risen and dressed the moment she discovered her brother gone from his bed in the cabin he shared with his father. She left her mother and roamed, finding her big brother at the side of the boat where the paddle housing made the gangway narrow and provided a secluded corner. For some time she watched Trance stare longingly at the vibrant young thing they had watched dance the evening before.

"Did you like my songs?" Vanity was asking, keeping her lively brown eyes trained on the deck and wishing her cheeks would not radiate her excitement so blatantly.

"I'll never forget you," Trance said.

"But we'll be seeing each other again, I know it!" Vanity whispered, looking longingly up into his blue eyes.

"Pa's taking us off at the next stop."

Vanity's heart fluttered. "Promise you'll visit me when…"

Trance looked away. "After a couple of days you'll forget all about me."

"I won't! I'll wait right here on this boat, going up and down this river until you come. Just you wait. Someday I'll be grown…" Her cheeks reddened again.

Trance smiled. Impulsively he cupped her cheek, looking as if he wanted to tangle his hands in her curls. "You're not like other girls. You're wild, free. I feel myself bound in chains!"

"Then promise me!" she whispered, leaning into his palm, closing her eyes and willing herself to be instantly sixteen so that he would take her desires seriously. "Set yourself free, with me!"

"My father says folks who are different don't mix."

"I don't believe it!" she said, flouncing away. She scrambled onto the railing and swung her legs back and forth.

Trance folded his arms and scowled. Finally he met her eyes.

She tossed her hair. "You'd best look me up just to be certain, because next time you see me I won't look anything like I do now!" She smiled defiantly at him, wondering herself what she would be like if they did meet again. "Just you watch. I won't look like anybody you ever saw in your life!"

He moved to take her into his arms. He looked serious, almost angered by her words, as if he wanted to believe her and wanted to prove it.

"John Travis Holloway! Unhand that young harlot this instant! Come away with me!" Trance's father shouted. He was standing at the bottom of the stairs leading up to the cabins on the saloon deck. "I should've known I'd find you here, dallying with her sort."

Trance turned from Vanity. "I mean to visit with my friend until we reach the next landing, Pa." He held his head high without a sign of worry on his handsome young face.

Theophilus Holloway went purple. He regarded his son with fury, then stalked away.

Trance leaned over the railing and stared down at the river. Vanity perched beside him, swinging her legs. They said nothing more until the whistle hooted, sending its mournful echo up and down the river valley some hours later when Trance straightened and finally whispered good-bye.

The *Natchez Trace* nosed up to a forlorn clearing. There the preacher and his family disembarked. Moments later the side-wheeler eased back into the river's strong current. The tow-haired youth on the bank raised his hand. The young girl at the boat's railing stood motionless, watching, her chestnut curls playing in the breeze.

Five

In the stillness of dawn, fifteen-year-old Mary Louise Mackenzie, known to all now as Vanity Blade, slipped from her cabin on the Texas deck. Barefoot, and wearing only a lace-trimmed batiste chemise, she tiptoed down the steps to the boiler deck and scampered toward the stern, where the huge red paddle wheel stood motionless.

The thick, moist air caressed her bare arms. Golden sunlight was just beginning to slant across the white railings and gingerbread trim, bathing the boat in its warmth. On the river where mist rose like the last of the night's frail fantasies, the light tinted the sluggish water deep amber.

There, where Maxxmillon Blade's magnificent new stern-wheeler patiently waited on an unanticipated sandbar, the river's banks stood solid and tranquilly dark. Serene blue-gray clouds smudged the pale sky. The scent of summer, heavy with the rich, muddy odor of the river, filled Vanity with a sense of daring.

Marooned for a second morning, she could no longer ignore the water's seductive beckoning. Glancing around to be sure Maxx's deck hands were still asleep, and that the old pilot was up in his pilothouse grumbling about low water, and that all the passengers were still in their staterooms, she stripped the delicate white garment from her sleek body with a giggle and dropped it in a soft heap at her feet.

Vanity leaped feet first from the railing, dropping beautifully pale and naked into the brown Mississippi. She drew up her feet the moment they touched the silty bottom and went under, holding her breath, to strike out for the bank.

By the time she had had her fill of swimming, someone would be standing at the rail, summoning her back with a fleecy towel and a frown. It was likely to be Sharona's maid, Lubie. The men on deck would be instructed to gaze at the opposite shore from the other side of the boat, and Maxx would be in the captain's quarters grinning out his window like the doting, captivated papa he had become.

Vanity reached the riverbank and pulled herself from the water. She made her way along the pebbled shallows to a sheltered spot where she splashed and played like a child.

Finally she sat on a smooth boulder and pitched pebbles into the water. The familiar plunk and the ripples smoothing out into the river calmed her restlessness.

Life aboard Maxx's boat had taken on a maddening predictability. Since Maxx had sold the *Natchez Trace* and dismissed the young ladies kept for his patrons' pleasure, the life of abandon she'd anticipated hadn't materialized, for after Maxx fitted out his new boat in the grandest manner, Vanity could only sing one show a week.

Maxx still welcomed gambling aboard his boat, but it was more refined now. As a result, his new patrons were several cuts above the old, and his profits infinitely bigger.

Vanity had certainly enjoyed the fitting sessions for all her new clothes, but when at last she did join Maxx in the grand saloon it was only for a few precious moments after supper. She was not considered a singer but a proper young lady who belonged in the sanctuary of the ladies' salon in the stern.

From the first, Sharona had interfered with everything Vanity wanted to do. Her list of *shoulds* and *should nots* grew longer each day.

Thinking of Sharona, Vanity petulantly tossed a handful of pebbles into the river. She gazed at her reflection. Sunlight glinted gold on her waist-length chestnut hair. Her dark brown eyes, still large and beguiling, with their long, silky lashes, were by far her most arresting feature.

In two short years Vanity had also developed a breathtakingly sensuous body, with delicate rounded arms and sleekly tapered legs. Her shoulders were straight, square, and white as cream. Her waist was trim and her hips flared perfectly. Her belly was taut and smooth, her skin flawless as satin.

Best of all, her puppies were just like mama's now! She had lusciously plump pink nipples that swelled with her secret dreams of young Trance Holloway, that preacher's son she had met so long ago. She touched herself, watching her reflection, and longed for Trance to materialize and make love to her.

Aboard Maxx's new boat, which he had named the *Vanity Blade* in her honor, Vanity seldom met men who interested her. She often saw the handsome but overweening Jules Pearson and was glad only because Quarter Dollar was always with him. Otherwise, she took no interest in the increasing number of planters, gamblers, and travelers disposed to eye a woman beneath the age of consent.

Startled from her thoughts, Vanity noticed the pristine riverboat jolt and then suddenly float free of the sandbar. Quickly, she waded into the water and started swimming back. She had had her fill of thinking. What good did it do to wish she could do that which they all insisted she must not?

As she expected, Lubie waited at the railing, her attractive dark face like a thundercloud. Lubie lowered her chin and glared at Vanity, her lips pursed. Near as anyone could guess, Lubie was about twenty-three. Her dark curly hair was always caught up in a blue bandanna. Sharona liked her to wear a plain blue calico gown with no adornment save a starched white linen apron.

Laughing, Vanity waved and swam into the current. In a few more strokes she was hauling herself up a knotted rope and standing dripping on the deck. She listened with half her attention as Lubie scolded, "Ain't no telling *what* the likes of you'll be up to next!"

"And good morning to you, too," Vanity said, accepting the napped towel. She let Lubie scrub the chill from her arms. It reminded her of the wooden tub in her mama's cabin and the long-ago day when she debuted with her on Broken Rock's stage.

A sharp twinge of homesickness swept over her, and the memory of her mother's wistful face filled her mind. Then it was gone, leaving her restless again. She wished that Lubie would leave her alone. Trying to be ladylike was as dull as church.

Lubie's soft words droned on as they both hurried to the privacy of Vanity's cabin on the Texas deck. "Wouldn't catch me *dead* swimming around in that dirty water, *naked* as the day you was borned. And just as brazen as a Natchez floozy! I'm going to catch hell for letting you out of my sight. Likes as not, you don't even care! Some folks just don't use they head like they ought." Lubie's eyes narrowed. "I ain't *nothing* but a lady's maid, but I got sense, I do. Get on in that cabin 'fore you catch your death. Had to be at least a half dozen gents eyeing you as you jumped in, naked as you please. Just you *watch!* You ain't going to catch no kind of husband, no sir-ee. Mark my word, you is in for one heap o' trouble this fine morning. Can't say *what* Mistress Sharona is going to say to you this time…and you just about as full-growed as you is ever going to *get*. Must be cotton bolls between your ears!"

"Just hush," Vanity said, flouncing into the cabin and wanting to slam the door on Lubie's words. "I'll swim if I want!" She stamped her foot.

Lubie waited, her frown even darker. The maid was popular with the black men who frequented the gambling boat. Maxx had no quarrel with freedmen, and he played high-stakes poker with any foolish enough to risk it.

Lubie had friends among Maxx's deck hands, too, though nothing seemed to go on between them. No breath of scandal ever touched Lubie's proud head. Lubie even held herself above white gentlemen interested in her favors. Had it not been for Lubie's instruction, Vanity would have exposed her lack of upbringing far more often that she already had.

The sweet thick fragrance of jasmine softened Vanity's impatience as she paused in her cabin. An iron tub painted white stood before her, brimming with bubbles. Vanity's clothes for the day lay across the lace counterpane nearby. Lubie retired to her adjoining cabin; Vanity never let a servant wash her.

Vanity dropped the towel and slipped into the tub, relishing the silky warmth of the oiled water. Romantic thoughts of Trance teased her. Would she ever see Trance again? Would he even remember her?

Jasmine hair soap suddenly stung her eyes. As she fumbled for the towel, her cabin door snapped shut.

Sharona's voice was an angry whisper. "I saw you out there in the river."

"Just make yourself at home," Vanity said sarcastically. "Don't bother to knock." She braced herself for yet another scolding. "Lubie! I've got soap in my eyes again!"

Lubie returned at once to pour a pitcher of clean water over Vanity's head. "Miss Vanity wasn't gone long, Miz Sharona," Lubie said hastily. "I had my eye on her the whole time! I *surely* did!"

"And was I asking you anything, Lubie?"

"No'm."

Vanity's temper flared, but she pressed her lips together, knowing it was useless to argue with Sharona. Maxx wouldn't like it. Besides, Sharona always seemed to know the answers. Vanity couldn't best her.

When her eyes were finally clear of suds, she looked up. Sharona was wearing her favorite morning gown, a simple shell-pink silk that set off her pale skin and black hair.

"I didn't do myself or anybody any harm by taking a swim!" Vanity said vehemently.

Sharona put her hands on her hips. "The gentlemen on board will be thinking you're a cheap little twist. If ever Maxx is forced to call out a man to defend your honor—"

"Every time I breathe, you say Maxx will have to fight a duel!" Vanity huddled beneath the suds, fury pulsing through her. "But it hasn't happened yet, and it never will! Swimming isn't wicked! I'll swim whenever I want." She shivered, angry because she had to restrain herself where her papa's *woman* was concerned. To the devil with Sharona! she wanted to say.

"It's swimming in the nude that's doing you harm," Sharona hissed. "The time will come, Miss High-and-Mighty, when you'll be wishing you knew how to behave." Sharona moved behind the tub.

Vanity tried to catch Lubie's veiled, cautious glance. "Bring my dressing gown now, please," she said, hating the quaver in her voice.

Lubie moved to obey, but Sharona waved her away. "Leave us a moment. It's something private I have to say to this young lady."

Trapped, Vanity fixed her stare on her glossy wet knees sticking up from the sudsy water. Lubie swished out, pulling the door closed.

Sharona arranged herself on the dressing table's white-fringed stool. She took up the silver-handled brush lying on the mirrored silver tray and toyed with the soft bristles. "You're not understanding how such behavior makes you look. A decent woman would rather die than strip herself naked in public!" She paused, watching for a response, which Vanity refused to grant her. Sharona sighed and went on. "We've had these discussions before. Your songs are always too bawdy. Your dances have been downright vulgar. Maxx indulges you, but I can't be letting him! It's thinking scandalous things, folks are, when they hear a young girl knows about sex. Living on this boat is soiling your reputation enough without—"

"You'll never get me off this boat!" Vanity erupted, and stood up. Suds and water coursed down her arms and dripped from her hair and fingertips onto the carpet. "Papa wants me!"

Sharona sniffed and shook her head. "We're both knowing he's not your papa. Your coloring's not right. You haven't a drop of Creole blood!"

Vanity stepped out and grabbed up her dressing gown. "I don't care what people think! I'm not any of those names you call me. And he is my papa…you…you…black-hearted mivvy!" Vanity shuddered with satisfaction. She had no idea what a mivvy was, save that it had been Belle's foulest name for a woman.

"You'd best be lowering your voice!" Sharona snapped, setting the hairbrush aside. She glanced toward the door, fearful Maxx would hear them. "A lady never raises her voice."

"I don't care! Papa should know how you treat me! I've got half a mind to tell him. He thinks you're so refined. He doesn't know the half!"

"It's for Maxx that I'm trying to help you," Sharona said with maddening civility. She stood and drifted elegantly toward the door. "It's keeping you from bringing him shame, I am."

Vanity whirled. She'd need hours to puzzle over Sharona's meaning and motives, and then only in the night would she imagine suitably scathing retorts. "I'll never shame him!" Vanity spat, quivering with a half-formed terror that in her ignorance she just might. "He takes me just as I am."

"And what might that be?" Sharona asked haughtily. "In two years you're still not reading above the first level. If you count, it's in deuces, treys, kings, queens, and jacks. And who will you be marrying—a gambler who will drag you from saloon to saloon and pawn your valuables every night…if not your body…to get enough money to play poker?"

"You would know!" Vanity shouted, laughing, then blushed in astonishment to see Sharona wince. Suddenly Vanity was sorry.

No one had told her where Sharona came from. She was just Maxx's woman, beautiful, clever, superior. Yet her secret past now lay bare in her anguished eyes, easier to read in that revealing moment than any words in any book.

Vanity turned away, afraid that Sharona might be right about her future. Would any decent man want her if she defied society's rules? Would Trance Holloway ever consider her seriously?

Sharona's voice penetrated Vanity's jumbled thoughts. Her tone was deeper and more grave than Vanity had ever heard before. "I do know that kind of life, Vanity. I care enough about the girl Maxx calls daughter to try to keep her from it. You'll be thinking what you will of me, Vanity, but I do have Maxx's best interests at heart. And yours."

Sharona left then, and Vanity hugged her dressing gown to her shivering body. Sharona had said nothing outright, but Vanity knew she was trying to get her to go to school. Vanity couldn't bring herself to agree. The thought of leaving Maxx filled her with terror.

She crossed the cabin and threw open the battered traveling trunk she'd brought from California. It stood in the corner, a weathered reminder of her past. She could almost feel herself back in Tenderfoot as the dusty, musty smell of the empty trunk reached her nostrils.

The cabin was such a glorious array of loveliness, with rich mahogany woodwork, a thick Wilton carpet, brass lamps, oil paintings in gilt frames, and a French porcelain basin and pitcher painted with pink roses on a genuine Louis XIV washstand. The trunk was a fit reminder of her crude beginnings, a relic more real than anything else she had.

In her armoire were gowns in every pastel shade of silk, India muslin, and lustrous satin. Packed away in paper wrappers were her mother's dingy gowns. Vanity no longer opened the wrappers as she once had. Now she could see how audacious the colors had been, and how clumsy the stitching, how blatant the styles. Still, she bitterly resented Sharona for educating her tastes enough to see the truth of her mother's life.

If she must go away to school…Vanity threw off her dressing gown and pulled on cambric drawers trimmed with six rows of fine Malines lace. She tied the thin white ribbons of a sheer cambric camisole over her ripe young breasts and adjusted the lace-edged shoulder bands. Then she wrapped herself in a whalebone corset and cinched the laces until her waist was scandalously small, her hips swelling seductively and her puppies bulging invitingly above the camisole. If she must…

She jerked on the loathsome plain dark stockings and hooked her ankle-high shoes, both symbols of her waning girlhood. Sharona said she couldn't wear a full-length skirt until her sixteenth birthday.

As Vanity pulled on her white linen gown and surveyed herself in the looking glass, she saw only the calf-length hem of her skirt, the peep of her lacy pantalets, all announcing she was still a child to be ordered about and insulted because of her upbringing. "I won't go to school!" she whispered vehemently, making a ferocious face at the looking glass. "I won't ever!"

Splintered rainbows of light from the three massive crystal chandeliers showered the intent heads of gamblers assembled in Maxxmillon's grand saloon. Three games of poker had already started as Vanity sashayed in that evening from the ladies' salon.

As she crossed the stunning black-and-gold carpet, threading her way among the tables, the men looked up, their laughter ceased, cigars dangled from slack lips. They watched her pass, then cleared their throats when she was out of earshot.

Against the cream walls and the expanse of freshly washed windows that looked out on the lights of Milliganie Point a discreet distance south of Memphis, and the gilded filigree that ornamented the lofty ceiling, Vanity looked tantalizingly innocent and lovely. She presented herself beside Maxx, who was conducting a straight game of three-card monte for a group of well-dressed Southern gentlemen who had boarded at Memphis.

Vanity waited patiently for Maxx to finish the current bid. When he looked up she gave him her most beguiling smile. Any scowl of disapproval that indicated she had once again invaded what was supposed to be the strictly male domain of his gaming saloon melted away, leaving Maxx wearing an indulgent grin.

"How's my little catfish this fine evening, hmm?" he asked giving the monte players a wink before looking up at Vanity again.

"You promised to visit with me tonight," she said, giving him a playful pout. "Come and sit with me awhile—Oh, excuse me," she said, remembering she was supposed to wait to speak only after Maxx introduced her to the gentlemen eyeing her short skirts. To all looking on, she was in the full bloom of womanhood and the skirts did much to disappoint their hopes.

"Gentlemen, may I present my impetuous daughter, Vanity," Maxx said as she paused. "Catfish, honey, this is Mr. Charles Wakely, a most renowned banker from Tennessee. Former Senator Eli Baylor…" He indicated a grinning wren of a man. "Hylan Claiborne of North Carolina, and Mr. John Simpson Moffat of our great state of Louisiana."

The gentlemen rose and bowed, eyes alight. There followed the usual clamor for information. Vanity had grown used to Maxx's two-year-old story of her arrival, laced heavily with gleeful chuckles and winks.

Two of the gentlemen excused themselves and headed for the bar. The others, sensing Maxx's desire to reprimand Vanity privately, drifted away but glanced back, speculating how soon she'd be of age and available to them.

Maxx attempted a fierce expression. "Myself, I have said many a time that you no longer belong in this room. For true, if you have it in your head to give us a song, I'll arrange for it later…"

Vanity snagged a curve-legged chair of European design and plunked her cloud of tulle ruffles and flounces onto it. "You promised to spend some time with me tonight. Hang the rules! I never get to see you anymore! I can't sing or dance without falling over Sharona's frown. She's not my jailer, Papa. She's a jaybird, always scolding! Can't we have just one little ol' dinner together like we did when I first came to you? Please?" She was quite good at imitating his Creole accent.

"Language!" Maxx said, his eyes twinkling over a forced frown. "Some of the finest gentlemen in the South frequent my boat. Would you embarrass them?"

Vanity shook her chestnut curls. Lubie had taken the best part of the morning to arrange them, and the best part of the afternoon to rearrange them after Vanity spent two hours at the wind-whipped railing with her cane pole. "I know you don't care what they think, Papa!"

"I care what they think of you, catfish," he said softly, taking up her dimpled, manicured hand and kissing it. "Forgive ol' Maxx, but a man must find his way in these troubled times. The clever General Polk has denied me half the river by stretching that damnable chain across it. My sympathies are ever with the South, for true, but in time only Yankees will have money to lose at monte and poker. I do indeed have to concern myself with the thoughts of my patrons. So should you."

"Great snakes! Am I to sit back in the salon yawning until the war's over? I don't even get to fish with you. It's talk, talk, talk all day with your banker and investment friends."

"Can I help it I have money to invest? Catfish, you're acting more like a woman every day. For true, you are." Now his eyes were less merry.

She felt stung more sharply than if he had struck her. She knew his opinion of addle-pated women with no concerns save for their own amusements. But she did so want to be with him—and avoid Sharona—and to have him dote on her. "Bet you can't beat me in draw poker, Papa!" she said, determined now. "I haven't forgotten a thing you've taught me. I don't see why I had to stop playing. It was all in fun. Let me sit with you tonight. I'll be as good as gold!"

"I was wrong to teach you poker," he said, looking as though he did miss those long afternoons when she first had arrived. He had taught her everything he knew about gambling, an innocent pastime that had ignited Vanity's penchant for dramatics. She had adored being the center of attention, a child indulging in a forbidden adult game, but even more so, she loved knowing how to control the game by skill and device.

Maxx had taught her to be a judge of men, too, if not women. She could read the eyes and thoughts of a man with comparative ease. Now she saw that Maxx was eager to have her join him, but was allowing a false sense of propriety to hold him back.

"I'll just sit here quiet as a mouse while you play," she said, giving him her dearest smile. She rose quickly, rearranged her chair at his side, and sat on it, trying to look as prim and innocent as a preacher's daughter.

Maxx chuckled. With a simple lift of his brow, he invited the gentlemen looking on to rejoin him. Quickly the chairs at the round table were filled. The gentlemen hungrily eyed the young lady seated with her hands folded, looking like the picture of demure innocence.

She read their thoughts so easily. They desired her, she knew! Listening with half her attention as Maxx shuffled a fresh deck of cards, had them cut, and began to deal out the first hand, Vanity watched the distracted gentlemen and knew that in a few months they, and dozens of others, would actively seek her favors.

Obediently she remained silent for the first few hands, but soon she couldn't help but watch the winnings begin accumulating in front of the dapper ex-senator. She dimpled and cooed as if she thought he was monstrously clever and watched as he flushed with boyish pride.

Maxx won his share and lost his share. As the bank, he never allowed himself to win conspicuously or to let another win more than he cared to lose.

Such was Maxx's skill. Vanity knew he was capable of playing a completely straight game, or one dealt entirely in his favor. For the most part he played honestly, and ejected any roving gambler who attempted to bilk patrons. Yet it was his very nature to play to win, and she watched him exercise control with the greatest of curiosity.

By the time Maxx had dealt a half dozen hands she leaned forward and said sweetly to her papa, "Might I join in this round? I'd like to see if I remember a single thing you taught me." Her voice was soft and playful, childlike in its innocence.

Maxx searched her face, as if trying to work out how such a seemingly innocent girl could be so calculating.

Feeling a flush rise to her cheeks, she looked away, ashamed to think she had just tried to trick him. Maxx could not be tricked. Now he would be angry, she thought, and her heart grew sore.

"You will not tell Sharona, no?" he said, his accent suddenly thick.

Surprised, Vanity lifted her eyes, puzzled that she could not read her papa's deepest thoughts. His expression was blank. She watched the cards gather before her, took up her hand, and realized that she could no longer tell if Maxx was dealing a straight or weighted game.

The hand ended quickly, with compliments from the gentlemen all around. Vanity was at a loss for polite banter, and so she remained silent, looking bewildered and tantalizingly artless while engaged in such a forbidden and wicked pastime.

Whispers reached the ladies' salon after several more rounds. Sharona arrived in a rustle of satin. Smiling and excruciatingly polite, she curled her fingers around Vanity's smooth arm and pressed. "Why, darlin', whatever are you doing here with your dear papa? I'm thinking it's past your bedtime."

Vanity shook off Sharona's hand.

Maxx shushed Sharona and invited her to sit to his right. "My pet, we're seeing how well Vanity can handle herself with a deck of cards. Life as we know it is on the verge of collapse, for true. When the Mississippi itself is bound up in chains, we must all fend for ourselves. I would not like to think our Vanity could do nothing to earn her way if ever I was not here to protect her."

A bolt of alarm shot through Vanity. Was this his way of showing her she had no future save gambling if she remained with him? Maxx dealt another hand and she took it up. Her heart leaped to see the straight he had dealt her.

"I fold," she said, slapping her cards facedown and edging her chair back.

The gentlemen tittered at her first major blunder. "Do wait your turn, my dear," Mr. Claiborne said.

Maxx put his big warm hand on her cold, suddenly trembling ones. "I want you to play," he said, quickly concluding the hand and then dealing another.

Sharona was silent, but her eyes were narrowed and sharp as she studied Maxx's closed expression and calculated how to deal with him.

Vanity's next hand was poor, but the one following promised to be a full house if she drew the proper card. The other gentlemen folded in short order, leaving Vanity and Maxx. Vanity won the hand, to the delight of the gentlemen. Maxx offered to deal Sharona in, but she declined gracefully, making Vanity feel like the crude little creature from Tenderfoot again for playing poker like a hussy.

It was her turn to be surprised when her next hand produced a flush. Maxx bet conservatively. Two of the gentlemen folded again and Vanity won the pot.

"I do believe this game has become a bit stiff for my tastes," Mr. Moffat said, removing himself from the table and bowing at Vanity and Sharona. "May I be permitted to observe?"

Maxx nodded, aware of how many others from the saloon had begun gathering around their table. Vanity was momentarily taken aback by Mr. Moffat's exit from the game. Foolishly, she whispered, "Are the chips worth more than I think, Papa?"

"Don't trouble your head about details, catfish," he said, trying, with a sharp glance at each player remaining, to convey that he did not want Vanity to know just how high the stakes really were.

"I do believe your papa is playing us for our very life's blood," Mr.

Claiborne said, rising quickly and asking to observe the next round as well.

As Maxx dealt the next round, Vanity studied his face. What was his purpose in this game? she wondered. Was he trying to frighten her? Was he hoping to teach her a lesson?

Her hand was worthless and she folded quickly, watching Maxx lose unexpectedly to the gentleman from Louisiana. The crowd had grown thick around them. As Maxx gathered in the cards and shuffled, Sharona whispered to him. He shook his head and she turned and glided away, murmuring pleasantries and finally calling for a sherry at the bar.

Vanity took up her next hand. He had dealt her a royal straight flush, ace high, the highest hand possible. She could not lose. She knew then that her hands had been too good for Maxx to be playing her straight. He either wanted her to win—perhaps he thought she needed the money—or he was setting her up for a crushing loss. He knew she was clever with cards but lacking in hard experience; perhaps this was his way of teaching her she was no match for a seasoned gambler.

Whatever his motive, she began seeing Maxx's bets and raising with an expertise even she found startling. The last two gentlemen folded early on, leaving the battle of wits to Maxx and Vanity.

At last the large pile of chips before Vanity was transferred to the center of the table. With apparently supreme confidence, Maxx made a bet Vanity could not match. She looked into her papa's eyes, frightened by their bottomless depths, and by the lack of emotion she sensed.

"Papa, what are you trying to do?"

"Myself, I want to see if you can play poker, catfish," he said softly. "For true."

Sharona was summoned back into the gaming parlor. She gasped when she saw the heap in the pot and shook Maxx's shoulder. "Enough!" she said firmly. Finally she cast a scathing look at Vanity. "What are you trying to prove? Do you want her money, too?"

"Will you accept my I.O.U., Papa?" Vanity whispered, her heart racing with confusion. Would he publicly ruin her?

"Yes, I will," he murmured, motioning for someone to bring the small cards he kept on hand for such occasions.

Painfully aware that her handwriting looked like that of an illiterate, she consigned all her mama's earnings, deposited in a small St. Louis bank, to the card. She showed it to her papa, watched for even the slightest widening of his eyes, but saw nothing. He seemed unmoved. If she lost this hand, which she could not, she would be penniless. Did

Maxx know he had dealt her a winning hand?

"I do believe," he said at length, "that you have offered here more than enough to see my bet. Do I take it you have raised me the rest?"

She shivered and finally nodded. "There's nothing more for me to offer, Papa."

A murmur of disapproval rippled behind them. Some thought Maxxmillon Blade was going too far in accepting his own daughter's promissory note.

"To call your bet, Vanity, I must offer up the *Vanity Blade*. Do you accept?"

Vanity clutched her winning hand to her breast and stared at Maxx. "You can't mean it!"

Sharona jerked Maxx's sleeve. "Have you lost your mind? Maxx, darlin', think what you're doing!"

Her mind reeling, Vanity looked up into Sharona's panic-stricken eyes and knew the terror the woman was feeling. The riverboat was Sharona's security, her own comfortable and safe future. But with the war, was any future safe and secure?

Vanity knew then that *her* future did not lie with cards. Yet she couldn't back down from her papa's offer. She had signed the I.O.U. with the full intention of losing it if there was some possible way Maxx knew to beat an ace-high royal flush. Perhaps he had one of his own!

In the moments she spent trying to figure out Maxx's motives, Jim Hickory had fetched the boat's papers from the safe. Maxx laid them on top of the pile of chips and Vanity's crudely printed card.

"I have two pair," Maxx said, pausing as gasps of disbelief erupted all around him. Then he laid out two nines and two more nines, four of a kind and a worthy hand in any game.

Now Vanity could decide to show her hand and win, or fold without revealing her royal flush, a perfectly acceptable way to convince everyone she had not had a hand high enough to beat her papa.

The moments ticked by with agonizing slowness. She realized what it really meant to win, and to win from one she loved with all her heart. The boat and her mama's money would be hers, and the future it promised would be hers. In it she would have no hope of ever being a lady.

But if she folded she would be penniless. Had her mama saved thirteen years for that money to be lost in one hand of poker? Vanity had never seen her mama gamble with cards. She realized in another horrifying flash how beguiling the game could be. She knew Maxx would probably not take her savings, and yet any other man would, most assuredly, without a second thought.

She was about to lay her cards facedown and concede defeat, when an overwhelming heat rose up from deep inside her. She struggled—she felt paralyzed—but she simply could not accept defeat in any guise. Even from her beloved papa she must seize victory and security!

Lifting her head, feeling tears well in her eyes, she turned her cards face up, and heard the rumble of surprise rip through the crowd. Sharona turned sharply away, steadied herself on the back of a chair, and finally made her way from the grand saloon as if the deck were pitching beneath her feet.

Vanity saw nothing but Maxx's eyes fixed on hers. She felt barren inside, knowing her instinct for survival was so hideously strong as to take the one thing her papa loved most.

But suddenly he was grinning, his face radiant with triumph! The white and gray whiskers of his beard fairly stood at attention. His eyes filled with love and even grew slick with tears. He seized her shoulders and hugged her. "Little catfish!" he whispered. Then quickly, while the onlookers buzzed with questions, he signed over the boat to Vanity and pressed the papers into her cold hands.

After some effort, he rose and gazed happily at his astonished patrons. Then again he seized Vanity and crushed her to his chest. "Vanity," he said, taking her face in his huge warm hands, "when my time comes I won't be afraid."

Her heart twisted with horror. "Don't say such things!"

"The country has come to war," he said, suddenly growing so solemn that she glimpsed the true gravity of the war and went cold all over again. "Whatever becomes of me, you will survive!" he said. "Who among you has a daughter like this?" he asked, throwing his arm wide. "Drinks on the house till dawn!"

She was stunned to see they had played for more than two hours. Bewildered, she tried to comprehend what Maxx had been doing by losing the boat to her. She began to think the boat was the least important aspect of the game.

She had learned to win. She had had the courage to risk all! Feeling a blazing strength straighten her back, she stood tall beside Maxx, realizing she was very nearly eye to eye with him. Her mama had taught her endurance. Maxx had just taught her courage.

Vanity's throat filled with emotion. She clutched the *Vanity Blade*'s papers to her breast, knowing whatever happened, the future lay not in the boat, but within herself.

Six

Sharona paced the captain's quarters, her mind racing. When she heard Maxx's footsteps approaching along the gangway, she stopped and turned away, folding her arms in a protective gesture across her bosom.

"You're upset with me, no?" he said, coming into the sumptuous stateroom and closing the paneled door carefully.

She whirled, bewildered and frightened by his self-satisfied tone. "How could you be letting her win the boat? How?" she demanded, flinging her arms wide and taking in their comfortable, private place with her anguished eyes.

Maxx smiled as he approached, arms outstretched. "For true, I don't think my little catfish will put us off at the next landing."

"What possible use can this riverboat be to a girl her age?" Sharona turned away, refusing Maxx's touch. She was more angry than she had ever dreamed she could be with him. A sense of betrayal welled in her bosom, hot and dangerously explosive.

Chuckling, he lifted Napoleon from the bed pillow and stroked the black cat's back as if he had not a care in the world. "Perhaps, then, you should tell me what troubles you about the game we played tonight. Do you fear I have nothing left to give you? Have I not always given you everything you wanted? Sharona, my pet, turn your head and look at me."

She struggled to keep her voice low and calm. "Maxx, darlin', it was bad enough that you let her gamble. I've told you often enough what the patrons think, seeing her in the saloon. You know how important it is to be keeping her apart from all that. What would you think if—"

With a gentle wave of his hand, Maxx shushed her. Irritated, he crossed to their bed and sank onto it, letting Napoleon leap from his arm and curl once again on the pillow.

In the shadows, he looked pale and suddenly tired, and that frightened Sharona. "I'm grieved to think you trust me so little," he began, choosing his words with care. "Myself, I share all with you, but what can I share with Vanity? I give her a few gowns, a place to live. You and me, we both know she's not my child. What will the courts give her when I am gone? Nothing…unless I provide now while there is still time."

Sharona dismissed his bid for pity. He was healthy as an ox. "She has her mother's money!" Sharona snapped, thinking Vanity's fortune far and above what she herself had had at such a tender age, or any other.

"In a Yankee bank," Maxx muttered, sighing heavily then and lifting his silver head. "My pet, the impulse overtook me tonight. She's nearly grown and yet still a child. Myself, I know not what the war will bring. Can we survive it? I wanted to give her something of myself before it's too late. The boat is a small part of that—and fairly taken, I might add."

Sharona laughed bitterly. "That little fool may think so, but I know better! You dealt her the winning hand. You *gave* her the boat."

He wagged his head, making Sharona doubt what she'd seen in the grand saloon. "I dealt the cards, for true, but she called my bluff. I need have no fear for her now." He smiled sadly, longing for her to understand.

Sharona turned away, aching inside, aware of how her next words would sound. "And what about me? What have you given of yourself to me?"

"I don't know," he said flatly.

She was aghast. In the two years since Vanity had invaded their lives, Sharona had watched Maxx slip further and further from her grasp. She could not hold him with her love, her charm, her favors. Nothing turned his rapt attention from the fresh eager face of that woman-child Vanity.

Crossing the stateroom, Sharona dropped to her knees beside Maxx's gleaming black boots. She clutched his bony knees. "Darlin,' aren't you seeing how wrong we are to be keeping her with us? She has her mama's money. Now she has your boat to keep her in these bad times. I'm asking you again, for the hundredth time, do you want her to always be living on this boat, or one like it? Do you see her turning cards all the rest of her days? Where will it be leading? She's nearly heathen, and even more illiterate than I was at her age. Maxx, listen to me with your head just this one time. I'm a woman. Money and security won't be keeping her from the future that is surely hers on this boat. Gambling will take her straight to heartbreak and the bed of some low, no-account man."

He wagged his head again, trying to interrupt. "It wasn't the boat so much as her will to—"

"Maxx, she's a mere girl, more beautiful than I ever was, even at my peak. It's a world of wolves we're living in. She's a beautiful lamb who's just been given a gambling boat! In time, perhaps only a few months, one of those wolves will be taking everything from her. *Everything,* Maxx."

A pensive smile pulled at Maxx's lip. "Was I just such a wolf in your life, pet?"

"If I had had money, men would have come after me. But I had only a smile…and my body to offer. They came just the same. Maxx, she's deserving more than we can give her. You're the son of a trapper and chambermaid. I came from a ditch digger and a scullery maid. Vanity comes from God knows what! Her only future is this boat, or a house in New Orleans, or the back-street apartment of some rich planter—unless we do something now to change that future."

She watched the effect her words had on Maxx and hated herself for doing this to him. "What more can I do?" he asked.

"She needs education. She needs refinement. She needs introductions into the right families. That's something you *can* be doing for her. It will cost us, surely, to disguise her background and find her a proper school, but it can be done. It's the only thing that we can be doing if she ever hopes to marry a man of some standing."

He hesitated. She remained perfectly still, knowing he was envisioning Vanity as a voluptuous, sought-after woman of questionable standing aboard his boat, dealing poker in his grand saloon, drinking whiskey and dallying with a string of disreputable men. Then he imagined her demure and serene in some distant parlor, looking like the grand ladies who sat, so lovely and above reproach, in the secluded ladies' salon.

He was a man, after all. He knew far better than Sharona the sort of thoughts a man had about the women in the salon and the one in the saloon.

Neither was he so blind that he had not seen his patrons' eyes on the scarcely concealed physical attributes of his lovely and innocent daughter that night at the gaming table.

The silence grew long. Sharona's legs ached as she crouched at Maxx's feet, waiting. Finally he heaved a sigh of resignation, and sighed again. "You're right, for true, my pet. Myself, I would not want to see my dear little catfish tricked and abused by the sort I welcome as friends. Can she be made to go to school? Will she learn to be a lady? Or have I delayed too long?"

"She'll be going if you insist," Sharona whispered, the thrill of victory rising like a tide in her breast. She hugged his arm. "Tell her she must go *after* you've found the right place for her. I'll say I disapprove. That'll make her carry herself there as fast as she can run!"

He smiled, but pain flickered in his eyes. He patted her hand and stood to ring for Jim. "Myself, I have known for so long that I could not keep her. Sharona, you're good to help me keep my wits now when I must let go. An old man needs the help of his dearest friends at such a time."

Shamed into silence, Sharona rose. It was the first time she'd heard him speak of being old. With a shudder she realized he had called her "friend," not lover. Nothing she could do would ever remove Vanity from his heart.

Vanity stared down at the huge white linen table napkin spread across the lap of her strawberry-satin flounced skirt. Elaborately embroidered in white in a corner were the letters VB. Hand-painted in the center of the white china plate before her was a picture of the riverboat as it looked on a summer afternoon. Etched in the crystal goblet was the *Vanity Blade*'s silhouette, her tall fluted smokestacks, pilothouse, big stern paddle-wheel, and the lacework trim along each deck. A shiver went through her. For nearly a month she had been the owner of her own riverboat, yet little had changed except for the thrill she felt when she considered this. Maxx still refused to let her sing more than once a week. She was still a girl, forced to spend most of her time in the ladies' salon, or to wander the decks alone with her cane pole while Maxx met with gentlemen in his private stateroom.

Looking up, she watched as Maxx guided Sharona among the crowded tables and seated her across from Vanity. He looked especially jovial this evening, Vanity thought, at once on guard.

"You have mischief in your eyes, Papa," she said as Maxx paused behind her chair to kiss the chestnut curls massed on the crown of her head.

"For true," he said warmly, seating himself and signaling to his steward.

Soon he was sipping Bordeaux and making small talk with Sharona, who looked rather bright-eyed herself. Vanity drew back, wondering what the two of them were up to.

"Catfish, we have a surprise for you, or, rather, I have one." Maxx waited as small toast squares spread with *pâté de foie gras* were placed before him. With relish he began nibbling, that small smile still lurking in his eyes.

Sharona was oddly silent.

"A surprise!" Vanity said breathlessly. She almost knew at once, without knowing how, that he had found her a school. Quickly she looked to Sharona to guess at her hand in this, and she saw Sharona color self-consciously. The woman looked aside and busied herself examining her many large rings. Vanity's heart began to pound.

"I asked my oldest and most prominent friends for help in this, I did. At first I thought only of a ladies' college, but you're not going to become some schoolhouse teacher, and for true, your qualifications are lacking. Philosophy and Latin would be more than you need."

"Latin?" Vanity whispered.

"No matter. What we've found...my friends and I...is a finishing school. You, my beautiful little catfish, are going to learn just about everything your dear departed mama wanted for you: dancing, music playing on a real grand piano...that fancy stitching...and all the right things to say to ladies and gentlemen of quality."

Sharona cut in, her lovely face masked and strangely tight. "I'm thinking this school isn't right for Vanity," she said, looking only at Maxx, then gripping the sleeve of his black frock coat for emphasis. "Your plan will never work!"

"What plan?" Vanity asked quickly, pushing aside her plate. A finishing school like her mama had talked about! A finishing school Sharona didn't like! "Where is this school? When can I go?"

Maxx was momentarily stumped for words. "Why...why, catfish, you'd have to pretend you...you didn't spend the last two years on a gambling boat. That's certain for true."

"She'll never pull it off!" Sharona said, refolding her napkin and tracing the monogram. "In that school she'd have to be pretending she was from a quality family. Impossible. She's not an actress! Maxx, darlin', don't be leading her on this way! I'm sure if you let me handle this, I can find her a decent place to learn to read, maybe a common day school where she won't be noticed."

Vanity balled her hands into fists, swept away by her fears that Sharona would start controlling her life. "Tell me what I have to do!" she exclaimed, instantly prepared to prove to Sharona and the world that she could conquer anything, even a high-class Southern finishing school!

Du Barry Vale College for Female Refinement stood at the heart of what had once been a thriving cotton plantation some fifteen miles outside Natchez, Mississippi. The estate had been in the Du Barry family for nearly fifty years. Following the death—some claimed in a duel over honor—of the family patriarch, Raphael Du Barry IV, the house and acreage passed to his unmarried daughter, Prosperine.

Since this tragedy in Miss Du Barry's young womanhood, she had opened her college of female refinement, grooming young women to be young ladies at a most exorbitant but necessary cost to some of the finest families in the South.

Sharona had declined to accompany Maxx and Vanity to Du Barry Vale; instead, she had stayed on the *Vanity Blade*, anxiously awaiting Maxx's return.

Maxx hired an elegant black carriage with cheerful yellow running gear and a black driver in forest-green livery to take them out to the college. "I've met the headmistress," Maxx was saying as the carriage rolled along a dusty narrow lane between fallow fields and overlacing soft maples and bur oaks. "She welcomed me like a for-true grand lady. She'll talk about her illustrious family till your ears are full, but let's be duly impressed anyhow." And he chuckled.

With a forced, nervous titter, Vanity fell silent and picked at her lace-edged handkerchief. Then she patted her brow again. And squirmed. And resisted scratching her nose. And longed to be fishing over the railing of her riverboat.

Her ruffled lavender bonnet and lightweight lilac woolen cape had her sweltering in the early autumn warmth. She wore a new mauve wool challis gown with enormous hoops that took up all the floor space save for the corner where Maxx pressed against the Morocco-leather side cushions.

Her heart drummed in anticipation, leaving her breathless, overheated, and more than a little terrified at the prospect of meeting young ladies of her own age at last.

"I'm to tell them I'm just from California," she repeated, straining to remember the story Maxx had concocted to keep the truth of her background hidden. "And you're my uncle…I'm not to talk too much because I'm supposed to be from a good family that has already taught me some manners. And true young ladies only speak when spoken to."

"For true, that is so." Maxx nodded, looking tickled.

She clapped her mouth shut, overwhelmed by what had seemed like a game only days before. Sharona was right. She'd never pull off such a charade! She felt like a weed being transplanted into a formal garden. She'd be laughed at. She'd die!

The lane was thick with velvety dust as it climbed a gentle wooded hill, then turned to reveal a large white early Greek revival house tucked in a glade. The grass was dappled, pale lime to deep sea-green, and shaded by broad-trunked oaks. Ensconced deep in the Southland's heart, it promised Vanity safety from any war raging in Virginia.

When the carriage halted in front of the narrow veranda, Vanity went stiff with fear. When she heard the sound of a harp, she knew instantly she belonged in a common school.

She gripped Maxx's arm, pleading silently, but his face was impassive. This, after all, his expression said, was just another deal of cards. She could call or fold.

He climbed down with great dignity to the recently raked gravel carriageway, then handed her down. She steadied her swaying hoops and managed to swallow. Feeling her mother's benevolent spirit watching, she lifted her chin and shook her abundant corkscrew curls, putting on what she hoped was a ladylike smile. She grasped Maxx's elbow and he led her up the white gravel path to the iron fence surrounding the house like a warning.

Maxx let her in through the gate and helped her up the sweep of steps to the veranda. From there she saw the vast formal gardens stretching from the side to the back of the house. Almost hidden beyond the roses, dahlias, camellias, and azaleas were small brick dependencies housing the servants and work kitchens.

Just as Maxx raised his hand to lift the door knocker, several young girls in frilly pastel hoop skirts drifted into the garden. They talked in such sober tones, Vanity wondered if they were being punished.

A statuesque black woman in severe charcoal satin and a blindingly white turban and apron opened the hand-carved cypress door. "Miss Du Barry 'waits you in the reception parlor, sir," she said, ushering them inside the big house.

Vanity tiptoed across the entrance hall's parquet floor and gasped as she was guided through a pair of towering double doors to the outer visitors' hall. On either side were marble busts of unknown but illustrious personages on slim white pedestals. Near the window where the sunlight spilled onto a collection of fine old rosewood chairs with petit point seats stood a small escritoire.

A magnificent pink marble fireplace dominated the vaulted parlor. Vanity gaped at the huge gilt-framed oils on the walls while the maid waited patiently for them to follow.

The halls were wallpapered with French murals depicting scenes from Greek mythology. Vanity's head twisted and turned in an effort not to miss anything. On an impressive spiral staircase two girls in hoop skirts took each step with exquisite care. Vanity started when she noticed the heavy books wobbling on their heads.

"Miss Du Barry will see you in here," the maid murmured as she led Maxx and Vanity into yet another pristine, airy chamber.

The enormous oil painting over the white mantle was of a most dignified, aristocratic young woman. As Miss Prosperine Du Barry, dressed in slate-gray silk, entered from another door, Vanity saw at once the painting was of the headmistress, albeit in her youth.

A tiny dome clock on the mantle chimed the hour of two, at which point the remarkably preserved Miss Du Barry curved her lips and gave a startlingly savage tug on an embroidered bellpull. Then she drawled, "Good afternoon, Mis-tah Blade. You-all do me such an honor, suh." She moved like Queen Victoria herself beneath the light-catching prisms in the chandelier overhead. Splinters of colored light glittered in her snowy hair. "This enchantin' young beauty must be your darlin' niece...Mary Louise. What a pleasure it is to meet you-all, Miss Blade." She inclined her head and indicated two French brocade chairs flanking a lovely rosewood tea table that held a silver service of staggering opulence.

Miss Du Barry was well into her sixties, with a feathery cloud of white hair done in a style much favored during the previous century. She wore tiny gold-rimmed spectacles and peered at her visitors with very bright forget-me-not blue eyes.

Vanity's stare was met with a tight-lipped expression from Miss Du Barry. In spite of the obvious quality of her new gown and expensive kid shoes, Vanity felt naked.

When Maxx and Vanity had settled themselves gingerly onto the chairs, Miss Du Barry arranged herself on a velvet divan. She poured three cups of tea into fragile china as she exchanged pleasantries and spoke reverently of her family's history and the house. In time she approached the question of which classes Miss Mary Louise Blade might care to pursue, and nodded with what seemed to be approval of Maxx's choices.

The conversation turned briefly to war, and Miss Du Barry was sweetly condescending about those "unchivalrous Yankees not allowing the South a graceful secession."

Vanity's attention strayed to a nearby bookcase. She could scarcely make out titles of Shakespeare, Byron, and the History of Rome in one three-inch-thick volume. Later, she'd be relieved to discover that no student of Du Barry Vale ever opened a book. They only wore them on their heads to improve their posture.

Abruptly, Miss Du Barry stood, concluding what seconds before had seemed like an afternoon without end. "I shall arrange for Mary Louise's accommodations and leave you-all to your farewells." She exited with startling speed, leaving Vanity staring into her papa's face. Tears sprang to her eyes.

Maxx stood, clasped his hands behind his back, then rocked on his heels. "I see it's time for me to take myself away. I'll look after your boat as if it were my own, I surely will, catfish," he said, his accent thick again.

She was on her feet and clinging to his neck. "I don't know what I'm doing here!"

He pulled her arms gently from his neck. Holding her away from him, he gazed deeply into her eyes. "I cannot teach you to be a lady. Sharona cannot. Your dear mama could not. The upper crust has secrets I can't even guess at, catfish. I want you to come back to me and tell me these secrets, and sit with me in the grand saloon again, and show all my patrons you are a true lady. We'll have a most fine boat then." He patted her damp cheek and then drew one glistening tear onto his fingertip. "You can do it."

"I'll make you proud…" she said in a whisper, "…Papa."

He gathered her in his arms, pressing her head to his ruffled shirt. She heard his heart beating and raised her tear-stained face, afraid he was leaving her forever. But his eyes were calm.

She laid her head on his chest, drawing in the fragrance of him, the strength of him, and knew that no matter how difficult it would be, she'd strive to be a lady.

Abruptly he pulled away, took up his hat, and strode from the room. He didn't want her to see his own anguish. Her heart swelled, knowing he loved her. He might not really be her papa, but she loved him just the same.

After he had gone out, Vanity heard the discreet rustle of Miss Du Barry's skirts in the doorway. Vanity turned, her chin up, determined to play the part of a proper young lady to the best of her ability. It would be her grandest performance.

Miss Du Barry inspected Vanity with her keen eyes and an unpleasant smile spread across her colorless mouth. "Now that your uncle has taken his leave, Miss Blade, let me make our rules perfectly clear. You shall speak only when spoken to. You shall not venture any opinion other than those taught here. You shall refrain from any unseemly behavior. Most assuredly, you shall not grin like a simpleton or offer any laughter out loud.

You shall neither stare nor lift up your face in that impudent manner."

Vanity felt herself begin to wilt. She had an overpowering urge to run after Maxx's carriage.

"Lower your gaze in proper respect, young woman, and say, 'Yes'm,' before I cast you from my college in disgrace. Your learnin' begins this very moment!"

Vanity trembled, struggling with herself as to whether she should obey or curse the woman six, nine, twelve ways to Sunday! Why, the shriveled old mivvy had no business…

Maxx was hardly out the door and already she was failing in her attempt to be a person of quality!

"Yes'm," she said softly, angrily lowering her eyes. The farewell tears had dried on her cheeks. Resentment stiffened her spine, but for the time being she would not let the woman know it.

"Often, young ladies brought to me are of a highly willful nature and have done poorly at other schools. You must realize that I am aware of this immediately, so don't try to seize my pity. I have no pity for unladylike girls. We shall treat you here as you shall be treated in the social circle. Either you are our equal or our inferior. I suggest you do not open a single one of your trunks. I venture to guess all your belongings are as garish and bedizened as that rag you are now wearin'. By the very looks of you, Miss Mary Louise Blade, you are quite the most inferior excuse for a female that I have ever had the misfortune to meet."

Rooted to the spot, Vanity frantically tried to understand if she truly was all Miss Du Barry said, or if she'd gotten caught in a nightmare.

"Follow me," Miss Du Barry said without softening her waspish tone.

Trembling, Vanity followed the woman out of the serene parlor into the rear of the house. She followed her through a bewildering maze of passages and deserted rooms until once again she heard the trill of a lovely voice and the notes of a harp.

"I should imagine you have a most desperate need to learn etiquette," Miss Du Barry said, opening a tall white door. "As I have a class awaitin' me, I leave you in the care of Miss Ezley. Miss Thorogood shall see you next, at three. We dine at six. Someone shall instruct you as to the sort of gown we find…ah…acceptable."

Vanity stood on the threshold of a long, mirrored parlor. Seated on foolish little gilt chairs around the perimeter of the room were a dozen girls ranging in age from seven to Vanity's own. As she stepped into the room, all eyes fastened on her and her gown. Vanity had never in her life felt so miserably conspicuous.

Miss Du Barry lifted her brows to the vinegar-faced woman in mud-brown silk standing near the door. "This, unfortunately for us all, is Mary Louise Blade. Her...uncle is some sort of person from N'Orleans. He claims connections with the Spears family in Georgia, but I cannot say as I recall a single cousin of that already questionable line havin' Creole blood. Can you, Eppa?"

Miss Eppa Mae Ezley turned with heavy-lidded disinterest to Vanity. She was of an equally extraordinary age, gray-haired and wearing a lace head cap common nearly a generation before. Her gown was monstrously tight, revealing a waist and shoulders so very narrow she looked cadaverous.

"I have never taken to any of the Georgia-born Spears," Miss Ezley said in a voice that was soft but passionless.

Vanity was still staring at the woman's figure when she realized she was being unseemly again.

In spite of her gauntness, the sour Miss Ezley's facial structure suggested fine breeding. Her skin stretched sparingly over those bones. Vanity suspected that in all the woman's uncountable years she had never been exposed to direct sunlight.

At last Vanity cast her eyes down only to find her curiosity drawn to three girls across the room, and a fourth who sat apart from them. They wore wide-hooped pastel gowns that to Vanity did not seem any different from her own.

"I am puttin' Miss Blade in with Winifred," Miss Du Barry said, as if the arrangement was a deliberate and obvious insult. She turned with a queenly grace, then glided from the classroom.

For several moments Vanity was treated to a bewildering array of names as she was introduced.

Winifred Swaine Pinchot of the Galveston Swaines, formerly of Vicksburg, raised her blonde head long enough to be introduced, and smiled hesitantly at Vanity before she resumed studying her hands, which were clenched in her lap.

Sylvania Hunt Leighey rose to her feet and murmured, "Fancy! *What a color!*" She was from Natchez, of course, of the Natchez Leigheys, and quite the finest student at Du Barry Vale, Miss Ezley said.

To Sylvania, Miss Ezley said, "Upon being introduced, a lady refrains from remarking upon the color of clothing."

"Oh, but I was admiring it, to be sure." She smirked over her curtsy.

Sylvie had russet hair fixed in a complicated braid and tiny cornflower-blue eyes as hard as stones. She looked at Vanity as if forcing herself bravely to view something revolting.

Lynette Elizabeth Rice had dark cocoa-colored hair but didn't deign to look at Vanity long enough for Vanity to see her eyes. She and Sylvie were both sixteen. Lynette was of the Maconborough Rices, the fourth of five daughters, and attractive in a smooth, wintry way.

The last of the girls to capture Vanity's interest was Beverly Josephine Tayloe of the Port Gibson Tayloes. She was fourteen, with a refined, classic beauty, a fine head of golden curls, and a way of looking at Vanity that made Vanity narrow her eyes in readiness to do battle.

With introductions completed, the class proceeded. The girls were learning a complicated French cotillion. To Vanity's relief, she was allowed to observe the first round, and was terrified enough to watch all the moves carefully. Although she knew nothing about formal ballroom dancing, and understood none of the movement names, she followed the steps with few mistakes the first time Miss Ezley suggested she show what she could do.

Tripping only once, but raked with some of the coldest eyes she had ever encountered, Vanity survived her first hour without too much humiliation and without saying a word.

At three she hurried into a chamber across the passageway where stocky young Miss Viola Thorogood taught the finer points of embroidery with expensive Chinese silks on the most delicate handkerchief muslin. Vanity had no hope of blundering her way through the class and so exposed herself immediately as ignorant in the skills of sewing. She spent the remainder of the time learning to thread a needle meticulously to Miss Thorogood's impatient satisfaction.

To Vanity's relief, she was released from class at five. The silent Wini, her roommate, guided Vanity to the second floor and their bedchamber. They were to share the commanding rosewood four-poster with its heavy wooden canopy and thick counterpane. The chamber was as high-ceilinged as all the others, papered in a yellow print. It overlooked a side garden. No personal effects stood displayed on the wide rosewood dressing table, and no paintings graced the walls.

Vanity's trunks, all new and imposingly large and handsome, had been delivered but not unpacked. She felt an overwhelming wave of homesickness for the comfort of her riverboat cabin and the security Maxx had given her. Desolate, she sank to the edge of the bed, wishing she could be alone to cry.

"We're not allowed to sit on the beds," Wini whispered, blushing. Then her expression brightened. "Do you have anything old and ugly to wear? It'd please everyone to gossip about your clothes. No one here likes to be outdone by a newcomer."

Vanity sprang to her feet and smoothed the bedcover. She heard what Wini said and then opened her mouth in astonishment when she realized what the young woman had meant. "Then my dress is all right?"

"It's a very nice dress, surely," Wini said. "Of course, nothing you wear will suit the girls, or Miss Du Barry. It's useless to try to outsmart them...unless you're like them," she added with a bit of dismay. "I'm not like them at all. That's why they've taken me out of Sylvie's room and left me in here alone. I-I'm afraid of the dark, you see, and every night Miss Du Barry takes my candlestick herself. I'm frightfully afraid of being alone. I was never away from my family for a day before coming here in June." She bit her lip and turned away.

"Where's Galveston?" Vanity asked, throwing open her first trunk. She wished she had one of her mama's purple or red gowns to set the tongues to falling out of their sockets in this place.

"Southern Texas," Wini said, going to the looking glass and smoothing her plainly dressed blonde hair.

With an exclamation, Vanity began telling Wini of her trip across Texas two years before. Then, with a gasp of horror, Vanity stopped. She'd been telling how she recited from her primer to the coach driver!

"Do go on!" Wini said, her eyes lighting up at finding a fellow foreigner.

"I wasn't supposed to...I mean..." She stopped, frightened and confused, trying to remember the story Maxx had made up for her. She was supposedly from a fine Georgia family newly settled in California. They hadn't discussed whether she could speak of her travels.

When the silence grew long, Wini moved toward Vanity and whispered, "Do you tight-lace? We're not supposed to. It's s-sinful, some say, but all the girls here do. It's...terribly wicked fun! Sylvie laces to sixteen inches, and she got me to twenty one night. I fainted. They were my friends then. But then...I didn't want to do...everything, and so I..."

"Tight-lacing?" Vanity asked, watching the girl blush scarlet. What could be fun about getting squeezed to death and fainting?

"You haven't heard of it? Here, I'll show you. Unhook my bodice..." Vanity obeyed.

When Wini had removed her bodice and corset cover, Vanity saw that the girl wore clinching corset stays much smaller than she needed. "We don't tight-lace during the day. Miss Du Barry would expel us, but after hours, we all tighten...It's...it's very arousing. I'm still not sure I like it. I think I do. Sylvie said I should. We sleep with our stays on, to keep our waists tiny, and sometimes we play a naughty game…Sylvie taught us. I mustn't tell you. You might tell Miss Du Barry."

"I don't think I'll be telling her a thing," Vanity grumbled, remembering the woman's bewildering change in disposition after Maxx had left. Besides, she had to wonder if the girls were playing tops and bottoms with one another. She'd heard of that once, back in Tenderfoot, before she could imagine what it might mean.

Wini grinned. "Oh, good. We could play it together, then. Sylvie used to wake me during the night pretending to be Miss Du Barry. It's how the game started, you know. We're all sure this is true—that Miss Du Barry punishes with whips. Real carriage whips of black snakeskin! We're all so wicked, Sylvie says, that we have to prepare ourselves…I can take fifteen strokes without a tear. Miss Du Barry will never break my spirit!"

"Strokes?" Vanity whispered in horror. "Great snakes!"

"Oh, yes! We take everything off but our stays, and Sylvie punishes us with a riding crop. She says husbands do it to their wives regularly, when they talk up…or refuse. Do you think that's true? My mother never hinted at such a thing, but then who would…talk about such things? Sylvie says we have to get used to it. You will try it with me, won't you?"

Vanity stared at her. She hadn't heard about such things occurring in marriage or fine finishing schools. Physical constraint and punishment with whips sounded like the depraved practices of a port city bawdy house!

A gong interrupted Vanity's thoughts.

"We must hurry! Miss Du Barry's severe if we're late even a minute! I don't mind where you're from, Mary, or why you're here," Wini said as Vanity followed her out of the chamber. "We all have our secrets. No doubt Miss Du Barry knows why you're here in any case."

Vanity caught the slight girl's arm and held her back. "What kind of school is this, anyhow?"

Wini smiled a bit. "Why, we're all wicked little misfits! Weren't you told? Didn't you guess that was why you were being sent away? But you mustn't let anyone here frighten you. They're all just the most horrid creatures, but no better or worse than you or me. Do remind me to tell you what each has done to find herself in this fine, upstanding place!"

Wondering if Maxx had any idea of the true nature of this school, Vanity waltzed into the dining hall to the impudent, unmasked stares of thirty-seven misfits. She wasn't afraid of a single one. She had finally found her saloon for children and felt wonderfully at home!

Seven

Vanity's trunks, filled with luscious new gowns and exquisite underthings made by Sharona's expensive Natchez dressmaker, still hadn't been unpacked after a week. Miss Du Barry's college for female refinement boasted a great many industrious maids who served to show the belles— if they didn't know already—just how idle life would be for a well-behaved future wife of quality.

But they were not to unpack Vanity's belongings on threat of a lashing with a stirrup strap, for Miss Blade's things were deemed "unseemly."

Finally Vanity hung up her own gowns, hurt that each was in some way found lacking by Miss Du Barry. The girls, too, made sure Vanity felt she was wearing rags. Vanity's clothes, however, were among the best at the school.

"She even has new steel-wire hoops," Vanity overheard one of the girls whispering.

Vanity had not thought young ladies of quality stooped to snooping and stealing. That her things began disappearing only made her think, at first, that they'd been "borrowed." What was more startling was how little effort the girls made to hide their jealousy and resentment.

Out of sight and hearing of the maids and old misses, Du Barry Vale's inmates displayed an eye-popping ability to swear like drunken miners. They treated one another with a crudity Vanity had not seen even among the lowest of the professional women she had known in Tenderfoot.

The fact that her schoolmates were so like professional women in their secret carnal interests and private vulgar language didn't make Vanity feel at home among them for long. She grew quickly estranged, saying little and confiding in no one, not even Wini, who at times seemed a bit teched.

For the first week Vanity's roommate said nothing more about the games involving tight-lacing. Wini had been the target of much abuse since her arrival two months before. Now it was Vanity's turn.

By the second week, Vanity's shortcomings were miserably apparent during her lessons on the Steinway grand piano. She had no talent for the harp either. "I could play a concertina!" she offered at one point, only to be stared into crimson silence.

"A crude concertina is unworthy of a lady," Miss Du Barry informed her.

All the young ladies agreed, kindling in Vanity a low-burning, dangerous anger.

Snicker at her, would they? They were nothing but finely dressed mivvies! Well, what she wouldn't say when Maxx visited! she thought as she fought to control herself.

At the singing lessons, however, Vanity excelled. Though the songs she learned were a universe away from those she'd sung since babyhood, Vanity did well enough to earn the grudging admiration of several younger girls.

In the classes on manners and deportment she proved hopelessly inept. The foolish behavior she learned made her giggle, but ultimately it was her inability to produce legible handwriting that brought her the worst criticism.

"How," Miss Ezley demanded, "are you to write a comely invitation if you cannot even hold your quill like a lady? A true lady is known by her hand. You, Miss Blade, will be recognized for your ignoble birth."

Luckily, Vanity had no idea what the woman was saying.

"Perhaps she will have a social secretary do everything for her," came a voice from behind her.

Vanity was startled to find Miss Sylvania Hunt Leighey, of the Natchez Leigheys, coming to her defense.

Miss Ezley stared Sylvie down with her pale eyes. "Miss Blade will hardly have need of a social secretary in the wilds of California. I cannot imagine a single family of worth in the entire state. I surely have not heard of any, and I know every prominent family in the South."

"Then I'll hardly need to write a comely invitation," Vanity murmured.

Bristling with indignation, Miss Ezley drew herself up, laid down the quill she had snatched from Vanity's hand, and turned her back. Vanity had never before felt such scorn. The sight of that rigid narrow back filled her with resentment.

That evening, after the "quiet hour" in the withdrawing room, where the girls practiced the fine art of conversation and learned the acceptable ways one might comment upon the weather, Sylvie indicated with a startling smile that she wished to be Vanity's friend. "I would so like to get to know you better," Sylvie said.

In Vanity's bedchamber that night, Sylvie settled herself cross-legged like an Indian upon the forbidden coverlet and listened with interest as Vanity repeated the story of her background as Maxx had dictated it.

"Is this California such a very large place?" Sylvie asked, nodding enthusiastically as Vanity described the areas she'd seen.

"And what does your house look like? Is it made of logs?"

"Oh, it's very fine," Vanity said, coloring as she began spinning the fantasies her mother had once spun for her. "I have one maid who takes care of the upstairs, and another who dusts the whatnots downstairs. I have a jolly woman who bakes me cakes seven days a week…" She was quite carried away with herself as she recited the details that had been etched into her mind so long ago.

"And your dear mother, is she beautiful?" Sylvie asked, her voice as sweet as cream.

Vanity described a cross between her vivacious mama and Sharona dressed in her best, forgetting that a born lady would never have worn the colors she described.

Sylvie seemed quite impressed.

All the while Wini said not a word but watched, fearfully, from the dressing table stool. Each evening Sylvie returned to talk with Vanity— or Mary Louise, as she was called—until finally Sylvie's closest friends, Beverly and Lynette, joined in to listen to Vanity's concoction of half truths and fabrications.

"You seem to get along awfully well with Sylvie and her crew," Wini whispered from the darkness of their bedchamber after one of those evenings. Miss Du Barry had just gone away with their candle. "Lace me tighter, please, Mary. My waist will bulge to twenty-three whole inches if you don't."

"Wouldn't you like one night's decent sleep?" Vanity asked, staring up at the dark underside of the canopy. The linen pillow beneath her head felt soft and comforting, but she longed for the rhythmic lap of river water or gentle wind in the pines of Tenderfoot.

"I sleep all right in my stays. Please, Mary, I want you to be my friend. How can you spend so much time with Sylvie? She'll turn on you just as she turned on me. She'll make you sorry you trusted her."

"I don't trust her, but she seems nice enough," Vanity said.

"But she's not. We were caught together…playing her game, and she swore on a Bible that *I* made it up! I never did! She's taught every girl in this school her indecent ways, but she acts innocent. You watch! When you least expect it, she'll draw you in and use you and your secret to get what she wants."

"You said *she* had a secret. It's hard to imagine she's anything so terrible," Vanity said.

"Maybe sometime you'll smell her breath," Wini said. "But if you tell her I said such a thing, I'll deny it!"

"What does she find to drink?" Vanity asked, ashamed of her own curiosity.

"She steals it, of course, from Miss Du Barry's own stock. You've never seen Miss 'Never Marry's room, have you? She has a cupboard filled with liquor! It's right next to the one where she keeps the whips and crops. Sylvie would know!"

"I don't believe that!" Vanity scoffed.

"It was the first place Sylvie showed me when we were first friends. Then she left me there to get caught! I was very nearly whipped myself. You ought to be warned about Sylvie. I've heard things about her. She'll learn your secret, just as she learned mine…and use it to make you do whatever she says!"

Vanity's heart hammered. "What makes everyone think I have a secret?"

"You have to, to be here. Girls come here only if they've caused a scandal and must be shut away. You've done something. If you haven't, then your uncle isn't so upstanding as you've led us to believe, because if he was, he'd know about the real purpose of this place. That's secret enough."

Vanity crossed her arms over the soft coverlet. She was growing to dislike Wini and was sad because she had hoped for a friend. "I can't figure what *you've* done to be sent here."

"I'll tell you, then," Wini whispered, turning on her side and grabbing Vanity's arm. "I'll tell you everything if you tell me why you're here when I'm done."

Vanity said nothing, knowing her secret was far worse than anything a born lady might find the mischief to do, and that included fantasies of tight-lacing and whips.

"I fell in love with one of Papa's vaqueros," Wini whispered, giving Vanity's arm a little squeeze. "His name is Castel. He's oh, so handsome! Papa said I couldn't marry him, no matter how long he was willing to wait. Castel's twenty and from a very fine Mexican family. His line reaches back to Spain, but Papa doesn't care. I-I let Castel kiss me...and touch me." She stopped whispering for a long moment, then went on sadly. "But Papa caught us. He didn't punish me, though I would've preferred it to this. Instead, he sent me here to live with these creatures."

"I've been kissed, too," Vanity whispered, finding her thoughts suddenly filled with memories of Trance Holloway and his gleaming blond hair. She was too embarrassed to ask Wini how much "touching" she had allowed. The only touching Vanity had experienced were fleeting pats from some of the "gentlemen" of her papa's acquaintance.

"Is that why you're here?" Wini whispered. "Because of that?"

Impatiently, Vanity shook her head. "I'm here to become a lady," Vanity said softly, no longer sure she wanted to be one if it meant this.

Wini flopped back on her pillows. "What I wouldn't give to jump on a horse and ride away forever with Castel! I would marry him tomorrow!" She turned suddenly. "Now tell me your secret!"

Vanity knew if she didn't confide something, she might turn Wini into an active enemy. "I'm...I'm a willful wretch, my mama once said."

"But why? Do you drink like Sylvie? Has someone soiled your virtue? We can't figure out who compromised Beverly. She won't say, but you can be assured her reputation is ruined. She'll go directly from here to an arranged marriage far from Port Gibson. And not to anyone of any sort of quality. Her family will never take her back."

"How sad," Vanity said, confused by the secrets. Aside from their catty jealousy and swearing, Vanity still believed the girls a social cut above herself.

"Was it a man?" Wini whispered, her soft, understanding tone inspiring confidence. "Have you been...fornicated?"

Vanity giggled nervously. Wini was such a peculiar girl! What could she say to satisfy her? Vanity wondered, straining to understand suddenly why she was here. She thought of Sharona's long campaign, to remove her from Maxx's doting care and wondered suddenly why the woman had opposed this particular school. Knowing Sharona, she would have thought it quite appropriate! Had Sharona tricked her?

"Really, Wini," Vanity said, beginning to simmer with the realization that Sharona had pulled a fast one. "I don't have any secrets that I know about."

"Then Sylvie was right. You're a bastard. Nobody wants a bastard in plain sight where she can get in the way and complicate things."

• • •

Stunned and wide-eyed, Vanity lay awake all night. She had known she was a bastard since she came to understand the word *papa*. She had known it so long, it seemed a natural thing to be. It concerned no one she could recall, and had ceased to be worthy of her thought.

But to be told matter-of-factly that in the east bastards were to be hidden, that bastards complicated lives...

For days afterward as she struggled through her classes, the horrible new thought stayed with her, gnawing away at her. She no longer wanted to write Maxx and tell him about the true nature of the school. He had abandoned her!

As she suffered her thoughts in silence, the other girls left her alone. Vanity watched everything with a keen new eye. Were the "creatures," as Wini called the girls of Du Barry Vale, really wicked, or merely bored, frightened, abandoned girls like herself?

The more Vanity tried to understand, the more bewildered she felt. She was afraid to see Maxx now, afraid he wanted to be rid of her. How long, after all, was she to stay? He had never said.

Finally, in her confusion, she reached out for friendship with the girls, her misfit equals. She progressed with her legible handwriting, her knowledge of the myriad manners needed at any of a hundred different social occasions, and her eye for fashion. Even her French progressed enough to win Miss Du Barry's meager praise.

In embroidery she still bled more frequently than was seemly, but in home management she came to understand the nuances of dealing with servants and tradesmen. She learned how to run a large household and which wines to order for her future husband's bountiful table.

She submerged herself in the elegant complications expected to arise in a lady's life. While Yankees and Confederates continued killing one another in Virginia, and fierce fighting broke out in Missouri, she learned to curtsy and flutter a fan.

As Charleston blazed, Vanity danced her first formal cotillion in a frilly tulip-yellow silk gauze ball dress with cocky young Confederate officers imported expressly for the occasion. She had a marvelous time sliding across the highly polished ballroom floor—much to Miss Du Barry's disapproval. Vanity even let one downy-chinned officer kiss her simply because she couldn't think of a good reason why he should not.

On the day after Christmas, Vanity received her first letter from Maxx. Overjoyed that she could read it by herself—and feeling relieved to learn he had not stayed away because he wanted to be rid of her—she was frightened to learn of all the fighting along the river near Missouri and Kentucky.

Maxx assured her he'd had time to withdraw her funds in St. Louis before the town fell back into Federal hands. He said at the first opportunity he'd convert everything to Confederate dollars—something about a gesture of loyalty—but didn't expect to be as far south as Natchez for some weeks.

By New Year's Eve, 1861, as Miss Du Barry's belles gathered for a recital, the whispered talk was of Federal forces headed for New Orleans.

The girls talked of nothing but the prospect of being ravished in their beds by occupational troops. Vanity couldn't tell if their eyes burned with fear or anticipation.

During those long, lonely months at Du Barry, Vanity's thoughts again turned to Trance Holloway. If he had gone to sea, he'd now be a Yankee seaman.

By March the South lost two important generals to the Union's Trans-Mississippi campaign. Fighting moved up and down the Union portion of the Mississippi in an effort to remove that chain at Columbus, Kentucky.

In April, the battle at Shiloh, Tennessee, brought the war so close the girls began packing in case they had to flee for their homes. Reports of deaths began arriving on black-edged letter paper. With trembling hands the girls opened black wax seals and their tears smeared the precious watery ink.

Vanity watched from her window as carriages arrived to bear away Cheleen Birkett to her home in Alabama and Suzanna Reabe to her home in Tennessee.

No letters arrived from Maxx. Vanity stole a map from Miss Thorogood and sent letters to Maxx at every landing where he might stop during his leisurely wanderings up and down the river: New Orleans, Baton Rouge, Vicksburg, Tallulah, Columbia, Friar's Point, Memphis.

Vanity's need for the hothouse misfits was over. She wanted to be home on the *Vanity Blade* with Maxx again. Hang the war, and hang school!

On April 25, New Orleans fell. More girls departed for their homes. The nearly empty classrooms were forbidding, and the few girls remaining searched for distraction. Sylvie was their imaginative leader.

Sylvie invited everyone into her bedchamber for a mock May dance in honor of the ancient pagan rite. Vanity was disinclined to go. She was busy planning her escape.

"She'll just talk about us if we don't go," Wini said.

"Let her talk," Vanity said, wondering if Miss Du Barry called out the hounds for wayward students as she did for the occasional errant house slave.

"You wouldn't say that if you heard what she says about you."

Vanity's blood boiled. Wini appeared to be such a sweet, helpless thing, but Vanity found her timidity wearing. She whirled from her place by the window. "Sometimes I think you've made up those so-called secrets. You were the one to call me a bastard, not Sylvie!"

Wini's face went white. "I thought you were my friend!"

"I'm trying to be, but I don't understand you. I don't understand any of you! I've never smelled anything on Sylvie's breath. At the cotillion I didn't see Lynette throw herself at any of the officers. I've never heard Beverly say an unkind word. How can you go on and on about them? Sometimes I almost don't believe you!"

Wini looked as if she had been stabbed. "Find out for yourself then. When you least expect it, they'll make you very sorry." As she went out, the door closed behind her with an ominous thud.

If she was being used, Vanity was sure Wini was the one doing the using. She was so tired of the pretense at Du Barry Vale that she decided she would join Sylvie in her bedchamber after all, with the intention of finding out the truth at last.

The older girls had gathered there in their frilly dressing gowns, their shining hair done up in curling rags and their scrubbed faces bright with excitement.

"Oh, I'm so pleased you could come," Sylvie said, drawing Vanity into her shadowed chamber. She tapped a beribboned riding crop against her leg. "Now we all can have a true celebration of the pagan. Sit here and tell us if you know anything about voodoo." She pulled off her dressing gown, revealing her tightly laced corset. Her waist was the tiniest Vanity had ever seen, an obscene distortion.

"Why would I know anything about voodoo?" Vanity asked, trying not to stare as each girl in turn removed her dressing gown to reveal bulging breasts, flaring hips, and tiny waists.

Sylvie swirled around the lovely bedchamber humming something that sounded like a chant. She blew out three lamps, leaving one candle burning with a flickering white flame in the center of the carpeted floor. "Your uncle's a Creole, part French, part Spanish, part Indian...and part Negro, surely. They know *all* about such things."

Wini had taken an inconspicuous place in the far corner. She hadn't removed her dressing gown. When Vanity glanced at her as if to ask if she'd repeated the few things Vanity had told her in confidence, Wini flinched.

Sylvie went on. "Isn't California just about the end of the earth? A place of heathen savages running about naked, devouring babies, and torturing men and doing unnatural, filthy things to innocent women?" She slapped her palm with the crop. "We wouldn't like to think you'd refuse to tell us about the secret practices that have surely been in your family for generations."

Vanity said nothing as Sylvie settled herself cross-legged before the candle on the floor. The nearly naked girl waved her hands over the flame, staring deeply into it. Her face looked haunted as the light brought her lovely features into garish and ghastly relief.

"Sit down beside me, Mary Louise Blade," Sylvie whispered, tapping a spot beside her with the tip of the crop.

Cautiously, Vanity sat down on the soft carpet.

"We're here tonight to discover just who you are, Mary Louise Blade," Sylvie whispered as the remaining girls made a circle on the floor. "Spirits, tell us Mary's secret."

"I have no secret," Vanity whispered, deciding to leave at once.

Sylvie seized her arm and jerked her back to the carpet. "You don't go until we know." She looked directly into Vanity's eyes, smiling like a demon. "If you don't tell us, we'll have to give you truth powder. Then you'll tell us everything you've ever seen, heard, done, and thought...for your whole life!"

Vanity shivered. The faint odor of alcohol masked with heliotrope cologne was coming from Sylvie's pretty little mouth. Vanity stopped pulling away as she felt Sylvie's nails dig into her arm.

Lynette leaned into the glaring yellow candlelight. "We know you're not from Georgia."

"I never said I was," Vanity said, her anger rising. "Maxx's people—"

Sylvie shook her head and flicked Vanity's cheek with the crop. "We know the Spears have no Creole relations from New Orleans—or California. Want to read the letters saying so?" She smiled very sweetly. "You're a liar, Miss Blade. Stand and remove your dressing gown. We give three strokes for a lie."

Vanity's mouth tightened. She jerked her arm from Sylvie's painful grasp. "You're pie-eyed!"

Laughing, Sylvie cocked her head. "That man who brought you here isn't your uncle. He's a gambler." She said the word in the same tone Wini had used for *bastard*. "That makes six strokes on your bare backside. Stand, Mary Louise, and take what's comin' to you. I guarantee you'll enjoy it…eventually. Let us lace you a bit more tightly before we begin."

Vanity touched her fingers to her tongue and pinched the candlewick, hearing the *sht-t-t* as the flame winked out. Instantly she stood, disoriented in the darkness, but knowing she must flee.

She crashed headlong into several strong-armed girls who held her and tore her dressing gown over her shoulders and started jerking on her drawers. Their frenzied giggles were more frightening than any nightmare.

"He's a gambler! You're a bastard! What we don't know is whether you're his bastard daughter, his dirty little mistress, or his child bride. Which is it, Mary?" Their whispering voices made her name sound like a curse.

Someone began jerking her laces. Vanity's waist was pulled in tighter and tighter. Her breasts began bulging forward as her hips were accentuated. Someone brushed something cool across the tops of Vanity's jutting breasts, sending a shiver of fear through her. She couldn't think or breathe. When the first blow of the crop stung her partially exposed backside, she erupted.

Flinging away the restraining hands, Vanity fought her way to the wall and struggled to the door. Throwing it wide and admitting dim light from the passageway, Vanity whirled on the girls crowded behind her, their faces wide with delight. "Light that damned candle!" Vanity hissed.

Wini scrambled from the darkness and struck a lucifer match, bringing the candle to life again. Then she backed away, her harshly lit expression saying she had tried to warn Vanity.

Vanity's heart thundered. Closing the door with care, she advanced on Sylvie and gave the laughing, unsuspecting girl a forceful shove. "Dirty mivvy!" she hissed, snatching the crop from her hands and snapping it in two. "Don't you ever lay your hands on me again or I'll tear out your hair!"

Tittering, Sylvie backed away.

Shoving her again, Vanity made Sylvie fall back against the edge of her mussed-up bed. The chamber seemed to be whirling. Darkness was all around save for the candlelit center ringed with upturned, gaping faces.

"I'm not his mistress or his wife!" Vanity hissed, circling the girls and watching each twist to watch her. "He's not my father, either. I just live on the riverboat. I own it—the *Vanity Blade*. That's who I am. You can all go straight to blazes. You're nothing to me! And you're not ladies, not a gull-danged one of you!"

Sylvie covered her smirk. "It's just too delightful," she started to say.

Vanity whirled, wanting to gouge the pretty face and cold laughing eyes of Sylvania Hunt Leighey. "You'd love to hurt me, but you can't. I'm free to leave any time I want. You're trapped. *You're* a lady. Your people will keep you prisoner here until you marry. You'll be trapped then, too, because you haven't got the gumption to go out and be what you really are—a slut!"

Vanity swung on Beverly. "I'm told your virtue's soiled, but you're not dirty. You're hurt. You're crying inside for someone to care, but no one does. Not here!"

Beverly twisted away, looking to Sylvie for defense. Sylvie's eyes narrowed and darkened. Wini started for the door.

"You," Vanity said, pointing toward her roommate, "are no better! They've made you like them, small and mean." Quickly she spun on Lynette. "And I can't forget you. I grew up with women like you who couldn't do anything different from what they'd been born to. You'll hide behind your family name while dirtying it with every man you touch."

Lynette whimpered. "Hit her, Sylvie! Make her stop!"

"You've said quite enough," Sylvie said from the shadows. She darted across the chamber and snatched a birch switch from beneath her bed. Whirling on Vanity, she swished it back and forth sharply in front of her.

"I haven't said the half! I'll never be like you, and I'm glad! You're right, I am a bastard! I stand alone as I am." Her voice had risen dangerously. "I could outdo you all!" she whispered, starting toward the door.

"Oh, do show us how you could," Sylvie said silkily. "We're frightfully sorry we hurt your feelings."

Vanity couldn't stop herself from turning and striking her most vulgar stage pose. Seizing a handful of her torn dressing gown hem to expose her legs, she strutted around the chamber, showing them a side of herself she hadn't known existed. "I have a beau, his name is Johnny!" she sang softly. "He comes at night and calls me honey. He gives me sweets and lots of money. Oh, say-y-y, have you seen my Johnny?"

The girls cooed with delight. "More!" said Lynette, her face lighting up.

"I have a beau, his name is Johnny. He holds me tight and calls me honey. He gives me love and lots of money. Oh, say-y-y…"

The door to the chamber creaked open. One stocky shadow and two frail silhouettes filled it. Vanity's voice trailed off.

"*What* is going on here?" Miss Du Barry croaked in strangled tones. "Light the lamps! Let me see your faces!"

The roomful of girls scrambled to cover themselves. Something overturned behind Wini and shattered, sending the sharp odor of spirits into the air.

Wini backed away, looking down with horror at one of Miss Du Barry's hand-blown glass decanters, which lay on the floor in pieces. "I didn't take it! I didn't! I don't know how it got behind me! They...they put it there just now! It's not mine, I tell you!"

Miss Du Barry stormed into the bedchamber and seized Wini's sleeve. "You shall depart this house at once, this very night! Harlot! Thief! Jezebel!"

"Just a minute! You can't send her away! She's done nothing! Look at the others!" Vanity exclaimed, realizing too late the other girls in the chamber looked innocent clutching their dressing gowns to their throats. "The decanter's yours, after all!"

Miss Du Barry's eyes bulged until the chamber trembled with her anger. "You dare to suggest...you filthy excuse for a female, you shall leave this night as well! I shall not tolerate your presence in my father's home another moment!"

Vanity stiffened, lifted her chin, and shook her tousled hair. "I wouldn't stay. You're a bitter, miserable old hag and you hate these girls. You keep them here and teach them stupid, useless things. You're dead inside from envy. You tried to make me feel low, but I'm not dirt under your feet. I'm better than you, better than all of you!"

Whirling past the woman, Vanity marched from the chamber and headed toward her room to pack. From behind her she heard a stinging slap and a cry of pain.

Vanity's departure was delayed because Miss Du Barry refused to let Vanity leave in one of the Du Barry Vale carriages. While telegraph dispatches were sent to all river landings likely to know of Maxx's whereabouts, Vanity was excused from attending any more classes. She ate alone in her room and Wini did not come in that evening to sleep. Vanity was waiting, still angry but feeling uneasy, the following afternoon when a black top-buggy called for Wini.

Wini didn't look up at Vanity, who was watching from the window, or wave as she boarded the buggy. Vanity had no idea where the girl was going. She was sick in her heart for not having trusted Wini, and she grieved to think she had brought her only friend such shame and heartache.

The afternoon was a long, miserable one in which Vanity imagined Maxx's scowling, disappointed face when he arrived to take her away in disgrace. How could she have ever thought she could pretend to be a lady?

Sylvie threw open Vanity's bedchamber door. "You're wanted in Miss Du Barry's office," she said, snickering.

Vanity turned from her window, wondering why Sylvie hadn't left yet. "What will your parents say when they come?" Vanity asked.

"Why, whatever makes you think I'm leavin'? I belong here, just as you so rightly said the other night. My father has enough money to keep me here forever if he so chooses, and that suits me because I have amazing power here. I might even teach here one day. Can't you just picture it, Mary? All those delicious little misfits comin' to me for punishment. And I'll be so very severe on their plump little backsides. I only regret I didn't have the opportunity to punish you. You're right about us all, you know. But we'll always have somethin' your 'uncle's' money will never buy. We have social standin'. You'll never be anythin' but an insignificant little bastard with no name, no family, and no place to call your own. You're a woman without station—"

"Do shut up!" Vanity snapped in a simpering accent, pushing past the girl and going down the hall.

The moment Vanity stepped inside Miss Du Barry's office, her body went rigid with surprise. Sharona sat across from Miss Du Barry's polished-rosewood desk. Her elaborate black twill gown contrasted sharply with the pastel Turkey-work carpet and the muted wallpaper behind her. She set a frail china cup back into the saucer in her left hand and finally looked up.

Such dramatics, Vanity thought bitterly, wanting to laugh. A black dress, a black-veiled hat, all for the occasion of her expulsion from Du Barry Vale. Though Vanity was delighted to leave the elegant prison, deep inside she was deeply hurt Maxx had not come for her himself.

Her resolve to be arrogant to Miss Du Barry wilted. Instead, she wanted to show Sharona she had indeed learned to behave like a lady. She would use the behavior now like an invisible gown she might put on and take off at will.

"How very good to see you again, Aunt Sharona," Vanity said in a sweet voice. She gave a small, graceful curtsy and smiled.

Sharona placed the rattling cup and saucer on a small gateleg table beside her. "I came the moment I…" Sharona paused, appearing unable to go on. Finally she summoned the strength to say, "Miss Du Barry tells me you were just asked to leave."

"I want to get out of here—I mean, I desire to leave this place in all haste, at your convenience, Aunt Sharona—"

"You may dispense with pretense, Mary Louise," Miss Du Barry interrupted, her voice hard as iron. "We know who and what you are. The matter of your dismissal, however, is no longer relevant. I regret to inform you that your…that Miss Doherty brings grievous news."

With a tingling of horror, Vanity's eyes shot to Sharona's black gown and veil, and to the letter she was pulling from the folds of her skirt. Vanity's heart began beating in a frightened rhythm. "Not Papa! Not Papa, too!"

The right side of Sharona's face tightened. She turned away as if to let a deep stab of pain pass. She didn't move as Vanity lunged forward to grab the letter and tear it open.

"My dear little catfish,

"How it does grieve me to be away from you all this time. This damnable war has kept me from visiting, for true, but I trust you've had a time learning all your dear mama wanted for you.

"Myself, I have been struck down, so I am told by the old physician standing over me, by a weakening ol' heart. You reckon you can go on without me now? I fixed it so you can. You got my boat, and your mama's money is in Confederate war bonds. Sharona will explain the rest. I got little strength to say good-bye.

"Don't cry, catfish…"

The last words were so difficult to read, Vanity felt as if she could see Maxx struggling with the last bit of his strength to write them. The letter wasn't signed.

Sharona sniffed as she fished into her reticule for something. "Here, he left you this." She held out a large dark copper penny. "He said it was blessed or something. I came straight from the funeral. It was his heart, as he said. It came on sudden one night. He was gone in two hours. He left a will."

Vanity clamped the penny in her clammy hand and let out with a heart-rending wail. "Not Papa, too! Dear God, I should never have left! God damn you for making me go!"

Sharona's eyes flooded. "I'm sorry, Vanity."

Miss Du Barry made no move to comfort either of them. Sharona looked away, a handkerchief pressed to her nose.

When Vanity opened her dry eyes and saw the two women with their faces turned away, she suddenly felt no hate. She was alone—utterly, irreversibly alone. No one could change it back.

Feeling stiff and awkward, Vanity made her way from Miss Du Barry's cool, impersonal office, out through the reception parlor. She didn't push over the pedestals with their pompous-looking busts. She didn't scuff her heels across the gleaming parquet floor. She went out through the wide front doors as if it was any sunny May afternoon.

The sky was pale, slightly overcast, the breeze cool against her burning cheeks and eyes. Sharona's hired carriage stood in the carriageway. Vanity climbed aboard, forgetting all except the penny in her fist. Gentlemen had always felt inclined to give her something the moment they set eyes on her.

Eight

1862

It had been three years since Trance Holloway had been on the Mississippi River. On that journey, when he had met lovely, beguiling Vanity Blade, he and his parents hadn't traveled as far south as New Orleans. Now Trance found the world of the Mississippi delta strange and warmly seductive.

Leaning against the gunwhale of the twenty-four-gun Union sloop, he looked across the wide brown river at the indistinct green banks where massive, twisted live oaks stood draped in Spanish moss.

Even without the war, the world of the bayou was filled with danger. Half his mates were down with dysentery, sunstroke, or malaria. When they went ashore, they were assaulted by Confederate men and women alike, and once, on a short run up the river, they'd seen, nailed to a tree, a sign reading BEWARE YANKEES!

Flag Officer Farragut's fleet had arrived only weeks before to blockade New Orleans. Trance had fought with the fleet to take the port city, but now, instead of pressing their advantage and moving upriver to take Vicksburg, they were dead in the water, making repairs.

Trance felt restless and impatient. His thoughts often returned to his parents and his sister, Rowena. His last night home—over a year ago—had been as painful as he had always feared it would be. He and his father had argued bitterly. His mother had wept and cursed him for breaking her heart.

In the end Rowena had urged him out the door, saying, "It'll be better for us all if you just go, quickly."

She'd been but twelve, yet in the midst of the emotional turmoil they had lived since returning to Cold Crossing to face the gossips, Rowena had possessed the only clear head among them.

Trance was wrenched from his thoughts by the deep, jovial voice of his bandy-legged friend Michael O'Donahee, a stocky, outgoing lad from Newburyport. "Lieutenant Holloway, sir, you're staring off into nowhere like always!"

"How's Andy?" Trance asked, thinking of the reckless mate who had been punished the past two days for insubordination.

"Still chafing in his irons and mad as a hornet, but behaving himself at last," Mick O'Donahee said. "Captain Morris is a hard, hard man, to be sure. I tried to tell Andy to take his orders without guff, but you know him—a head full of stones and stubborn as brass. He hasn't got the good sense God gives shavetail mules!"

"The captain reminds me of my father," Trance said, shaking his head and chuckling to think he'd come so far and still hadn't escaped authority. Turning from the gunwhale, he leaned back against it with a discontented sigh.

His long, fully matured body looked powerful and sleek in the flattering cut of his dark naval uniform. He had an arresting air about him now, with his distant, brooding gaze and handsome sun-bronzed features.

The advancing evening air smelled heavy and beguiling, reminding him of humid summer nights at home. He felt a vague uneasiness stirring deep within him, a need that went unfulfilled as he went about his solitary life.

Though he lived among his fellow seamen and snapped to the orders of his captain, his moody, turbulent thoughts as always were his own. His memories of another time on the river were haunting, for the particular memory he held most dear was little more than a blur, a sensation of longing, a flash of dazzlingly beautiful brown eyes that he always had to force himself to remember had belonged to a girl who was little more than a child.

Trance tried to shake off his disquiet. "I have leave to go ashore tonight. I was trying to decide what to do with myself in this occupied city. The last time I risked it, I was spat on by a Southern lady threatening me with her parasol."

Mick chuckled, his blue eyes merry. "My young bumpkin, I know places where the color of a man's uniform doesn't matter. It's the color of a man's money that counts. Indeed, it does!"

Trance smoothed back his wind-tossed silver-blond hair. He didn't mind being called a bumpkin. He knew he was one, and he had already gone on a number of escapades with Mick and the others in search of the ultimate in delicious lips, soft arms, and swelling endowments. "I thought you hadn't been to New Orleans. You sound as if you know the place well."

"Ah, friend!" Mick laughed aloud. "Every such city has these places!

They're as easy to find as any saloon. All a man must do is lift his nose to the breeze and follow the scent of sweetness and delight!"

Trance and Mick had staggered from the theater district to the nearest cock fight. Fleeing with their hated Yankee uniforms intact, they sought quieter amusements along shadowed, sinister streets, laughing and singing as if all the world should join in.

Mick bellowed the bass for "The Parlor Maid, She Is a Darling," as they fell over crates and cotton bales and hogsheads of sugar. There they saw tied up along the dark, deserted wharves the bulky white shapes of riverboats sympathetic to the Confederate cause.

Trance and Mick marveled at the beautiful boats whose lamplights dotted the water with so many pinpricks of light.

The boats were like grand dames bedecked in fine array, or sirens of the river, beckoning the wary and unwary.

As they wandered and stumbled, commenting upon females they had met—and passed by—Trance thought again of that long-ago day he met the girl in shabby green satin. He remembered how she had strutted across that gambling boat's small stage, and how he had envied her her breathless abandon.

What he wouldn't give to cast himself free from the parental chains around his mind and heart! He wanted to throw his arms wide to the sweet night air and sing out his yearning as Mick was doing.

But only a good Kentucky bourbon set Trance free, and then only for a few hours. By morning he would be riddled with self-contempt at his weakness. Yet he embraced his single vice, relishing his moments of intoxicated freedom and his taste for moral abandon. By day he was the most sober, dedicated officer aboard his ship, respected and trusted by all.

As they paused to laugh over something Mick was saying—sometimes Trance was so lost in himself he didn't bother listening—he focused his eyes with some difficulty and saw ahead the blurry white shape of a lovely side-wheeler.

She was lit from bow to stern, the beauty of her filigree trim and graceful design shimmering in the night air. The reflections of her lights winked in the inky water ahead. Then he heard a lilting young voice, and instantly his skin prickled with recognition!

"Sh-h-h!" he hissed, seizing Mick's sleeve and shaking him into silence. "Listen! Do you hear her?" Blindly he stumbled forward, following the teasing sound as it echoed among the shadowy shapes of warehouses and saloons.

"Me boy, you're not wandering off in your sorry state," Mick said, grabbing hold of Trance's collar and hauling him backward.

Pushing Mick's hands away, Trance straightened, willing his head to clear. The side-wheeler was magnificent, a star-lit dream. She had two tall proud black smokestacks with plumes on top, a gently curving deck, and all the promise of the gambling boat he remembered from three years before.

She was a smallish boat, beautifully fitted, and exuding an air of dignity—strange for what he knew must surely be a floating gambling palace. Then he squinted into the murky darkness, trying to make out the name emblazoned on the wheel house and pilothouse.

In red was written VANITY BLADE. A chorus of cheers echoed across the water, seizing his befuddled brain and dragging him forward a few more uncertain steps.

Trance knew nothing but the sound of that siren's voice! He scarcely felt his feet touching the ground. He no longer felt the sensations of his body or the moist caressing warmth of the night air. He was following an impossible dream, yearning for fulfillment.

He staggered up the stageplank and across the deck. Before he could get his bearings, he was stumbling up the main stairs to the saloon deck and into the splendid grand saloon, where the air was milky-white with smoke from half a hundred Havana cigars.

Standing in the great doorway, staring out across the assemblage of refined gentlemen seated around tables draped in gold cloths, the air above their oiled heads splintered by the refracted light of six softly swaying crystal chandeliers, naval Lieutenant John Travis Holloway looked like a crazed and hungry refugee.

His pale hair was wild, his naval uniform disheveled and faintly smudged thanks to the dark, dirty streets. His glazed blue eyes were wide, and his usually hooded expression was alive with hope.

He searched the amused faces turning toward him. His heart hammered. His blood rushed dangerously. His head reeled. Then the deck seemed to pitch beneath his feet. The grand saloon and all the glaring yellow lamps swooped and receded before his eyes.

Then he saw her. He had to be dreaming! She stood across the long, elegant saloon looking like a morning glory in a huge bell-skirted blue gown. Her dark chestnut hair was piled high in light-catching coils and rolls. Wisps escaped fetchingly at her temples and nape.

She saw him, he knew. She turned to face him, her creamy cheeks so radiant even at that distance he was struck speechless. A flush rose to her delicate cheeks.

Her shoulders were softly rounded and bare above the deep décollétage of her gown. Her skin looked luminescent in the light. She wore magnolias in her hair and at the cleft of her creamy, tantalizing bosom. She had been talking to a portly gentleman and laughing loudly, but now she straightened and stood stock-still, matching his stare from across the smoky expanse.

She looked soft, lovely and innocent, as vulnerable as he remembered, but a woman now of devastating desirability. She looked at him with direct brown eyes, challenging him to pick up his leaden, stupid feet and approach.

Come to me, her unsettling gaze said, and he found his body suddenly raging with power, his veins singing.

Yet as he drew closer he saw something worrisome in her lovely expression, a tightening at the corners of her voluptuous, infinitely kissable lips.

He saw something in those subtly amused eyes that made him want to seize whoever had wounded her and crush him! He wanted to take her cheeks in his palms and kiss away the knowledge that had changed her from a girl to a woman.

But all he could do was stop a few feet from her, his body coiled so tightly that he felt ready to explode. He wanted to say something profound, but an overpowering blackness washed across his vision.

A ringing filled his ears. He pitched forward into his dream.

"Damned drunken Yankee!" someone muttered.

Vanity swept her guests with a look of warning. "Perhaps this young officer has a touch of fever," she said in her "Sylvie" voice. "You'd be wise to step back."

Instantly, the area around the unconscious naval officer cleared enough that Vanity could crouch in her rustling gown and cradle his head in her lap.

He moaned and then went limp again. Another officer appeared and stood stupidly over Vanity and Trance, looking down and blinking.

"Do you know this young gentleman?" Vanity asked, her voice at its most ladylike. When the stocky man nodded, she went on. "Then be so good as to notify his commanding officer that he has been taken ill. I'll look after him until you can send someone for him."

Vanity cushioned Trance's head with someone's coat, then straightened. Thanking her patrons profusely, she signaled Jim Hickory, Maxx's former personal assistant and now the *Vanity Blade*'s saloon manager.

The dark man came forward and, with the help of several deck hands, lifted Trance Holloway. They bore him away to Vanity's stateroom on the Texas deck.

"Put him there on the bed and fetch a doctor," Vanity said.

Her heart thrilled to see Trance, yet she worried because he'd passed out. Might he really be ill?

"Want one of us to stay with you, Miss Vanity?" Jim asked, his usually jovial face creased with disapproval. "He's apt to get violent...or uppity once he wakes."

Vanity patted Jim's coat sleeve and then steered him toward her door. "I'll be fine! I know him. He's a preacher's son!"

"Them's the most uppity kind!" Jim said, shaking his head when he saw Vanity wouldn't be swayed.

Closing the stateroom door, Vanity turned, half fearing that if she dared look at the man on her bed he would turn out to be someone else.

But it was Trance Holloway sprawled on her covers, his head twisted crookedly to one side, his arms thrown out to each side, his legs splayed. For one hideous moment he looked dead. Then she saw his chest rise with a single soft breath, and she felt herself tingle from head to toe.

He had come back! She approached her bed with a sense of wonder, noting all the changes three years had wrought. The lean youth had become a man; the wide shoulders had filled out and were solidly muscled, the chest was broad and hard, roped with muscles from heavy work, and his legs were lean and as sturdy as prime oaks.

She straightened his head upon her pillow and smoothed back that wonderfully pale hair from his damp brow. Unconscious, his expression was open and faintly anxious.

She traced the hollow of his sun-darkened cheek, but then he gasped for breath and stirred, sending a thrill through her.

Blinking, he struggled upright.

She threw herself onto her knees at the side of her frilly bed and seized his arm. "You're all right! You're safe with me, and you don't have to worry about getting back to your ship! I told them you were sick. Lie back. Let me be your nurse!" Then she got up and sat on the edge of her bed, gazing down at him as he relaxed, transfixed, into her pillows.

He looked at her with the same wonder she felt. "It *is* you!" he whispered. "I thought I was dreaming!"

She couldn't stop herself from shivering with delight. She clasped his warm hand tightly in her own and smiled down at him. "Hello! I see you joined the navy. Was your pa terribly upset?"

Trance smiled and nodded. "Thrown into a torment."

His eyes went over her face with a tenderness that brought a lump to her throat. "I was sure you'd long forgotten me," she said haltingly.

"How could I?" Then his eyes strayed to her throat, and to her shoulders, and then to the creamy swells of her bosom. "How could I ever forget you?"

A starburst of desire went off in her chest as she watched his eyes travel over her body. Suddenly she was trembling all over, knowing what she could have, at last, with this man of her dreams.

Her eyes locked on his. He drew her close then, his breath coming rapidly, his eyes growing wide, his moist, seductive lips parting.

"I dreamed you'd come to me," she whispered, startled at the husky tenor of her own voice.

"I've thought of you so much…You've grown even more beautiful than I remembered."

"I've been away, you know. At school! But while I was gone, Maxx died…of heart failure," she said softly, looking away until the unexpected sheen of tears had left her eyes. "Sharona thought she was going to get this boat from me. She was my papa's…woman. She and I had a terrible fight afterward. The boat's mine, you see. Great snakes! She didn't like that."

"Why?"

"It was awful, the things she said about giving Maxx her best years and then getting nothing in return, like he was an investment. She got plenty! But she resented me because he loved me."

"What will she say when she finds me here in your bed?" Trance whispered, then grinned.

"She's gone." Vanity sighed. "When she left, she said the strangest things—something about making me sorry and, if I could take what was rightfully hers, she'd take what I had left. I thought she meant my mama's savings, but that's tied up in war bonds. I don't know where she's gone, but I do know this boat is mine! I'm famous up and down the river, just like my mama wanted."

"It was good of your pa to will you this boat," Trance said.

Vanity's lips curved. "Oh, but I won it from him! In a game of poker!" She watched his face for disapproval. "Does that shock you?"

"Nothing you could do would ever shock me," Trance whispered, his eyes adoring. Then his brow tightened as if he was in pain.

"Can I get you something? A toddy?"

He shook his head and tightened his grip on her fingers. "Just some time alone with you."

"That's something I can arrange," she said, grinning impishly.

He was about to draw her into the strength of his arms when a tapping sounded at the door. Instantly his soft eyes darkened. He drew away, gathering himself back into that brooding detached state she remembered from that first day at the revival meeting by the river. How she hated it!

He tried to get up, "You'd better see who that is."

"Lie back! *I* give the orders aboard this boat, Lieutenant!"

A bumbling doctor, fetched from some saloon near the wharves, came and went with a chuckle, pronouncing the Yankee lieutenant afflicted with "fever," but not of the sort his commanding officer would accept as a valid excuse for returning late to his ship.

Nevertheless, the old gent scribbled out a prescription for a draft of the quinine to ward off malarial tremors. "See to it you remain abed, my boy, for at least three full days. I'll send a message that you're not to be moved."

Vanity's eyes widened as she gave the doctor her loveliest curtsy, then showed him the door.

She spun around and gave Trance a heart-stopping smile. "Three days!"

She looked every bit the lovely fresh sixteen-year-old that she was. Though her gown was very sophisticated and her hair was done up in a fancy style, she radiated youth and good health.

"What shall we do, then?" she asked, rushing to the foot of her bed.

Trance sat on the edge where the doctor had examined him,

watching her hungrily.

"Where shall we go?" she asked huskily. "We'll get away from everything!"

"It's the middle of the night!" Trance said, clutching at his head as if it hurt.

"You need another drink," she said, and went to the door to signal a steward.

Moments later she held out a tumbler full of amber liquid to Trance, and felt her blood rush as her fingers brushed his. She thought of the hours ahead—alone with him.

"I shouldn't have more," he said, shaking his head.

"Oh, do! It won't hurt. Would you like to go out in the skiff? We could find a quiet place—I have a better idea! Let's take a run up to Natchez! I could show you where I went to school...and where Maxx is buried. You have three days, after all!"

"Can you leave New Orleans just like that?"

"Of course! You forget, this boat is mine. I pay the pilots, the clerks and stewards, the barber and stokers, right down to the last deck hand and monte dealer." She shrugged prettily. "Of course, I have a bit of help, but I give the orders! To Natchez!" she exclaimed as she whirled from the room like a princess.

Amid a flurry of activity and the departure of more than a few disgruntled patrons who did not care to go to Natchez, the *Vanity Blade* pulled away from the wharf and beat a frothy path into the darkness of the wide Mississippi at midnight.

Bullfrog, the boat's pilot, a man of considerable girth and voice, made the air inside the pilothouse sizzle with a fascinating variety of oaths, but the boat headed upriver anyway.

Huge iron baskets filled with burning rags hung out over the bow, casting a smoky light across the water. The riverbanks dotted with white mansions, expanses of tall breeze-bent cane, and the lovely old black oaks soon fell away. On the narrow Texas gangway, Vanity and Trance stood at the railing. Trance felt acutely aware of Vanity standing so close at his side and yet not touching him except where the hem of her wide blue skirt brushed his boots.

"I love this river," she whispered, her soft white hands clasping the railing as she leaned forward. "Do you swim?"

"Of course," Trance said, chuckling a little. "The swimming hole was my favorite place in summer. I got strapped regularly for going there Sunday afternoons. Do you?"

"I swim all the time." She leaned back and arched her beautiful back so that her full bosom stood out tantalizingly. She was well endowed for such a young woman, Trance thought, and felt his body come alive.

He wanted to seize her and hold her close. His thoughts seemed so powerful and overwhelming suddenly that he had to step away from her to keep himself from doing what his aching hands and body demanded.

"Oh," she said, pouting a little. "You disapprove, too. Everybody does, but it's fun! You know it is! I love the way the water feels, the way it slips over my body and runs through my hair. I used to swim even as a child. I can't tell you how often those old miners snatched me from the creek and gave me a good shake. 'Ketch yer death!' they always said. But I didn't. Do you want to swim now?" she asked excitedly.

Alarm ran through Trance. "No," he said, moving quickly and catching her arm. "Be sensible, Vanity! It's too dark, too dangerous."

"Great snakes! I don't care a fig for danger!" Vanity said, moving close and putting her hand over his. Then she broke free of his hold and started for the stairs leading down to the saloon deck. "I grew up always doing exactly as I wanted. I didn't have a worry if it was good or bad, right or wrong. When I was with Maxx, he let me do whatever I pleased. Once, he even let me take a puff on his cigar! Sharona nearly fell off her chair. You'd think she was Miss Du Barry's sister the way she carried on about ladylike behavior. I'm so glad she's gone!" She paused. "Though I do miss her a little. I don't really have any friends on this boat, just some people I see at the landings. Everyone's a bit afraid of me, I guess. Some think I'm wicked to live this way. Some so-called gentlemen think I'm... well, I do know a lot for my age! A man can't cheat that I don't notice! Only last week I threw a man off my boat for cheating. What do you think of that?"

Trance was at once fascinated and aghast. He watched her, his expression hidden by the darkness, wanting so much to touch her, thinking that he dared not for what would surely follow.

Quickly he followed her down to the boiler deck just off the water. He could almost imagine himself stripping to his underwear and diving into the black river. It would be like getting drunk, he thought, though he was drunk enough now on Vanity's beauty.

"Come on!" she said, seizing his hand with her small warm one and dragging him along the gangway, behind where the big red paddles turned gently. "A little tug on the right bell and we'll stop," she whispered. "I'm not afraid to swim in the dark. I've done it lots of times! Not many people are left on board to bother us. If they do, I'll order up a round on the house and they'll go on back to the bar."

He stopped her, holding her slim shoulders in his hands. He had never before realized how big and wide his hands were. They looked dark against her fairness.

His fingers slowly edged up to the lace at her neck, and finally he rested his palms fully on her shoulders, pretending he was holding down a weightless bit of sunbeam. "I won't let you go into the water, day or night. It's not—"

"Oh, don't say it's not seemly! Then I surely will jump in! You won't be able to stop me!" She squirmed away, laughing. "You haven't left your father. You're wearing him on your shoulder, and he's whispering in your ear, 'Have no fun, John Travis. Be dull and stodgy for all of your days. Don't let that Jezebel corrupt you!'" Vanity darted away and began yanking at the hooks at the back of her bodice. "I dare you to swim with me!"

Angered, Trance turned away, refusing to be taunted and tricked into letting her endanger herself. She was, after all, just a slip of a girl.

She bolted past him and he heard the faint jangle of the bell. The paddles eased to a stop. Without their threshing he could hear the chink of poker chips overhead. A man's voice drifted on the night air, and then a woman laughed, making his pulse race.

"Are you a Jezebel?" Trance asked, his head whirling from all he'd drunk.

He wished he was in possession of his wits, for he wanted to remember everything about this night.

Suddenly she was there before him, her beautiful face so close that he might kiss her. Her eyes were slits. "I should slap you for asking such a thing, John Travis!"

"Don't call me that."

"I will, whenever I hear your father speak through your mouth. And it's such a handsome mouth, too." She sighed. "I double-dare you to swim with me! We'll dive in at the bow and climb out at the stern. There are ropes to hold…"

"You'd never be able to pull yourself aboard!" he cried.

"Help unhook me, John Travis!" She presented her back to him.

He hated to hear her call him that. He felt so controlled by his father's hypocritical ethics that he couldn't have the one thing he desired more than anything on earth—Vanity!

His hands fumbled with the hooks down her lovely slim back. When he saw the whiteness of her sheer, embroidered corset cover gleaming at him, he was fully erect and terrified of himself, terrified he would seize her and ravish her like a drunken seaman right there on the deck.

She struggled out of the bodice, tossed it down, and dropped her skirts with heart-stopping speed. Her white petticoats gleamed in the darkness. Soon they, too, lay in a heap only two feet from his astonished eyes.

Her corset cover scarcely concealed the fullness of her plump breasts, forced up high by the tightly clinched corset. Her thigh-hugging lace-trimmed pantalets were like an erotic fantasy come true.

He swallowed, then felt himself break out in a cold sweat. He was sure his face, neck, and chest were glowing red with fire. Heat coursed through his body, inflaming that agonizing desire deep within him. He wanted her! He'd had just enough to drink to make him want to fall at her feet, to reach for that voluptuous, absolutely innocent young body.

Nine

She leaped from the railing recklessly, feeling her foot slip; she didn't drop gracefully, but plunged like a toppled crate into the inky water.

Instantly she was swallowed and the current seized her. She swam for the surface, disoriented and dazed. Panic blossomed in her breast. She felt the fool, and then she was breaking the surface and gasping.

Trance stood poised at the railing, a powerful silhouette in the moonlight, tearing at his white seaman's shirt until finally he gave up and threw himself overboard. Vanity wanted to laugh, but she was still embarrassed about her graceless entrance into the water. She had hoped to impress him.

In seconds he moved close behind her. He brushed against her, his hand closing on her arm. Then he let go, grazing her breasts, as if on purpose.

She started to pull away, felt her foot hit him solidly somewhere, and then he choked out her name.

"Trance?" she called, the dark water lapping against her chin and cheeks.

The current carried them swiftly along the drifting riverboat's hull. With the paddles stopped, they were safe from being drawn in and dashed to death, yet she was suddenly afraid he would be lost to the river's strength.

"Trance! Trance!" she cried, realizing her foolishness. He was still half drunk, and unfamiliar with the stern's configuration. He might drown! "Trance! This way!"

Then he was there, surrounding her with his arms, his hands first on her shoulders, then her back, and finally he was encircling her waist. She struggled, thinking first of the rope trailing nearby in the water, and then of the erotic sensations he caused in her body.

He caught the rope easily, aided by the full moonlight. Her breasts felt cool as they were crushed against his half-opened shirt. When she and Trance bobbed together, dangling now in the seductive current, pulled through the water as the boat moved, she felt herself bump against him, and suddenly her body was raging with desire to be touched and explored.

"Are you all right now?" he whispered huskily.

He thought he had saved her, she thought, wanting to laugh. Then she wanted to cry to know that he cared so. She put her arms around his neck. When the water pushed them together and then apart, she curled her legs around his hips.

The shock of his arousal so boldly apparent against her pantalets sent explosions of excitement through her. She didn't know whether to break free or continue holding him.

He needed all his strength and concentration to hold tight to the rough wet rope. They were heavy together, growing chilled and just a bit frightened of the power unleashed between them. "How long can we go on like this?" he whispered, his words muffled by the water lapping the hull.

"All night," she said, pressing her cheek to his shoulder, hearing the pounding of his heart. "I don't know how I can be thinking the things I'm thinking," she said, lifting her face and wishing he would bend to kiss her. But he was arched back, both arms up, hands gripping the rope as they drifted, locked together almost as lovers. "I've dreamed of you so often," she whispered. "I...waited for you. I'm not a Jezebel. I'm a virgin. Does that make you want me?"

The moonlight illuminated the tops of his brows, the curve of his cheeks, and the straight line of his nose. His hair gleamed like silver. The remainder of his face was dark.

He kissed her cheek and then strained to press his face into her neck and burn her throat with his lips. He trembled, arching against her...

She felt him shudder. He moaned as if in pain. She tightened her legs around him, nuzzling his chest.

"Release me, Vanity, please!" he whispered hoarsely.

She took the end of the rope he offered and hauled herself hand over hand to the deck. Below, he waited in the water.

Then, with powerful arms, he pulled himself up and stood with his trousers streaming water onto the deck. He peeled off his soaked shirt and unfastened the buttons of his union suit. He tore his arms from the wet, uncooperative sleeves and left the top half hanging back from the waist of his trousers.

His chest gleamed in the moonlight, his nipples small tight points, the pale hair across them catching the silvery moonbeams.

"You'll need to bathe now," she said, shivering. She snatched up one of her petticoats and held it before her, her teeth chattering.

His voice was flat. "We must go back to New Orleans."

"But you're under doctor's orders! Oh, Trance, don't be so…Trance! Trance!" she pleaded, rushing to him, not wanting him to spoil things.

He stepped back, a chasm of restraint opening between them. "Put me off at the first landing, then. I didn't mean for…" He shook his head and twisted away.

"Do you need another drink?" she ventured hopefully.

"I don't need anything but to gain control of myself! We're near strangers, Vanity! I-I can't marry you. There's a war, and I'll soon be in it. I belong back on my ship."

"We're not strangers! I've thought of nothing but you since we met. Trance, I'm not a floozy! I'm…I'm yours." The yearning in her voice surprised her. "I'm yours."

"We're still too different!"

Stung by his words, she wrenched free of his sudden grasp. She didn't want to pout, or, worse yet, to curse him, though she did, for being such a fool about propriety.

Yet he was of the strange world she so wanted to make her own. She was of that other world where manners and morals had never mattered—the world of the new, the raw, the untamed. He was bound up with everything she had grown to despise at Du Barry Vale.

She lifted her chin. "You can sleep steerage for all that it matters to me, John Travis." Leaving her gown, she ran for the stairs, her wet footprints like a trail of tears.

During the night she fretted, wondering if Trance had found dry clothes and a warm place to sleep. She knew Jim Hickory would look after him, for Jim hadn't failed to notice her interest in Trance.

She had a bath and retired when the stewards removed the tub. Lying there, with the riverbank slipping by outside her window, she remembered—and longed to recapture—that thrill she'd felt when Trance had shuddered against her.

Her body ached for that which she had never known. With Trance on her boat, she had no intention of proceeding to Natchez until her desires were satisfied.

He was so gull-danged foolish, yet she loved him for it. He had such a dear, agonized look in his eyes. Only she could ease it.

As the sky changed from inky-dark to gray, the birds chirped along the banks. She dressed quickly and went outside.

She found Trance at the railing, his hands deep in the pockets of snug trousers borrowed from a clerk. He wore a frayed but snowy-white boatman's shirt.

He looked as aloof as ever. What had her reckless behavior of the night before cost him? she wondered, peering up at him as he stood squinting into the shifting pale colors of the sky.

Saying nothing, she scrambled onto the railing and sat swinging her legs back and forth. He remained silent, his eyes on the forested point ahead.

She had ordered the boat to resume its journey. Shortly, black smoke began curling out of the twin stacks. The big paddles slapped at the brown water, and the boat eased from the safety of the river's edge into the current.

She peeked at Trance and caught him studying her. Color flooded her cheeks. She smiled provocatively. "Are you still thinking I'm some awful Jezebel?"

"I never said that!" He seemed exasperated that she had misinterpreted his silence.

She swung her legs around and dropped to her feet beside him. "Then you can damned well be civil! Meet me for breakfast in the dining room, or jump overboard right now. It's all the same to me. I won't change myself for you or anyone! I had my fill of trying to do that, I can tell you!"

He grasped her wrist as she turned away. "Vanity, try to understand. We mustn't give in to what we want."

She didn't move away. Finally she looked into his eyes and saw the torment there. And suddenly his lips were on hers, soft and tentative, then pressing urgently, filling her with a dazzling white light. But as quickly as he kissed her, he moved back and away from her again.

He tried to smile, and that eased her confusion, but clearly he was not going to be conquered in a few hours.

They had their breakfast together, but it was Vanity who was uncivil, taunting Trance until he had no choice but to agree to go ashore with her when they reached Natchez.

• • •

Trance urged their hired phaeton around a farm wagon pulled by two long-horned oxen. The tow-haired boy perched on the top of the cotton bale in the wagon bed waved as they passed. The black driver tipped his frayed hat.

Ahead, the road was muddy, but Trance seemed not to mind. Vanity sat back, letting him wrestle with the lines. She hadn't been to the cemetery where Maxx was buried, and now she thought she'd been foolish to force Trance to take her there. She felt gloomy and was afraid her mood would dampen what she had hoped would turn out to be a romantic afternoon.

They turned beneath an arch of brick and stone. Sharona had left Vanity detailed instructions on where to find the mausoleum, and Trance had no trouble locating the white structure. A live oak spread its moss-draped branches overhead. The air was heavy with damp morning heat. Trance stepped down and stood in the lane with his arms crossed.

"Eerie place," he said at length. He crossed the long grass and read the brass plate. "Esteban Blade," he murmured, rubbing at the engraving. "Can't make out his dates. Marie Barclay. Delance Barclay." Trance straightened up. "I feel as if I'm being watched."

At the sound of Trance's deep voice, Vanity's mood lifted. A shiver of desire ran through her. She tried to ignore it, thinking it wicked to yearn for Trance in such a sacred place. "Surely a Yankee is safe here," she said. "Natchez surrendered amicably, so I heard."

"Come look, and then we'll go. A man doesn't like to spend too much time in a graveyard during a war."

She watched his eyes come to rest on her. Perhaps he was realizing at that very moment that life was hauntingly short. Right or wrong for each other, they had very little time.

Trance handed her down to the narrow lane. She expected to feel repulsed by the sight of Maxx's name engraved on the brass plate, but she felt strangely comforted.

She touched the letters. "I had him only two years. My papa."

Turning, she went into Trance's arms and clung to his warm strength. The sun beat on her hair and shoulders. She lifted her face. Trance's eyes seemed to swallow her. She pressed herself against him, knowing he wanted her now, that he had abandoned his reserve.

Quickly, he handed her up to the buggy seat and settled beside her, his solid arm brushing hers, his jaw determined. He caught up the lines as if angry.

"Where can we go?" she whispered, unashamed of her yearning.

He slapped the lines against the horse's rump and urged the buggy out through the archway and back down the road toward Natchez.

They drove most of the afternoon, exploring the town, driving past Du Barry Vale, then going back to a sheltered place on the bluffs where they could look down at the curve of the brown river and the huddle of shanties, saloons, and warehouses below on the bank called Natchez Under the Hill.

They talked of unimportant things. Beneath their easy banter was the knowledge that they wanted to be together, that their time was precious.

As dusk fell, Trance placed his navy revolver between them on the seat and eased the buggy down a deserted lane. They didn't know what they would find, but they knew what they needed: a private place to make love.

When they came upon the one-room plank cabin, dusk had cast its soft gray-blue light. All around them was a cypress wood. The dirt track leading to the cabin door looked as if it hadn't been used in months.

"Stay here," Trance whispered, climbing down and taking the revolver. "I'll look around."

Swallowing nervously, Vanity nodded. The cabin appeared in good repair. A truck patch to the side had been planted but was now weedy and overgrown.

She heard Trance moving about in the brush behind the place, and then she heard his heavy boots on the floor of the cabin. When he didn't come out, her heart began to hammer. "Is anyone in there?" she finally called.

He emerged onto the porch, the gun hanging limply from his hand, his expression unreadable. He approached the buggy and stopped to look up at her. He was having second thoughts, she knew. "Can I ask someone I find so special to go inside that place with me? Is it dishonorable to want you so much?" he said at last.

Then he turned away abruptly, as if angry with himself.

"Is it safe?" she asked, putting her hand along his cheek.

He looked up at her again, his eyes softening. "I don't know if I love you, Vanity," he said, tucking the gun into his waistband. "I only know I've always wanted you. We don't have months or years to court. All we have is this night, and I have to have this night with you. I-I'll stop if you want, I just know that I must hold you. Now."

She fell into his arms. He held her there on the road, letting his hand travel the length of her slim back from her neck to her waist and then farther, to the rounded curve of her bottom.

Then he was crushing her against him, taking her face with his free hand and tipping it up so that he could plunder her mouth with his lips and tongue, his determination and desire to possess raging unchecked within him.

She met his kiss with an urgent desire of her own, pressed herself willingly against him, thinking of nothing but the joy she felt being close, so close. She was his—wanting him, needing him, demanding him. She gasped as his mouth moved to her throat. And finally he pressed his palm against her breast, moaning softly as if he'd finally found what he had been searching for.

Abruptly, he tore his lips from her throat, slid his hand around to her back, and held her tightly. She sensed the conflict raging within him—his desire against curbing natural yearning.

She brought him beyond the edge of reason, arched against him and watched the response in his eyes. He made his decision; he gathered her into his arms and carried her into the small dark cabin.

Someone had left the place swept clean. A crude table stood along one wall. A broad, shallow box was in the opposite corner, once filled with straw and used as a bed.

Trance set her down in the middle of the room. His eyes were eager, hungry now. He wouldn't—couldn't—turn back now. They were there together and they would become one.

"I'll tether the horse," he said, his voice husky.

When he went outside, Vanity surveyed the barren room, wondering how they would manage without a bed.

She removed her heavy velvet skirt and spread it on the floor. Her petticoats were so thick and ruffled they were actually soft to sit upon. She removed her bodice and sat in the circle of velvet and lace, and was unpinning her hair when Trance appeared in the doorway.

The door closed, leaving them in utter darkness. She heard his rapid breathing and the soft rustle of his shirt as he pulled it off. One boot thudded to the floor. The next was placed there more quietly. She heard his tentative footsteps.

"I'm here," she whispered.

He crouched and patted his way toward her, encountering her leg first. Her pulse leaped as he touched her. It was a dream made real. As his hand moved up the inside of her leg, she reached out with a gasp of fear and yearning.

They fell into each other's arms, their skin hot and moist, their mouths eager, exploring, clumsy with inexperience, but learning ever so quickly to seek and receive the pleasure they brought each other.

His hands were quick, darting, slowing, finding her warm breasts, now freed of the corset's squeeze, and fondling them as exquisite instruments of pleasure for them both.

Then boldly she surveyed him, slowly, timidly—the satiny feel of his warm solid shoulders, the corded strength of his arms, the hot smooth skin of his neck, the faint stubble on his hard jaw, the gentle moistness of his lips, the brush of his lashes against her fingertips.

She was nearly naked in his arms now, lying on the hard floor, feeling the lacy edge of a ruffle tickling her cheeks, the soft air on her bare legs.

His chest was so broad, heaving with each breath. His belly was hard, taut with desire. He gasped when she explored further, and her own body was suddenly alive with anticipation when she thought of receiving so much unrestrained strength into herself.

"You're the first," Trance whispered raggedly, seizing her, plunging into her, holding her a prisoner of his need.

She moaned and tightened her legs around him, wanting him to give her time to adjust, but the onslaught was relentless. His power was uncontrolled, a consuming thing, tearing her from herself and dragging her into a deeper, inner darkness where all she knew was this union, his arms holding her, his body owning hers, his lips drinking in the satisfaction he had dreamed about.

Suddenly she was splintering in a rain of light and fire, and he was lost, too, to the blaze of his need. They were one, spiraling from the darkness into the pure white tingling warmth of satisfaction.

Their thirst quenched, their urgency receded like the calm after a hurricane. They lay together, limp, dazed, overawed by sensations they had never dreamed existed.

In Vanity's heart was only peace, perhaps the first she'd ever known. He lay heavily upon her, taking in the night air in great gulps, waiting for his heart to slow. She savored his warmth, kissing his neck just behind his ear where the blond hair was so like a child's.

She felt tender and affectionate—and frail and lovely. "Trance..." she whispered, nuzzling him and feeling her nipples suddenly tingle with renewed awareness. "Love me again!"

· · ·

She opened her eyes to see Trance's flat stomach, with its golden hair spreading downward, and caught her breath. Illuminated by the light pouring through the open doorway, Trance was pulling on his boots.

She thought he was going to go out without speaking to her, but he paused and looked down, thrilling her as she lay curled naked on her rumpled petticoats.

His eyes softened and he knelt beside her, gathering her into his arms. He held her that way for a long moment, savoring her, then drew back, gazing into her face.

She put her hand on his chest near his nipple and watched it tighten to a small point. Her own body responded. They were linked by an overwhelming yearning for each other. She felt moved to tears, and safe, so very safe from the uncertainty she'd known since Maxx had died.

Then Trance went out. She pulled on her corset cover and pantalets, noting that the waistband was torn. A tingle went through her as she remembered the power of their first union. And he had loved her again in the night, more slowly, but with the same passion.

When Vanity finished dressing and went out, he was stroking the horse and looking down the road.

"Is someone coming?" Vanity whispered.

"No, but I'm uneasy. I'd feel better if we were on our way."

She went to him and slid her arms around him. "I want you even more than before!"

Smiling, he lifted her face. She saw true joy in his eyes. The change was remarkable, exhilarating. If she had thought him handsome before, he was more so now.

"I don't care what anyone thinks," she said. "You must stay in my stateroom tonight. My bed is so soft!"

"Vanity, no," Trance said. "Your reputation."

"I have no reputation! I own a riverboat, and I'm only sixteen. I know what those old gamblers think, but I don't care. I run a decent, high-class boat, just like Maxx did."

Trance didn't meet Vanity's eyes as he handed her up to the buggy.

As soon as they started back along the road, Vanity clenched her fists. "Don't spoil it by saying you're sorry, or that you've dishonored me! If you dare, I'll shoot you dead with your own revolver!"

Startled, he laughed. Then, though they were within sight of town, he halted the buggy. "Vanity, I'm not sorry. I only wish we could be together forever. If you're sure you won't be scorned, I'll stay in your stateroom tonight."

A satisfied smile came to her lips. She had conquered his propriety. At last she had freed him to accept her love as his due. Clutching his arm, she gazed up at him. "Tonight it won't be so damned dark!"

The muscles in his arms went taut. He snapped the lines sharply, causing the horse to start. "You make me forget...everything!"

That was how she wanted it, she thought, grinning as they drove through town toward the steep road down to the waterfront.

The *Vanity Blade* splashed away from the wharf at noon for her return to New Orleans. Vanity had ducked aboard, knowing her tangled chestnut curls were a testament to how she'd spent her night.

During their absence, Jim had had Trance's uniform cleaned and his boots shined, and had left them in Vanity's stateroom. It was as if Jim had known Vanity would be welcoming Trance to her bed when they returned. Jim had even ordered a special dinner for two to be sent to the stateroom that evening.

Vanity had spent the afternoon preparing. She was bathed and perfumed, her hair done simply but beautifully, her nails buffed and her cheeks pink with anticipation.

She wore a butter-yellow Swiss muslin gown with a daring décolletage. A band of yellow silk roses ran from her left breast to her waist and then down the side of the skirt to the flounced hem.

Trance arrived just as the music began in the grand saloon. They ate in near silence. Dinner seemed to be the least of their concerns. Trance was noticeably impatient, while Vanity was coy and self-conscious. Her gown, while very pretty, left little to the imagination, and Trance's eagerness and hunger for her were palpable.

"I'd like to sing for you tonight," she said finally.

Trance looked bewildered, as if he had expected her to disrobe as soon as they stopped eating and sipping the expensive claret. But Vanity wanted to prolong the ecstasy of their last evening together. It might be days or weeks before she saw him again. One of the memories she wanted to sustain her was the look on his face as she sang.

Trance nodded and gulped the last of his wine. But when he put his glass down, it seemed to Vanity that he had changed again, into the watchful and withdrawn Trance she'd first known.

She worried that she had angered him because of the delay or because she was still performing. But she pressed on, finishing her dessert gamely and then rushing him down to the grand saloon, where she was startled to find a crowd and a lot of betting under way. For her, the world had stopped when she'd moved into Trance's arms.

She whispered instructions to Jim, who relayed them to the musicians. By the time she had seated Trance at a conspicuous table, the fanfare on the slightly raised stage had begun.

Trance ordered bourbon and tossed it back with a vengeance. He was downing a second as Vanity swished her way into the glare of the footlights. As the tune she had requested began, doubts assailed her. Was she wrong to remind Trance that she was not like other women?

But then the joy of performing came rushing back. She felt her mother's presence near at hand and thought of Broken Rock Saloon, with its cigar smoke and cheap whiskey. She longed to recapture the security of that happy time, or of the many happy nights she performed when Maxx sat puffing on his Havana, smiling indulgently.

She wanted Trance to love her. She wanted him to say it passionately, and to mean it from the depths of his soul. She wanted him to love everything about her—her birth, her past in the boom camp, her bawdy songs and carefree dances. She wanted to be cherished for what she was and not what she was supposed to be.

She began to dance as her mother had danced, feeling her mother's yearning, her abandon, her desire to be loved and accepted for all that she was.

The music went on until she paused to sing the words her mother had made up so many years ago.

"Where is my love? He's gone away-y-y. Though I do need him, he's gone to stay-y-y. Where is my love? He said good-bye. If I don't find him, my heart will die."

She sang three more stanzas, each sadder than the last. Vanity had never thought about the words before, she had simply loved the tune and the angelic look on her mother's face as she sang it, softly, sweetly, longingly.

She heard her own voice grow hushed with yearning. The musicians followed her lead beautifully, letting their accompaniment fall away to a whisper as her voice took over. The thunderous applause startled her. She looked up and knew Trance was staring at her. She felt naked, her emotions exposed and vulnerable. What if Trance could not love her as she was?

When she stepped from the glare of the footlights, Trance sprang to her side, as intense as she'd ever seen him.

The applause had not ended when she left the saloon on Trance's arm, but neither noticed. Arm in arm they climbed the stairs to the Texas deck and the stateroom that had once belonged to Maxx.

When the door closed behind them, Vanity went into Trance's arms at once and felt herself being propelled backward to the bed.

She gave herself up to his passion, welcoming it with the innocence and joy of what she knew to be love. She accepted his power and impatience, savoring being the object of his need.

He was there for her in every way, showing her startling new passions, until they were tightly joined on the bed, locked together, soaring to the heavens.

Ten

In the diffused pink light of dawn, Trance watched Vanity's sleeping face turn against the white pillow next to his.

Her long lashes lay against the perfect curve of her cheek. Her lips looked red still, and swollen from his violent kisses hours before. Her chestnut curls, their gold highlights glinting now, were in a riotous tangle around her lovely face and bare shoulders.

She stirred, moaning sweetly. She was only sixteen, he reminded himself. Until the day before, she'd been a virgin. The gift she had bestowed upon him awed him, for he didn't feel worthy.

He had hurt her, he was sure. She'd cried out so and clutched at his back, but he hadn't been able to stop himself!

But now he felt something new as he looked down at her, something more than a physical need, although, certainly, that need was undeniable—and constant.

His sense of protectiveness surfaced more strongly than ever. He wanted her safe always. He winced when he thought this was where she lived, that this was the only place where she thought she might belong. She deserved so much more—a real home, true security, and his complete devotion.

He felt warmth for her welling in his heart. He wanted only the best for her. He wanted to see her happy and safe in a decent place where she didn't have to dance to gain a stranger's approval.

What a delicate, sweet thing she was, he thought, smoothing her tangled hair from her shoulders. His ardor swelled. He tried to hold back, to think of something else, but his eyes were drawn back to her face, her throat, her rounded shoulder and bare arm lying along the edge of the quilt.

His eyes were drawn to the delicate swells almost but not quite hidden by the quilt. Finally, overcome by desire, he tugged the quilt away until her smooth white breasts were bare before him, softly rising and falling with each breath she drew.

This time he would be gentle, he told himself, thinking of nothing and no one else in the world but Vanity lying so innocently beside him.

He bent to kiss her breasts, first one, then the other, and then he buried his face between them like a child, lost and in need of comfort. She smelled of him, he thought, feeling exhilarated and touched almost unbearably. She had become part of him, one with him!

He felt her draw in her breath deeply and knew then she was awake.

Lifting his head, he saw that her deep brown eyes were open and filled with joy. He didn't want to ravish her this time, he wanted to savor her. Suddenly, reality intruded. This was their last day! He wondered if he could bring himself to go back to his ship.

"What a delicious way to wake up," Vanity murmured, running her slim fingers through his hair. She drew his face close for a kiss.

As his lips closed over hers, his hand ran deep beneath the covers. She arched with desire when he cupped her warm, sweet secret places.

He kissed her all over her face, tasting every inch of her until he had memorized the contours of her forehead and cheeks, her chin, the arch of her brows, the fullness of her lips. He tasted deeply of her mouth, found himself growing impatient again and made himself pull back.

"It's all right," she said.

He shook his head against her neck, forcing himself to regain control simply to explore her. She uttered delicious little sighs that made him reel. Her hands clutched at him, but still he held back, fascinated suddenly with the feel of her, with the responses that he could draw from her by the mere touch of his fingers or lips.

She was so free, he thought, watching her close her eyes and arch her head back into the soft pillow. *She abandons herself even to this and delights in it.* His own abandon had been violent and hurried, almost stolen. Now as he watched her, he wondered if ever he'd be free enough to love her, good enough to deserve her.

He kissed her, longingly, as if she was already waving from the railing of her boat, leaving him behind as she had that day three years before. How many nights had he dreamed of this, of holding her body and making it his own?

Suddenly she was clutching at him urgently to join her. He rolled to his back and drew her on top of him, letting her find her own way with him and watching as if in a dream. Her breasts were so delightful, bouncing against his palms. He wanted her naked forever!

And then her own violence came and he saw her face, saw the

almost drunken delight with which she thrust herself against him, finding that which he resolved she would never find with any other man. Moments later the welling of his passion drew him into a knot of blinding convulsions, and he spent himself so thoroughly he felt he could not move.

When he was able to open his eyes, the stateroom seemed to be spinning. He was trembling, overcome by the things she could make him feel.

As he held her tightly on top of him, feeling his heartbeat slow, he kissed her neck and said softly, "I love you."

She snuggled against him, finally growing heavy as she fell into a contented half sleep.

He eased her back to her pillow and climbed from the bed. At the window he watched the green riverbanks slip by. The whistle of a nearby paddle-wheeler made him start. Then he saw a lot of activity along the bank, indicating they were coming into New Orleans.

His heart sinking, he turned back to Vanity. Perhaps if he dressed quickly and left, he might spare himself the agony of saying good-bye to her. How long he'd be forced to stay away, he didn't even want to venture a guess.

He did dress, his every movement heavy with reluctance, his heart weighted with the dread of being parted from her. He had lost a part of himself to her, he thought. He belonged to her now more surely than he belonged to himself.

Elated to be among the few to find such a treasure, he went quickly to the door. When his hand closed on the cold porcelain knob, he couldn't turn it. He couldn't bring himself to leave without seeing her eyes one last time, without watching her lips just before kissing them, without holding that delicate naked body against his once more.

"Vanity, I'm going now," he whispered, finding his throat choked with emotion. He loved her. He loved her!

She sat up, blinked, then flew to his side, clutching him. "I'm going with you! I want to see your ship. Please wait while I dress. Please!"

Trance could only nod.

Vanity insisted on taking the reins of the hired buggy. She lashed them playfully against the rump of the unsuspecting horse, and laughed with delight as the buggy leaped and then hurtled along the planks of the wharf and finally onto paving stones.

Trance steadied her as she stood, whipping the air just above the horse's rump. His face was flushed with emotion, his smile easy.

She shook back the tendrils escaping her loosely knotted hair. "Great snakes! I love this!" she shouted above the clatter.

But as quickly as she gave vent to her happiness, she was forced to slow. She sat back in her seat, trying to maintain an expression appropriate for one returning an ill seaman to his ship.

There simply was no way Trance could appear wan and recently risen from his sickbed; the unmasked desire in his eyes was impossible to hide. He pulled Vanity to him and kissed her soundly moments before they came into sight of his ship. Immediately he slumped forward, feigning a fairly convincing look of one who'd recently been delirious with fever.

A number of mates leaned over the gunwhales, nudging one another as Vanity struggled with her skirts and finally managed to get down from the buggy unassisted. She was wearing a finely tailored willow-green day dress with a full-length shawl trimmed in forest-green braid, and a truly delightful confection of feathers and ruffles on her head.

She made great show of helping Trance to the ground and then steadied him on her arm as they approached the seamen gathering near the gangplank.

"Well, Lieutenant, I see you found yerself a real case of fever, all right," one of the men said.

Trance stiffened. Vanity paused, hoping he would ignore the remark.

She smiled sweetly at the impudent man and was pleased to see his suggestive leer give way to an embarrassed grin. Her beauty was a weapon she had learned to use well since her departure from school.

"Let us pass, please," she said quietly and looked at the ground in front of her so that those watching didn't realize how confident she was. If she had learned anything since coming to the river, it was that men were manipulated best when they felt *she* wasn't aware of much of anything! The men stepped back and resumed their smirking. Vanity felt Trance balk as she attempted to lead him up the plank. Then she looked up into the grim face of the commander, a most imposing man with narrow eyes and a goatee.

"Lieutenant Holloway." The commander's voice was unforgiving.

"Fever of the worst kind, Captain," a man muttered behind Vanity.

"Common kind, more like it," another interjected.

Vanity's heart leaped as Trance reared up. "Don't, Trance! Moan and collapse forward or you'll fall into the river!"

Trance didn't restrain himself.

"We should be ailing so," someone said, snickering. "What's the price of yer fever, honey-pie? I heard tell of Southern hospitality. Don't keep it all to yerself, Lieutenant! We showed you a time in Boston. Turnabout's fair play."

Vanity reacted with surprise and hurt to think Trance had lied about his virginity, but she didn't have much time to think about it because at the same moment Trance exploded from her grasp.

He whirled on the plank and faced the men standing below on the wharf, then leaped into their midst, knocking the three loudmouths down. All Vanity could see were a lot of feet, fists, and dust.

At once the ship was alive with shouting men rushing to the gunwhales to watch and then tumbling down the gangplank to join in. Vanity nearly landed in the water.

She managed, with the help of several overeager hands, to make her way safely back to the wharf. Trance was pummeling the man who had spoken first. She shouted for him to stop, but already the commander had ordered those not fighting to tear Trance free.

Four men dragged Trance away and held him. Vanity was frightened by the savagery in his face. He was still furious about the insults directed at her. Then it dawned on him that he'd done something for which he'd be made to suffer. Vanity saw a muscle in his cheek jump.

He looked to her, and she saw how much he regretted what he'd done. His commander strolled down the gangplank, hands clasped behind his back, regarding Trance as if he were just so much filth. Glancing only briefly, albeit scathingly, at Vanity, he jerked his head toward the ship. "Have him flogged."

Vanity rushed at him and tore at the man's braid-decorated sleeve. "He was defending my honor! Your men have the manners of savages!" Gone were any notions of simpering and groveling.

The commander looked away, unmoved. "This is no longer your concern, madame."

"It was a delirium! You mustn't flog him. I won't allow it!" She ran after him and caught hold of his sleeve. "Oh, do reconsider, kind sir! Do! Do! He was only being a gentleman. You would've done the same."

The commander lowered his gaze sufficiently to give Vanity a clear view of his steely-gray eyes. "His dalliance with your sort is a minor offense, unworthy of brawling with his fellows. Release my arm, young woman, before I have you arrested and thrown into a military prison, where I should think you would prosper nicely."

The force of her palm striking his whiskered cheek sent reverberations of pain to her shoulder. "I'll not stand here and be insulted by a damned Yankee!" Her accent now lent her words aristocratic authority.

"Indeed, a Yankee, madame, and a proud one. Take your hand from my sleeve."

She released it as if it were covered with slime. "You're not fit to command! You won't have a sick man flogged! I'll telegraph President Lincoln myself!" She started up the gangplank, determined to rescue Trance, but her way was blocked by a dozen burly seamen, all of whom were enjoying her reckless outburst immensely.

She was seized from behind and placed firmly back on the wharf planks. She felt her helplessness so keenly that she burst into tears.

"If you will be so good as to provide the name of the doctor who examined Lieutenant Holloway, perhaps I will reconsider the punishment," the commander said, then strode up to the deck of his ship without looking back.

"Dr. Ignatious Langworth, sir!" A flood of relief went through her. Surely the old gentleman would remember how well he'd been paid to report to the *Vanity Blade* at such an inconvenient hour.

She turned away, faint and exhausted. As she staggered back to the hired buggy and paused to catch her breath, she saw a familiar-looking man ambling toward her. She brushed quickly at her tears and stood defiantly. Here was a person she did *not* want to see at a time like this.

He wore an especially glossy tall silk hat, a tailored frock coat, and very snug buff breeches that hugged his hips and thighs and accentuated a prominent part of his anatomy, causing Vanity to blush and turn away.

"Might I be of some assistance?" he asked, tipping his hat. "I saw that you were havin' some difficulty with that damned Yankee bastard and thought perhaps I might call him out for you."

"The coward wouldn't appear," Vanity snapped, using her best school accent on Jules Pearson, Esquire.

"Can I assist you into the buggy, Miss Blade? I would be honored to drive you wherever you'd like to go." He turned a charming smile on her.

His eyes were alert and direct, his lips tight with what appeared to be forced congeniality. Certainly he was handsome. She knew she could expect him to protect her from the further abuse of that Yankee commander.

She gave Trance's ship one last look, now certain that once the commander contacted Dr. Langworth he'd retract his order to punish Trance.

Then she nodded to the solicitous Jules Pearson. "You're very kind," she said, as he handed her up.

"May I?" he asked, indicating the empty seat beside her.

She declined politely. She had no intention of allowing anyone to occupy the place where Trance had been only moments before. "I'm quite recovered now, thank you ever so kindly. I must be on my way."

Then she turned the buggy and clattered away, her thoughts consumed by worries about Trance's fate.

When she arrived at the *Vanity Blade* it was nearly noon. She was exhausted. Had it only been a few hours ago that she lay in Trance's arms, waking to his deliciously tender kisses?

Some of the boys working her boat loitered on the busy dock, sipping at their whiskey ration. One helped her down from the buggy and took care of returning it to the nearby livery.

Vanity scarcely noticed a second buggy drawing to a stop some distance behind her. She trudged up the stageplank, determined to sleep until evening.

The mustachioed gentleman in the tall silk hat alighted from the buggy and paid the driver with an air of detachment. He squinted up at the fine gilding on the *Vanity Blade*'s saloon deck, and watched as the ravishing young woman in willow-green let herself into the stateroom on the Texas deck.

Vanity paused before closing her door, remembering how she'd pushed Jules Pearson into the Mississippi mud at Crystal Point three years before. With Jules in the vicinity, Quarter Dollar would surely appear soon. She looked forward to seeing him again, even if the presence of Jules Pearson made her uneasy.

For three days Vanity hired a buggy and drove out to see Trance. Each time she was turned away, not even allowed aboard the Union sloop to speak to the captain.

Sick with worry, she returned each day to fret over her own misspelled messages that were sent back unopened.

After a week she received a communiqué which read:

Lt. Holloway does not wish to receive you. Desist in your attempts, madame.

Never had Vanity felt so desolate. She stood at the railing each afternoon, staring across the brown water, wondering if Trance was angry. Had he been punished after all? Was he blaming her?

Her anguish was so complete that she entered the grand saloon each evening to bolt a quick whiskey to buoy her strength.

Talk was of the battles upriver to free Island Number Ten to the persistent Yankees, and each night the gambling was feverish, as if her patrons were pretending doom was not upon them. "Vicksburg's big guns will hold the blue bastards," the men boasted.

Vanity made her rounds, sipping whiskey, charming her patrons. During her late performance she stumbled fetchingly about the stage, singing her mother's old songs in a slurred, suggestive voice.

At the poker table, Jules Pearson raked in profits while eyeing Vanity. At midnight, when she was tired and numb at last, she consented to sit with him. She watched, saying nothing, as he dealt his shaved cards and bilked the unwary drunks foolish enough to play with him.

When the last of the fools had departed empty-pocketed at the end of the week, Vanity leaned forward from her chair, exposing a significant amount of bosom. She rested her chin on her hand. "You're quite the man with a deck," she said in her best Du Barry Vale accent.

He leaned back and regarded her from beneath lowered lids. His thin moustache bristled. "I've seen you play a few advantageous rounds yourself, my lovely hostess," he drawled.

"Keep cheating, however, and you won't be welcome aboard my boat, Mr. Pearson," Vanity said. "Perhaps Maxx didn't watch you as closely as he should have."

He raised his eyebrows. "If a man was to say such a thing to me, I'd be obligated to call him out. The meadow behind my father's house grows lush on the blood of my insulting but very dead acquaintances."

"Do what you like, Mr. Pearson," Vanity said, smiling broadly. "But you've been warned. I can have you thrown off whenever I tire of you."

His mouth spread into a grin. "Oh, do try, dear lady. I'd so enjoy it!"

She rose, her bosom heaving, her head spinning, but she kept her voice soft and even. "I haven't liked you since I pushed you into the river. I let you cheat this week, but only because I'm distracted. Please, take yourself away before tomorrow night, or I'll have my men make short work of you!"

He stood, too, and bowed elegantly. "Would you care to escort me off your precious boat, Miss Blade?"

She was taken aback by his cooperation. But with Jim Hickory always nearby, and her deck hands as loyal as any crew on the river, she felt safe leading the way out of the saloon into the humid darkness of the broad gangway.

At the bottom of the wide sweep of gilded stairs on the boiler deck, Vanity turned, only to inhale sharply when she found Jules so close to her. A ripple that was as much thrill as it was terror ran down her spine.

"I like a female who stands up to me," he whispered, taking her shoulders in his slender hands.

Repulsed, she twisted away and started for the stageplank, where she intended to push him into the river a second time.

Jules watched and then bowed again. "Would you throw me off without letting me retrieve my belongings from my cabin?"

"Why didn't you say so before?" she snapped.

"Because..." he said, moving closer. "I, too, was distracted." He yanked her against his chest. He looked deeply into her eyes, making sure she was aware of her breasts crushed hard against the front of his coat. Then he roughly pressed his lips to her mouth.

The short whiskers of his moustache brushed against her upper lip, and another thrill of alarm went through her. She was tempted to cry out and slap him, but just as quickly he released her and stepped back.

"Pardon the liberty, Miss Blade. I thought you would taste as delicious as you look. Regretfully, you leave me passionless. Someone should teach a creature as lovely as yourself how to kiss."

Her open hand sailed toward his cheek, but he deftly caught her wrist. He didn't look passionless at all.

"I'm putting you off at the first landing!" she hissed, fighting tears.

"We shall see," he said, turning on his polished heel and taking the stairs two at a time.

Shaking, Vanity went to the railing and stood staring into the murky darkness, her heart twisting beneath Pearson's insult. Could it be she didn't know how to kiss? Was that why Trance had tired of her so abruptly?

She clenched her fists, then turned away and rushed headlong to the Texas deck and the safety of her stateroom.

Now she feared she had been nothing but an amusement for Trance. She fell across her bed, hurting, fighting her tears and then finally giving vent to them. She fell asleep and dreamed of Trance coming to her from the shadows, but she couldn't hear what he was saying.

During the night the *Vanity Blade* nearly overran a skiff that had no running lights. But Vanity slept through the shouts and awoke just past dawn to remember she had said she would put Jules Pearson off at the first landing.

After rising and changing her rumpled gown for a silk morning wrapper, she marched down to fetch Hickory and two of her sturdiest men. Together they rapped at Jules's stateroom door, expecting resistance.

Jules was roused from his bunk after Hickory unlocked the door. He scowled as Vanity folded her arms and scowled back.

"I asked you nicely last night, Mr. Pearson, to get off my boat. We're coming to a landing now."

He walked over to her, his silk drawers leaving little to be guessed at. His chest was bare.

Hickory and the men closed ranks behind Vanity.

"And what is it I'm supposed to have done?" His eyes were flinty, startlingly so in the early morning light.

"Aside from insulting me, you were cheating at cards."

His mouth tightened into an impatient half smile. He stared at her, his expression calculating and strangely inconsistent with the amusement she'd seen in his face the night before.

Then he snorted. What a truly horrid man he was! How could she have felt even a moment of attraction for him the night before? It had to have been the whiskey!

Jules's voice was silky with control. "I see you have me at a disadvantage, Miss Blade. I should remember that fact when dealing with the only woman who has ever gotten the upper hand with me in the past. Don't think I've forgotten that unexpected dunk in the river."

He dressed behind a screen and then gathered his belongings. She saw him slipping a thin-bladed knife into his boot. Drawing back her hem as he sauntered out, she watched him limp away and wondered why she hadn't noticed it the night before.

Following him to the boiler deck, she watched with relief as he made his way leisurely down the stageplank.

One of the deck hands hefted Jules's trunk halfway down the stageplank and then gave it a mighty heave that sent it plummeting into the mud.

"Good riddance!" Hickory muttered, turning away as the stageplank was hoisted up. "Never trusted that one. There's something about him… Can't put my finger on it."

In seconds the boat's paddle wheel dragged them back into the current. Jules flung himself down onto a stump to await the next boat.

"Sweet Susie! You put him off where?" Quarter Dollar's eyes were round as saucers.

Vanity sidestepped the impatient passengers pouring down the stageplank from her boat at Hillsboro Landing. She tugged Quarter's arm. "He won't be angry with you, will he? You had nothing to do with it!"

Quarter wagged his head, clutching at his forehead with a trembling hand. "You don't understand. My boss man, he's powerful fearsome when he's in a temper. You don't think he keeps me 'round just to tote his trunks, do you? I've known the strength of his fists." He went on wagging his head. "Sweet Susie! He's going to want a piece of my hide just to be satisfied. He can't take it out on you now, can he?"

She wrung her hands. "I-I…I'm awfully sorry. I never dreamed… it's plain you mustn't go back with him! I'll buy you and give you your freedom! I should've done it months ago!"

Quarter paused, squinting at Vanity in disbelief. His brown eyes gentled. "Don't worry about me. I'll handle him." He stepped back to admire her. "You're looking mighty fine these days, Miss Vanity. Tell me all about your doings since I seen you last."

Vanity brightened, feeling her worry drain away. She clutched at Quarter's ragged sleeve and coaxed him away from the confusion along the landing. "You'll never guess who I've seen, who I've been with!"

She insisted he put down his boss man's trunk. They strolled along the lush bank well out of sight of the landing. She chattered happily about Trance falling drunk at her feet. Giggling, she modestly conveyed how close she and Trance had become.

"But he hasn't been back since I took him to his ship. Why would he stay away?"

"I can't feature it."

Vanity went warm with embarrassment. "Was I wrong to give myself?"

"Can't say, Miss Vanity," Quarter said, his eyes darting to the side when she tried to catch his gaze. He smiled uneasily. "A lady can't be too free with herself or some men get the wrong idea."

Vanity shivered. "As those stupid seamen on the ship did?" She hated herself for being so foolish. "I shouldn't have taken him back myself."

"No'm, maybe not, but it's done. Chances are good boss man will head for New Orleans in a day or so. I'll see what I can find out for you."

"Would you? Oh, I'd be so grateful! You're a dear, Quarter! I need a good friend."

Quarter ventured a smile.

They went on talking until Quarter glanced at the sun. He heaved a sigh. "I got to find me a way of fetching boss man from the landing. The longer I wait, the worse it'll be. But don't you fret. I'll steer him clear of you awhile and he'll forget."

"I wonder," Vanity said, wishing she could talk with Quarter longer. "Can I hire you a boat or buggy?"

Quarter's eyes went warm with gratitude. "No'm, I can manage. Thank you kindly, though. You just look after yourself and that beau of yours. I recall he was a rare one."

Before she had the chance to say good-bye, Quarter trotted away toward Pearson's trunk. By the time she returned to the landing, he was nowhere to be seen.

Though the *Vanity Blade* hadn't completed its circuit of the part of the river open to Southern navigation, Vanity ordered an immediate return to New Orleans. She wanted to be there when Trance came to her. She would have a few choice things to say to one who stayed away so long when he claimed he loved her.

The river looked positively green in the noonday haze. Gnarled oak branches jutted over the water like arms; their reflections looked like black snakes wriggling in the water.

Everywhere it was green, so rich and lush as to appear unreal. Trance, in a terrible mood, felt set apart from the world. He dreaded seeing Vanity again. He had been forced to stay away from her for over two weeks, with no chance to get word to her. He knew she'd be hurt and angry, but what was worse...he had dreadful news for her. She'd likely never forgive him.

The gentle rhythm of the crickets singing and the earthy odor of the banks filled him with longing. He had crossed the long, crowded wharf looking for her riverboat, and found it tied up some distance away.

His heart pounded as he drew near it. He paused a long moment, looking up at the white craft. He almost turned away, thinking to lose himself in the canebrakes and cypress swamps. What could his commander to do him then? How could he go to Vanity now and tell her what he'd been sent to say?

Trance straightened his shoulders. He was no coward. Pain radiated across his back, but he ignored it. For now, he thought, he would just think of seeing Vanity again.

Instantly, the leaden feeling in his heart lifted. He strode toward the riverboat with only one purpose—to satisfy his longing to touch his beloved one last time.

He looked for her on the Texas deck, knocking at her door but getting no answer. A steward happened by, giving Trance a look of contempt, and then nodded toward the far side of the boat.

Trance went to the railing and saw a fishing line trailing in the brown water. He tumbled down the stairs to the boiler deck like an eager schoolboy, and came up behind her, out of breath, to find her dressed to the nines in a gaudy turquoise-checked pongee silk over an enormous crinoline.

She twisted from her perch on the narrow railing, looking like the precocious, overdressed child he had met three years before. The anger he'd dreaded and expected tightened her pink lips.

Her huge skirt billowed in the breeze. Her petticoats showed in a froth of lace like clouds around her dark-stockinged legs. Trance forgot his reason for coming and gazed at her, a starving man looking at a splendid banquet.

Vanity didn't speak. She looked at him, her dark perceptive eyes boring into his with deadly accuracy. Chestnut tendrils tickled across her creamy cheeks in the gentle breeze.

She drew up her line finally and dropped the pole onto the deck. "I thought you weren't coming back." Her voice was controlled, masking her hurt and bitterness.

Trance felt anger tense his shoulders. He had secretly hoped she'd understand, that to see him would be enough. "Can you come ashore? We must talk."

"No," she said firmly, swinging around and showing her pantalets all the way to her thighs as she hopped to the deck. "I waited days and days. I sent messages! If you didn't want to see me then, why should you want to talk now?"

He refused to tell her he'd been in irons. "I came as soon as I could!"

He was tempted to turn on his heel and leave, but he was under orders to stay and endure her anger. He had to tell her. "We'll talk here, then, where anyone might overhear us."

"Talk away." She strolled along the gangway, her expression stormy.

Trance paced to the bow, wondering again how he might break the news to her.

"You're no better than *him*," she said at length. "Staying away and giving no good reason! Why, Trance? I thought you'd stopped loving me!"

How could she think that? He lost the train of his thought and whirled around in indignation. "Who am I like?"

She brushed her skirt down over the broad hoops. "The bastard who broke my mother's heart!"

He caught her arm and watched her lovely dark eyes blacken. She loved him, he thought. How could anything else matter but that? "I didn't stay away because I wanted to, Vanity. Won't you believe that?"

"Why did you, then?"

He couldn't tell her, he knew, so he said nothing. He only wanted to kiss her, to regain that wonderful security he had felt with her that last morning they were together.

"Vanity, please, I have something very important to talk to you about. Where can we go?"

She was very still. "We could take the skiff," she said finally.

"And when we're someplace where we can be alone, will you listen to what I have to say?"

Her nod was so slight he almost missed it.

Eleven

Trance rowed downstream to a secluded bayou where oaks sagged beneath their moss garlands. Ashore, shade beckoned. He climbed out, helping Vanity to the muddy bank. Before she could draw a breath, he pulled her close.

"What did you come to tell me?" she asked, squirming away.

It could wait, he told himself. He tore open his coat and pulled it off. His shirt was soaked with sweat. He pulled that off, too, and threw it over a nearby tree branch.

Searching for a way to begin, he turned and watched Vanity sit on a fallen log, regard him thoughtfully, then unbutton her shoes. As she peeled off her dark stockings, Trance tensed.

Her hands trembled as she opened her bodice and shrugged it off her shoulders. Standing up, she stepped out of her skirt and untied a half dozen snowy petticoats.

Among the dark oaks, she looked like an apparition. Her underthings stood out stark white against the shadows. His throat constricted as she unlaced her corset. Turning away, she pulled the boned muslin from her slim torso and stood with her naked back dappled in sunlight.

She slid her pantalets to her knees and stepped out of them. Trance went weak. She looked so frail, so vulnerable. She turned then, letting him take in all of her as she stepped into the shallows, lifting handfuls of water to her arms.

She found solid footing several feet from shore and stood waist-deep in the brown water, pulling pins from her hair. Trance was drowning in desire. If he had any other purpose in seeing her, he couldn't remember it.

Quickly he stripped off his clothes. He was powerfully aroused, and stood only an instant beneath her wide-eyed gaze before plunging into the water. He splashed to her side and gathered her fiercely into his embrace. "I love you, Vanity!"

Her breasts felt cool and slippery. He kissed her hungrily. She clutched his back, pressing her quivering body against his. The heat of his passion rose out of control. He drew back, wanting to prolong the intensity of his pleasure.

They moved together in the water like two fish gliding back and forth, standing at times to view each other, then sinking again into the privacy of the murky water, where his hands moved on her and hers on him.

Guiding her toward the shore, he rested her against some rounded boulders, parted her knees, and took her. In ecstasy he plunged, his mouth locked on hers, his hands cupping her bottom, her breasts brushing his nipples.

She dug her fingernails into his back, but he felt no pain. He knew only that he was part of her. For those exquisite moments there was no past or future, only an incredible, satisfying present.

Only after he staggered backward, spent and exhilarated, and turned to see if anyone was passing on the river, did Vanity draw in her breath. She laid her hand on his shoulder. "Your back!"

He twisted away and shrugged. Mick had told him the lash marks were gone. "Aboard ship, the captain's word is law. I was wrong to fight."

She pursued him through the muddy water. "Let me see. Oh... Trance." Her voice was like a balm. "Does it hurt?"

"Not now."

"This was what you came to tell me. Forgive me!" She pressed her lips again and again to the ten welts. "I'm sorry I was angry."

He feasted his eyes on her breasts as the water lapped at them. "Cover yourself so I can think!"

She gave him a teasing smile, but when he didn't smile in return, she waded ashore. He devoured her beauty, feeling wanton to hunger after her so.

Draped with her half-opened corset cover and pantalets, Vanity took a seat on a fallen log. She lifted her hair and ran her fingers through it, allowing the breeze to dry it.

She gazed at him, so tall and lean, among the shadows and sunlight. The blond hairs on his legs lay in wet lines down his muscular thighs and calves.

Vanity watched his backside tighten as he stepped into his trousers. He turned ever so slightly as he drew them up, hiding that thick, golden thatch and the shrinking evidence of his spent passion for her.

When he turned, his expression was dark.

"You're not going away!" she cried, standing and running to him.

His skin felt cold.

He shook his head. "No, though we'll go upriver soon."

"*That's* going away!" she insisted, pressing her face to his chest. "You're cruel to come back to tell me that. I was just getting used to you being gone!"

"Listen to me," he said, urgently prying her arms from him. "Sit over there. I can't think if I'm holding you."

Hurt and uneasy, Vanity returned to the log.

"I didn't come to say good-bye," he said suddenly, as if he feared that was what she might think.

"But you're going to do battle, and you could be…" Vanity couldn't complete the sentence.

He shook his head, his expression growing hopeful. He crouched before her. "Nothing's going to happen to me! I've feared death, but now I know I'll live because I have you!"

Her heart twisted. She took his cheeks between her palms and placed a tender kiss on his forehead. "I love you, Trance."

"Marry me, Vanity!" He looked surprised, as if he hadn't intended to propose.

She didn't have to think. "Oh, yes, Trance!"

"I-I…" His troubled thoughts returned and his eyes clouded. "I shouldn't have asked! We have no time to get married. You'll think I'm toying with you, and I've never been more serious!"

"I'll wait. I'll wait a week or a month or a year…as long as it takes!"

He pulled her to him, holding her and pressing his face between her warm, still-damp breasts. He kissed them, relaxing in her arms, and she began to feel less panicky.

Finally he drew away and chewed his knuckle. "What would you say if I asked you to leave the river till the end of the war?"

"I'd have nowhere to go!"

"Soon the war will be here. If we take Vicksburg, the South is doomed. Vanity, would you consider waiting for me in a safe place…at my parents' home?"

Stunned, she couldn't think of an answer.

He rushed on. "My sister's there. You'd like her. I don't know what else to suggest. It's too dangerous to stay here."

"But your parents!" Vanity whispered. "To live in their house? Would they have me?"

"Would you go?" he asked, gripping her arms tightly. "Do you love me that much?"

"I love you with all my heart...but your parents' house! Your parents think I'm a...a..."

"If I want to marry you, they'll accept you. They'll have to if they want me to return to the family."

She stared at their muddy footprints along the bank. She hadn't intended to make love to him. She had only wanted to talk, but he had an effect on her that made her strip away her clothes and give herself to him again.

"You want me to wait at your parents' house...and get ready to be a...a proper wife."

"You're all I could ever want in a woman, in a wife," he said quickly. "You don't have to change. While I'm doing my duty for my country, I just want to know you're safe. If I was worried about you..."

She finished the sentence for him. "...you wouldn't be safe yourself. Of course, I'll go, then," she said, feeling uneasy even as she agreed. "I'll go the moment you return to your ship. Do we have much time?"

"We have no time. I'm already overdue, but I couldn't tell you what I was sent to say without...without preparing you."

Her stomach knotted. "There's more?"

He nodded. Now his face looked ravaged. At last he lifted his eyes. They were so blue, so earnest, and so tortured.

"My commander has ordered me to commandeer the *Vanity Blade* to be outfitted as a ram...and used in case there's a siege at Vicksburg. It's likely to be damaged, maybe sunk. I know how much Maxx's boat means to you. God, if I could prevent this..." His chin dropped to his chest.

She watched the breeze ruffle his hair. "Commandeer...I don't understand. What does that mean?"

"The Union has the right and power to take any vessel it needs to fight the war. You'll be paid, of course, after the war. But you wouldn't need a boat if you were married to me. I see you walking down the stairs into our front parlor wearing a beautiful white gown with a skirt so big you'll hardly get through the door! We'll be happy, Vanity! Believe that!"

"There are a hundred riverboats your commander could use! Why does he want mine?" But she understood only too well. "Because I slapped and insulted him," she answered softly. She shuddered. "If you don't deliver my boat into his hands, what will he do?"

Abruptly, Trance stood up and paced. "I'm not concerned for myself, you understand. I'm thinking of my parents and sister. If I brought shame upon their heads, Rowena would never make a good marriage." He ran his hand through his hair, then curled it into a fist. He whirled.

"Either I take your boat and hurt you, or I humiliate my family. Try to understand, Vanity! Give up the boat without a fight, but not because I'd be court-martialed. Do it for our future."

"Court-martialed?" she whispered.

"I had to agree to be the one to tell you! If I refused, it could have been interpreted as treason. I could have been hanged...This is so ridiculous! The commander of a Union naval vessel engaging in petty vengeance...Vanity, tell me what you're thinking."

She tied the ribbons of her corset cover and reached for her petticoats. When she finished dressing, she crossed the muddy riverbank and took Trance's hands. His brows were so tightly knit over his blazing blue eyes that she wanted only to comfort him.

She slipped her arms around his neck. "It's only a boat. You're what's important to me!"

He exhaled, his mouth broadening into an incredulous smile. "You'll go, then?"

"How much does the Union pay for a side-wheeler of the finest caliber?" she asked, forcing a light note into her voice.

She forced herself not to think of losing something so filled with precious memories. This was what her mama had wanted for her, an upstanding man of character to take her as his wife.

Trance pulled official papers from his breast pocket, and they sat down together to discuss the terms. When Trance handed her a small leather wallet containing all the cash he had in the world, her heart twisted to see how little it was.

Then her heart blossomed with love to think he would give her everything he possessed. Giving up her boat was well worth his love, she thought, accepting the money and kissing him. She wouldn't mention she had plenty of money of her own in Confederate war bonds.

Finally Trance helped Vanity back into the skiff and rowed back to the Vanity Blade.

As Vanity walked aboard moments later, she saw troops waiting. She felt faint at the thought that she would have no time to adjust to this. Trance bowed stiffly and joined the uniformed men.

Jim Hickory was the first to accost her as she stood on the deck. "Is it true they're taking the Blade, Miss Vanity?"

Wearily, she nodded. "Call everyone to the office, please. I'll pay double. If ever I have another boat..." She would soon be Trance's wife, she reminded herself. Her life as a riverboat entertainer was coming to a mind-stunning halt. "You've been such a good friend, Jim!"

Not trusting her emotions, she rushed up the stairs, pausing only a few seconds in the grand saloon's doorway. The aroma of cigar smoke still lingered. She could almost hear Maxx chuckling.

Forcing back tears, she hurried to the Texas deck. In her stateroom, she packed quickly, her mind occupied with what to take and wear.

When she had finished, she took her strongbox to the office to pay her crew, feeling no resentment as her cash reserves were depleted.

Holding his satchel in well-manicured hands, and with sleek Napoleon making figure-eights and purring around his ankles, Jim Hickory was the last to go. "You've been a pride to know, Miss Vanity," he said, shaking her hand. "If there's ever anything I can do…"

"If you see Quarter Dollar, tell him I've gone to Ohio to marry Lieutenant Holloway."

She wanted to explain, but there was no time, for Union soldiers were already on her boat, tearing out the fine furnishings as she waved good-bye to Jim and Napoleon.

Without searching the desk, without thinking of Maxx or all he left behind when he died, Vanity walked slowly to the gangway and ordered a lanky boy in a blue uniform to carry her trunks off the boat.

This new life was all she had ever wanted, she told herself. Trance would come for her soon. How trying, after all, could living with his parents be?

The Yankee troops stared at her as she picked her way down the stageplank in her cherry-red traveling suit. On the wharf, waiting in a pile, were her trunks, the three new ones she'd taken to Du Barry Vale and the battered one from California.

Trance was nowhere about. She stood for some time watching the Yankees, wondering how her boat would look fitted out as a ram. She wondered where it would sink.

Then she saw Trance racing along one of the gangways.

"I'm here!" she called, her heart soaring. Soon, soon they'd be married! She waved, her heart leaping at his relieved smile.

He came headlong down the stageplank, stopping long enough to catch his breath. "Stay near a day or so…I can meet you!"

"I'll send a message to let you know where I'll be," she called, beaming.

• • •

SAMANTHA HARTE

Vanity found a marvelous little hotel not far from the wharf. Beyond the arched doorway that opened onto a courtyard was a riot of summer flowers. She took a small, high-ceilinged room on the second floor overlooking the dusty street.

The room was wonderfully plain, with a tiny anteroom and a bedchamber taken up entirely by a beautiful brass bed piled with pillows and embroidered coverlets. Above it hung a mosquito-net canopy.

After unpacking, Vanity paid a maid to deliver a message to Trance. When the girl returned, she couldn't say when Trance would arrive.

Vanity paced away the afternoon. At length she fretted about her gowns, thinking how awful they'd look in a small town. The only outfit suitable for a preacher's home was a calico dress she had worn while fishing with Maxx on hot afternoons.

She had neither the ready cash nor time to order more suitable clothes. She would arrive in Cold Crossing wearing a braid-trimmed Holland-blue wool that would surely label her a floozy!

At eleven she ordered supper and then fell into bed, naked, with a bottle of wine. When the bottle was drained, she slept beneath the netting with the covers thrown back.

Near dawn she awoke to the sound of footsteps in the anteroom. Rolling over onto her back, she saw Trance in the doorway. Through the netting he looked out of focus, like a dream.

She opened her arms wide and he joined her there, embracing her. "Love me! Love me!" she said eagerly, trying not to think that soon they'd be parted, perhaps for months.

His touch was delicious, his timing superb. When she could stand no more and wanted only to be with him, he was there for her, sure and slow, giving her all of himself.

Afterward, they lay spent and shaking. He talked of the life they would share in Cold Crossing, of their cottage and children and the years of happiness they would have.

Vanity lay beside him, lost in the dreams he spun for her.

In the night their passion rose again and they tried to make their last night endure forever.

By noon the next day he was gone.

They said no good-byes, only farewell. She didn't even get out of bed. He had wanted to remember her as a naked vision behind the netting.

When the last of his footsteps faded down the narrow stairs, Vanity lay back on the pillows still scented by their lovemaking, willing her tears not to flow. She would not weep when her greatest joy waited in Cold Crossing, Ohio.

154

Twelve

Vanity found no buggy for hire at Cold Crossing's landing. The day was gray and dismal, a fair representation of her mood as she abandoned her trunks in exasperation and started for the center of the sleepy river town.

The trip up from New Orleans had been long and nervewracking. She had been forced to make her way through Yankee-held territory at great inconvenience to herself.

She didn't look forward to seeing Trance's parents again. Though she bore a letter of explanation from him, still she wondered at the reception she would get.

As she made her way along the deserted, wheel-rutted lanes to the outskirts of town, the sky darkened. Trance had told her the way, and with each step she tightened her fists.

At the corner of Mulberry Lane her stomach knotted. She saw a whitewashed church in a plain grassy yard. In need of repair, it had one wide door at the end, three colored-glass windows on the side, and a tiny bell.

Next to it, a weathered picket fence surrounded a gray frame house. As she stiffened her resolve, the sky opened, dropping a heavy load of chilling rain. Her bonnet ruined, her curls melting to wet chestnut strands clinging to her shoulders, Vanity dashed for the protection of the small porch.

She nearly overran Trance's sister sitting on a bench, a bowl of snap beans in her lap. The girl leaped to her feet.

"Why, you're that girl in the green satin! The one who sang dirty songs on the riverboat!" Rowena Holloway exclaimed, backing away and grinning.

Vanity smiled. "That's me, all right."

"What are you doing here? Have you seen Trance? When is he coming home?" Rowena spilled half the beans as she struggled to open the door. "Come inside and take off that wet bonnet. Mama will think it's brazen, but I think it's wonderful!"

Vanity hesitated, summoning her courage.

"Papa's writing his sermon. Are you going to stay? Oh, do stay! Your dress is just wonderful, but Mama won't like it, either. Did you have it made? Was it expensive? We have to sew everything here ourselves."

Vanity made a face as if to say the dress was unimportant. Then she stepped cautiously into the scrubbed entry hall. Her heart was pounding so hard she felt sick.

Trance's mother came through a door at the end of the hall, wiping floured hands on a ragged dishtowel. About to ask who was calling, her large eyes fell on Vanity, who was dripping water all over her floor. She gasped, then went haughty, a frown carving her face into sour lines.

"Look who's here, Mama! It's that girl, do you remember...?" Rowena's lively blue eyes snapped with excitement. "Aren't you surprised?"

Mrs. Holloway regarded Vanity with supreme tolerance. "Indeed, I remember. May I ask why you've come to my home?"

Vanity pulled Trance's letter from her soggy reticule. Suddenly she was very glad she paid some attention to Miss Du Barry. "Excuse me if this is an inconvenient time, Mrs. Holloway. I'm just off a packet from St. Louis. I've been on a train, two wagons, and a coach from New Orleans. Trance is there, as you know, and..."

"I did not know that. John Travis has not bothered to send a single letter in over a year." Then she appeared to check her bitterness. "Is he ...well?"

"Oh, yes, he's fine. I'm sure he meant to write, but they were fighting so long..." She shivered and was grateful when Rowena helped her out of her dripping cape.

Rowena fussed over Vanity's wilted ruffles, cooing over the elaborate ruching along the hem and the elegant sweep of Vanity's bustle.

"Would you care to step into the parlor?" Mrs. Holloway asked, sliding the doors open to display a chilly chamber short on comforts. "Rowena, fetch your father. Tell him Miss...I don't recall your name."

"I'm..." Vanity faltered, reminding herself that the woman would soon be her mother-in-law. "I'm Mary Louise Mackenzie. I've just been with...I've just come from seeing Trance, and I...I have some rather surprising news."

Vanity sank gratefully onto an ugly horsehair sofa. Rowena brought a painted tin tea tray with white china cups and whispered that the water would soon boil. Vanity nodded, wishing she could ask for something a bit more bracing.

Trance's father appeared, wearing a threadbare black frock coat and a forbidding expression.

His wife gave him a look Vanity couldn't interpret. "You recall meeting Miss Mackenzie when we were traveling the river." Mrs. Holloway's tone conveyed that the episode had not been resolved.

Vanity stood and thrust out her hand. "Good afternoon, Reverend Holloway."

He shook once, limply. "Miss Mackenzie..." The bags beneath his eyes had deepened with the years. He looked balefully at her and didn't attempt a smile.

"I'm delighted to see you again, sir," Vanity added. "I've come a long way."

"Why are you here, young woman?" he asked, clasping his hands behind his back and pacing the length of the parlor.

When Vanity found herself unable to speak, he paused, as if he already knew the answer. "If you have taken up with John Travis, I pity your immortal soul. I must say before you speak a word that you have no place with us. Even if you find yourself in a...situation, you will find no refuge here. I have disowned my elder child, my only son. He will get nothing more from me, and neither will you."

Rowena, who had been eavesdropping, darted into the parlor. Scarlet, she curtsied before her father, acting as if she hadn't heard a word. "Excuse me, Papa! Isn't it wonderful? She's seen Trance! She knows where he is! I'll bet he's coming home any day now." She turned to Vanity, her efforts to avoid an unpleasant scene obvious. "When's he coming home, Miss Mackenzie? Are you going to marry my brother?"

Vanity laughed nervously. If this minx could bluster her way about this staid house, Vanity would certainly hold her own.

"Reverend Holloway," she began, lifting her face and feeling a lot better, "your son's fighting for his country. I don't carry his child, as you so indelicately implied, but it would be a sorry thing indeed if he was killed before we married and produced one to carry on the line. He sent me here to live with you, believing you would take me in. He's planning to come home as soon as possible to marry me. I can certainly wait for him somewhere else, if that's your wish. But he won't feel as kindly toward you if he finds I haven't had your hospitality. He felt very strongly that I would be safe here with you."

Trance's mother scoffed. "Do you expect us to believe our son would expect us to take in a—"

Trembling and angry, Vanity offered Trance's letter. Then she sat down, determined to give them ample opportunity to remember they were Christians. If she had not loved Trance quite so much, and if she didn't intend to fulfill her mama's dreams for her, she would have slapped Theophilus Holloway's self-righteous face—and Submit Holloway's, too—before leaving without a parting word.

After reading the letter, Trance's father found his way to a chair and sank into it. "Forgive my rudeness, Miss Mackenzie. I offer my humblest apologies, and my heartfelt thanks. In this letter John Travis indicates he is coming home to live by the principles I hold dear."

Submit Holloway's eyes went very round. Speechless, she snatched the letter from her husband's hand and read it quickly. "She *must* be carrying his child! Why else would he marry the likes of her and come home after all those horrid things he said?"

"Perhaps, my dear, he wants her because she does not have a waspish tongue. Would you be so kind as to show her to the guest bedroom, and have the Christian decency to make her feel welcome?"

"I won't have this hussy in my house!" Submit shouted, flinging the letter to the threadbare carpet. "I see what's already going on! Just look at her! She's seduced our son, and now she's weaving her spell around you! You're a disgrace to your pulpit!"

Reverend Holloway grasped his wife's arm, steering her from the parlor. Vanity could hear him whispering harshly in the hall.

All the while Rowena was positively gleeful. She sidled up to Vanity and plucked at her beaded and fringed reticule. "Don't be offended. They're always like this. Are you a hussy, Miss Mackenzie?" Rowena whispered.

"If you ever ask such a thing of me again, *Miss* Holloway, I'll show you how girls fight. I'll tie your hair in knots. I'll blacken both your eyes, and I'll bite you where it hurts a girl most! I'm here to wait for Trance, and…and…"

Mrs. Holloway appeared in the doorway, her face rigid with reproach. "Would you follow me upstairs, please? You're welcome to stay as long as you like."

"And not a moment longer," Vanity muttered as she marched, head high, from the plain parlor. She felt Reverend Holloway's eyes fixed on her back as she climbed the steep, narrow stairs.

• • •

The guest room was over the kitchen in the rear, a cramped but serviceable chamber with pine walls and a carpetless floor of broad, scarred planks.

She had two windows, one overlooking the vegetable garden beyond the kitchen yard and the other looking out at the church. A plain iron bed, a chest of drawers and an unpainted washstand completed the room's furnishings.

All the rooms in the house were equally plain. The Holloways lived like poor folk. At least, to a young woman used to gilded filigree, European carpets, and hand-painted tableware, the Holloways' mode of living appeared meager, their days comprised of endless menial chores.

Vanity's first weeks in Cold Crossing would have seemed an eternity without Rowena. The girl never left Vanity's side, and never tired of her tales. Save for the unending Sundays perched on a pine bench in the whitewashed church, Vanity could almost say she found simple living relaxing. She was even reminded of the years in Tenderfoot. Without nightly poker games and the constant piano songs, she had time to think, plan, and dream.

She thought of Trance, and their future in a comfortable if simple house where they would live with no particular fanfare or routine. She spun a web of silvery dreams, of sun-drenched days and love-warmed nights, all revolving around Trance and his love for her.

Rowena helped Vanity perfect her reading and ciphering and taught Vanity dozens of Bible verses, intended to convince the Holloways of Vanity's sincere desire to conform.

When two months passed and Vanity's waist didn't thicken, Submit Holloway's expression softened. Vanity learned quickly how eagerly the neighbors whispered of the Holloways' most intimate secrets. In time she realized they spoke confidentially to her only to learn what they could of her—and to pass it along. Too late she realized she should have lied about her past. She came to be called "that Southern woman" waiting for John Travis, who was "no better than she should be."

Thereafter, Vanity gave up trying to befriend the gossips. She used what little cash she had remaining to buy plain cotton dress goods. At Mrs. Holloway's stiffly polite suggestion, she took up the painful art of dressmaking.

With a sewing needle in her hand, she still bled more than was seemly, but after a week she produced something resembling a fitted bodice and gathered skirt homely enough to please the most puritan of tastes.

No more did she wear elaborate ringlets and corkscrew curls. Her center-parted hair was twisted back into a severe knot. The effort made her look years older, and afforded her a bit more respect. Certainly, it was easier to tend without a maid. She wondered if Trance would like or disapprove of the changes.

When no word came from him, Vanity settled in, determined to wait out the war itself if necessary. She learned how to cook stew and how to bake, mend and turn a fine hem, hunt eggs, milk goats, wring and pluck chickens, and dust, beat, and scrub a house into submission, all in anticipation of tending her own hearth.

She could also mend a sock, hang a bed linen on a line, simmer soup stock, and put up an apple butter to rival that of any marriageable young woman in several states.

She could finally read above the primer level, write in a legible hand, and recite passages from the Bible. She no longer boasted that she could play poker with the best riverboat gamblers, or catch and gut a catfish, or distinguish a smelly five-cent stogie from an aromatic one-dollar Cuban Havana. Her nights of strutting, singing, and showing her legs were ended. Most certainly, she forswore her taste for Kentucky whiskey and French wine, and said good-bye forever to the mildest forms of blasphemy.

She felt ready to take on her new role as Trance's wife. She only wished that he would send some word as to when he would arrive.

Week after week passed, but still there was no word. Vanity passed her seventeenth birthday with little celebration; she wasn't certain of the day, and that occupied dinner table conversation for a week—that and repeated requests that Vanity get baptized.

Rowena proved to be a delightful companion. But as the miserably cold days of winter melted into spring, Vanity grew melancholy. Had Trance survived the many river battles around Vicksburg? Would she ever see him again?

In early summer, Rowena turned fifteen. Soon after, she met a young man, and the change in her behavior suddenly strained the cordiality at Cold Crossing's parsonage.

"Do you think it's wrong to kiss, if you're in love?" Rowena asked, leaning on the handle of her hoe and gazing intently into Vanity's flushed face.

The girl never ceased with her provocative questions. Vanity's impatience flared with the heat of the summer sun on her neck. "A person might think you had a beau."

"And if I did, would it be wrong to kiss him?"

Vanity threw down her own hoe and stomped into the shade. "Wrong? Great snakes! No, but don't tell your mother I said that. I don't want her after me today."

Rowena abandoned her work, too, and joined Vanity. "His name's Ethan. I love him! I've kissed him!"

Vanity forced away her jealousy. "Tell me about him."

Rowena beamed. "He's everything Papa hates! He hasn't been in school in years. He works on his father's farm, and he's very brawny." She gave a little squeal. "I love his hands, especially when...Papa thinks him and his people are crude, but I love him! He's talking of going west. Him and his whole family are leaving in only a few days, and I...I don't know how I'll stand it!"

Suddenly Rowena's secretive behavior of recent weeks came into focus. "You've been wanting to tell me this for days, haven't you?" Vanity asked.

Rowena nodded. "I know you're worldly, Mary. You could tell me what I need to know—about men."

Coloring, Vanity let the statement go by without comment. "You're thinking of going off with him, aren't you?"

Rowena looked away. "There's no use telling me that I shouldn't. I already know that, but it's what I want to do. I love him."

"You can't wait until he gets settled and sends for you?"

"Folks die on the trail. I'm not taking any chances." She turned to Vanity and looked imploringly into her eyes. "I know we were meant for each other the way you and my brother are. If I don't go, Papa and Mama will do something to make sure I never see Ethan again. If I don't go away from here...soon...I'm lost!"

Vanity swallowed. "It is a trial to live here, that's sure."

"It's not just that. It's this whole way of life I hate. It's not right for me. I can't be stuck in one place like this. Ethan wants to see the world, and he wants me at his side. You've already seen the world, Mary. You don't understand what it's like to remember all I saw on the riverboat and know how much more is out there just waiting for me! And besides, I love him. I need to be with him, and if I'm not married to him, well, I'm not strong enough to live in sin. If I don't go, he wants a token of my love. Tonight." Rowena lowered her face and whispered, "I mean to give myself. Is there a way I can be safe?"

Jumping up and rushing back to her hoe, Vanity began attacking the recently planted garden. After a strained moment, Rowena came to Vanity and tugged at her sleeve.

"I heard once that certain women know. I...I know you're not one of those kind!" she added hastily. "But you met a few in your time, in that saloon out in California. You said so! Vanity, is it a sin for me to want to keep from having a baby if I can't work up the courage to go off with Ethan? I couldn't get in a fix like that. It'd kill Mama. But I'm either going off with him or I'm—"

Her words were cut off as the back door of the house slammed. Submit Holloway came out, her face red from baking. "I need both you girls inside as soon as you're done here. Rowena, where's your bonnet? You're getting sun!"

Rowena hastily put her bonnet back on. With furtive looks at Vanity signaling her to keep her silence, she finished hoeing and then hurried inside.

Her question plagued Vanity. Though she'd heard such information was available, she'd never been old enough to be told—or to need it.

Long after they had washed and dried the supper dishes, had meditation, studies, and prayers, and gone to bed, Vanity lay awake, grateful she hadn't come to Cold Crossing unmarried and carrying Trance's child.

Near midnight, Vanity heard her door open softly. Rowena stood there in her traveling hat and cape, a carpetbag clutched in her hand. Putting it down, she closed the door and tiptoed to Vanity's bedside.

"I couldn't go without saying good-bye!" she whispered. "Don't tell Mama and Papa I'm gone until morning."

"He'll fetch you back," Vanity warned.

"I'll make sure Papa won't want me back," Rowena whispered, taking Vanity's warm hand and crushing it between her cool ones. "I know you've been with my brother. Will I be afraid?"

Vanity was glad for the darkness. "Not if you really love him."

"Will I feel pain?"

"Not if you really want him, and if he's...gentle."

"Was Trance gentle?"

"Trance is very passionate, but I wanted him and I...I would've let him do anything. It can't be wrong if two people are really in love." She squeezed Rowena's hand, not believing the girl had enough courage to go, especially if she was honest with her. "A man gets big, and he makes your blood rush so fast you don't care what he does. You just want him to do it! He...he goes inside..."

Vanity suddenly ached for Trance and began to cry. "You'll feel like one body, and it changes you somehow. Rowena, be sure Ethan's the one! Nothing will ever touch your soul like this."

For a long moment Rowena was silent, her hands still holding Vanity's. "Thank you. Thank you!" She pressed her lips to Vanity's cheek, then rushed out, leaving Vanity afraid.

At dawn, Vanity was near exhaustion from lack of sleep. She could hardly drag herself to the kitchen to begin breakfast, and she dreaded every creaking floorboard in the house, knowing that at any moment Rowena's absence would be discovered.

She had completed both Rowena's and her own chores when Submit walked into the kitchen clutching a carefully penned note. The woman stopped just short of walking into the table in the center of the room and stared blankly at the words her daughter had written.

Moments later Reverend Holloway came in holding his worn Bible in preparation for morning prayers at the table. He seated himself and folded his hands before looking up at his wife's ashen face. Then he saw the note in her hands. "What is it, Submit?"

Quickly, Vanity drew a chair up behind the woman and guided her onto it, glanced at the note, and saw enough to know Rowena had spared her mother no detail of her shocking plans.

Vanity's heart went out to the woman when she saw huge tears rolling down her thin cheeks.

"Both my children," Submit whispered, crushing the note to her bosom, "both gone. Both gone from me. Dear Lord..." She went on mumbling something that sounded like a prayer for strength.

Her husband rose and snatched the note from her. Then he turned on Vanity. "You knew about this, didn't you?"

Vanity gave no indication that she had or hadn't. She avoided the man's eyes, determined that if he spoke one harsh word she'd leave.

But Theophilus Holloway gathered his wits quickly and left the kitchen. They heard him go out the front door. His wife went on weeping softly at the kitchen table.

• • •

Vanity made herself scarce during the two days Trance's father was away looking for Rowena. She did most of the cooking and cleaning, then retired to her room over the stifling kitchen to gaze from the window and think about the river and Trance.

When Reverend Holloway returned, he didn't speak to Vanity for hours. She overheard him saying angrily that Rowena was beyond his recall, that she had been duly married and was on her way with Ethan Tinsley's family to Independence, Missouri.

"We won't be seeing her again," he concluded, walking away from his wife, his back like a ramrod.

Vanity wondered at such a family. Theophilus Holloway had disowned Trance and now didn't want Rowena back. What kind of man was he?

She was still brooding a week later, staying alone in her room and avoiding evening prayers when Reverend Holloway came to her.

With head bowed, his manner stiff with forced sincerity, he closed the door and regarded her from the shadows. "My dear Mary, I've had little opportunity to discuss matters with you since Rowena took her leave of us. I feel you had a hand in this, however innocent."

"I had nothing to do with it," Vanity said indignantly. She crossed her arms, remembering what Trance had said about his father so long ago.

"I'm sure you feel you did nothing to encourage my daughter to become so rebellious. By your mere presence, you disturbed the order of our household. I'm not saying that I wish you should leave us, too. On the contrary, I want you to stay…most sincerely, I do."

Vanity moved from the rocker by the window to stand beside the table, putting as much distance as possible between Trance's father and herself. The man had a queer look in his eyes.

"You've brought us the shadow of wickedness, Mary Louise. I saw it that day we met by the river. You've come far since that day, but you're still a heathen woman. I have meditated long on how I can help you become truly the wife my son deserves—if he returns."

"I've obeyed all your rules," she said, edging against the wall.

He moved closer. "I can help you, Mary. We must pray together. I have healed wayward women like yourself before." His deep, hypnotic voice lured her, but it was the strange odor of anise that made her realize he was trying to hide alcohol on his breath. As he moved into the pale moonlight falling through the window, she finally saw the secret side of Theophilus Holloway. She wondered if he would even remember this encounter.

"Healed?" she whispered, looking for a means of eluding him.

"We must begin with an admission of all sins. You've had carnal knowledge of my son, have you not?"

Vanity's pulse began racing. She pressed herself against the wall so hard her shoulder blades stung. "That's none of your business."

"I can touch you and remove the taint of sin from your body."

"You can?" she asked, unable to believe he was saying such things. The pious old hypocrite!

"By the laying on of hands…" he whispered, holding out his palms so that he would be pressing them against her breasts in another step, "…I can make you clean again."

Before she could gasp or protest or even laugh at his audacity, one of his hands closed on her breast. Lightning-fast, the other pressed between her thighs.

"Let this woman be—"

She twisted away. "Get your hands off me!"

He continued to grip her painfully, pressing his hard, grim mouth against hers. Words poured from him, but they weren't the sort to come from the pulpit.

Her anger blossomed and made her strong. Gripping both his wrists, she dug in her nails and wrenched her face away from his. "If you don't let up on me, there won't be any way for you to explain why I bit your mouth! I'll spread this all over town! It'll probably kill your wife, but that'll be on *your* head. Your son and daughter will disown you, just as you've disowned them. You're no kind of preacher! You're a dirty old masher!"

His grip on her breast tightened enough to leave bruises. He left her no alternative but to knee him, and certainly he must never have encountered a woman with enough experience to do it half so well as a girl bred in a boom camp and raised on a riverboat.

With a howl, he doubled over. "Merciful heavens! You've unmanned me!"

"Get out of my room!" she hissed, rubbing herself where he'd bruised her. "You so much as look me in the eye again, and I'll be gone! You'll never see Trance again. The only reason I'm staying is to help your wife until she comes to her senses. I'm staying because I love Trance enough that I'd sleep in the devil's own house to please him. Your way of getting with women would make them howl from New York to San Francisco!"

• • •

A letter mailed in August from Missouri arrived in September saying Rowena was happily married and on her way west with Ethan and his family. Submit Holloway wept again, but, strangely, she seemed to rally each time she read the letter.

"I longed to marry young," she mused. "But I was almost twenty-seven when I married Theo. He was the first man to meet my exacting standards and my family's, but, unfortunately, I never truly suited Theo. I think I would have liked going west. I've tried to be a good wife, but… to fail with both my children is a terrible burden to bear."

"I wouldn't say you've failed," Vanity said softly, punching down bread dough.

"In any case, I've lost them both. I knew they would one day grow up and move away. If John Travis comes home from the war, I hope you settle nearby."

"Trance is coming home," Vanity said resolutely.

"That he hasn't written his parents doesn't surprise me, Mary. That he hasn't written his intended is something else again."

As the weeks wore on, the woman's words cast a pall over Vanity's hopes. Vanity endured at the Holloway house until the spring of 1864. With news from the war as grim as it had ever been, and the Mississippi River long freed to the Union, a dispatch arrived late one afternoon by messenger.

Spring snow swirled outside as Submit closed the front door and stared at the sealed message. "I can't read this," she whispered, taking it to her rocker by the heating stove in the drawing room and holding it in her lap.

Vanity stood nearby, her heart pounding. "May I read it, then?" she asked. It was about Trance—she knew it!

"That's all right, Mary. I don't need anything."

Had the woman lost her mind?

"May I read the message, please?" Vanity asked gently.

"I could use a cup of tea," Submit said, her voice soft and cordial. "If you would be so good."

"I want to read the message! I know it's about Trance!"

But the woman wouldn't release the paper…

Hours later when her husband came down from the bedroom where he'd been writing a sermon, Submit was still rocking and staring into space. Reverend Holloway snatched the paper without ceremony and tore it open.

"Naval Lieutenant John Travis Holloway confirmed missing, believed dead…"

At first Vanity refused to believe the words Trance's father read as if he'd expected it all along.

Dead?

She retired to her room. She felt nothing—no pain, no heartbreak, no grief. She simply sat, whispering at intervals that she didn't believe it, that it couldn't be. Such heartbreak wouldn't come to her a third time.

She thought of nothing and no one. For hours, she stayed in the rocker by the window, rocking just a little and remembering in exquisite detail the moments she had shared with Trance.

"This can't have happened," she whispered again and again.

When a letter came from Trance's commander confirming that he had not been seen since November, Vanity's heart sank.

A week later, she packed her trunks and walked away from the frame house on Mulberry Lane in Cold Crossing without even so much as a good-bye.

She was scarcely missed.

The crushing weight of realization and grief splintered her heart just as she reached New York State by rail. For a month she recuperated alone in an Albany hotel room. She ran up a bill she couldn't pay and yet convinced everyone by her creased, two-year-old gowns and jewelry that she was well-heeled.

Seeking solace in whiskey, noise, and familiar distraction, she found a small saloon where she drew a crowd by playing, and winning, poker. With bills paid, and new gowns ordered, she set about building a new life without Trance. Her first and only thought was to become the star her mother had wanted her to be.

Laughed out of every theater and burlesque house, she learned quickly that her quaint songs and untrained dancing routine labeled her a rube. As the Union sliced across the Confederacy, humbling the dashing rebels and bringing the war to a close, Vanity Blade once again gambled, now to pay for much-needed lessons with the most renowned honky-tonk entertainers in the east.

Her days filled, her evenings taken up with a profusion of solicitous gentlemen of varying quality, she seldom dwelled on might-have-beens.

She lived the life she knew best, drinking a bit more than she should and understanding only too well how her mother had come to live out her last days in an isolated place like Tenderfoot. She sometimes thought she would live out her days playing poker in Albany saloons.

In time, she told herself, the simple life with Trance would have paled. At last, with her routines perfected, her voice honed to a saucy, sultry seductive whisper, her body bedecked in audaciously expensive gowns copied from the latest Paris styles, her hotel suite lavished with flowers and tokens of esteem, she embarked on a real career in the Albany Rialto Burlesque.

She gave no more thought to propriety.

Thirteen

1866

At the sound of a discreet tap at her dressing room door, Vanity turned from the looking glass. "More flowers?" she called, smiling a little as she resumed applying fresh lip rouge for her final performance that evening.

Her maid, Elsa, ventured in with an armload of four dozen red roses. "Mr. Addison sent these! Won't you please see him? It breaks a girl's heart to see a grown man get down on his knees!" The thin woman with the curved spine, whom Vanity had taken in from the streets, smiled from beneath her mop of graying brown curls.

The frown that instantly darkened Vanity's face softened. "Oh, Elsa, don't tell stories. He didn't get on his knees!" She adjusted her breathlessly tight, ruffled, and beribboned black corset. "He would never do such a thing."

"But he did, miss!" Elsa insisted, turning to drag in another arrangement of freshly cut spring flowers so large it came in a wrought-iron floor stand.

"Great snakes! Who sent that?"

"I don't know, miss. Isn't it wonderful! There's a card."

Elsa handed Vanity a small cream-colored envelope engraved with an initial so elaborate Vanity couldn't read it. She was about to tear it open when Elsa rushed to the gentleman poking his balding head in the dressing room door.

"Mr. Addison! You mustn't come in yet! Miss Blade is indisposed. If you'll please just wait…" The tiny woman pushed him out.

Vanity put the card aside and slipped behind a screen where she adjusted the black lace garters at the tops of her patterned black stockings. Mr. Addison was proving to be quite a nuisance.

Her hair had been cut in a fringe that framed her face now, and her curls were dressed with silk flowers and creamy pearl stickpins. Her cheeks were highly colored, and her eyes were lined with false lashes so that her lively expressions onstage could be seen in the highest box and farthest dollar seat.

Vanity began tying on her voluminous scarlet petticoats. "Send Lloyd in now, the dear old thing."

Elsa had been holding the dressing room door closed. She stood away, stumbling over the enormous bouquet, and whispered out the door to the aging financier. "She'll see you for just one minute! Hurry! It's nearly curtain time!"

Vanity took a deep breath. She scanned her tiny backstage chamber, hung with huge feathered bonnets and dazzling costumes. Lloyd's overpowering West Indian bayberry hair tonic filled the air.

The small, rotund gentleman came in grinning. "My very dearest Vanity, I—" He spied the overlarge floor bouquet and his expression wilted. "Ah. Now I understand. You have a new admirer."

"Not at all, Lloyd, dear! Did you have something urgent to tell me? I don't have much time…" She patted his cheek.

He thrust a small, beautifully wrapped package into her hands. "This is for you, my dear!" He drank in her loveliness, letting his hungry little eyes rest on her luscious bosom.

Feeling uncomfortable, she took the gift. "Thank you, Lloyd, but…" She turned away. Hers was a careful performance, one intended to avoid angering him if possible.

She did like the cheerful old man. The diamond stickpin in his cravat was large enough to make Vanity's rivals incredulous when Vanity insisted she had no intention of becoming his mistress.

Past fifty, he reminded her of Maxx and happier times, and because he did, she didn't think of him as a potential lover.

"Lloyd, you're too generous," she said sweetly, as she returned the package to his plump, dimpled hand. "I've tried to explain I can no longer accept your gifts."

His lively brown eyes clouded. "I want to know the real reason why! And who sent these flowers?" He kicked the stand over. A puddle formed beneath the scattered blooms and greenery.

Not wanting to be undressed in front of him any longer, Vanity had been struggling into her elaborate black skirt. At his unexpected outburst, she went still, holding her skirt, her bosom thrust out by the specially designed corset. A single deep breath would make her breasts pop free, almost into his scowling face.

"I think you should leave," she said softly, with narrowed eyes. "I do *not* belong to you."

His voice was controlled. "My dear, this is my last offer."

"For an apartment of my own and an allowance?" Vanity asked, recalling the dozen offers he'd made in the last months.

"A very generous allowance," he added.

Vanity crossed to her wardrobe and lifted her bodice from the hanger. She was only too aware of the breathtaking effect her nearly bare breasts, her tiny clinched waist, and blossoming hips had, but she was determined not to be late going onstage.

Without Trance, nothing mattered but the remnants of her convictions, and a silent vow she had made in her hotel room nearly two years before. She would never love another man. Until she found someone suitable to marry—love would have nothing to do with that—she would live a celibate life. She would never lower herself to being a mistress. That was one step away from being a harlot.

She considered calling Elsa back into the room and then decided against insulting Lloyd that way. This battle had been raging between them since the first evening eight months before when Lloyd lumbered backstage expecting she would be honored to grace his bed that night.

What a surprised man he had been! Her indignant tirade had left him speechless—and intrigued. He looked even more surprised and bewildered now as she continued to refuse him and his offers.

"I'm grateful for your generosity, Lloyd. Nothing would give me greater honor than to be by your side..." She didn't add "as your wife." He might actually propose, and the week before she had realized she simply couldn't marry. Not yet, anyway.

His nose and cheeks went purple.

Worried he was about to become violent, Vanity ducked behind the screen and jerked the bellpull to summon Elsa. "If you'll forgive me, Lloyd, I have a show in—"

"I know you have a show! A woman as beautiful as you needn't work! I can give you everything! I'm offering you comfort and ease! You...you must know I can't ask you to marry me!"

She stopped trying to hook her tight bodice. "Why not?"

His face twisted as he forced out the words. "I...I already have a wife! Are you satisfied? I have now been more honest with you than any other woman—or man. Say you'll let me take care of you. Say you'll be exclusively mine! You're my dearest, sweetest, most beautiful love!"

He looked as if he was about to get down on bended knees.

"Don't!" she said, slashing the air with her perfumed hand. She hurried to hold the dressing room door closed so that Elsa wouldn't walk in just yet. "You're *married?*"

He sighed. "She lives in another city. She's—"

"Don't tell me she's an invalid, or that she refuses you, or that she's with child, or ugly, or inhibited! I've heard it all before!"

"I don't like your tone, my dear."

Vanity wanted to throttle him. "I actually believed you were being honest with me." She jerked the door wide open. "Please, be so kind as to leave. Knowing you've misled me, that you are the sort of man who would, I would not accept you now under any circumstances! Good-bye, Mr. Addison!"

He swept out, turned, and fixed her with a glare. "I'll see you ruined in this town!"

"Do try!" she snapped, slamming the door and sagging against it.

She was heartily tired of men assuming she was desperate to offer intimate relations in return for money. She wanted no more of it.

When Elsa tapped, Vanity let her in. Without talking they finished preparing Vanity for her final evening performance. Elsa knew when to hold her tongue.

Moments before curtain call, Vanity sank to the stool before her dressing table and lowered her face into her hands. Then she saw the engraved envelope.

"Can I get you a nip of something, miss?" Elsa whispered, tidying the overturned flowers.

"No, I'm fine." She lifted her head and snatched the card from the envelope.

> My darling Miss Blade,
> Your fame has reached to the corners of our restored union. May I extend my sincerest congratulations and beg your beautiful company whenever you find yourself in New Orleans.
> Fondest regards,
> Jules Pearson, Esquire

Embossed in the lower right corner was a side-wheeler. Beneath that was the boat's name, *J. J. Pearson*. Vanity reread the card, a smile lighting her face.

"I'm better than fine!" She laughed, thinking that the arrogant Southern gentleman she'd once pushed backward into Mississippi mud was now actively soliciting her attention! What she wouldn't give to show him just how expertly she kissed now, and that she had no trouble rejecting generous favors from exceedingly wealthy gentlemen. Her company? Jules Pearson should be so lucky!

"Have you ever seen the Mississippi River?" Vanity asked.

"No, miss! I don't know any place but this town."

"Would you be willing to travel with me? I'm thinking of going on a trip. I miss the river. I miss riverboats!"

"But everyone here loves you, miss! Hear them stomping for you?"

The sound was so like what Vanity remembered—boots stomping impatiently for her mother to perform at the Broken Rock. She stood and threw back her head. "I'll give them a performance to remember me by!"

"When will we be leaving, miss?"

"Begin packing now. We're leaving tonight, for New Orleans."

The side-wheeler *J. J. Pearson* had been on the river less than three months when Vanity and her maid arrived in New Orleans in April.

The magnolias were in bloom, and every tree in the land, save the mossy live oaks, was a riot of colorful blossoms.

Since arriving in New Orleans, Vanity hadn't been able to contain her exuberance. Though war had changed the South—on every street corner gathered ravaged ex-soldiers, some still in uniform, with empty sleeves and pant legs, eye patches and invisible scars—Vanity did not see the burned, deserted plantations or droves of former slaves still thinking "freedom" meant never having to work again.

She saw only the brown river, heard the lilting mixture of voices, smelled the deep earthy aroma of the South that brought back delicious memories of Maxx and their happy years together.

The wharves were choked with sea traders, freighters, barges, coal flats, rafts, sloops, and "photograph" boats making likenesses of the snakelike river and all who cared to have their faces immortalized in sepia and black.

And though the railroad had taken away more and more freight and passenger traffic, the splendiferous white packet steamers still stood side by side along the docks, gushing black smoke to the sky, hooting importantly, and beckoning to all for a swift but comfortable journey up the wide old river.

Grandest of all was the *J. J. Pearson,* a crack riverboat nearly three hundred feet long. Vanity liked thinking she had not come south solely to see Jules Pearson again; he was still not the sort she cared to encourage, but his invitation had intrigued her. She would see him, in time. Meanwhile, she couldn't stop herself from hiring a buggy to take her out to the wharf to gaze at the monstrously large boat.

The boat's promenade deck was a full fifty feet above the waterline. The saloon deck was decorated with the ultimate in complicated wooden filigree painted white. The boiler deck held all manner of freight, and nearly spilled over with steerage passengers awaiting the daily ran to the Memphis races.

The *J. J. Pearson*'s twin side paddles were enclosed in giant round wheelboxes hand-painted with a colorful panorama of Natchez's skyline and bluffs. But for a gaudy, noisy array of guests lining the gently curving upper decks, the splendid boat had a formidable air about it.

After only two days, Vanity grew weary of accompanying herself to places where it was really only proper to have an escort. Grudgingly, she admitted she was impatient to see Jules, to impress him.

She booked passage to Natchez, on the excuse of going to put flowers on Maxx's tomb, and found herself standing on the wharf with her carpetbags and bandboxes only to see the *J. J. Pearson* pulling away, thrashing its way north into the sultry afternoon heat.

"Why didn't he wait!" she exclaimed, snapping open her silk foulard parasol to shield her pale cheeks from the Southern sun.

Gritting her teeth and narrowing her eyes, she watched the gilded beauty move ever farther away.

"Knowing him, he'll have my trunks thrown into the nearest mud. Elsa, did I ever tell you I once owned a boat like that, not so big, of course, but far more beautiful? I won her in a poker game."

"No, miss!"

"Oh, yes, and it'd serve him right to invite me south, leave without me, and then lose that ol' boat to me in a few rounds of draw poker." She chuckled to herself. "I suppose we'll have to book passage on another boat, or wait until tomorrow."

Elsa darted forward, pointing like a child. "Look! They're lowering a little boat. Do you suppose it's for us?"

Vanity's spirits soared. That was better!

The river was high, and the light-skinned black rowing against its surging power had plenty of trouble returning to the wharf. At length, Vanity found herself looking down into Quarter Dollar's warm welcoming eyes. She squealed for joy!

"Sweet Susie! Would you look at yourself!" Quarter said, snagging the steps and hauling himself up to the wharf.

Vanity embraced her friend, delighted to be embarrassing him in public. "Now I know why I came back! To see you again!"

He grinned, eyeing the startled deck hands watching from nearby boats. "You've done all right, by the looks of you."

"And surely you have, too, but what are you doing still with Jules? You're free now. A war was fought for that!"

He shrugged off the comment. "Looks like the war hasn't laid a hand on you, Miss Vanity. We got your trunks early this morning, and when we pulled out just now I told boss man you hadn't come aboard yet."

"I know what he's about," Vanity said, chuckling. "He's trying for the upper hand, but I've come south to show him just who his betters have turned out to be. Tell me what you've been doing with yourself!"

He indicated the skiff. "He's still steaming, Miss Vanity. He doesn't care if I break both arms rowing you out."

"Then we must hurry!" Vanity exclaimed, gathering up her wide skirts and letting Quarter help her down the steps. For the first time she truly felt like a lady, helpless and encumbered by yards of expensive silks.

Quarter still wore a white castoff silk shirt, though now his trousers fit, even if they were far below the standard he deserved.

When Elsa was settled next to Vanity, and the bandboxes and bulging carpetbags were piled in the middle, Quarter started out into the river, his powerful shoulders rippling beneath the worn silk as he cut the oars into the water.

"Tell me everything that's happened since I saw you last," Vanity said.

Quarter only laughed and went on rowing. With surprising speed, as if he'd rowed against the current all his life, Quarter brought them to the hull of the *J. J. Pearson*. "You've done mighty well among the Yankees. I surely was pleased when boss man took it in his head to send you a card." He panted as they tied up.

"I'm rather notorious in New York," Vanity said, her cheeks coloring. "How long has Jules had a riverboat?"

"This here's our second. The first almost got took by the Yankees, same as the *Vanity Blade.*" For a moment his eyes became veiled and he looked away from her. "We outsmarted them, luckily, but only to snag a few weeks later. The *Louisette* went down six miles north of Epson Point."

"And the *Vanity Blade?*"

Quarter lifted his head, smiling sadly. "She went down proud, Miss Vanity. Rammed a Yankee gunboat just as if she'd been born to it. Her bow was piled with charges. She went in a shower of flame. They were clearing wrecks from around Vicksburg for months afterward. In the end, the Yankees got the best of everyone, but it was a grand show. Now all that's past." He shook his head. "It surely is fine to see you again. What I can't figure is how come boss man found you singing in New York. Last I heard, ol' Jim Hickory said you were headed for Ohio to marry up with Mr. Trance."

Vanity thought Quarter's eyes looked uneasy as he spoke of Trance—as if he knew Trance was dead and wasn't sure if she did.

Brawny, shiny-faced deck hands helped Vanity and Elsa aboard. Quarter directed one of the men to show Elsa up to Vanity's stateroom.

"Then you didn't hear about Trance," she said when they were alone. She watched Quarter's face carefully.

"No'm. Is there something I should know?"

She found her grief hard to put into words and realized she had not spoken of Trance's death to anyone since she had left Cold Crossing. "It's been almost two years. A telegraph dispatch came to his parents' house. I was there…waiting." She put trembling fingertips to her lips. "He…he was…I stopped waiting."

Quarter's confused face fell in disbelief. "Ah, Sweet Susie! No. Not Mr. Trance. Here, all this time I've been thinking you and him were up north making babies—Excuse me! I won't speak of it anymore." He went nimbly ahead of her on the boiler deck. "This ol' river hasn't been the same without you, Miss Vanity! No, siree!"

Relieved to have him trying to distract her, Vanity put aside the grief buried in her heart. She drew a breath, turned, and savored the broad water before her. The faint breeze tickled her cheeks. She wanted to weep, but not so much from sadness as from a longing for things past— Maxx, Trance, her lost childhood.

"Where am I likely to find Mr. Pearson?" Vanity asked, blinking away the sad thoughts.

Quarter put his hand on her arm. "You've always been good to me, Miss Vanity. Would you take a bit of warning from a friend who cares the world for you?"

"Of course," she said, smiling. "Warn away!"

"Don't…*don't* tangle with my boss man."

Unlike the gambling whiskey boats Maxx had kept, the *J. J. Pearson* was fitted like a respectable passenger steamer packet. The grand saloon was as fine as any Vanity had ever seen, with a rare Brussels carpet, French walnut furniture, and the faint aroma of Cuban cigar smoke.

Gambling was allowed in private suites along the outer walls of the grand saloon, and these resembled the secluded parlors kept for such purposes in hotels.

Quarter agreed to tell his boss man Vanity had boarded safely. She retired to her suite near the stern where Elsa waited, still unpacking what Vanity would need for dinner.

While Elsa readied several gowns taken straight from Vanity's stage performances, Vanity went from the door leading to the grand saloon to the door opening onto the gangway. She felt like a child returned to her favorite playground.

At length Vanity frowned over the gowns spilling from her trunks. The almond silk was tempting, but the fragile fabric would wilt after only an hour. She wanted to appear fresh all evening.

The scarlet satin did wonders for her eyes, lending them a fiery quality men found irresistible, but the color was a bit bright for her purposes this evening. She didn't care to have Jules Pearson mistake her reason for coming.

In the end, she chose a demure blue muslin, sheer and ruffled, and drawn back slightly at the hips into a bow that caught up the lower half of the skirt into a bit of a train. She had given a good many performances in it, but it still looked like new and was a color most becoming to her hair and skin.

When she emerged from her stateroom two hours after boarding, she felt and looked like the queen of the Albany stage. Though her lace-topped high-button shoes pinched a bit, and she missed the rocking sway of large hoops now out of fashion, she knew she was every bit the most beautiful woman on the river.

Her hair was caught up in a complicated style of curls and braids that had taken Elsa a long time to arrange. She had tiny spit curls beside her ears, and dangling, genuine diamond earbobs that winked as the light caught them. Down her back ran a series of tiny blue bows any man would yearn to pluck open!

Quarter waited on the gangway as she started toward Jules's private gaming suite. He looked worried, but Vanity gave him a confident smile. She had outwitted more men than it was decent to mention.

"I'll be fine, you'll see," she said to reassure Quarter. How peculiar it was that he was so concerned when she felt perfectly safe!

As Vanity tapped at Jules's door, Quarter hung about the shaded gangway, still trying to figure out why his boss man had taken such pains to lure Vanity back to the river.

When Vanity disappeared inside the suite, Quarter hurried up to the sun-drenched promenade deck, where he had a safe place behind the smokestacks.

Trance Holloway dead? Quarter hadn't expected to hear that. Settling himself in the shadows, Quarter chewed his knuckle and thought back to the second year of the war when the Yankees were still shelling Vicksburg.

His boss man had been up to his usual capers, traveling the river for his clandestine visits to wealthy parlors, looting drawers and sideboards for silver, strongboxes for cash, and jewelry boxes for tempting earbobs and the occasional diamond.

About that time he got the idea of traveling on a single boat instead of booking passage on a different one every night; it seemed a more efficient way for a gentleman thief to make a living.

Quarter still was not privy to the particulars, but one day his boss man took ownership of a quality stern-wheeler called *Louisette*. Quarter suspected his boss man's daddy had financed the enterprise. The aging gent would do anything to keep Jules on the river—away from the family plantation in Louisiana.

For Quarter, the daily routine didn't change. He still rowed his boss man from boat to shore and shore to boat in the thick of the night, with sheriffs, posses, and hounds baying at their heels, but boss man's modus operandi had never yet failed. Always they came away clear.

And then, while boss man slept away the better part of the day, Quarter sold the stolen goods at whatever landing or port was most handy.

The war had done little to change all that—until boss man ventured too close to Vicksburg and found the *Louisette* boarded one day by a tall, tow-haired Yankee naval lieutenant charged with commandeering her for the Union's ram fleet.

"Paid after the war? I don't believe I care for the way your so-called commander does business," Jules had said, leaning back in his chair while the young lieutenant stood at attention before him. "I suggest you take yourself off my boat in all haste, sir."

Looking uncomfortable but officious, Lieutenant Trance Holloway had produced the necessary papers. Jules had scoffed, kicking them away. Then he had risen to his feet, an ugly dueling pistol ready in his hand, primed and cocked.

"We'll just see what colors fly from this jackstaff come morning," Jules had said as a half dozen of his burly deck hands moved into his office at his signal, preventing Trance from leaving.

Moments later, Lieutenant Holloway, with Jules beside him, was ordering his detachment of troops to debark and await further instructions. Quarter had been near enough to see the gleam of the pistol muzzle hard against Trance's ribs.

That night the *Louisette* quietly steamed away, not to be seen again except in the bayous near Epson Point, where she soon snagged and went down.

Quarter still got a chill remembering that night. He'd been watching, unsure if he would be able to help Trance escape his boss man's hold. He had just returned in the skiff, nearly missing the *Louisette* riding with no lanterns in the shallows off the point. He found Trance pistol-whipped and unconscious on the stern deck.

Above him stood Quarter's grinning boss man, a Louisiana pig sticker in his hand ready to gut Trance. The stones to fill his belly were piled on the bloody deck nearby. It was likely Jules had made Trance select them himself from the muddy bank.

At great risk to his own life and limb, Quarter had rushed in. "Boss man, think how truly fine it'd be to have a Yankee officer tucked up your sleeve like an ace?" Quarter had jabbered, thinking only a few words ahead of himself. "We've had some mighty close shaves in the past weeks, what with Yankees, Rebels, and Jayhawkers falling all over themselves in these parts. I'd hate to think of what would happen if you were taken in by an ornery rebel sheriff who's just been thinking Yankees are looting in his jurisdiction and come to find out it's one of his own compatriots. Sweet Susie! Such a sheriff would be cross with you!"

Jules had snarled at him to be quiet.

"But think on this, boss man," Quarter had pressed, Trance's life hanging in the balance. "If we had us a Yankee naval officer trussed up tidy somewhere, we might make us a real advantageous trade. You'd get off scot-free!"

"I won't be taken by any sheriff," Jules had said darkly.

"No, like as not, you won't. But supposing you got taken by Yankees for questioning…about not turning over the *Louisette,* or for anything else they might want. They don't need reasons to interrogate a Rebel sympathizer. Think how glad they'd be to get back one of their own. I-if you was to keep Mr.—this here Yankee officer handy, you'd be safe coming and going, so to speak."

Slowly, Jules had straightened, finally sheathing his long, thin-bladed knife. "I do believe you have a whiff of intelligence about you, boy!"

The idea, born of desperation, had saved Trance's life. He'd been kept aboard the *Louisette* until she snagged. After nearly drowning in the shallow draft hold as she sank, he'd escaped, or so Quarter's boss man had claimed. Quarter hadn't been on hand to assist with that. He'd been selling goods in Buck's Creek.

Now, after all his efforts, Trance Holloway's body was probably moldering in a bayou somewhere, gutted and weighted with stones. Or he'd been shot. Or maybe he had been set free as boss man said, and caught a Minié ball while on his way to the Yankee lines.

Quarter clutched his head, grieving for one of the very few white men who had ever been truly kind to him. What sadness to think he had not survived to marry Miss Vanity and live a happy life.

Now Miss Vanity herself was below, walking right into one of his boss man's well-oiled traps. What Jules wanted with her was unknown to Quarter. Since childhood he hadn't been able to predict his boss man's moods or desires. Perhaps he still wanted revenge for being pushed into the river, or for being put off Vanity's boat for cheating. The Pearsons were long on memory.

Whatever the motive, there was no kindness or mercy in it. Vanity was in danger, and Quarter didn't know how to protect her. All he could do was wait.

Inside Jules Pearson's suite hung the familiar pall of tobacco smoke. Along the nearest wall of the anteroom stood a French walnut credenza aglitter with crystal decanters.

Throaty male laughter came from beyond the fringed portieres hanging in the archway between the rooms. Vanity made her entrance, her skirts rustling, and paused in the doorway as each man looked up. "Gentlemen, good afternoon," she said in her most sultry voice. "May I join you?"

At once Jules's guests were on their feet, falling over themselves to help her find a chair.

Since she'd last seen him, Jules Pearson's sharp, insolent face had filled out, giving him an indulged decadent air Vanity found unappealing. But at thirty, with dark curly side-whiskers and the pencil-thin moustache above a mouth that could be very appealing, he was an attractive man.

He wore a snug cutaway coat with a ruffled silk shirt, and trousers, as always, accentuating his manhood in a startlingly vulgar manner. "Miss Blade, my guests. Gentlemen, may I present Miss Vanity Blade, late of

Albany." His left eyebrow lifted and he drawled, "I hear you found your way to the burlesque stage, Miss Blade."

She nodded. "You were good to send such lovely flowers. They reminded me so of the South, I had to come back for a visit."

"And how good of you to grace me with your attentions," he said, smiling at her with those mocking eyes. "Each time I see you, you have grown more beautiful."

She nodded her thanks, wondering just what he expected now that she was there.

Quickly the conversation turned to her recent performances in Albany. Each man insisted she sing for them, then and there, but she declined. "Perhaps another time," she said, fixing her gaze on Jules. "Might we play a few rounds? It's been quite some time for me. Would you indulge me?"

The gentlemen around the table were only too eager to consent. She accepted a tumbler of Kentucky sour mash and nursed it through the first of several tentative hands while watching to see just how straight Jules kept his private games. Unless he had invented tricks Maxxmillon Blade had not known and taught her, Vanity concluded after an hour that Jules was dealing and playing fair.

They played two hours before Vanity grew hungry enough to suggest a recess and a light meal in the dining room. "Let's eat here," he said, only too pleased to order Royal Poinciana Pompano with shrimp stuffing. The fish was served with a cream sauce and marinated French cucumbers.

Afterward, Jules accompanied Vanity on a tour of his new boat.

They were running at quarter speed, in no hurry to reach their destination. Dusk had fallen, making the river look gray. The banks were shrouded in mist. When they paused at the bow and looked upriver, Vanity was very aware of Jules. She had wondered if she would feel attracted to him.

"I'm intrigued to think you came so far at my invitation, Vanity," Jules drawled. "I thought you didn't care for my company."

Vanity tilted her head and smiled. She watched the effect her beauty had on him, and she felt satisfied he was in her thrall. "Your behavior hasn't always been that of a gentleman, Mr. Pearson. Perhaps I hoped you had mellowed as you gained maturity."

"And have I?" he asked, moving closer so that she could see his black eyes moving over her, taking in her bosom, her diamond earbobs, and her gold necklace.

"Perhaps. Why did you invite me here?" she asked.

"Shall we say I was unable to put your considerable charms from my mind? If I have mellowed enough to suit you, might I hope that you would smile on me in more than a practiced way?"

"Practiced! I'm insulted!" she said, embarrassed to be discovered play-acting with him. He was more astute than she gave him credit for.

He bowed. "I most humbly beg your pardon." As he straightened, his breath brushed her lips. "I simply expect more than the usual flirtations from my women."

"Your women! Oh, my, we are vain!"

"Indeed, we are." He chuckled. "You came in such haste. That tells me I'm something more than an amusement."

Realizing he was right, Vanity turned away.

"You're very lovely when you're demure, Miss Blade. What an asset to be a woman and play the coquette when it suits you. Look at me. Why did you come?"

She met his eyes squarely, deciding he was so utterly vain that to him the truth would sound like an expert lie. "I was bored. And I needed to escape the attentions of a gentleman who did not accept 'no' very well. When your card came, the idea of returning south struck me. Naturally, I would acknowledge your invitation. You're hardly a forgettable man."

His mouth tightened into an unsettling smile. She thought momentarily that he was angered, but then he took her shoulders and stared into her eyes. He was memorizing her face, looking hungrily, speculatively, at her lips. She hadn't been kissed by a real man in far too long. She began tingling all over.

He lowered his face to hers and lightly brushed her lips with his. She expected a response, but oddly it was not arousal but a welling of denial that made her draw away. In spite of her physical needs, she could not stand to kiss Jules or any other. She would never love anyone but Trance! She had been a fool to think she ever could.

But she was alone now, and her body longed to be touched. Jules was, perhaps, one of the only men other than Trance who had ever stirred her. Why, now, did he frighten her so?

His lips closed more possessively over hers. The moist river air caressed her cheeks and throat. The river water slapping the hull far below made her hope she might regain a fraction of the happiness she'd known with Trance.

But when Jules's arms closed around her, and his body arched against hers, she knew that though he aroused her still, she could not yet be intimate with a man.

She pulled away and gave him a practiced smile that would have worked on any other man. "Perhaps we should resume our game."

"You're a good gambler," Jules said, his voice thick.

She knew he was aroused, and she felt vulnerable. "I learn most things quickly."

"You'd be a credit to any man. May I be so bold as to ask why you haven't married?" He guided her back along the gangway toward his suite.

"I'll tell you what I've told all the others."

He chuckled, his tone once again suave and beguiling. "Oh, do."

"I'm waiting for one very special man. When I meet him, I'll know him, because he'll be the one to give me what I desire most."

"I do believe I must know what that is!"

"True love."

"Ah." Jules sighed, smiling. "The lady is a romantic."

"No, I'm practical."

"Perhaps you're not so unique as I first thought."

"I am—among the women you know who gamble and play by their own rules. I settle for nothing less than what I want. Do you play by the rules, Mr. Pearson, or do you bend them a little?"

Jules grinned as he swept her into the suite and planted a playful kiss on her lips. "I, my lovely, cheat when it suits me. I'm not an honest man. If I were you, I would not trust me any further than you can see me. I'm said to be a man of mysterious moods. You would do well to take yourself from here, the sooner the better. You think you're very clever, but darlin' Miss Blade, if I so desired, I'd have you for breakfast."

She regarded him from under lowered lids. Her tone was soft, her lips pouting. "I'm terribly frightened, Mr. Pearson."

"So you should be. For now you can play the tease, but later perhaps you should be more careful. Allow me to tell you when I'm in the mood for your games."

She went on gazing at him, her expression having an uncontrollably erotic effect on him, one he could not act on now that they had rejoined his guests.

"I'll be so very careful, Mr. Pearson."

She saw a muscle twitch almost imperceptibly in his jaw. Vanity seated herself, smiled at each man in turn, locking eyes with each for a second of intense personal contact. She heard Jules's voice grow strained as he began the first round.

He might have her for breakfast, she thought, but she would serve him up for tea!

Fourteen

As the clock neared midnight and the suite emptied of players, Jules called for another recess. He slipped out, his eyes dark, his mouth set in a hard line, his thoughts clearly elsewhere.

Claytie Tullis, one of Jules's guests, offered Vanity his arm and led her out onto the gangway for a breath of air. "It's dark as the inside of the devil's heart out here," the man said and chuckled at his wit. He stroked his side-whiskers that met up with his moustache, making him look as if he were wearing a muffler under his nose. "Yes, indeedy, it is some kind of dark out here, all right."

"Tell me what brings you to the Mississippi and the *J. J. Pearson*," Vanity said, stifling a yawn. She went to the railing to breathe in the heavy river air.

Jules Pearson was proving to be a formidable opponent; she hadn't won a hand in two hours. She wondered if she ought to retire, but that would be admitting defeat.

The gentleman from Georgia chattered on and on about his strained circumstances since the war, and the loss of his wife to a marauding Yankee. He overcame his emotion the moment he thought Vanity's lack of attention meant his story had grieved her.

"I do believe I see our host on his way back already," Mr. Tullis said, disappointed that he hadn't had more time alone with the beautiful Vanity Blade.

Vanity turned to see Jules step out of the darkness of the forward gangway. When he looked down at her, his lips curled into something resembling a smile. As he strode into the suite, leaving her alone with Mr. Tullis, he glanced back, as if looking for something beyond the railing.

Vanity looked, too, but saw only the black river. The boat began slowing as fog swallowed the banks. Within a few minutes the boat was enveloped. Their only safe course would now be to edge toward the shore and tie up; otherwise, they'd risk bottoming out on a sandbar,

184

or snagging.

Mr. Tullis patted Vanity's hand. "Pardon me if I'm speaking out of turn, my dear, but I've been asking myself why a lovely woman like yourself with a reputation to protect would indulge in the masculine pastime of poker playing."

She lifted her eyes, bestowing the gentleman with one of her sweetest smiles. "I simply have an inclination for the sport of chance and enjoy pitting my wits against fine minds. Men who gamble are surely the most clever of their sex, wouldn't you agree, Mr. Tullis?"

Delighted with her flattery, he squeezed her shoulder, "Call me Claytie, Miss Blade!"

"Shall we rejoin Mr. Pearson?"

"I must confess to being a bit weary, my dear. I don't suppose I could interest you in a little private conversation in my cabin. I have a rather fine French Bordeaux in my possession. It deserves someone very special indeed to appreciate it." He pressed against her side.

"You're very kind, but…"

"I confess, too, that I don't care much for the way Mr. Pearson plays." He edged toward the suite where they could look in and watch Jules dealing. "He's a changeable man, and he's been known to cheat."

"I know," Vanity said and smiled. "I've been watching every hand he's dealt, but so far everything has been from the top. Of course, a clever man like yourself already knows that."

"What an exciting creature you are, Miss Blade! But lookie there. He's not dealing off the top now." He gave her shoulder another squeeze and pointed.

Jules brought a face card from the bottom of the deck in the same clumsy manner she'd seen years before. She gave Mr. Tullis's arm a friendly pat. "I hope you sleep well. If Mr. Pearson has changed his tactics, I'd best sharpen my wits. Good night."

The gentleman stared admiringly at her. "I should like to watch."

"By all means."

Together they strolled back into the suite and resumed their seats. Jules gave Vanity a look that chilled her, then smiled wickedly. "Shall we continue?"

"Indeed," she said sweetly. "I never quit until I'm clearly the winner."

Jules's eyes did not warm to her playful challenge, although he did go on smiling. His black eyes raked her throat and bare shoulders as if he meant to rape her there on the table. Vanity felt as if she'd stepped in street droppings.

What was he about? she wondered. He frightened her, and this made her angry. If he had stirred her before, he failed to do so now. To invite her there, make her wait on the wharf, kiss her, and now…if his purpose was only to make her a fool, she just might play to win his boat.

Taking her seat, she played her first hand into a straight and won the pot with ease. Jules appeared startled to see her do it, and so did the other gentlemen.

Straightening, Jules dealt again. She played with determination, knowing her greatest asset was her distracting beauty and apparent innocence.

The longer they played, the more determined she became to see if she could, indeed, win Jules's boat. At dawn when one of her hands proved to be a full house, she won an enormous pot that sent the last of the night's players away to their cabins, clearly disgruntled.

By ten that morning, while the boat was still enveloped in a white shroud of fog and drifting near the shore, Vanity and Jules continued playing, enjoying no casual banter now but dealing and betting with a seriousness that sent whispers of excitement among the bored, impatient passengers.

By noon Vanity was exhausted, but Jules seemed willing to continue, although she had caused his stacks of chips to dwindle.

They took another brief break at three in the afternoon. Shaking with fatigue, Vanity changed into the cream silk and her finest pearls, and sat nodding as Elsa revived her hairstyle. If Elsa spoke, Vanity was too tired to remember. She knew only that she had decided to win Jules's boat, and win it she would.

Jules spent some minutes at the railing as if trying to see through the wet, clinging white fog before reentering the suite. He was obviously preoccupied, and his game continued to deteriorate. Vanity read his brooding expressions with ease, calling and folding when necessary until Jules had very little resources left.

Several more gentlemen had joined them in the suite, adding new resources to the stakes. And other men had come in, hoping to find a seat when the current players grew weary.

All talk aboard the boat centered around the game and the fog that was keeping them from their destination. Passengers who had been occupied with games in other cabins stopped in occasionally to comment on the young beauty—a burlesque singer from Albany—who was trouncing Jules Pearson at his own game.

During the remainder of the afternoon and on into the evening, whenever Vanity playfully suggested they end the game with her the winner, Jules shuffled anew, saying, "We're here to play," with a look that said he would make her very sorry she had bettered him.

By eight that evening, Vanity's wits were dulled, but still she won more often than any gentleman seated at the table.

The game was twenty-four hours old, and the riverboat drifted with the current, the paddles still, the boilers hissing with steam only in the event they neared something to be avoided. The fog was so thick that one could not see the bow from the stairs.

Vanity felt as if time had stopped, that her life had become this endless game. The pile of chips and markers from various gentlemen who had been forced from the game was heaped before her. She idly stacked everything in thousand-dollar piles.

Jules's boat was worth roughly twice what she had won so far, but she was now in a clear position to get it. She had cash reserves in her cabin, and was good for substantial markers to her bank in Albany. A number of those markers were already among her winnings, since she had lost to Jules at first.

Vanity refused all drinks, preferring not to muddle her thoughts. "We might eat a little supper, though, if you please, Mr. Pearson," she suggested at nine.

The eager gentlemen who wanted to engage her in something other than the loss of their hard-earned money agreed. "We can adjourn for an hour."

She patted her throat with her hanky. "If Mr. Pearson insists."

Jules shook his head. His damp hair fell into his eyes. His jaw had darkened with stubble, and the light in his eyes was almost feral.

In the past several hours he had grown jittery, starting at every sound on the gangway, and watching the door as if expecting someone.

Nervous, Vanity tried to win the friendship of the gentlemen she was defeating, in the event that Jules drew the pearl-handled derringer tucked in his waistband.

Supper was brought in but they didn't stop; they ate while playing. The cabin grew stifling. Men retired from the game only to take up a place behind Vanity. She could hear their whispers, indicating they saw Jules produce a stray card now and again.

That Vanity didn't challenge his cheating, and continued to win, only piqued everyone's interest.

At midnight, Vanity trembled noticeably. She defeated the remaining gentlemen with four of a kind, convinced the game was at last over. She felt profusely grateful as each man rose and bowed to her, murmuring admiration for her astounding skill.

Jules dealt again.

She moved to stand. Jules's hand shot out, catching her wrist in a grip that hurt her.

"We are not done yet, Miss Blade."

Wearily, Vanity took up her hand. The symbols on the cards swam before her eyes. She went on staring at them, and then like that eerie, menacing fog, she sensed a queer energy emanating from the admiring men behind her. She focused on a queen-high royal flush.

Adrenaline leaped through her veins.

She straightened. It was the nearly undefeatable hand she needed to end the game! Surely, Jules had dealt it to her. He likely had a royal flush of his own.

She raised her weary eyes, looking for a sign that Jules was aware of her hand. His lips were white, his face gray, his eyes flickering constantly from his cards to the door. He had begun to sweat.

The men gathered behind him had expressions of unremarkable interest, but they showed curiosity about the suddenly electrified men behind Vanity.

Vanity bet timidly at first, testing Jules to determine his degree of faith in his cards. He saw her watching him, narrowed his black eyes, and bet as recklessly as he had all evening.

"I do believe you've given me something to work with this time," Vanity murmured as she called his bet and raised enough to take all that he had remaining before him, which was a considerable amount.

He hesitated, glanced at the door, drew a deep breath, then let it out slowly as if avoiding a sigh of exasperation. He looked as if his teeth were clenched and aching.

The hair on the back of Vanity's neck prickled. He appeared to be listening! She watched his eyes widen ever so slightly. At once his facial muscles relaxed as if he had thought of something, or heard something he had been expecting since the afternoon before.

Vanity listened, too, hearing nothing but footsteps along the gangway as passengers strolled about. Perhaps those footfalls had a certain sinister quality about them, fading as they did when nearing the door to the suite. She expected, if she turned, to find a throng watching from every available inch behind her.

Abruptly, Jules pushed his remaining winnings forward into the center of the table. He twisted a diamond pinkie ring from his left hand and tossed it into the pile. Then he pulled the gold-nugget stickpin in his wilted cravat and tossed that in, too.

Finally he fixed his bottomless black eyes on her and waited, eyebrows raised in a clear dare.

With remarkable calm, Vanity met his bet and raised. The pot was hers. The game was hers. It was now only a matter of moments before she put Jules Pearson, Esquire, in his place.

Jules scribbled out an I.O.U. marker and, as if it meant nothing, tossed it into the pile. He grinned, tensed and waiting on the edge of his chair, raising her bet.

She raised again.

Jules's eyes bored into her. He took out his pocket watch and studied its face a long while. He seemed to be thinking, or waiting. "Might I retire to my cabin long enough to replenish my reserves?"

The hubbub behind her proved negative. "The little lady wasn't granted rest at dinner," someone said.

Abruptly, Jules dropped his watch onto the pile, a Juergerson worth nearly a thousand dollars. As an afterthought, he added his silver derringer.

Tingling but undaunted, Vanity raised with a flair for the dramatic; she rose ever so slightly from her seat, bending over her winnings just enough that her bosom was displayed like fine porcelain. Pile by pile she pushed every last bit of her winnings to the center of the table.

The men gasped.

With exquisite care, Vanity removed her earbobs, necklace, and bracelets. She tugged a tiny gold watch from a hidden pocket in her skirt and placed everything on top of the pot.

When she was done, she tilted her face, almost as if offering her lips. "I wouldn't be troubled at all if you retired to your cabin for more cash, Mr. Pearson, but only if you also bring the papers for this fine boat. I believe I have raised you so much that the only item you have left to call my bet is the *J. J. Pearson* itself." She gave him her sweetest, most delightful smile. "I would accept that."

Except for the murmur of voices coming from other suites and the sound of banjo music emanating from the grand saloon, the night seemed to have stopped.

Jules stood. Eyes unfocused, he swayed toward her. Then without speaking, he swung away and staggered from the suite, jerking the door open as if he expected someone to be waiting on the other side.

Vanity sank into her chair and accepted a whiskey.

She gazed with a sense of accomplishment at the mountainous pot waiting in the center of the table. A gentleman touched her arm. "Someone's calling you, Miss Blade."

She twisted to look.

From the gangway door, Quarter anxiously waved to her to come out, his face wild.

Her heart skipped a beat, but before she could stand, he was thrust aside, the sound of the blow and a grunt evident to all in the cabin.

Jules filled the doorway.

He glared at her with supreme contempt. He closed the door, a nasty smile playing at the corner of his mouth. Striding into the suite, he sat and took up his cards.

Vanity looked for evidence of a weapon, certain he had returned to kill her. Though he still seemed to be waiting, it was now as if he knew that which he waited for had arrived. He gazed with casual interest at the heap of chips, markers, and jewelry piled in the middle of the table.

Then he locked eyes with Vanity, taking in the rapid rise and fall of her bosom. "If I place the papers for my boat on the table to call your bet, Miss Blade, I do believe the amount is in excess of your raised bet. Do you agree?"

"I don't know the value of your boat, sir," she said sweetly. "I have only a few baubles left in my cabin to make up the difference. If you'd like, I'll get them, but in my case, I do believe I have the winning hand...sir."

He smiled coldly. "I was not suggesting that you offer up your jewels to equal the price of my boat. Might I make myself plain, then?" He nodded when she agreed.

He opened the papers, making a cursory show of them to the men watching, proving they were, in fact, the papers of ownership for the *J. J. Pearson.*

"Let us say that if you have the winning hand, ownership of my riverboat and all its contents shall become yours. If, on the other hand, I have the winning hand, my boat will remain mine. The contents of this pot will become mine, including...yourself."

She lifted her chin. Her curls fell back, exposing the length of her unadorned throat and the bareness of her squared, white shoulders. "By myself, you mean...me?"

"I think my meaning is clear to every person in this suite. If you like, I can be more explicit."

She never took eyes off him. She knew she had the winning hand. "Very well, Mr. Pearson. I accept the terms."

With nearly imperceptible hesitation, he placed the boat's papers on the table. "I see your bet and raise that small remaining value I spoke of."

"I call," Vanity said, her voice strong, every trace of weariness gone from her body.

For more than five seconds silence rang loud in the suite.

Before either of them could display their hands, however, a gunshot pierced the stillness.

A woman in a nearby cabin shrieked.

Every man lunged toward the door. The sound of running footsteps on the gangways outside and on the lower deck sounded like thunder. Several more shots rang out.

The suite erupted in chaos. Men burst in from the gangway, flooding the anteroom and crowding around and behind Vanity. The table tilted, spilling everything into her lap. She was lifted from her chair, and by then she could see the intruders wore flour sacks over their heads. Their mingled odors were rank, their attire that of beggars and thieves.

Squawking with surprise, she was dragged to her feet. A hand closed over her breast. She shrieked and fought, hearing poker chips rain down on the carpet. Two more shots were fired in the suite.

Someone across the suite slumped into the arms of Mr. Tullis, blood welling from the place he clutched on his shoulder.

The acrid smell of smoke filled her nostrils.

A pistol pressed hot against Vanity's cheek. "No trouble from you, girlie. Come along!"

She cried, "I won't!"

She erupted with flailing arms, but a flour sack was thrown over her head, blinding her with dust. Her arms were twisted back, thrusting her bosom forward. She heard someone's muffled words: "Gather up that there fortune, if you please, gents! And then be so good as to empty up yer pockets."

Vanity felt herself being pushed. "I won't go!" she shouted through the sack.

One of the river pirates stumbled sharply against her, pressing his fist into her belly in a mock blow. "I think you will!"

She thought it sounded like Jules speaking. "I won that hand! The money's mine!" she shouted.

She was dragged through the anteroom and thrown forward. Pitching headlong, fearing she would fall over the railing, she crashed into a support post and was knocked senseless.

When she came to, she was again pinioned from behind, her bosom again thrust forward. Then fingers cut into the taut neckline, tearing it, nearly baring her.

When someone gathered up her ankles, she was lifted and trundled face-up down the gangway to the stairs. The sack fell back over her face, finally dropping behind her as she was handed from one group of hands to another aboard a small dirty keelboat that waited alongside the *J. J. Pearson*. It had no running lights, and it looked like little more than a shadow drifting in the thick blanket of fog.

She had only an instant to see the hem of a pair of fine woolen trousers and well-buffed kid shoes before she was struck from behind.

She lay stunned on the deck. Her hair had come free of the pins and was tossed in a tangle about her shoulders. The front of her dress was torn from neckline to waist, leaving her snowy corset cover exposed, and one breast bared.

The darkly clad, ragged men scuttled about, throwing aboard their dark craft all the loot taken from the *J. J. Pearson*. Then they all leaped aboard. A man from the side-wheeler shot into the fog, but instantly three of the river pirates retaliated, peppering the big boat with pistol shots.

Then they were shoving off, drifting away into the white, with nothing to give them a bearing save the direction of the current. The men poled into the murky whiteness, finally jerking the sacks from their heads to reveal shaggy hair and beards. All save one.

The fog rolled over them. Vanity lay still on the wet deck. When she stirred, she was lifted and carried by the one in kid shoes. Later she would remember his softly hissed words: "I *never* forget an insult."

Fifteen

Vanity awoke to darkness. She was lying on her back, her wrists bound together above her head. Somewhere nearby she heard what sounded like mice scratching. She heard no lapping water, but felt herself on solid ground, perhaps on a thin mattress.

As she listened, spritely piano music came from nearby, and from far away she heard the mournful whoop of a paddle-wheeler. She stifled her fear, trying to understand what had happened, and what she could do about it.

Twisting and jerking, she found she could not bring her arms into a more natural position. With her head throbbing, she managed to roll onto her stomach and get herself into a kind of sitting position. Her wrists were tied with coarse rope to an iron dray pin driven deep into the ground.

At the sound of a key turning in a padlock, Vanity tensed. She had to keep her head if she expected to survive this captivity.

A slice of binding yellow lamplight slanted across what appeared to be a one-room shed with an earthen floor. A man wearing kid boots, fine woolen trousers, and a white silk shirt open at the throat stooped to enter. A flour sack with eye holes burned into it covered his head.

He stood for a long time just looking at her and chuckling softly. She felt vulnerable and afraid, but she stuck out her chin, determined not to show it.

He kicked the door closed. It bounced against the frame and opened again, admitting enough light to outline the man's silhouette. He had broad shoulders and powerful arms.

Her fists ached. "Just what do you think you're doing with me?" she asked calmly.

Without ceremony, he seized her ankles and wrenched her onto her back again. Partially straddling her, he tore away the last fragments of her corset cover, completely baring her breasts.

She gasped. "A…a man with shoes as fine as yours shouldn't have to resort to rape!" she said sarcastically. If, indeed, he meant to rape her, there was precious little she could do to stop him.

His hands were sharp and cruel on her breasts. He leaned heavily on her, rubbing his sack-covered face against hers. "A woman as beautiful as you shouldn't flaunt herself so."

With a growl of impatience, he tore off the mask and smeared her face with lips that tasted of whiskey. Despite the faint light, she still couldn't see his features.

"Y-you're a miserable excuse for a man. You'll be sorry you took Vanity Blade prisoner!"

"Shut up!" he hissed and slapped her.

The pain was stunning, and her bravado wilted.

His determined fingers were just finding their way deep within the tangle of her skirt when the door swung wide.

Another shadowy figure plunged in. She caught a glimpse of grasping hands as she closed her eyes and squirmed.

"Goddammit! You'll damned well wait for my go-ahead!" someone with a drawl shouted.

Vanity bucked beneath her attacker. "Just get him off me!"

The second man lunged, dragging her attacker away. His boot grazed her side painfully. The men fought, and one stumbled across her, crushing her.

"You'll do it my way!" one hissed, jerking the other one up and punctuating his words with sickening body blows.

At last one man dragged the other from the shed and pushed him headlong into the brightness beyond the door. Then for a long moment he stood bent over in the doorway.

Vanity didn't know which man had prevailed. She couldn't speak.

He rubbed his bruised jaw. "I expect you to remember this." Then he was gone.

The key turned in the lock. Vanity sagged back, panting, not wanting to weep. But she was overcome. What was a captive to do but wait for the next chance?

When next she awoke, it was dawn. Pale light, swirling with dust, slanted from a small window behind her. She lay with her numbed arms twisted back. Her stomach growled.

Sighing with exasperation, she wondered if she'd have to wet herself if someone didn't soon tend to her needs. She tugged at her bonds until her wrists and ankles burned, and finally she lay still, listening and waiting.

When she thought she couldn't wait another moment and would wet herself, an odorous woman in a frumpy flowered-silk dressing gown unlocked the door and entered, groaning and heaving a weary sigh. One look at Vanity and she laughed harshly.

"Ain't we pretty! Ain't we, though! Need to piddle, do you? I figured as much. Lay still there or I won't oblige you."

Vanity watched the woman waddle around the mattress. Vanity figured the woman to be about thirty and of mixed blood. Wheezing, she crouched, tied a grimy handkerchief over Vanity's eyes, and undid the ropes attached to the stake.

Stumbling along with the woman, Vanity was led out and down a shadowy corridor to a plank door leading to a muddy, barren yard. The privy was a horrid place. Vanity was relieved when she came out, but when she tried to break free and run, the woman cuffed her smartly about her blindfolded face.

"Damned little mivvy. You won't be running off from ol' Atty, you won't. Keep a cool head or you'll be dead before night."

"I'll be out of here faster than—"

"Ah, girlie, shut yer face! I'll take none o' yer guff. Inside with you!" She shoved Vanity back into the hall, then nudged her all the way back to the shed, where she sent Vanity headlong onto the mattress and reattached Vanity's bonds to the iron stake.

When the woman started out the door, Vanity called to her. "Wait! Don't go yet! Tell me why I'm here. How long will I be kept?"

Saying nothing, the woman snickered and disappeared, then returned with some surprisingly good-smelling gumbo in a chipped china soup plate. "Eat up before I take it away. I know how to keeps prisoners in line, I do."

With her dusty bare toe, the woman nudged the plate closer.

"How I am supposed to eat this?" Vanity snapped.

"When you're hungry enough, you'll figure it out."

Vanity put her face in and slurped up the food, feeling it drip down her chin when she lifted her head.

All the while the woman chuckled. "What're you doin' here? I'll tell you. You're here at the pleasure of my boss man, and he'll do whatever pleases him. Soon as he's done with you, I'll get you. And I'll treat you good, I will. Better'n him. I'll give you a clean dress, and good doctoring when you need it.

"You'll be a prize, you will, with them titties. You won't want fer nothin' in my house. I got the best place under the hill, and a good clientele. Real gentlemen from all over take up with my girls. You'll like it…if you're smart. If you're not, well, I'll get my share anyhow, and then…" She leaned close, grinning. "Boss man takes his long pig sticker and goes like that!" She thrust her hand into Vanity's belly, drawing a square. "Yer guts'll fall out. He'll fill you up with stones, and you'll see what the underside of Ol' Muddy looks like. Plain enough for you?"

Vanity's stomach rolled as she nodded.

At twenty-four, Quarter Dollar knew Natchez Under the Hill better than any place on the Mississippi. Situated along the river's edge below the tree-studded bluffs of Natchez, the dingy frame-and-brick buildings along Silver Street were as dilapidated and crude as the creatures inhabiting them.

Few trees punctuated the gaping expanse of mud where the scattered buildings stood. At the foot of Silver Street were always docked the proud beauties, the white riverboats. And, as always, the unwary passengers who chanced to spend an evening gambling or whoring at the unlovely landing more often than not returned to their packet by morning, poorer and very much wiser. If they returned alive.

No place, save Cave in the Rock to the north, was as dismal and dangerous as this one muddy, sloping street where the weather-worn shacks, saloons, and warehouses tilted drunkenly in the mud.

By day it was a quiet place, with shutters latched, dogs lazing in the sun, and crude wagons waiting for nothing at all.

By night, tinny pianos rattled while rubes from the North played three-card monte, trying to "pick the baby," carrying home whispered tales of Natchez Under the Hill, the most depraved quarter-mile on the Mississippi.

From a dark alleyway, Quarter waited for a wagonload of white men to pass before darting across the street to a broad brick building that was shuttered in the noonday heat.

Alongside the gambling "palace" ostensibly belonging to one R.D. Wannamaker, was a shed with an iron roof over the door, and a crudely lettered sign on the boarded-up front window that read KEEP OUT.

The "warehouse" belonged to his boss man and had been their

headquarters for years. Quarter knew it was no coincidence that Vanity had been aboard the *J. J. Pearson* when the river pirates robbed them. They'd come at boss man's request. It was likely that Vanity was being held in one of Atty's cellar rooms.

When he could, Quarter stayed clear of that crazy old whore. He had lost count of the number of unlucky souls boss man and Atty had let waste away in her cellar since they had taken up with each other ten years before, back when Atty still had her looks. That octaroon had always been an eager accomplice.

As Quarter had feared, his boss man hadn't forgotten how Vanity had pushed him into the river. Neither had he forgotten being put off at an isolated landing to wait and fume for two days in the heat. If Quarter didn't find Vanity and quickly arrange for her escape, she'd disappear or die.

He rounded the shed and looked in the rear window before climbing inside. He was startled to find Vanity curled on a pallet on the shed's dirt floor. Her fancy gown was in shreds, the bodice gaping. He wanted to wake her and untie her wrists, and reassure her that he'd soon have her free, but he'd never before tried to steal away one of his boss man's captives. If he failed, it would mean his life, and his mother's. He needed time to plan.

Until then, Vanity was the personal, very private property of his boss man.

Vanity awoke to the sound of movement and twisted around in time to see a shadowed figure climbing out the window. "Great snakes!" She sighed, sagging back on the mattress. She wished she was anywhere else, even back in Cold Crossing, scrubbing Submit Holloway's kitchen floor.

Overhead were cobweb-covered rafters, and to all sides were strewn heaps of trash, broken trunks, smashed crates, bundles of clothing, empty whiskey bottles, and two wagon wheels with broken spokes.

Atty was late with supper, Vanity thought, just as the low doorway swung open, admitting the man with the flour-sack mask. "Comfortable, Miss Blade?" came his muffled drawl. He plucked the sack from his head and smoothed back his mussed black hair.

Vanity went weak with surprise. "Jules! How did you find me?"

Grinning, he moved behind her. "We're not so lovely today,

are we? Were you taken in a game of poker, or did you have a run-in with river pirates?"

Suddenly she understood. "You sent for them! You didn't want me to win your boat!"

He nodded. "Excellent reasoning, my lovely." Like a conquering lord, he straddled her. "Since this is my operation, I can tell you without a doubt that you'll never leave this shed alive without my favor. If I give it, you'll have to convince me that you have some feeling for me, and be very convincin' indeed, because I've learned what a pokerfaced little bitch you can be."

"You have to let me go. It's your duty as a gentleman!"

He laughed. "I'm no gentleman! Surely you know that by now. My only duty is to myself. No one will miss you, after all. I've sent your maid on her way. I said you'd abandoned her. She was quite cross, stupid thing, said something about not gettin' paid. I suggested she take your gowns and sell them, since you had no more use for them—or her."

"Surely she didn't believe I'd do that!"

Jules smiled to himself. "Most women believe everything I say." He strolled to the window and looked out, touching the dust on the sill. He turned. "I warned you I'd cheat, and I did. I'm not the man to anger. In addition to keepin' what's mine, I now have what I wanted when I wrote you—your money. Your precious person has proved an unexpected bonus."

"Someone will find me!" she hissed.

"Pray, who?" He turned slowly and regarded her. "You seem a bit worse for the wear. Have you been fed regularly? And have you been safe?"

"You know very well I haven't!"

"Oh, did I tear your dress like that? I must've been drunk. Let me get you something a little more comfortable and accessible. One of Atty's girls must have some old chemise you can wear. I'll show you just what you're good for."

"That other man tore my clothes."

"Of course, how stupid of me." He ventured closer, watching for her slightest movement. "Are you suitably grateful, Vanity?" Crouching, he grabbed her bound ankles, straightening her legs with a jerk. Quickly he leaned over her, watching the terror flare in her eyes.

He brushed her cheek with his lips. "You taste dirty, my lovely. But I must admit, you're ever so appealing. I had no idea you could be so docile. Are you docile, Vanity?" He seized her hair and jerked her head back, exposing her throat and full bosom. "They're exquisite. May I?"

She said nothing, but kept her eyes on his. Slowly he cupped one of her breasts. Holding her breath, she endured it.

"You're not afraid?"

"Should I be? Who was that other man? Your underling? Or your partner?" she asked. "You don't seem to have much control over what he does."

His hand tightened on her breast. "Never mind him!"

She gasped as he jerked her head back and covered her mouth with a kiss. Then he was kneeling over her. Her arms were still twisted back and useless. He was so high on her chest that she couldn't breathe.

"Pleasure me, Vanity," he whispered.

"I'd rather be dead!"

The cold hard muzzle of a small pistol pressed against her temple. "Very well."

"Then shoot!" she screamed, going clammy. "If you think you have all my money, you're a fool!"

He bent over her face, opening her mouth with his finger. "Tell me. How much more money do you have?" He kissed her again.

"W-Why? Do you need it? Or are you just greedy?" she spat, her voice shaking.

He released her hair, shifting his weight to her hips. "If I ceased degrading you, would you think more kindly of me?"

Her breath went out in surprise. He almost sounded sincere. "I might. You'd expect something in return."

He chuckled. "You're so right. Do you find me attractive? I find you exquisitely so."

"No woman could help but find you attractive, Jules," she responded, trying to maintain her composure. She would say *anything* to avoid what he had wanted moments before.

"You're as good with words as you are with cards, my lovely."

He moved against her breasts, gratifying himself. At the height of his arousal, he leaned against her, his chest against her face. "I'm not fool enough to think you'll just hand me your money. But if we were married, it would be mine by rights," he whispered.

Vanity's hands curled into fists. Surely he was joking.

Moments later he stood and straightened his clothes, leaving her torso damp from his passion.

"I will not…"

He turned and aimed the silver derringer at her face.

She would have to play his game until she found her escape, she thought. "I will not…object to that," she lied, her eyes fastened on the hollows in his evil face.

Night crawled across the river, blackening the water, shrouding the dismal saloons and warehouses along Silver Street. In Wannamaker's the traffic upstairs to the many private rooms went on all night.

It was rumored that somewhere in the musty cellars, or along the rubble-strewn alleys, were places where a man might lose himself from the law. Women were sometimes held for ransom in subterranean chambers. In fifty years, untold numbers had been hidden away to keep them silent or to further some criminal cause, only to be forgotten.

Beneath Wannamaker's warehouse, owned by Jules Pearson and managed by Atty Sheehan as a bawdy house, was a warren of such cells reached by a single door and narrow wooden staircase leading from a rear hall.

Here, Atty subdued troublesome hirelings, or instructed unwilling initiates, or held businessmen who refused to pay, or who cheated her or tried to close her place, or otherwise aggravated her.

Atty was sometimes prevailed upon to incarcerate certain persons of potential value. If asked by her boss man to keep someone alive, she took the task to heart, never relenting in her personal care.

She trusted no one else to deliver the food to her charges. Each evening she made her rounds, and on this evening she had a complement of seven unfortunates. Having only six cells in her cellar, the seventh languished in the storage shed. But soon that prisoner would be moved below, there to await boss man's pleasure.

Atty gave no thought to her charges' daily comfort save for providing nourishing food. She cared nothing for their fate. Her only concern was her pay.

One such captive had brought in cash money for over a year. What his value was, she didn't know or care. But sometimes curiosity got the better of her, and she would stand at the door to his cell, listening to his endless muttering, or ranting, or sermonizing, or hymn-singing—or his disquieting silence—and wonder what he had done to live out his life in a cell known to take water to the beams when the river ran high.

On this evening he chose to remain silent. With unflagging strength he finished his exercises and then stood on tiptoes to gaze out the spattered, barred window high on the back wall of his cell.

The window was too small to squeeze through. It looked out on a rear yard where Atty's whores hung wash and went to the privy.

Three days before, Atty had led a new bare-breasted girl, her face covered with a rag, out to the privy. He stood watching for them now, flexing his arms to preserve his strength another day. He believed a moment of escape would come. Each day he stood ready, awaiting deliverance.

In the neighboring cell a man lay snoring. A tax collector, he would likely die there if no one paid for his freedom.

In the next cell was a woman who did nothing but weep and pray. He prayed for her, too, but in the sixteen months he'd been a captive in that cell, he'd heard more than one hapless girl weep—and then submit.

At times, he, too, sank into despair, but then he would try talking to those captives willing to pour out their stories. "When you get out, tell someone I'm alive!" he would always implore.

He didn't know the rest of the prisoners. Some came and went quickly. Others faded into silence. He knew one thing: Jules Pearson was a man without a shred of pity.

In the early months of his captivity, he believed himself held by Confederates. He had been dragged from the hold of the sinking *Louisette* and carted into town, supposedly to a doctor. He woke up in the cell and hadn't been out since.

In all that time, Jules Pearson hadn't deigned to visit—until a few weeks before.

"Atty tells me you've been raisin' a ruckus about gettin' out of here. I admit forgettin' what I needed you for. Remind me," the man said, ambling into the sodden cell, a pistol holding his prisoner at bay.

"You don't need me to trade to the Yankees or Confederates! Write my father for a ransom. He'll do his best! And…and Vanity might have money. I'll say nothing of this place! On my honor, as a gentleman!"

For a moment Jules Pearson had been quiet. "You need a shave, Lieutenant. Vanity, you say? What is your connection with her?"

"She's waiting in Cold Crossing, Ohio, to marry me. If anyone can raise a ransom, she can! She claims to play poker like a wizard. You might know or remember her."

Jules had nodded. "Indeed. You're speakin' of Vanity *Blade*."

His hopes flared. "Yes! Yes! Send a message in care of my father. They'll pay all they can! Just tell them I'm alive!"

Jules Pearson had smiled as he strolled away into the dimness to the stairs a few tantalizing feet away. Atty's muscled bouncers relocked the cell door, leaving Lieutenant Trance Holloway almost afraid to hope.

Trance had been waiting on the edge of his nerves since then. He yearned to return to his parents and make amends. He longed to be with Vanity again. He dreamed of the life awaiting him and prayed he hadn't placed his loved ones in danger by asking to be ransomed.

His blood sang to think that soon he might be going home again. Even if he did look like a savage, with milky-white skin and his once-proud frame gaunt, he would soon get back his color and put on some weight.

While looking out the barred window, he heard a paddle-wheeler whoop in the distance. He felt he would explode with impatience. Sixteen months of his life! If he could be alone with Jules Pearson just a few minutes...

He broke into a sweat waiting for Atty to lead her newest captive to the privy. In spite of his efforts to cast physical needs from his mind, the familiar ache of desire never left him for long. The sight of Atty's new girl had aroused him, for she reminded him of Vanity.

When he saw Atty and her charge cross the barren rear yard, his loins were at once on fire. With an angry grunt, Trance turned from the window. Dear God, if only he could go home!

Angry and frustrated, he denied himself sight of the girl and threw himself onto the pallet in the driest corner of his cell. Lately he'd been feigning weakness, hoping to lure Atty into his cubicle so that he could overcome her and escape. Hopes for a ransom were fading with each dismal dawn.

Shortly he heard her lumber down the narrow stairs, her keys jingling. She opened his door and brought in a bowl of gumbo.

"Still feeling poorly?" she clucked, not venturing close enough for him to leap up and grab her. She put the gumbo on the packed earthen floor near the door.

Then she went out, locking the door on his exasperated sigh.

Vanity was asleep when Atty came for her. After she was untied, she was jerked to her feet and stood in the yellow light that came in through the door.

"Just mind your own business and I won't have to get rough," Atty muttered, pulling Vanity roughly through the door.

"I'll be as good as gold," Vanity snipped, excited because she had not been blindfolded.

The woman yanked her down a dimly lit hall. It made Vanity think of a warehouse. At the far end was a narrow stairway. Crates of empty bottles were stacked on nearly every step.

At the top they turned into another dingy hall lined with open trunks and heaps of trash. It looked like a cheap hotel. Vanity was pushed into a plain chamber with two rusting iron beds, a dresser, and, in the middle of the room, an iron hip tub filled with steaming water scented with Indian violet.

"If you think I'm working for you, think again!" Vanity exclaimed. "I'll jump out the window first!"

Atty laughed. "Working will come soon enough. You can't get married looking like a pig!" The woman pointed to a cracked looking glass hanging next to the door.

Vanity glanced quickly at her filthy reflection before lunging toward the window. "I'm not marrying anybody, either!"

She found the window nailed shut, and shuddered to think of all the poor girls who must have hoped to jump from it, only to turn back as she was forced to do.

"Off with everything," Atty said, grinning.

Determined not to show any fear, Vanity shed her tattered clothes and sat in the tub. When she was clean and dry, she donned finely stitched underthings and allowed Atty to tie several flounced petticoats around her waist.

"Who did you steal these things from?" Vanity asked as the woman lifted a cream satin gown from a trunk in the hall.

Vanity sidled toward the open door but the woman gave her the back of her hand, and Vanity stumbled away, holding her cheek.

"Put this on, and no guff," Atty muttered. "Preacher's waiting."

Feeling trapped, frightened, and furious, Vanity struggled into the gown. When she was dressed, with a lace-edged veil over her damp chestnut waves, Atty prodded her out the door with the muzzle of a Colt revolver.

Reluctantly, Vanity inched along the cluttered hall as someone began to play the wedding march on a piano downstairs.

Through a small unpainted door they emerged into the main upstairs hall, which was decorated in gaudy scarlet plush. Oil paintings of scantily draped nymphs graced the walls.

Left facing the staircase, Vanity looked down into a bored throng of half-dressed prostitutes. Behind her were the bouncers, patting clubs into their ham-sized hands.

Vanity edged down the stairs into an assortment of frock-coated gentlemen who ogled her and made snide comments.

She must be dreaming, she thought. How could she go through with this? Beyond the foot of the stairs was the main door, and it stood open a few inches. With her eyes fixed on it, her muscles tensing to bolt for it, she was startled from her concentration when a dark-skinned man poked his head in.

With one sweep, his quick, keen eyes took in everything. Just as Vanity was going to call out his name, he put his finger to his lips. Then he slipped out and closed the door.

Quarter Dollar! Her heart leaped with hope.

Gasping for breath, her heart hammering, Vanity made her way through the gawking patrons and smirking women. On the far side of the smoky parlor stood a makeshift altar where Jules waited, wearing a white cutaway over gray-and-white-checked trousers.

The homely, pickle-faced preacher adjusted his spectacles. He glanced nervously at two bearded men holding pistols on him. "Dearly… Ladies and…Uh-h, we are g-gathered here…"

Jules held out his hand. Vanity tried to draw a breath.

"…in the sight of this…uh…company to join in…uh…matrimony this m-man and this…woman. Do you, Jules Christopher Pearson, take this woman as your lawfully wedded wife?"

Jules smiled. "I do, indeed!"

"Do you…" He leaned to the side and hissed, "What's her name?"

When Vanity didn't reply, one of the men stepped forward and jabbed his pistol against her cheek. "Talk up."

"Vanity Blade!" The muzzle pressed deeper. She winced. "M-Mary… Mary Louise Mackenzie!" Ringing filled her ears.

"Do you, Mary Louise Mackenzie, t-take this man as…your lawfully wedded husband?"

Fully supported by Jules now, she reeled.

"Say 'I do,'" the preacher prompted. "Let her speak of her own free will, sir! Do you take him as your lawfully wedded husband?"

The grip on her arms tightened. Blinding waves of pain radiated through her body. Jules shook her, his grip crushing, until she whispered so softly the preacher leaned forward and asked her to repeat: "I-I…do!"

Sixteen

Nights had always been hard for Trance. The rats were plentiful, and often when the weather was wet, he stood in water to his knees.

This night, though he was comfortable and his pallet dry, the haunting strains of a wedding march echoed from the floors above. What sort of people got married in a bawdy house? he wondered.

A few moments later, he heard someone on the stairs. He paused, listening, and backed up as footsteps stopped outside his door. The padlock rattled, and then his door creaked open, flooding his cell with blinding yellow light.

"Who is it?" Trance called, shielding his eyes.

Two of Atty's oversized thugs plunged in and seized him. One held him in a bear hug, while the other twisted a gag across his mouth. He was thrown face first into the dirt, his arms wrenched behind his back and bound.

Unable to speak, Trance twisted his head enough to see the legs of a man strolling across the pool of light. He was wearing checked trousers. Trance shut his eyes tight, bracing himself for a shot to the head.

He heard the man breathing, and smelled aromatic cigar smoke. Opening one eye, he found Jules Pearson squatted beside him, his white cutaway looking ridiculously out of place in the mud-and-timber cell.

The man lifted Trance's head by his hair and grinned. "Good evenin', Lieutenant. So sorry to wake you. We're havin' a little show upstairs I thought you might like to see."

The strains of the wedding march faded.

Atty's men jerked Trance to his feet and he was driven from the cell with dread in his heart. He stumbled up the stairs. In hopes of still escaping, he made quick note of all he saw as they pushed him up a second flight and guided him along a dim corridor lined with trash and trunks. At the far end of the hall, Jules opened a floor-to-ceiling panel two feet wide.

"I think you'll be comfortable in here. After you," Jules whispered, grinning as he helped Trance edge sideways into the narrow space. Trance wondered if the space was between false walls.

Jules entered after him, jabbing Trance's ribs occasionally with a pistol muzzle.

"Now you can just wait here quiet as a mouse," Jules hissed after they had moved in the pitch-dark for ten or fifteen feet.

Trance heard a panel sliding, and dim light illuminated the lower portion of the wall he faced.

Crouching, Jules crawled in through a low three-foot-square opening, his cutaway dusty now. He slid the panel closed, leaving Trance in the musty, utterly black space.

Trance leaned his head back until it bumped against the wall. *Think, think!* Trance said to himself, gritting his teeth and trying to breathe normally. If Jules had meant to kill him, he would have done it straightaway. This was, perhaps, the moment of escape for which he had waited four hundred eighty-two days.

Dizzy, confused, Vanity stared at the silver fountain pen in her hand. On the table before her lay a marriage certificate, and on it was her drying scrawl.

Someone supported her as Jules plucked the pen from her numb fingers and signed his own name. He kissed her cheek. "Congratulations, my lovely."

Laughter echoed all around.

They were man and wife. All she possessed belonged to Jules Pearson—her money, her body, her life. When he smiled with those faintly amused black eyes, she collapsed again, wanting only refuge from this nightmare.

She awoke, seemingly moments later, in a gaudy bedchamber with Jules standing before a huge looking glass, removing his cutaway. He untied his black cravat and tugged it from around his neck. "Care for a drink, my lovely?" He unbuttoned his trousers, his smile broadening.

Fighting voluminous skirts, she scrambled off the bed and darted for the door. Yanking it wide open, she flung herself into the dimly lit hall, where two big men, caught unaware at first, managed to break her flight and carried her back.

"Where do you want her, sir?" one asked.

"At my feet, thank you."

Vanity was dumped on the floor.

"I'm not your wife and never will be!" Vanity shouted as the door closed and was locked.

"Be good and take off that ridiculous white gown. You look like a virgin. We both know you're not."

Scrambling up, she flounced to the heavily draped window, jerked the dusty brocade aside, and found nails studded along the sash. She looked out at the darkness, wondering if Quarter could save her in time.

"Come to bed now, Vanity. Unless you prefer the shed."

She turned, finding Jules's hard, muscled body naked and aroused.

To humor him, she gathered her patience. "Perhaps a drink would help."

"Of course." He poured something and then lounged on the four-poster, holding out the tumbler. "I promise to be gentle."

Taking several unwilling steps, she faltered. "Where does that other door lead? I don't want to be w-watched."

He swung his arm wide. "Satisfy your curiosity."

Trying not to hurry, she crossed the dark, musty chamber and yanked open the paneled door. Inside, a globe lamp on a mirrored dressing table was turned low. A rack of suits and dresses stood across the way opposite a divan. A hip tub heaped with laundry stood in one corner.

Dashing in, she flung the door closed but found no key in the brass plate. Racing to the far corner, she thumped recessed panels, listening for hollow ones, hoping to find a secret door. No bawdy house patron cared to be trapped in a dressing room during a raid, she thought...

Hearing a chuckle, she whirled and saw Jules standing in front of the rack of clothes. She was certain she had not heard him come in. He had thrown on a white silk dressing gown that accentuated his swarthy coloring. His suit lay in a heap nearby, and that confused her because she was certain he had undressed in the other room.

"Jules, if you have any honor, don't do this to me!"

He stubbed out his cigar on the scrap of carpet. "Honor, sweets?" His black eyes were so utterly cold he looked suddenly ugly and remorseless.

"Let's go back in the other room," she said softly, faint with terror. She would say anything now to delay him.

"Let's not," he said, lunging and catching both her wrists in a biting grip. He pushed her backward onto the divan.

His mouth came down on hers so savagely she couldn't catch her breath. Then her gown was tearing. She felt mashed as he thrust his weight against hers, pinning her thrashing arms and legs. When she bit him, he reared back, patting his torn lip.

She saw his fist…and knew nothing more.

Paying the grizzled ex-slave to wait, and praying the old man wouldn't lose heart and pole away on the only raft to be found at that hour, Quarter pounded up the bank, back toward the scattered buildings, noise, and lights of Natchez Under the Hill. Darting between buildings, he dashed across the dusty street, the humid night air clogging his lungs. He stifled the urge to cough.

If he was lucky, fog would cover the river in another few minutes. If he was very lucky, he'd have Vanity out of Wannamaker's in time to lose her—and himself—in the mist.

This was his last-ditch effort. Taking Vanity from his boss man would mean the end of the line for him. No more selling stolen goods along the river. No more rowing to and fro, taking boss man to towns and riverside estates to do his midnight thieving. If Quarter got caught, there was no telling the death boss man would dream up for him, and for his mother, who was back on the Pearson plantation.

But if he got away clean, he might leave the river forever and start a new life.

He squirmed in through the shed window and moved noiselessly to the door opening onto the rear hall of Atty's bawdy house. He found everything ominously quiet, as if it were already too late.

The door to the cellar stood open, and he found that disquieting. He didn't go down, though he would have liked to free the unfortunates wasting away below. If the door was open, however, Atty or one of her brainless thugs was surely there.

Silent as a shadow, he slipped up the narrow, cluttered stairs and paused to make sure the upper hall was deserted. Then he tugged the pocket pistol from his waistband, reassured himself it was loaded, and moved fast down the hall to the place in the wall where a panel opened to the false wall along the main bedchamber. His boss man had slipped in and out of there many a time, as did countless other patrons.

He pressed the panel open, edged inside, and pulled it shut. Scuffing sideways, he suddenly felt the hair on his scalp prickle. "I get the distinct feeling I'm not the only fool in this hell of a place," Quarter whispered.

He heard something, reached out his left arm, and inched farther along. He touched a sleeve, then felt the person flinch. Patting his way up the shoulder to the bearded neck and cheek, he felt the twisted piece of cloth in the person's mouth.

"Sweet Susie! Have they taken to leaving folks in here to die? Seems it'd stink up the place more than ever." Shaking, Quarter tugged a folding knife from a concealed pocket along his trousers seam and cut away the gag. "Please don't yell out, or you and me will never see the light of day again."

The grimy gag came away in Quarter's hand.

"Quarter! It's me!" Trance hissed, pressing against his friend and whispering a few vital details of his captivity since the time when Quarter had saved his life on the *Louisette*'s deck.

Quarter went cold. Stunned and horrified, he finally silenced Trance. "We got all the time in the world for that later. Promise me you'll stay right here…" He began sawing at the rope binding Trance's wrists together. "I'm trying to save a friend in there. No matter what you hear, don't stick your nose in. We'll all get away in good time, I hope."

He felt Trance nodding and then couldn't stop himself from taking time to embrace his friend.

"I'm mighty glad you aren't dead, friend," Quarter said, stooping to slide open the lower panel. "Sit tight…"

He crouched and entered the dressing room beneath a tangle of clothes hanging on a rack. He froze when he saw a man slumped on the divan, clutching his head. Seconds later, another man slammed into the dressing room and stood over the one on the divan. They were the same height, the same build. One was naked, and the other wore a disheveled white dressing gown.

Quarter cringed as the naked one doubled his fist and struck, sending the other sprawling.

"By God! You'll do it my way or this time I'll kill you!"

Quarter's blood ran cold. He hated his boss man more than any two creatures on God's earth. They were a murderous pair, had been since they were small boys on the plantation dressed in identical velvet-and-lace suits, wearing fancy little curls and all the while inflicting the most exquisite torture on their slave Quarter Dollar. That Quarter shared their daddy's blood only made them hate him more. He wished the twins would murder each other and be done with it.

Backing out, he patted Trance to reassure him, then crept along the secret passageway to another panel leading to the adjoining room.

Emerging in darkness beside the four-poster bed, he found Vanity sprawled across it, unconscious. Before he could drag her out through the hidden panel as he had hoped to do, his boss man—in the darkness he didn't know if it was Jules or Jock—yanked open the dressing room door.

Quarter had only enough time to slip his pistol beneath the pillow cushioning Vanity's head. He eased himself back into the darkness behind the sliding panel and drew it closed as Jules or Jock strolled to the foot of the bed and looked down on her.

Vanity awoke in the dark, lying on the bed, wearing only her underthings. Naked again, Jules paced at the foot of the bed.

"You said you'd be gentle," she whispered, her jaw swollen where he had slugged her in the dressing room.

"In time you'll understand, Vanity," he whispered. He placed his drink on the nightstand, then sank to the bed beside her. "Let me show you how I meant for it to be."

Leaning over her, he kissed her with cold, tense lips. His moustache bristled against her tender upper lip. With exaggerated care, he lifted her bound wrists and placed them above her head. She snatched at the pillow, wondering if she could endure what was going to happen. Her fingers brushed something metallic and cold beneath the pillow.

Her pulse raced.

Jules explored her with expertise, burying his face between her delicious breasts. She was holding her breath as she gathered the small pistol into her shaking hands. Could she commit murder to prevent rape?

"I hear your heart hammering. Do you want me, Vanity?" Jules whispered.

Her arms felt wooden. She tried to ease the pistol from beneath the pillow. Jules's mouth closed around her nipple, sucking until it stung. Moaning, she twisted away. He lifted his head and smiled, his tongue still toying with her nipple.

She endured kisses that trailed lower. Though her legs were locked rigidly together, he pried them apart. She felt his breath through the delicate fabric of her pantalets. Then he kissed her there...

"No!" she screamed, bringing her bound hands over her head. She took aim. The pistol muzzle was an inch from his temple. "No!"

He lifted his eyes..."Very well, my love—"

"No!"

Vanity's last memory of him was his eyes going utterly round.

She didn't consciously squeeze the trigger. She only said "No" softly, but with more emphasis, and felt a stunning, bone-splitting shock course through her arms and shoulders.

She saw a brief flare of fire and heard the deafening explosion. When she opened her eyes, Jules was slumped against her shins.

Choking with revulsion, she squirmed from beneath him. The dressing room door flew open. A man in a white dressing gown stumbled out, but he was struck from behind and collapsed to the floor.

Confused, Vanity heard shouts of alarm in the hall and the frantic rattle of a key in the lock. Someone stood over the man on the floor, raining powerful angry blows...again, again! And again!

Then Quarter straightened, gasped for breath, and finally fell over his feet lunging for Vanity. "Follow me!"

Catching hold of her wrist, he dragged her through the dim dressing room. He pushed aside the rack of clothes, exposing an opening in the paneled wall. Crouching, she crawled into darkness and felt someone take her arms and push her sideways through cobwebs.

"Drop it! Drop it!" Quarter was saying behind her.

She forced herself to release the pistol.

They burst into the narrow hall that she remembered led to the stairs. With shouts close behind, she followed a tall, bearded blond man to those stairs, tumbling down them, scattering crates of empty bottles, to the low doorway that led to the shed.

"You two go on. Head south along the bank. There's a man with a raft..." Quarter didn't wait for them to nod their understanding. He threw himself down the cellar stairs. "I'll meet you!" he shouted.

The bearded man looked momentarily confused. He stared after Quarter. Then he turned to look at Vanity in her underthings, blood spattered across her shins. His eyes widened in horror. She saw his teeth clench beneath whiskers that surely hadn't been cut in years. He looked like a beggar.

Boots thudded on the stairs behind them. If the beggar wanted to wait, he was welcome to, she thought, darting into the shed and going to the window Quarter had left open.

The beggar was close behind her, and he helped her climb through. In seconds he, too, was out.

"This way!" she hissed, pulling her camisole closed and scuttling across the street to the safety of shadows between two buildings.

Then they were running behind the buildings to the muddy barrens along the wharf. Three paddle-wheelers were tied up, smokestacks sighing. Though the man following her didn't appear weak, he seemed confused, and he loped after her.

Fog lay heavy on the river, advancing in layers against the banks. Behind them was an unnerving silence. Pistol shots rang out then, and Vanity felt sick to think Quarter might not get away.

Her bare feet pounded across dirt, pebbles, and weeds. She'd committed murder! She'd signed her name to a marriage certificate and put a bullet in a man's brain!

Murder! Murder! Murder! The word echoed in her mind with each footfall.

The shelf of silt grew narrower and narrower, finally ending in weeds and trees black with shadow. Now there was only the broad, dark river, and across it the far shore—and safety.

"There!" said the man still running behind her.

She stumbled to a stop, seeing a black man stand up from behind some brush and motion them to the water's edge, where a raft rocked gently. She gasped for breath, twisting to look back at the distant lights of the landing. She pressed both palms to her mouth to keep back her screams. Murder!

The tall, gaunt man motioned toward the raft.

"Go! I'm waiting for Quarter!"

Then they saw him, his legs pumping, his face a mask of determination. "Go!" he shouted in a high voice. "They're on my ass!"

The bearded man grabbed Vanity and flung her onto the raft. The man tending it cast off the ropes as the bearded man leaped on after her. Quarter flung himself into the shallows, pushing the raft out until he lost his footing and had to crawl aboard.

"Down!" he hissed, flattening Vanity to the damp boards. They drifted with the current until finally they were beyond the point. The lights of Natchez Under the Hill were swallowed up in the fog.

In trembling silence, they moved with the current until Quarter sat up, looking all around as if he was trying to get his bearings.

"Swee-eet Susie! What a night!" He gathered Vanity close. "Now, don't you fret yourself, missy. You can't change nothing back. It's done, and that's it." He lifted his sweat streaked face and clapped the bearded man on his shoulder. "Look here, missy. Just get hold of yourself for a little minute and look into the eyes of this creature in rags. Tell me if you haven't seen him somewhere before on this earth." Quarter flopped onto his back, panting. "I still don't believe it myself."

Holding her mouth to keep back the horror of what she'd found the strength to do, Vanity turned to the man with the angular, bearded face. Though he was filthy beyond description, his hair was a remarkably pale shade like…

She let go a shuddering gasp of pain and twisted away. Why must she see Trance in every man's face, especially one with ghastly white skin so taut over the temples and cheekbones, and the rest masked in a scraggly beard?

Then a tingling sensation started in her blood. She lifted her eyes, squinted through the darkness, leaned closer, and drew in her breath until her head was pounding. Those eyes…those dark blue eyes!

The man stared back at her, having already recognized her from Wannamaker's back hallway. His gaze swept over her, lingering on her blood-spattered feet and ankles. "Vanity, what are you doing here?"

A wail of recognition erupted from her throat. She didn't hear his question, only the gravelly tenor of his voice. She flung herself against him and felt tattered fabric covering thinly fleshed bones.

Rearing back, she looked again into those eyes. "How did you— You're not dead!"

He shook his head. "I've been a captive for sixteen months. And months aboard a riverboat before that. Do my parents think I'm dead, too?"

She fell against him, feeling his tentative touch on her arms. "I don't believe it! I can't believe it!" She sobbed for joy.

When she could finally bring herself to pull away from Trance, she began to comprehend what he'd said. "Jules Pearson had you prisoner, too?"

The conversation became fragmented, with bursts of nervous laughter and happy weeping as each tried to explain. Again and again, Vanity vowed she couldn't believe Trance was alive and in her arms.

"Look what he did to you," she said, plucking at the vestiges of Trance's uniform. She caressed his beard, ran her fingers over those features she'd known so well, and touched his mouth gently.

A tide of hate welled in her breast for Jules Pearson. She was about to say, "I'm glad I killed him!" And then the enormity of all that had happened sank in. Trance might understand that she had been forced to sign her name to a marriage certificate, but would he condone murder, even of such a one as Jules Pearson?

Seventeen

Silently, Quarter guided the raft miles downstream, gradually crossing the broad, dark expanse of water, headed for the far Louisiana shore. Well into the night, he roused Vanity and Trance. "We'll be there soon. You'll have to be quiet."

Quarter labored with the pole, gradually steering them toward a sagging wooden pier. As he poled in close, Trance caught a piling and looped a rope over it with an expert seaman's knot. He scrambled onto the rickety boards and helped Vanity up. Quarter climbed up after them, motioning toward woods.

After tramping through what seemed like swamp for a mile, they emerged along the edge of a fallow cotton field. Here the fog hung in the treetops, white and ghostly. Quarter took off at a trot, with Trance and Vanity close behind. On the far side of the field they could see the back of a plantation house perched on a rise. There, on a slight slope, were a string of once whitewashed-brick slave cabins.

Quarter went to the nearest one, tapping lightly at the door. After a few moments he was admitted, and then he motioned for Vanity and Trance to follow. "We can stay here awhile." He indicated a frail, lovely, middle-aged black woman lying in a homemade bed in the corner. "My mother, Opal," Quarter said, looking as if he was about to cry. "She says she's dying."

Forgetting the way she was dressed, Vanity went to the woman. "You have a wonderful son! He's been my best friend for years. My only friend!"

The woman patted Vanity's hand. "Thank you. You're very kind. We'll do anything we can to help you."

Vanity turned back to Trance. She felt overcome with excitement and was suddenly shivering so hard Quarter had to lead her toward a low fire burning in the hearth.

"I'll bet you both could do with a nip of good home cooked corn liquor!" he said, grinning. "Sweet Susie! It does my heart good to be here with my mama and my two fine friends!"

Vanity awoke at dawn. She had slept curled tightly against Trance's back. Now she was alone.

Hurrying from the cabin, she found him at a trough across the muddy, dawn-lit yard, shaving before a scrap of broken mirror tacked to a post.

Trance turned at her approach and smiled. He'd changed into someone's loose, tattered shirt and baggy pants, but to Vanity he looked wonderful. She slipped her arms around his chest. "This must be heaven," she whispered.

"I'm not much to look at," Trance said, having shaved most of his beard away. He studied the hollows in his cheeks, drawing his knuckles along his bony jaw. Then, as if hating the sight of himself, he lathered his face to shave again.

They had talked about Trance's captivity. Though Vanity knew Trance didn't yet understand how she had come to be a captive of Jules Pearson, he hadn't asked about it. She knew now that they were alone she'd be expected to explain.

Not wanting to destroy their happiness, Vanity moved away from Trance, wondering how she could tell him of her swift retreat from Cold Crossing, or of the intervening years on the burlesque stage. It was all so far from what she had expected to do, so terribly different from what he must have imagined her doing all the while he was captive in that cellar!

Trance turned from the mirror, watching Vanity's face cloud with her thoughts. How he loved that sweet, anxious face! Her eyes were so dark and beguiling, he felt drawn away from the shame of how he looked, and from the humiliation he felt because in all those months he hadn't managed to make his own escape.

Judas! She was more beautiful than ever. Those were the eyes he had summoned on countless sleepless nights. Those were the lips he had kissed a thousand times in his fevered imagination.

And that body he loved so...the desirable body he had begged God to make him forget...that body he had sworn never to lust after again if only he might be delivered for a single hour from bondage.

He had made such sincere promises. His stomach knotted now to think he wanted to abandon them all to be with Vanity. Every vow that he would return and make peace with his father, every fervent hope that he would make his mother proud—they all wilted and vanished in the face of his love for Vanity.

His throat constricted. He didn't want to look at her, but his eyes sought her face. He noticed an ugly bruise along her jaw—Quarter had rescued her from Jules Pearson's bed…

"Vanity!" he cried, trying with all his strength not to ask how she had come to be with that vulture. His breath came in gasps as his imagination filled with possibilities. "I thought you went to my parents…"

"I did, Trance," she assured him quickly, kissing his forehead and then his tender cheeks. "But then the message came…you were believed dead…" She shook her head. Her voice became small. "I *couldn't* stay there."

"Whose blood is all over you, Vanity?"

She was about to speak when Quarter emerged from the cabin. "Missy, we got you some clothes. Suelyn will show you where to wash. Then I got something to show you. The grits are cooking, Mr. Trance, if you're hungry."

Given a reprieve, Vanity went with Suelyn behind the cabins where she washed beneath a pipe from a raised wooden cistern filled with rainwater. Free at last from the lingering stench of bawdy house toilette water, she put on a threadbare, once-red calico dress that clung to her unbound breasts and uncorseted waist like a lover's eyes.

After breakfast, Quarter entertained them with tales of his childhood on the Pearson plantation. His best story was about a gentleman thief known as Ghost, a man said to be well born and who had plagued the residents along the Mississippi River for the past ten years.

During the afternoon, Trance and Vanity slept, recovering from the turmoil of the evening before. At dusk they ate a delightful meal of pine-bark stew rich with chunks of catfish, onions, and potatoes. Afterward, when Quarter's friends left to attend to chores, Vanity remembered Quarter had said he had something to show her.

"Don't know how I could have forgotten that." He grinned.

Leaving Trance sipping at a good wine they had dug up from the secret stores behind the big house, Quarter drew Vanity outside.

"After I show you these things, you can tell Mr. Trance. I just thought you'd like to read everything over first by yourself," Quarter said, looking excited. He plucked a battered strongbox from the doorsill outside and led her away into the evening shadows.

From inside the strongbox he took a packet of water-stained papers and handed them to Vanity.

She untied the stiff white string holding them together and unfolded the first letter. Though the text had run, the signature was Maxxmillon Blade's!

Her attention leaped. "Where did you get this?"

"Bought the strongbox off a Yankee who'd just come from the *Vanity Blade* after she was done getting fitted as a ram. You probably hadn't even started north yet!"

Vanity puzzled out two lines. "He was asking for information from someone," she said. Unfolding the next, less damaged letter, she drew in her breath. "This is the reply! From California!"

After reading half the letters, her heart was racing. "He was asking about me!" she cried, unfolding another and then another. "He never told me he was trying to find out who I was!"

The final letter left her shivering.

> ...have determined that Mary Teresa Mackenzie, her father, Sandbar Mackenzie, a former Mississippi riverboat pilot, and her mother, Louise, arrived in San Francisco harbor in 1844. Mackenzie had brought in the schooner's hold a dismantled riverboat which he later fitted for use on the Sacramento River.
>
> Weeks after their arrival, Mary Teresa disappeared and was never heard from again. Some believe she had a lover aboard the schooner.
>
> Mackenzie now owns a small freight packet...

Vanity leaped to her feet and spun around, squealing with delight. "My mother's name was Mary Teresa! Great snakes! Do you know what this means?"

Quarter nodded, his eyes warm with happiness for her. "You may have a grandpappy still alive back in California!"

Vanity threw her arms around his neck. "I'm going to find him! How can I ever thank you?"

"No need. I would've told you sooner, but I had to traipse all over creation with boss man...and when I wrote you in Ohio, my letters only came back."

She threw her head back. "That story you were telling us this morning about the gentleman thief and the river pirate headquartered in a Natchez bawdy house..."

"You were a-gazing at Mr. Trance like your brain was nothing but grits," Quarter teased.

"You were telling us about your boss man!"

Quarter nodded.

"And you were forced to help him?"

"Since I can remember."

"I wish to God I hadn't been the one to kill him," she whispered.

"He needed killing, missy."

She crushed the letters to her chest. "I've got to get away from here, don't I? I don't want to hang. And…and Quarter, Trance must never know what I've done!"

"I won't be the one to tell him, missy. Boss man's dead. H-he can't hurt either of us no more."

"I've got to leave for California right away. Trance probably doesn't have any money. I lost all mine. I'll have to win more if you don't have any put by." She saw Quarter's bewildered expression. "You're coming with us, of course!"

"Miss Vanity, I'm honored to go as soon as I've buried my ma. She won't last much longer. But I'm worried about Mr. Trance. He's a prideful man. Use your wiles and let him think up going to California for you."

"Nonsense! Trance won't want to go back to his family, not after he hears that his father disowned him and how he treated me!"

Quarter held her back. "Don't tell him too much. Not just yet. Think, missy. *Think* what it means to a man to be a captive. Don't push him. He's going off half cocked, same as you."

"I'm thinking with a perfectly clear head!" she exclaimed. "Trance will be delighted to know I've found some kin."

Moments later, Trance came out of the cabin, his eyes astonishingly blue in the ghastly paleness of his face. "What are you two whispering about?"

"Shhh! I love you! Let's take a walk!" Vanity said, drawing him away from the cabins. "Quarter, is it safe?"

"Keep to the path," he said, pointing in the direction of the river.

Moving beyond the dismal collection of brick cabins, Vanity and Trance skirted dense canebrake, following the footpath to the river.

The moon was rising huge and orange behind them. Vanity danced happily at Trance's side, her arm linked possessively with his. "I'm so happy I could cry! Give me plenty of cheer, Trance! Give me all you got!"

He pulled her to a stop and gathered her into his arms. "I don't want to hear any more bawdy songs, Vanity. I want to forget the past two years. Tell me everything you've done."

"There's time later. I've something amazing to tell you!"

"You're right." His lips touched hers tentatively. "I dreamed of you every night. Memories of you kept me alive."

"Oh, Trance!" she whispered, kissing him fervently. She twined her arms around his neck, wanting to recapture the passion and abandon they had shared those last days in New Orleans before she went north.

But Trance felt wooden in her arms, as if his bony frame shamed him, and as if he'd forgotten how to be tender.

"Love me, Trance. Love me again like you did before!"

He kissed her, his body melting against hers just a little. Finally he pulled away and buried his face in her neck. "I want to, Vanity, but there's too much I don't know." He untwined her arms from his neck and studied her face. "Why did you leave my parents?"

She sighed. "I want this to be a pleasant walk."

"Telling me why will be unpleasant?" he asked, his face in shadow.

She squirmed free and walked on ahead. She crossed her arms, feeling chilled. "I left because I believed you were dead. I had no more reason to stay. Mama wanted me to be a star, so I became one, in Albany. I sang in a burlesque theater. And I *was* a star! A very sought-after one. Are you angry?"

He ran his hands through his pale hair. The moonlight glinted on it, making it look white. He looked so like his father, she shuddered.

"I suppose it's hard for you to realize why this bothers me so," he said. "I lived on daydreams. I believed you were there with them, waiting. I imagined the four of you at the dinner table, or working together in the garden. I expected you to like Ohio, and wanted you to make my home your own, even if you thought I was dead. After so long, I knew you had to think that."

Vanity cast her eyes down. "We both know I could never have stayed there long, not in their house. You and I might've been happy in a place of our own there. You were once very unhappy with your parents. Don't you remember?"

"I was a rebellious boy! I'm a man now. A changed man."

"We can still be married! We don't need to go back to Ohio! You'd feel trapped there, just as I did, as you once did. Your father is so self-righteous—"

Trance shook his head, cutting her off. "I have to go back! I vowed that if I escaped Jules Pearson, I would go home. I'm bound by that pledge, Vanity! I have to make peace with my father."

Vanity stormed along the path. "You've been away from him too long. You've forgotten—"

Trance followed. "Listen to me! It'll be different there when we're together. We'll have our own place. We'll raise a family—"

She whirled. Everything in her screamed to say *yes,* she would go with him anywhere to have his love, but she couldn't return to Theophilus Holloway's false piety. "I won't go back!"

"I was wrong to desert my parents!" Trance shouted. "I dishonored my father and hurt my mother. I promised God to make up for those things."

Vanity gave an exasperated snort. "What if, after all your promises, you're not happy there?"

"I will be, if I have you! You can learn to like the simple life, if only you'd try!"

"Life is not so simple in Cold Crossing, Ohio, when a preacher cleanses sin from women by having sex with them!"

"That is something my father alone will have to live with," Trance said, his eyes dark with anger.

"Not if he's trying it on me!" Vanity clapped her hands over her mouth. "Forgive me! I should never have said that!"

His eyes rounded.

She turned away, unable to believe she had said such a hurtful thing. She still wanted to make love, but now surely he would hate her and turn away. "It's true," she whispered in a small voice. "I can't live near that man. If we marry, we must live somewhere else. Your father's antics are really only a small part of it. I could never tolerate a family that disowns a son, and erases the name of their daughter from the family Bible when she elopes. Family is too important for that." She raised her tear-filled eyes and nodded. "Rowena ran away, too. Trance, try to remember why you left."

Trance was shaking his head. "If family is so important, then you must know why I have to go back."

She began to tremble. Could he be right? She shook her head, not wanting to give in. "Trance, please come to California with me! For the first time since Maxx died, I have kin again! You can understand how I feel! My grandfather may still be alive! I want to find him."

Trance didn't seem to hear what she was saying about her grandfather. "You won't go home with me?" he asked softly.

"If you were...yourself, you wouldn't ask."

"I have to honor the pledges I made to God and myself. You understand that, don't you? I pledged my *life* in return for escape."

A shudder went through her as she thought of Trance languishing all those months in a cellar, not knowing if he would live or die. "I do understand, but when I tell you that your father—"

"I can't—I *can't* let that make any difference. I am honor-bound to do what I can to…to…" Trance turned away.

"Then go home, but don't try to be something you're not. I won't ask that of anyone, Trance. You shouldn't ask it of me. If you can't come to California with me, then you can't." She rubbed tears from her face. "I tried to become be a lady at school. I tried to be a scrubbed and wholesome wife in Ohio. I tried to be a…an independent woman in Albany, and got in too deep with a man who would not leave me alone. When Jules wrote, I thought I could go back to a life on the river as some kind of poker queen." She laughed at herself. "I was in the middle of another high-stakes game when Jules had me kidnapped!"

She didn't dare say anything more. She had to leave before she was arrested. Trance could never know the woman he loved had murdered her bridegroom in a bawdy house in Natchez Under the Hill!

"One thing is certain—I'm never going to Cold Crossing again, John Travis."

Calling him that had a sobering effect. "You refuse to come with me and you refuse to try living in Cold Crossing again?"

"If saying yes, I'll marry you, means pretending to be something I'm not for the rest of my days, then no, I won't marry you."

She burst into tears. This was not what she thought they would be doing alone in the moonlight.

She held her breath, praying he would see the senselessness of returning to a life he had once rejected. He looked bowed by his thoughts, weak and tormented by the things she had said.

When he straightened, he turned to her with the eyes of one in the unrelenting grip of a desperate pledge. "I pledged my life, Vanity. I can't go to California with you. My place is with my parents—until they die. You will either come with me to be my wife, or we will say good-bye here."

Her entire body began to shake. He looked so like his father, she was frightened beyond reason. He was no longer the man she had loved and grieved for with such intense fidelity.

To give in to his demand now and go with him would be to forfeit forever what little truth she had learned about herself. No man was worth such compromise. No man should ask that much.

The violent trembling eased. She relaxed her fingers and found herself straightening. "John Travis...Trance...I love you more than any man I have ever known. I could've loved others. I could've married, but I was content being widowed in my heart because I always believed you wanted the best for me, that you truly loved *me*. But if your love requires that I change to suit you and your family, then you don't really love me. You love a fantasy woman. You should marry a woman born and bred in your hometown, not someone like me, born in a saloon, raised on a gambling boat. I'm going to California. When I find a man like me—born and bred like me—I'm going to marry him!"

Except for a shading of surprise in Trance's eyes, his expression didn't change.

Vanity let her arms drop to her sides. With a sigh, she started back toward the cabins, brushing past Trance's rigid form blocking the path. The mental discipline that had kept him alive in the cellar had made him unbending.

She didn't hear him follow. She longed for him to. She prayed that he would suddenly throw aside his zealous decision and chase her. She would fling herself into his arms...

But there were no footsteps behind her. Her tears ran hot on her cheeks, but she didn't turn around. She and Trance had changed. Now, as before, when she believed he was dead, her future was her own.

They waited in silence at the landing. All was quiet, green, languid. The morning was hot and still.

Quarter had found Vanity a bonnet, and she assured him that one winning hand of poker would net them enough traveling money to get them to California by way of the finest transportation they fancied.

Trance stood to the side in some tall grass, unswerving in his decision. Quarter had found him enough money for passage north, and Trance had already sworn to repay him the moment he reached Cold Crossing.

"I'll keep after you if you don't," Quarter teased, though his eyes reflected sorrow that the two people he liked best couldn't settle their differences.

Vanity watched the upper point, hoping a riverboat would soon splash into view so that she would be the first to leave. She didn't think she could endure being left behind, not so soon after finding Trance.

After an hour, a broad white side-wheeler whistled and rounded the point. Quarter signaled. The steamer edged toward the dense green shore. Gushing black smoke from twin stacks, it eased into the shallows and dropped its wide stageplank.

Trance turned for just a moment as Vanity started up it. Her chestnut hair was caught back with a snapping yellow ribbon, making her look still so young and innocent. Her eyes were huge with heartbreak, and hauntingly beautiful. Her lips were pressed tightly together, but he didn't budge from his stand. He had made a vow and must keep it. His honor and self-respect were at stake.

But as she stepped onto the sweeping deck, and the stageplank was lifted behind her, Trance felt a pain in his heart so acute he almost sank to his knees.

Forcing himself to remain upright and endure watching her go for the third and last time, he remembered that day so long ago when she was only a girl. He had thought he would never find her again, that she was so rare, so far beyond his reach that she was more myth than reality.

It was true she was like no woman he had ever known. She didn't defer or obey. She stood proudly, alone.

He thought of that day she left him to go to Ohio. She had been so radiant, so sure that she would fulfill his hopes. Then she had been the sort of woman he understood. She had been so demure and sweet, almost like a child.

He had expected to go home to her, his little wife-to-be waiting in gray skirts and a floury-white apron. He had dreamed of having tow-haired sons and apple-cheeked daughters by her, and a cottage not far from his home where he'd be welcomed and respected.

Vanity would have done anything for him then, but she had been changed in ways he couldn't accept. He had become a stranger to himself, too.

Were those dreams that had sustained him in the cellar wrong? If his vows were costing him Vanity's love, should he risk going back on his heartfelt pledge to God and himself? Why did she have to be so headstrong?

Why did he have to want her so?

This time she did not wave. She stood on the deck, looking like she might not even see him.

Would she not call out his name? he thought, wondering if he could endure life while knowing that somewhere she laughed, lived, and loved—with another man.

She wouldn't marry another, he assured himself. In time she'd come back to him. He would only have to go home and wait.

He smiled a little, lifting his hand. His heart wrenched as she turned away. She lifted her hem and started toward the stairs where he could see her no more.

She was a woman, he thought. Yet he did not know what that was, apparently, for in his foolish heart he had imagined her a delightful, gratifying, delicious plaything.

But beyond her womanhood was a human being, just as beyond his manhood he was first a creature of God. He had loved Vanity first and foremost for her uniqueness. Why had he wanted to reshape her? How could he have driven away what he loved?

The whistle blew. The boat pulled away from the landing, growing smaller and smaller until it rounded the lower point, leaving only the broad expanse of brown water bounded on all sides by hazy green banks.

"I'll see to it you're settled before I join her," Quarter said, startling Trance from his thoughts.

"You're going with her?" Trance asked. His throat tightened. By God, he did love Vanity!

Quarter nodded. "Somebody's got to look after a sassy little thing like that."

"Should I have gone?" he asked. He loved her!

"In my book, it isn't good for a man to chase after his woman until his heart's in it. Do what you must, Mr. Trance. Like I said, I'll keep in touch. You'll always know where to find her."

Trance wanted to weep. He loved her! "Will you write if she plans to marry?" he whispered.

Quarter thought a minute. "I'm done being in the middle. I'll let you know where she goes. I can't do more than that. I got me a new life to build. I'm going to settle down, have me a woman and some babies, and earn a real living. My war's over. I'm finally free."

"The war's over," Trance mused, hearing another riverboat whoop.

His heart leaped. He fancied that Vanity had forced the boat to return to the landing.

But it was another, smaller boat laboring into view. Quarter hailed it. In a short time, Trance was aboard, stepping into a small dark cabin and remembering a night so long ago it seemed like a dream. He remembered crashing, drunk, at Vanity's feet.

After he closed the door, he dropped to the bunk, forgetting to go out and thank Quarter for his help. He did not look up from the floor until long after the boat had steamed away from Ashland Landing on the Louisiana side of the Mississippi River.

At the clearing, Quarter paused to gaze at the crumbling brick cabins. This had been his first memory, this wide, muddy yard where he had done his first chores as a slave boy belonging to Mr. Jason D. Pearson, the cane planter.

It had once been a proud place. In California, he promised himself, he would have a real house. He would bring to it a fine young woman, and he would treat her with love and respect.

His twin boss man was dead. Vanity had shot Jules and he had smashed Jock's head. A pattern of crime stretching back to his boyhood was broken. Quarter's dreams burst into full bloom.

To the north, in a Natchez hospital, lay a man with black hair and a pencil-slim moustache. A white bandage covered a particularly destructive contusion on his left temple. For days, Jock Pearson lay near death. The doctors tending him shook their heads. To them, he was merely another casualty of that wretched place known as Natchez Under the Hill.

But in time Jock recovered. Save for a nasty scar on his temple, he looked the elegant gentleman once again. Though quiet and courteous to all, he hadn't forgotten his miserable half brother, that spawn of his father's lust for a gentle slave named Opal. He hadn't forgotten what Quarter Dollar had done to his head.

Leering crookedly, Jock Pearson, Esquire, owner of the *J. J. Pearson*, and the thieving half of a gentleman thief known as Ghost, strode back to his riverboat dragging his right foot so slightly even he did not notice the imperfection.

He was on his way to exact a very ugly justice on those responsible for the murder of his better half.

Eighteen

1867

Traveling to California by ship around the Horn of South America proved more tedious than Vanity had expected. She grew weary of her thoughts and found her cramped cabin confining. She expected the nightmares but eventually even they lessened.

She resigned herself to her secret guilt. If Jules Pearson was capable of holding an innocent man captive for no better reason than the remote possibility of trade to save himself, he was not a man worthy of her conscience.

Quarter's company was most welcome, but she found herself strangely unable to pretend contentment.

Impatient to find her grandfather, and then perhaps her real father, Vanity spent long hours at the gunwale. When at last they were in sight of San Francisco Bay, she felt at loose ends, uneasy, unsure, and, most of all, very lonely.

In her heart she was resigned to her decision to let Trance go. For him it was best, his only recourse, but for herself she felt sad and disappointed. He had changed too much.

She and Quarter debarked and took a steamer to Sacramento, and there she booked a room at the unlovely but solid Federal Hotel. By day she searched the riverfront, asking after Sandbar Mackenzie at every boat and in every saloon.

By evening, dressed in gowns of better and better quality, she plied her skills with her companion, Lady Luck, at the more respectable gambling establishments such as The Chrysanthemum and Oakly's Billiards and Fine Spirits, "respectable" being a relative term.

Her name became quickly known. She was said to travel about town with a black bodyguard calling himself 'Lija Quarter—Quarter Dollar had renamed himself, though Vanity swore she'd never get used to the change.

Vanity made a fair living, enough to pay her board and amass an attractive though not ostentatious wardrobe.

Quarter quickly found himself to be a successful trader, bringing together those who needed to buy with those who needed to sell. Within weeks he knew everyone of any import within twenty miles of the town, and well up the Sacramento, American, and San Joaquin rivers.

It was during a particularly lucrative deal in redwood lumber that he heard of a freight pilot calling himself Mackenzie. He lost no time getting a message to Vanity.

Vanity waited at the wharf, watching the weathered stern-wheeler *Louise* chug into Sacramento with a load of hides from the ranchos to the south. She had fitted herself out in a snugly tailored tan bombazine bodice devoid of trim save for two bands of brown braid at the cuffs, and a leaf-brown foulard silk skirt draped back over an understated bustle.

With a discreetly plumed hat, buff kid gloves, black high-button shoes, and silk-lined parasol, she looked every bit a lady of quiet, respectable tastes. Her rich chestnut curls were combed back severely from a center part, and twined around the back of her head in a coronet-style braid.

She wore no jewelry except a small brooch at her throat. She believed herself to look quite plain, and hoped the man she had come to meet took her for an ordinary sort of person. She didn't want to be welcomed because she looked wealthy.

If she didn't take to Sandbar Mackenzie, she told herself for the thousandth time, he would never think to connect her with the increasingly notorious young woman fresh from New Orleans who was so bold as to enter strictly male gambling halls and beat the pants, boots, and neckerchiefs off nearly every man unfortunate enough to sit at a poker table with her.

If she did find Mr. Mackenzie worthy of her respect, she hoped he would find her respectable enough to welcome her as his granddaughter.

With her heart aflutter and her chin up, Vanity boarded the *Louise* as it was being off-loaded. It was badly in need of paint. The boilers wheezed dangerously. The deck hands were scarcely civil to this most unwelcome hindrance to their beeline to the whiskey ration.

Vanity climbed to the pilothouse, where she found an aging gentleman with bushy eyebrows leaning against his motionless pilot's wheel, puffing contentedly on a corncob pipe.

When he turned, his face drained momentarily. With effort, he brightened. "What can I do for you, little lady?" His voice was gentle.

She stepped into the tiny pilothouse and gave him a dimpled smile. Her heart thundered, making her unable to speak at first. The way he stared told her clearly how she resembled her mother, that he could not help but think of her as he stared into Vanity's face.

"I'm told you did a little piloting on the Mississippi, sir," she finally managed.

"Aye, I did, but I had more bad luck than was right for a man. They called me Sandbar in those days." His eyes looked sad, his smile humble. He was nothing like the profane, arrogant, self-important river pilots she had known.

"They call you Smoky now," she said, already thinking that she liked him.

"Aye. More bad luck, I'm afraid. My first boat brought from the east burned. This is a rough, raw land, little lady. What can I do for you?"

"I've just come from the east myself," she said, wondering how she would introduce herself. She bought time with small talk. "I was on the Mississippi many years, too. Did you ever hear of the gambler Maxxmillon Blade?"

The old man's face drained. "I-indeed, I have…and on more than one occasion. I was piloting one time, and he was on the boat. A proud young buck, he was, with a head for cards. There wasn't a man to match him on the river."

She nodded proudly.

"I heard tell he once won twenty thousand dollars at one sitting. Why do you come here asking after him? Is he about?"

"Oh, no, he's dead now," she said, suddenly feeling sad and uneasy. "I have a reason for speaking to you now, but I suppose I'm worried about what you'll think. Have you a family, Mr. Mackenzie?"

"Aye. My first wife, Louise, has been dead some eleven years now, God rest her soul. I've remarried. Do I owe you money? Is that why you're here?" He looked nervous, his long graying side-whiskers quivering.

Finally she laid her hand on his sleeve, feeling an instant spark of kinship with the kindly old man. "You don't owe me a thing, Grandfather."

It slipped out softly and hung between them like a gunshot. He stared blankly at her a full minute before stepping back and taking hold of the big pilot wheel.

"Lord have mercy!" he whispered. "You're my Mary's girl, the babe she went away to bear in shame. Believe me when I say I searched for her!" he added, as if afraid Vanity would condemn him with her next words. "Mercy, how we searched for her! Her mother died a broken woman without her. It...it humbles a man."

"I haven't come out of bitterness," Vanity said, her own voice beginning to break. Tears spilled from her eyes.

She felt herself shaking, fearing, in spite of his words, that he would reject her. She longed for him to embrace her, and as he straightened from clutching the wheel, he looked equally afraid that she would not accept him.

They slipped easily into the warmth of each other's arms. He smelled of Bull Durham tobacco and probably had a taste for a nip of rum on occasion. His body was wiry and thin. She felt his bones through the worn cloth of his shirt and heavy wool coat—and thought of Trance.

When Vanity pulled away to look into his eyes, she saw her mother's features and wept for joy. She had come home!

"Tell me how you came to find me," he said softly, looking as though he would like to make her feel welcome but had only the hospitality of a hard bench behind the wheel to offer. She took it gratefully, feeling weak and unsteady.

"I lived with Maxxmillon Blade two years as his daughter; when I was five, my mother told me he was my father. Only a few months ago I learned he traced my true identity here, and that's how I found your name."

His eyes widened. "As his daughter? Impossible—"

"I know now that she only told me a story, but..."

"I think, little lady, that I have a surprise, then, for you." With a twinkle, he tugged her to her feet and led her down to the boiler deck.

Waving to his deck hands and calling that he'd return in a few hours, he eagerly led Vanity off the dilapidated stern-wheeler and along the rows of warehouses to a modest cabin on a quiet dead-end street a few blocks away.

"What do you call yourself?" he asked, looking at her again and again as if to convince himself that he wasn't dreaming.

Vanity explained her mother's chosen name, watching how her words settled on the man's fleeting expressions of wonder, joy, heartbreak, and regret. "When I went east, I took her name, and that of the man I thought was my father. I'm called Vanity Blade."

"A remarkable name! A stunning name," he said, tapping at a humble plank door and then letting himself in. "I'm back!" he called, scarcely able to contain his excitement. Then he turned back to Vanity. "You took this name, Vanity Blade? What did my Mary call you?"

"I was christened Mary Louise," Vanity said, thinking how like this man her mother had looked when she was surprised. Vanity couldn't understand, however, why he was so excited.

"Ah, Louise…my dear first wife's name, God rest her soul. If only she could see you…" He seemed to want to say more but held himself in check. He led Vanity into a small front room too simple to be considered a parlor. When a woman in a plain cotton skirt and tailored bodice entered from a kitchen, he turned with an outstretched hand. "My wife…Sharona." He beamed.

Vanity fought the sickening thud of her heart. She lifted her eyes to the tall, raven-haired woman standing in the doorway, drying her hands on a tea towel.

Sharona said nothing for a moment but let Vanity take in her subdued hairstyle and her unadorned face before coming forward. Then she put her hand on the nearest table to steady herself. "I wasn't expecting…you look well, Vanity. H-how did you find me—us?"

"What are you *doing* here?" Vanity cried, suddenly confused and very disoriented.

Sharona went to her husband and put her arms around him possessively. "You know who she is, then, darlin'?"

The old man gazed adoringly into Sharona's face. "It's a miracle…" Then his expression darkened. Suddenly his brows knitted and he took a step back. "You've known of her all along! You've known she was my Mary's girl and said nothing! Tell me, why?"

"Sit down before you work yourself up too much. I'll be making us some tea and we can talk." She led her husband to a chair and settled him into it. Then she turned to Vanity, a strange pleading look on her face. Quickly she turned away toward the kitchen.

Vanity felt as if she was being asked to reserve judgment. She took an offered seat at a modest table set for two with simple crockery and waited the long moments while Sharona boiled water in the back room. As the moments ticked by, Vanity braced herself for Sharona's explanation, expecting lies.

The room was so spare, Vanity thought, nothing like the luxury Sharona had enjoyed on the *Natchez Trace,* or on the *Vanity Blade* with Maxx. Impatient to learn why Sharona had come to Sacramento, of all places, and had found and married her grandfather, Vanity fidgeted.

At last Sharona came back into the room carrying a simple wooden tea tray. She served and then seated herself. Leaving her cup to cool, she looked first to her husband and then to Vanity.

"When I left, Vanity, I was a bitter, grief-stricken woman," Sharona said softly, pleating the fabric of her skirt. "Maxx had left me so little of what I thought was important in those days. But to be sure, I've changed!" she said, lifting her face. "I came here seeking revenge, I did. I was saying to myself that you had got all that belonged to me—Maxx's affection and his attention. You got his boat from him, and so much of his funds." She paused, shaking her head. "I was such a fool."

"You knew, then, about the letters he'd written here. You knew about my grandfather and didn't tell me," Vanity said, reeling to think of the years she'd spent wandering when her kin was known.

"I know what you're thinking of me," Sharona finally went on. "I did know of your grandfather, but I kept it from you...out of spite at first. It's as simple as that. I believed that if I found your grandfather I might get my hands on whatever he possessed...I convinced myself he was rich, and he was—is—though not in money. I wanted to be taking what belonged to you, Vanity. You took what I thought belonged to me. I wanted to hurt you."

Vanity's grandfather looked bewildered. "But you said you loved me, Sharona!"

"And I do, darlin'! With all my heart! I came here to you, wanting to take all you had..." Her face softened as she looked into her husband's face. "All you had was that old boat and a lonely heart. You, my darlin', truly needed me. I fell hopelessly in love. I came for revenge and found salvation instead. Can you be understanding what it's meant to me these past three years to have found that?"

Vanity almost believed the woman. "If you had such a fine change of heart, Sharona, why didn't you write later?"

Sharona took her tea with a shaking hand and sipped it. "I suppose I thought you would never be finding us here. What you didn't know would not hurt you, so to speak. And...and I didn't want to lose him to you as I lost Maxx."

Vanity stood suddenly. "You never lost Maxx. You were simply too selfish to share him with me! I don't believe a word of this!"

Startled and embarrassed by her own statement, Vanity started toward the door.

"In time I hope that you do," Sharona said softly.

"You're not going!" Vanity's grandfather said, rising and following her. "You must stay and tell me of my Mary!"

Vanity threw back her head and regarded Sharona with a suspicious eye. What had become of her innocence and trust? she wondered. Suddenly she was uncomfortable with herself, realizing she was behaving coldly, harboring a bitterness that would surely drive her grandfather from her.

The time for pridefulness and revenge was past. She forced herself to smile at the eager, sad-eyed old man and finally she embraced him. "Would you like to go to Tenderfoot with me and see her grave?"

His pain was visible, and his brown eyes grew moist. "I was foolish to hope…How long has she been…gone?"

"Eight years," Vanity whispered, feeling the sting of her own tears. "I've fulfilled nearly all her dreams for me."

"We'll go tomorrow," he said, taking Vanity's arm as if it was made of glass and gently guiding her back to the table, where they talked far into the night.

In the mountains, the air was crisp and sweet. Vanity closed her eyes and breathed deeply, savoring being home again.

Though the sky was overcast, the day was lovely and serene, the banks of the river golden with late-autumn color. The familiar threshing of the *Louise*'s paddle wheel made Vanity feel as if she had returned to more than home. She was herself again, feeling the exuberance of her childhood welling up from the desert of all her disappointments.

Standing at the bow, Vanity waited for the familiar stretch of cabins, shacks, and warehouses lining Tenderfoot Landing. But the years had changed the river. New towns had sprung up where nothing had been before. And where she expected a town often was now a collection of abandoned, wind scoured buildings gradually being swallowed by tall yellow grass.

When her grandfather nosed the boat toward the banks and a rotting wharf, Vanity thought he was stopping to take on wood. But when the wheel stopped slapping the water, and the stageplank was lowered into thick brush, Vanity had the eerie feeling this windblown stretch of new timber was the place where she had been born nearly twenty-two years before.

Leaving the crew in charge of the boat, Sandbar Mackenzie heaved a sigh as he stood in his pilothouse high above the river. The place had been all but abandoned for five years now, if he recalled correctly. Few boats stopped here anymore. If the old-timers needed something, they took the road to Elizabeth Landing, two miles downstream.

Uneasily, he made his way down to the boiler deck, where Sharona sat waiting for him.

"Don't be worrying so," she said. "There are no ghosts in places like this."

"An old man still has his thoughts. I turned out my own girl, and she's been dead these many years. She'd be with me now if I hadn't been such a fool."

"Has Vanity asked after her real father yet?"

Sandbar shook his head and pulled at his lower lip.

"What will you be telling her when she does?"

He shrugged. "Let's not talk of that just now. My mind's on my lost girl and the fool who was her father. Do you think Vanity will stay on with us when we're done here?"

"I'd lay odds she's back in Sacramento to stay. Will you still be loving me when you've forgiven me for not telling you of her, Sandy?"

He chuckled at her endearment. "'Tis better she found her way to me of her own free will, you know that. If I had gone to her, I would have always wondered if she really wanted anything to do with the one who cast out her mother. This way I know she needs me…" He kissed Sharona's soft cheek. "But you, lass, you gave me back my life. After I lost my Louise I thought my life was over. I'll not be turning my back on you after all the happiness you've given me in my old age."

"I told you," Sharona said, hugging his arm. "I like older men. Always have. And you are such a dear to me. You've given me so much I almost think I can afford to share with Vanity this time. She's changed so. She was a wild creature when she came to Maxx and me. Now look at her…"

They stood a moment watching Vanity at the railing. She strained toward the grassy expanse of land along the river where a few weathered cabins still stood, but where so much more lay in heaps and piles of rubble beneath the waving gold of the grasses.

"She's a woman now," Sharona whispered. "She's known hard times. She's been hurt. I hate to think that Howard Collins will be hurting her still more. Can't you lie and say you know nothing about him?"

"My dearest," he said, moving toward the stairs, "I can't see why the man would not accept her as I do."

Sharona sniffed. "Then you are a foolish old man, because you have no idea the effect a woman such as the infamous Vanity Blade will have on one of the more stalwart members of Sacramento's City Council."

"Pooh! What man could resist that face?" Sandbar said, gesturing toward Vanity, who turned and waved. She was wearing a rich blue gown that highlighted her hair and made her look like a demure, dark-eyed angel.

"Beneath that sweet exterior beats the heart of a seasoned gambler, a woman who plays to win, a woman who would bet all to get what she wants, and would take from the man she called 'father' to get it. You have never watched her play poker, my darlin' Sandy."

"Poker, is it? I'll have you know I'm a fair—"

"Don't you dare draw a card with her, or I'll leave you!"

Sandbar blinked. He saw that Sharona was serious and hugged her. "If that's how you feel, I'll keep my distance from her, but only at the card table."

Vanity had left the boat and was picking her way, skirts high, along what had once been a wagon track. "The hill is nothing like I remember!" Vanity called. "It used to look like a mountain! And everything is so small, so sad-looking. I'm sure that's where the first Broken Rock Saloon stood. Look there! The new one. There by those trees. That's it! And…" she squealed, "…it's still occupied!"

Vanity scrambled onto a rickety boardwalk in front of the old two-story saloon. The place had never been painted, and the new sign had faded so that she could scarcely make out the letters.

The window glass was cracked in a dozen of the front panes. She pushed her way inside, finding the haze of dust there startling and depressing. Expecting to enter a vaulted room filled with tobacco smoke and raucous laughter, she was unprepared for the cramped, musty old room she found.

"What can I do for…you?" a man asked, eyes widening as he came from the back room. "Parched, are you?" He pushed back his black derby.

"Where's Doby, and Belle, and Gardenia? What of Otto?" Vanity thrilled to say their names.

The man spat into a cracked porcelain spittoon and screwed up his face. "Hell! They ain't been 'round here in a donkey's years! What you want with them ol' horsethieves, anyhow? Owe you money, do they?"

"They were friends!" Vanity said, bristling.

He raised his brows and looked her up and down. "I see. Well…" He nodded to himself. "Them ol' whores is likely down in San Francisco scrubbing the floors of the courthouse, these days. Doby, that ol' sonuvabitch, is probably slinging suds in some other danged place. If he ain't dead. Ain't no money in here, that's sure. Who the hell this Otto feller is, I hain't got no idea. Did you used to work this place?"

"I was its star—me and my mama!" She rushed back to the door and dragged Sandbar and Sharona inside. "Give me plenty of cheer, boys! Give me all ya got!" She pranced in a circle, swishing her skirts and whooping with excitement. "Heaven's mighty far, boys, but hell is nice and hot!"

She clattered onto the stage and nearly fell through the rotting boards.

"I oughta warn you about that stage. It's likely to swallow you!" the bartender called, grinning at her with interest. He hadn't seen one of her kind in the place in six or seven years. "Need a job, honey?"

Vanity jerked her heel free of a board and climbed down. The memory of her mother backstage, and all those happy performances they gave together, was hard to sustain now that she was here in the dismal and seedy place. No longer was it the wonderful old saloon Vanity kept tucked in her memory.

"Thank you, sir, but, no." She turned to her grandfather. "I'll take you to our shack, and then we'll find the graveyard." She placed a thick gold eagle on the battered bar. "For your trouble, friend," she said, winking. "You can tell folks you met Vanity Blade."

He found the gold coin more impressive.

The track had been all but washed away by years of heavy rains. She expected to climb a good while before coming upon the shack she and her mother had called home, but almost before she knew it, she'd passed it.

Glancing back, she felt a shiver run down her back. It was so dilapidated now that it would probably collapse in another year or two. What she had remembered as a spacious one-room cabin appeared to be little better than a crib, with a tin roof, gaping doorless doorway, and one primitive window.

"Great snakes! This is where we lived," Vanity whispered as her grandfather and Sharona puffed up the hill behind her.

Leaving them there, Vanity picked her way to the promontory where she used to look out over the town. By closing her eyes she could almost hear the rattle of wagon wheels coming up the road. The wind whispering in the pines almost rang with hauntingly soft strains of piano music.

But, upon opening her eyes, she saw that it was all gone. Her childhood lay far behind, overgrown by all she had learned and all the places she had been. There was no going back, no recapturing the gentle, happy times when her mother was alive, sparking her imagination with stories of a glittering future.

Vanity had had her glittering future, and it had not made her happy. Only Trance's love had made her happy. But that, too, was gone forever now, a relic of a time when all seemed possible.

Turning, she could see her grandfather and Sharona waiting on the road and she felt depressed.

To have Sharona here gave Vanity an eerie, uneasy feeling. Sharona had kept her from Maxx when he had so little time left. Vanity worried over her grandfather's condition, wondering if Sharona might do something again to keep her away.

Vanity would have to be careful, she thought, as she rejoined them. "The graveyard is this way," she said, climbing ahead of them. She'd already spied the ridge and the twisted tree where her mother had buried her money.

They entered the graveyard, which was enclosed by a surprisingly sturdy knee-high iron fence. All the wooden markers had fallen over and were so weatherworn that not one name remained.

Vanity stooped by the tiny marble lamb beside the place where she knew her mother lay. They had placed a small wooden marker over her mother's grave, and now it was only a piece of gray wood with faint markings on it.

The lump in Vanity's throat swelled. "I'm all that's left of her," she whispered. "Me, the songs she taught me…and this." She ran her hand over the faint carving meant to resemble fleece on the lamb.

She looked up, thinking she would ask why he had sent her away if he had loved her so, but the question went unasked. She knew why. And, besides, it was long done.

He stood, hands folded before him, his shoulders rounded, his face a study in pain.

She went to him quickly and put her arms around his shaking shoulders and held him close. She knew when he buried his face against her neck that he was embracing his dead daughter.

"Heaven forgive me," he said, sobbing.

Vanity felt helpless and looked to Sharona, suddenly glad of the woman's presence. When Sharona took her grandfather and comforted him, Vanity turned back to the windswept grave.

What would she have done in her mother's place? she wondered. For so long she had revered her mother, thinking her a misunderstood saint. To think that her mother might have been weak and foolish— and disastrously proud—and that she, in fact, had wasted her life frightened Vanity.

She had always thought she could do no better than her mother. Now she saw that she had done more with herself than her mother had ever dreamed.

She turned away from the grave. The past was dead. She picked her way back to the boat.

When Sandbar was able, he and Sharona walked, arm in arm, back to where Vanity stood, gazing downstream to where the towns still throbbed with life.

"Thank you for bringing me here, Vanity," her grandfather said, wiping his eyes with a red kerchief. "Can you tell me how she died?"

Vanity looked into his face, loving him already. "She was shot," she said softly.

As she expected, he flinched and walked away.

Sharona's voice was hushed. "Can't you be more gentle?"

"When I can," Vanity said, feeling cold and uncertain about her future again. "What about my real father?"

Sharona shook her head.

"I know him," her grandfather said. "I went to him when I learned my Mary was in trouble. I expected him to marry her. I even took a pistol. I found him working in San Francisco. I could've shot the man, but I held out hope she'd go to him when the time came. She was a very prideful girl. Got it from me, she did. But she was never seen again."

"Is he still in San Francisco?"

He shook his head. "Sacramento, with his wife and family. He was married when he compromised my Mary. That's why he couldn't marry her."

Vanity's eyes narrowed.

Nineteen

At fifty, Howard Collins had delusions of becoming California's governor. A clean-shaven man considered handsome by the women in his social circle, he had a hooded expression many thought too suggestive for one with political ambitions.

He kept himself comfortably in a brick Italianate home on Sacramento's finest residential street, priding himself on possessing the most elaborate grounds, finest carriage, and best-dressed wife in town.

On this particular morning he was waiting in his study, expecting a visit from a hopeful suitor for his daughter, Audrey, a green-eyed beauty of twenty-four. She had great potential as a wife, but so far had picked the most dismal prospects. The one he had to interview today was a penniless merchant who rented a dry-goods store.

At the sound of tapping at the door, Howard turned from his cluttered rolltop desk. His wife, Cora, entered, smiling apologetically.

"Excuse me, dear." She looked upset and turned away, as if trying not to weep.

"What is it?" he asked, rising quickly and going to her. Such a little fool she was!

He noticed how wounded her eyes looked. "Some...*woman* is here. I can't imagine who she is. Howard, dear, if you have something to tell me, say it now. Don't make me wait."

Confused and irritated, he went to the door and looked down the hall. All he could see was a flashy satin skirt. A charge of alarm went through him, but he controlled himself. "I can't see her face, dear. Did she give you a calling card? What did she say she wanted?"

His wife was maddeningly slow in answering. "Why would she come here, to our home? What will I tell my friends?"

"If you tell me her name, perhaps I can ask her in to my study and learn why she's here. Whatever possesses you today?"

His wife whimpered and rushed from the room. Oh, not to be

burdened with a suspicious woman, he thought, starting out into the hall. "Good afternoon, my dear. How can I help you? I'm always eager for political supporters. Have you a contribution for me?" he asked, thinking her one of the many he had flirted with at certain exclusive functions at his club.

She turned, but said nothing. She had lovely dark hair styled to accent the rich reds in her chestnut curls. Her long cape was stunning, and her skirt was bustled so high in back she reminded him of a great, lovely ship. When she moved it was with a theatrical grace he knew he himself lacked.

"Good morning, Mr. Collins. I hope you'll forgive the intrusion. Might I speak to you privately on a matter of some importance to me?" She smiled agreeably, and he warmed to her.

She had a beguiling Southern accent, and sounded so cultured he was immediately persuaded to think she was quite important, perhaps even rich.

"Do come into my study, Miss…"

"Oh, but the parlor is so lovely. Your wife keeps a delightful home. I understand you have children, sir."

"You have the advantage, my dear," he said, uncomfortable at the thought that his wife and servants were probably memorizing his every word. "I have no idea who you are."

But there was something familiar about her, he thought. Her face was a work of art, flushed with innocence, the eyes large, brown, and hypnotic.

He found himself eager to please her, eager to sweep her out of sight of his wife.

He had been faithful to her since failing to protect himself while visiting a "professional woman" in San Francisco the year before. The humiliating cure he took had caused him to alter some of his romantic habits.

The sense of recognition continued to plague him as he guided the lovely creature into his wife's elaborate parlor.

"I am called Vanity Blade by most," she said, lifting her face and appraising him openly. "I understand you made your fortune shipping goods from the east and selling them to the miners at enormous profits. Three dollars an egg. One dollar per potato and onion."

Howard quietly closed the parlor door behind him. He was not so sure now that he liked this creature. "I'm very pleased to meet you, Miss Blade. If you care to transact business, I would advise you to come to my office in town. This is, after all, a Sunday, and my day with my family. I am also expecting a caller."

"I won't keep you. I have no business with you. I only wanted to meet you, to see you, to hear your voice…and ask myself…" She turned scarlet and lost her poise for some moments. She looked away.

He revived at the sight of her discomposure. She was not so frightening as he first thought. She was merely a young woman of intense beauty. He had no need to fear her.

"I will be blunt, Mr. Collins." Her eyes hardened to large brown jewels when she looked at him again. "A man calling himself Sandbar Mackenzie sailed here from New Orleans some years ago with his wife and daughter. You were a seaman aboard that ship. Am I correct?"

"I worked my passage to California, yes," he said.

At once he felt ill, and groped for a chair. His head began to reel. Memories assaulted him, memories of Mary.

"You…you need say no more, Miss Blade." He loosened his collar and opened his coat. The parlor suddenly felt warm and close. He dropped his voice to a whisper and made a fist. "I used to wonder… How much do you want?"

The silence was heavy with tension. Howard gripped his stomach, his mind plunging back into his past, to the long voyage around the Horn from New Orleans, to the breathtaking young girl he had met aboard ship. He had fallen completely in love during those brief but intense months at sea.

Mary Mackenzie had made him forget all his responsibilities, his wife, Cora, his two-year-old daughter, and the one who died while he was at sea, his values—such as they were—and his marriage vows. Most of all he had forgotten about Mary's father, who never forgave an indiscretion born of hopeless, tender love. He had not understood what might become of his starry-eyed Mary when she took home news of her condition.

It was all so long ago! Sometimes he thought about it when he was in San Francisco, or when he'd had too much sherry, or when Cora refused him as she had the night he left home so long ago.

Now he saw Mary's face in the young woman glaring at him from across his respectable parlor. His daughter. His "other" daughter.

"I never expected her to…get…After a time, her father came asking if I was keeping her somewhere. I wasn't. I had no idea where she had gone. And I was very sorry about her…predicament, but as you can see, I could do nothing. I was already married, and a father. I…I never dreamed *you* would find me, not after all this time. H-how much do you want?" he asked again.

Her silence drove him crazy. Wasn't she there for money? Wasn't that all people wanted, especially beautiful women like…like her?

She stood, her hands clenched together, her face as hard as marble. Going to the door, she flung it open, only to come face to face with a woman very nearly her own age and size.

"Oh, good morning," the girl said, tilting her head and eyeing Vanity's attire.

Audrey Collins had rich auburn hair. Her eyes were green and soft, her lips full and lovely. She shrank back demurely at being discovered in the doorway. She looked disconcerted but secretly amused to find her father closeted in the parlor with so lovely a young woman. "Excuse me, Father," she said, her voice as sweet as a spring wind. And then she stood aside. "Were you leaving, ma'am?"

Howard raised his eyes, undone at the thought that his two children had met at last. He stood, feeling his blood pool in his legs. He felt light-headed and nauseous.

Miss Vanity Blade disappeared out the front door in a swirl of satin, slamming the door behind her. She had said nothing.

He avoided Audrey's eyes. Should he have waited to offer Miss Blade money? Should he not have offered it at all?

Then Cora was there, whispering for Audrey to do some small chore for her. When Audrey obeyed and left, Cora turned her accusing eyes on him. This time he did not look away or even attempt a denial. All these years he had had a daughter he was too much the coward to acknowledge. He had not known where to find her in any case, nor had he cared.

What had become of his young love, Mary Mackenzie? he wondered as he suddenly longed to see her fresh innocence again.

"I'm leaving you!" Cora hissed, shaking with rage. "I always suspected…but to see…to have one of your bastards come to the door. Were you always unfaithful to me?"

"Yes, but it's not necessary for you to go," he said, walking from the room, feeling ten years older. "I shall be gone before supper."

"But you…you can't abandon us!" his wife cried, following him up the curved stairs and into the bedroom, where they fought for the next two hours.

• • •

In the end, he admitted nothing. Cora wept herself into a headache that forced her to take to her bed. In another few days they would be back to normal, he thought. He was rather glad now that Cora knew.

Ah, how Miss Blade had looked like Mary! Why hadn't he had the courage to divorce Cora when he wanted to? He would have been happy with Mary Teresa Mackenzie. Now all he had was his money, his reputation, and his ambitions...

Then the name registered. Vanity Blade, the female gambler. His daughter!

He felt a deep chill in his bones and knew without a doubt that if her connection to him was ever discovered, he would never become California's governor.

Vanity went directly to her grandfather's house from the bank. She marched at a brisk pace, her head back and her bonnet ribbons snapping in the wind.

Heads turned as she passed. Some of the gentlemen she knew, and some were worthy of her eye. Others were impudent strangers, and to them she gave not a flicker of acknowledgment.

The street where her grandfather lived with Sharona was modest, to say the least. They had a four-room frame house shipped ready-cut from back east.

Sharona, however, had transformed the place into a quaint haven, and played the part of housewife so convincingly that sometimes Vanity forgot her suspicions that the woman was still plotting to hurt Sandbar.

Certainly, Vanity's grandfather seemed delighted with his life with Sharona, giving back all the tender love Sharona seemed to have missed with Maxx.

They were waiting for Vanity when she rushed in, her face alight with excitement. "I've gotten the loan," Vanity said, waving the papers that would enable her to buy one of the finest side-wheelers on the Sacramento River, and not with funds earned on a table covered with green felt. She felt like a legitimate citizen again. "And you, Grandfather, must be my pilot!"

Her grandfather looked happy at first, but then his face clouded. "But I can't, Vanity. I'm bad luck. And I'm old."

"Nonsense! I won't have anyone else pilot my boat. I'm going to name her *Pacific Princess*. We'll have gambling and entertainment..."

featuring me, of course!" She laughed like a child. "Except that we'll be respectable on Sundays. I'll bring in the finest cooks, hire the best Chinese stewards. It's already fitted to the nines! I've wanted a boat of my own ever since losing the *Vanity Blade* to the damned Yankees." She fixed her grandfather and Sharona with a determined gaze. "I don't care a whit for what Howard Collins thought of me. I thought he was a snake. This is what I was born to do, and what my mama dreamed of for me. By heaven, I'm going to conquer Sacramento, too!"

Sandbar rose from his chair and went over to Vanity, who was pulling off her bonnet in preparation for having supper with them. "And what of Collins? Will you see him again?"

Vanity paused, remembering the impressive house and the distinguished-looking, handsome man. She had seen his timid wife, whose eyes were so like Trance's mother's it had given her the shivers. She tried to imagine her mother loving such a man and couldn't.

No matter, really. She had disliked him the moment he spoke. She hated him for offering money, and hated him for leaving her mother to such an end, even if he was already married.

She had no more desire to see Howard Collins again than she did to see Theophilus Holloway. They were of the same cut of cloth—opportunists who used innocent people.

"Vanity...we've tried to wait until you were ready to tell us what happened with him." Sharona's voice, as always, was maddeningly reasonable.

Vanity tried to control the flood of anger that engulfed her. "He offered money. That says it all, I think."

"We're sorry, darlin'."

Vanity shivered, thinking for the first time that in her awkward way, Sharona was as much a mother to her as her own had been. "Let's not talk of him again. I'm glad I never knew him."

"Your bitterness will make you hard, Vanity," Sharona said.

Vanity shook her head. She drew off her gloves a finger at a time. There was no name for the kind of woman she intended to become, but she was certainly a cross between an adventuress and a lady. Vanity took the nearest chair and fixed her grandfather with a shrewd eye. "Will you pilot my new boat?"

He smiled. "How can a man resist you?"

"Some do. Now, all we need is a captain," she said happily.

Twenty

1872

Ace Malone—with his big grin, graying temples, straw hat, and striped trousers—was no match for Luther Gant, captain of the *Pacific Princess*.

At least Luther thought so that evening as the gambler seated himself across the green-felt-covered table.

"What'll it be, Malone—five-card stud or draw poker?" Luther sized up the prosperous gent, who was probably too slow with that derringer up his sleeve to be a threat. Luther never played straight. At thirty-five, he matched any man daring enough to venture into the *Pacific Princess*'s game rooms.

Ace offered Luther a Virginia cheroot. "What can you tell me of the woman called Vanity? I've heard a mighty lot about her since coming back to California."

Luther accepted the cigar, lighted it, leaned back, and thought a while. Then he shuffled the cards. "You're the second man this week asking after my boss. I can't tell you much," he said evenly. "I manage things here on her boat. On slow nights, I amuse myself with Lady Luck."

"Where might I find her?" Ace asked, showing plenty of teeth as he smiled.

Luther's shoulders tensed. He intended to save Vanity for himself! He'd been working on her for four years. Who were these men after her, this old coot in striped pants, and that muckworn guy loitering on the dock several nights before?

"Why might you be looking?" Luther asked.

Ace accepted the cards Luther dealt, his manicured hands fanning them. Luther's hands were manicured, too, but worn from years of scrapping for a living in every major eastern city. He'd even tried his hand at prospecting in the west, too, for a week.

He'd found his niche in California's saloons until the day Vanity entered and played poker with a battalion of political weasels at the

Lucky Hill Men's Sociable Club. Smiling like a schoolgirl, she'd cleaned them out.

From that moment Luther had wanted her. Weeks later she noticed him when he boasted of being the finest riverboat captain ever to set foot in the place.

He'd eventually learned how to captain a riverboat, too. He found Vanity a challenge; he wanted all the things she owned, including her beautiful body. He believed no woman that tasty, and in the prime of her womanhood, should sleep alone, though to his knowledge she still did.

"Where does Vanity live?" Ace asked, suspicious of Luther's reluctance to offer information. "I've tried to book a table for this Saturday night, but can't for love or money."

Luther smiled. "With so many aboard, we damned near sink on Saturday nights. You want to hear Miss Blade sing, book a table two weeks in advance. She has a look about her that..." Luther paused. Sometimes he worried that he even loved her. "She has a look that makes men want to gather her up, but, friend, she's pure Alaskan ice."

Ace regarded Luther. "When I knew her, she was warm as a summer night. If you'd simply tell me where she can be found for the remainder of the week, I'd like to pay my respects." Ace placed a hundred-dollar bill on the table. "As a surprise."

Luther took the bill. "She has a house in Sacramento, but I'd be careful, friend. We found Bullo, her butler, prizefighting on the San Francisco docks two years ago. He has his instructions, and he's dumb enough to follow them to the letter. You're not the first to try calling without an invitation."

Ace stood, clapping his straw hat onto his graying waves. He winked. "Nice talking with you, friend."

On Saturday night as the *Pacific Princess*'s boilers gathered steam for her evening excursion to San Francisco, Vanity waited in her phaeton. Her footman, a young protégé of Quarter's, opened her door and bowed as she swirled her skirts and high, bow-trimmed bustle down to the rough wharf planks.

She wore a tailored bodice so tight her waist looked two hands small. Her bosom bulged tantalizingly. The black-and-white-striped satinette gown was trimmed with wide black velvet bows, point lace, and a deep hem flounce. Her hat was trimmed with feathers and white silk roses hand-twisted in France.

Whenever she stepped from the phaeton, her mother's voice came to her: "A maid to tidy your upstairs, another to dust whatnots in your downstairs. A jolly lady cooking you cakes, a man to open your door…"

Vanity had all that and more. Her dressmaker kept her in fine gowns, day dresses, bonnets, and underthings. The rest was shipped from San Francisco: high-button kid shoes, Brussels lace shawls, Chinese silk fans.

Whatever Vanity wanted, she had. She had a magnificent house, a fine buggy, and the company of nearly any eligible man who struck her fancy.

She was as rich as ever in her life. The *Pacific Princess* brought in good income, and she still played poker to keep life interesting.

Mounting her side-wheeler's stageplank, she felt proud of her beautifully appointed boat trimmed in red, but a sense of loneliness always dogged her. Every man in the city yearned for her. Women from the social circle where Audrey Collins reigned as a scandalous yet still respectable divorcée envied her beauty. Even whores on the line coveted Vanity's notoriety.

But Vanity was alone. Since bringing east coast burlesque to the *Pacific Princess*'s small stage, she'd not had to worry about money. Yet she trusted no man who paid her court. Only Luther Gant, her captain, seemed unaffected by her charms. He wanted his pay and nothing more.

Though she was rich and beautiful, those were common enough things. No one seemed to want her for the qualities that made her uniquely herself.

In the five years since she'd come home, she felt more lost than ever. Nowhere did she feel that sense of belonging she remembered from her childhood.

Her beauty and wealth set her apart. Her admirers carried her name to Los Angeles, New Orleans, Albany, New York. She had her pick of gentlemen, yet she kept to herself, watching, waiting, for one man to step from the throng and set himself apart.

She couldn't name what she sought. It couldn't be love. Men loved her on sight, showering her with gifts—and grew wearisome. She was accused of destroying marriages with a smile, of turning the heads of decent family men who had never strayed.

She still had her youth, but, like her mother, that which she pursued had proved less than enough. To be loved by all was to be loved too much. She wanted to be loved by one. She just didn't know where to find him.

On that particular evening she found Luther waiting for her in the private salon on the promenade deck where Vanity rested before her performances and hid afterward.

Already the salon was littered with flowers. She read the cards, smiling at the audacity of a judge, the sweetness of a shopboy, the caution of a traveler begging an hour of her time at any price she might care to name. Always there were those who assumed too much.

She whirled and caught Luther watching her. She tossed the cards into a basket; her social secretary would acknowledge them all within two days with an array of standard responses.

"You're staring," Vanity said, unpinning her hat.

He puffed on the cheroot. "She's restless tonight, the lovely, lonely Vanity Blade. Though rich men and beggars alike come asking about her every night, she spurns them all."

He tugged a bell cord and a steward brought Vanity her standard drink, a baby titty, a concoction of anisette, creme yvette, whipped cream, and a red cherry.

She hated it, but its appearance never failed to redden the faces of any men who saw it—an experience she enjoyed.

"What's bothering you?" Luther asked, clearing his throat.

She looked up at him, wondering what it was she liked about him. He couldn't play straight poker; it wasn't in him. He prided himself on cheating. He was attractive enough, though his eyes were unsettling.

She shouldn't like him. He was a liar extraordinaire, and had conned her into hiring him as captain when he'd never set foot on a river craft in his life! His competence now was questionable.

At poker she could beat the suspenders off him—and boots, socks, and drawers, too, if she had a mind. But perhaps, after all, it was that knowing, suggestive leer of his that told her she could trust him by distrusting him.

He made no excuses for what he was. She admired that most of all. He was ambitious, lazy, lusty, often vulgar. He could startle her, and make her laugh when she felt gloomy. His popularity with certain brash females was well known, but she didn't care.

He appeared to be filled with dull, unimportant little secrets. If he had a weak spot, she didn't know it. That he had contented himself to work four years for her had some significance. She just didn't know what it might be.

"Vanity, you're looking at me in a way that fills me with need," he said, giving her that look of his and then laughing as if the last thing on his mind was her body. "Tell me what you're thinking."

"I'm thinking I like you," Vanity said.

He nodded. The gears in his brain moved with ferretlike speed. "What does that mean?"

"If I ask you a question, you'll tell me the truth or an outrageous lie. Because I can't tell the difference, that makes you…ah…interesting."

"Ah, interesting, something I've always wanted to be. What's your question? I'll tell the truth."

"What's wrong with me?"

He laughed at first, watching her sip the creamy drink and lick the white foam from her upper lip. "Vanity, you're badly in need of a good…"—he lifted his brows as if censoring himself—"…a good romp between the sheets."

She sputtered, feeling herself go red. "Sex does not solve everything."

"No, but in your case, you need something you won't buy, and seem unable to…settle for. You, baby titty, are a fine wine turning slowly to vinegar."

She moved to slap him.

He caught her wrist. She glared at him, fearing he was right, that she needed love but also needed to ease a certain unmentionable pressure.

"I suppose you think I'd take the likes of you to my bed," she said wryly.

"Oh, I'm not so conceited as that. But I do wonder why you don't take a lover. You would be ever so much more beautiful with that faint glow of passion lighting your fair cheeks. Do you know how dull the skin of a loveless woman gets?"

"You needn't be so horrid!" she said, twisting away. "Why don't you kiss me and see if my color returns?"

"Why, indeed? I'm the one man for a thousand miles who doesn't fall asleep every night mentally stripping you."

"Get off this boat! You're fired!"

He only laughed. "I think you'd miss me. Other men drool at your feet, whining for a smile or a kiss. I wouldn't."

She was outraged. She flung herself at him, thinking to scratch his face so as to stop him from smirking.

"Oh, my, we are tense!" He caught her wrists, forcing her arms back. Holding them with one hand, he caught her chin with the other. "This is what you want. Why you forbid yourself such a simple comfort, I can't imagine. You do everything else an ordinary woman does—scratch, bathe, eat, piss, sleep, bitch, cry, swear. Why not this?"

Luther bent her to him, jerking her just a little before softening his hold and lowering his face to hers. She could see into his laughing brown eyes.

He was drunk, she thought, faintly disgusted and yet aroused. He made her heart flutter. She hadn't felt that since...

She closed her eyes to drive out memories of the man she'd turned from five years before. Five years was long enough to wait, to hope...

"Open your eyes, Vanity. Watch me kiss you. I'll bother with this only once," Luther whispered.

Her eyes flew open. She saw his lips part, his tongue pink and moist. Then he was kissing her and her body was responding in spite of her fury. His tongue invaded her mouth, plunging deeply as if, since she wouldn't sleep with him, he wanted to give her something to remember.

She moaned. He was strong, moving his thigh between hers, kindling her need if not her love.

Luther released her suddenly and moved away. He forced his voice out softly. "It's late. I'll get us under way."

"Luther!" Vanity staggered to a chair, hating her body for its need. "Don't go just yet."

Before opening the door, he turned, looking strangely unlike himself. "Vanity, marry me."

That was not what she had expected him to say. No standard refusals sprang to her lips. She stared, openmouthed, wondering if he was joking.

"No, not tonight," she said, as if joking herself. "But I will... next month."

Luther smiled; he was finally raking in the profits from a very long game of five-card stud.

Before a pressing crowd of passengers that made the *Pacific Princess*'s grand saloon unbearably close, Vanity stood alone on the limelit stage. To her left was a man squeezing an old concertina. She was breathless from her performance, distracted and wishing that she could retreat quickly without fanfare.

"...so take my hand, my darlin'," she sang in a voice husky with emotion, "and lead me to your love, far-r-r away."

The song had always provoked in her a deep melancholy. And because she had a concertina accompanying her, she often felt as if she stood on two stages, this lovely gleaming one and another dusty creaking one up in the mountains.

The saloon erupted with applause. She curtsied and blew kisses, but instead of giving an encore, as she was often persuaded to do, she gave her admirers a pleading smile and skipped offstage.

Luther and several other husky men were there to protect her as she made her way past hopefuls clutching armloads of roses. She hurried to her private salon for her cape.

Luther followed. "Your singing was off tonight. Anything to do with me?"

Vanity pinned her hat and grabbed the cape. "I feel...smothered. Give everyone a free round. I'm going home."

He stepped in front of her, his eyes dark. "Were you joking when you accepted my proposal?"

She blinked. "I wouldn't joke about such a thing. I will marry you. You were right about me. I do need what you can give me." She swallowed and forced her way past him. She was sorry, she thought. If she needed what he could give her, she didn't need it immediately.

He moved closer. "We'll make a good team."

"Yes, we will. Good night." Vanity wanted to get off the boat before the passengers realized she was leaving. She slipped down the stairs to the boiler deck and rushed down the stageplank.

Her phaeton drew near. As she gathered her skirts and stepped up, she shivered. Holding the doorframe, she twisted, squinting into the shadows between the pools of light illuminating the wharf.

"Something bothering you, Miss Blade?" her footman asked.

She shook her head. "N-no, it's nothing."

But once inside the coach with the door safely latched, she rolled up the leather window cover and looked out.

The *Pacific Princess* sat like a majestic candle-lit wedding cake on the river. She could hear the lively banjo music, and she saw her patrons waiting for her encore.

Why should she feel so uneasy? she wondered, as she tried to shake off the sensation that someone was watching her. She had agreed to marry Luther. There was no danger in that. As he had said, they'd work well together, and she'd...find release.

She reached for the pistol stored beneath the cushion opposite her seat and tapped the roof, signaling her driver to carry on. "Hurry!"

Twenty-One

Vanity embraced Mathilda and then Quarter as they came into her entry hall. "You're both looking so wonderful," she said with an unexpected tightening in her throat. "How are you feeling, Mathilda?"

Quarter's lovely young wife patted her thickening waist. "I sure don't feel like I got three more months of this!"

Quarter looked at Vanity. "I get the feeling we're here for something special," he said.

Vanity glanced nervously at the floor and then smiled a little. "Go on into the dining room. I've already seated Sandbar and Sharona. You know my grandpa. He doesn't like to wait for his dinner!"

Vanity found herself shaking as Quarter seated his wife and took a chair beside her. Sandbar stopped chuckling over something Sharona said and everyone turned expectantly toward Vanity.

Clutching the back of her chair, Vanity wished she had decided on an easy way to tell her "family" her plans. Finally she found her voice. "I want all of you to be the first to know. I've decided to marry."

Mathilda jumped to her feet and rushed to Vanity. "I just knew if you married up you'd be happier. Didn't I say that a hundred times, 'Lija?"

He helped her back to her place and nodded. "I sure have thought so."

"Well, this is an occasion!" Sandbar said, thumping the table. "Let's get this celebration going!"

Sharona placed her hand on his arm, quieting her husband. "We're very happy for you, Vanity, but…"

Vanity tensed, having feared that Sharona might have some objection.

"But who are you going to marry?"

Vanity laughed a bit too loudly. "Luther, of course."

Startled, Sandbar nodded as if he should have guessed, but just as quickly, his bushy brows drew together over his eyes. He had never liked Luther, and still didn't.

Quarter looked distracted, and Mathilda seemed a bit confused. Everyone tried to look enthusiastic, but as Vanity had feared, they didn't understand why she would marry a man she didn't love.

Sharona looked ready to comment. Vanity wanted to keep her quiet and signaled for the dinner's first course to be brought in. She took her seat and fussed with her napkin.

"Vanity," Sharona asked softly, "if this is your engagement dinner, where is Luther?"

Blinking, Vanity raised her head, a flush of embarrassment announcing to all that she had forgotten to invite him.

"How soon?" Quarter asked, moving his chair back.

"A few weeks. A month at the most," Vanity murmured.

Quarter stood and placed his napkin on the table. "I've forgotten something. Mind if I step out for a few minutes? I'll be back before you get to the main course."

He slipped out after giving his wife's shoulder a reassuring pat, leaving behind an awkward silence that prevailed until the soup plates were empty.

By the dim light of the flickering carriage lamp, Trance Holloway reread Quarter Dollar's two-week-old telegram. Moments later the hired carriage rocked to a halt. Trance tucked the paper into his breast pocket and stepped out.

The *Pacific Princess* stood lit up and gleaming among the other riverboats along Sacramento's riverfront. Though a lot larger, it looked much like he'd imagined. He quickly joined the excited throng crowding toward the stageplank.

Trance shouldered his way past the immaculately dressed people eager to hear Vanity Blade sing that night. She had done well for herself, he thought. She deserved acclaim. She had always been so vivacious, so lovely...

He forced his way past a knot of gentlemen in tall hats and hurried aboard. Already the boat staggered beneath the weight of passengers. The wide stairway leading up to the saloon deck was so thick with people Trance could only rein in his impatience as he worked his way up, hoping he'd find a secluded table where he could watch Vanity before revealing his presence.

Perhaps, after all this time, his feelings for her had dimmed. Though after receiving Quarter's message he had booked passage west aboard the first train, and had endured a rough stagecoach ride, he might find, after seeing Vanity in person, that he no longer loved her. In such case, he wanted to do nothing to interfere with her marriage to Luther Gant.

The boat was truly beautiful. He had never seen more elaborately carved gingerbread trim. As he squeezed through the wide doorway to the grand saloon, he smelled fresh seafood, heady wines, and expensive perfumes. He was reminded of the first time he saw Vanity, and felt a sharp twinge of nostalgia.

In the center of the crowd near the stage stood a distinguished gentleman in a black Merino frock coat. Beside him stood an auburn-haired beauty in a sea-green silk that caught the light and fairly glittered.

Trance hadn't expected to see Vanity before her performance. Suddenly he decided to confront her, so he sidestepped ladies in feathered hats and rushed up behind her.

The gentleman turned, his shrewd eyes narrowing as Trance advanced. Was this her betrothed? Trance wondered, a bitter taste coming into his mouth.

"Do I know you, sir?" the man asked from around a cigar.

The auburn-haired woman turned. She had the same voluptuous lips as Vanity, and round, beguiling eyes, but hers were green. Vanity's were dark brown.

Taken aback, Trance faltered. "I beg your pardon...sir...miss! I mistook you for someone else."

The woman looked enough like Vanity to be her sister, but her eyes were veiled and calculating.

"May I introduce myself?" the gentleman said, assessing Trance with a knowing sweep of his shrewd eyes. "I'm Howard Collins, a city councilman. We're here at my daughter's insistence. She's quite determined, you might say. So often she's mistaken for the famous Miss Blade we thought we must see her for ourselves. Surely you didn't think my daughter was Miss Blade! May I ask your name, sir?"

Trance extended his hand. "John Travis Holloway of Ohio, sir. I'm here for the railroad."

"Ah, in that case you won't feel very welcome aboard a riverboat packet. Railroads are stealing away the river trade."

"They'll never provide entertainment, I fear," Trance said, smiling, impatient to find his table and alarmed that he hadn't remembered the exact shade of Vanity's hair. "I did think your daughter was Miss Blade. I beg your indulgence."

The woman lowered her eyes and fluttered her lashes. She was remarkably lovely in her own right, Trance thought, bowing to her.

The councilman indicated their table. "Please join us, Mr. Holloway. May I present my daughter, Audrey?"

"I'm a divorcée," Audrey declared boldly.

Her father stiffened. "I'm sure Mr. Holloway has no interest in that!" He nearly pushed her to her seat.

"My condolences, Miss Collins."

"Audrey Collins Whitney," she said, waiting for Trance to assist her with her chair.

"I'm honored to make your acquaintance, but…"

A graying gambler in a straw boater and striped trousers brushed past the table, knocking Trance aside. "Excuse…" He seized a chair at the foremost table.

Voices rose excitedly as the steam whistle whooped. With a faint jarring motion, the boat got under way.

"I'd be honored to join you, but I'm meeting someone after the show. Another time, perhaps." Trance tipped his hat to the woman's inviting smile.

Howard Collins fished an engraved card from his vest pocket and offered it. The councilman would be an important man to know for business purposes, Trance thought, making his way to the reserved table nearby.

He ordered a short whiskey and downed it. Five years…five *years* of unbearably lonely nights…

The aging gambler at the front table twisted about excitedly as if he, too, couldn't wait to see the toast of Sacramento. Though Quarter Dollar had written twice a year telling Trance of Vanity's notoriety in California, Trance had thought his old friend exaggerated. He hadn't wanted to believe she was sought after by so many, and had taken secret comfort year after year when she didn't marry.

He patted his breast pocket where the dispatch was tucked. "Vanity engaged! Come now or never!"

At thirty-two, he had rebuilt his life. He had honored a thousand self-imposed promises, yet he remained unsatisfied, yearning for something kindled thirteen years before when he first saw a girl in green satin hiding behind an oak tree on the Mississippi riverbank.

He had done all that was required of him. He had lived the life expected of him. He had sent his parents to their graves believing they had raised a son at last worthy of their highest hopes.

Still, deep inside, he searched for that last corner of himself, the place where his true heart lay. In that private part of himself waited his love for Vanity. He had found it there every time he looked.

He sat in the secluded corner, his presence protected by a cluster of potted ferns, waiting to see her bewitching face once again. If she had changed too much, he would go away.

Trance was scarcely aware of what he ordered for dinner. He declined a third whiskey, and nodded absently at Audrey Collins Whitney when she tried to flirt with him.

Then the banjos jangled a fanfare. All eyes strained toward the brightly lit stage. The side door opened…

Thunderous applause greeted Vanity's entrance. She wore a plunging black evening gown of chambray silk, with a magnificent flounced bustle and long train accented with yellow satin rosettes. The fit of her bodice accentuated the ripe swell of her bosom, and the skin above it was as pure as cream.

She wore a pearl choker accented in the center by an onyx brooch sporting one large dangling pearl directing Trance's starved gaze back to her alluring cleavage.

Her rich chestnut hair, crimped into a soft frill along her forehead, was roped with pearls. A fresh yellow rose trailing black ribbons was pinned above one ear.

On her slim wrists were a king's ransom in gold bracelets, and on one hand a stunning diamond ring flashed and sparkled. As she snapped open a black lace fan, strolling and swaying to center stage, she lifted her lovely face, sending shivers of desire through Trance.

She had not changed. Her eyes were still so vulnerable! She swept her audience with a direct, friendly smile. Trance wanted to fall at her feet all over again.

Stepping lightly to the music's rhythm, she taunted her audience with her playful smile. He felt no shame in wanting her. He had fought his need, run from his need, tried with all his strength to forget his need, but still it thrived, now more powerful than ever.

Unaware of the amused stares around him, he drank in her beauty. She paused in the middle of the stage, looking up into the lights. Her youth and innocence shined through, though the years had slimmed the girlish fullness of her cheeks.

"I've been waiting for, oh, so long, I just don't know what to do. Where will I go to find you?" she sang. "Then will you love me, too? Oh, yes, yes, yes, I've been waiting for, oh, so long, to taste of your tender kisses. How long will I dream of this? When will I get my wish-h-hes…"

She had begun strolling forward, but her voice trailed off abruptly as if she'd forgotten the words. She stopped and frowned into the footlights.

Trance thought she'd spied him, but her astonished gaze was fixed on the aging gambler in the striped trousers.

He gaped at her, too. Standing, he said, "You're not Vanity Mackenzie!"

The musicians fumbled through several notes, watching to see if Vanity would resume the song. Seeing her preoccupation, they went on loudly, trying to cover the whispers rising from the puzzled audience.

Vanity's fan clattered to the stage. She squinted down at the gentleman. "Vanity *Blade* to you, you low-down son of a snake!" She yanked her hem so high much of her yellow satin petticoats showed. She marched to the far end of the stage and ran down the narrow steps.

Swirling her black skirts indignantly as she weaved between the tables, she stopped directly in front of the gambler. "Smiling Ace Malone!"

The banjos stopped. The piano player's dark fingers hovered over the keys.

Ace scowled at Vanity. "You're not old enough to be—"

"You're damned right! My mother's dead, no thanks to you. And your baby, too. Get off my riverboat before I have you shot!"

She made a fist and swung. Ace didn't even duck. Her knuckles crashed into his cheek and nose, sending a spray of blood into the footlights.

She fumbled beneath her petticoats, exposing a leg covered with a black stocking embroidered with intricate flowers. In the black-and-yellow-ruffled garter above her knee she had tucked a tiny silver derringer.

Jerking it free and cocking it, she gestured with the weapon toward the grand saloon's door.

"If you're still in Sacramento tomorrow, I'll kill you myself. My mother was only twenty-three when you went away. I'll hate you till I die!"

Ace staggered back, looking from her face to the tiny pistol.

Trance was on his feet. He had nearly reached Vanity when she forced Malone at gunpoint from the grand saloon and waved him on toward the railing.

The night air was sweet, the lights from the boat reflecting on the black water far below. The steady threshing of the boat's paddles was loud outside the saloon.

Ace backed to the railing. "I can't swim! Mary, remember how I piggybacked you—" Afraid she'd fire, he leaped backward. "I couldn't do anything for your ma! But I never forgot her—"

Trance moved into the shadows outside the brilliantly lit doorway. Each window was filled with curious onlookers.

He was at Vanity's side now. Gently he grasped her shoulders, whispering softly next to the sweet-scented yellow rose pinned in her curls. "Send him away in a skiff. Your mother wouldn't want you to commit murder in her name."

He felt a violent shudder go through her. The derringer wavered in her hand.

"Someone tell my pilot to turn around. I'm done for tonight."

Trance saw a steward nod and hurry away. Another burly steward motioned to Malone, and the two slipped into the shadows. Vanity stared into the blackness beyond the railing. The pistol's muzzle dipped. Finally she eased the hammer down and dropped her arm to her side. Trance felt the tension drain from her shoulders. He was suddenly aware that he was touching her, and a current of desire shot through him.

Her voice was astonishingly calm. "Thank you. He wasn't worth killing."

She turned, moving from beneath Trance's light touch. Still she didn't look up. At last she held out the derringer as if not trusting herself with it. "My mother died loving that bastard. I hope he rots. I need a drink." Her voice softened. "We Mackenzies love long and hard."

"Is that true, Vanity?" Trance whispered.

She stood stock-still, not believing her ears. She turned, and her beautiful dark eyes went wide, her expression brightening with recognition and delight...before becoming anguished.

"Trance..." She said his name like a prayer. "How can this be?"

Her eyes swept over him. He knew he looked thinner, and that his face was lined, his eyes more hooded.

He didn't think he was handsome anymore. And he had been told he kept himself too aloof to be loved. But for that beautiful instant as Vanity looked into his face, he felt young and filled with hope once again.

She lifted her hand and brushed aside the blond hair on his forehead. "Your hair's a little darker!" She smoothed twin lines between his brows. "You've worried." She trailed her soft palm along his cheek, kindling his desire, then brushed her thumb across his lips. "Trance, you're still suffering. What are you doing here?"

"I had to come," he said.

She looked blank, as if she'd forgotten that what she was doing might be of any interest to him.

The whistle whooped. In moments the boat was turning and heading back to Sacramento.

"Am I too late?" he whispered.

She was about to speak when a stocky man with slick dark hair pushed his way through the onlookers and took Vanity's arm, turning her roughly.

"Who the hell was that? You broke his nose!"

She stared into the man's face as if she didn't recognize him. "Oh… I'm glad. Luther…" She blinked, and looked so beautiful, so confused.

Trance looked into the man's face, wondering how she could settle for him, lower herself to him—even talk to him! He was wild to think she'd agreed to marry a weasel so obviously after her money.

"I need a drink," Vanity murmured. "A double. Luther, this is Trance Holloway, someone I knew long ago. Trance, this is Luther Gant, my… uh…captain. Trance, how did you know where to find me?"

"Quarter writes twice a year."

She smiled. "I should have guessed."

"Is it true you're getting married?"

Luther grinned. "It sure is. We're getting married right here on this boat in just three more weeks. We're already booked solid. It'll be a sensation! One hundred dollars a plate. The best food and music. If I get my way, Vanity will sing every night like she did in the beginning! Even Councilman Collins was in the audience tonight," Luther snickered. "You'll be in every morning newspaper! We've only *started* to make our fortune." He took her arm and shot a pointed look at Trance before trying to lead her away. "Great for business, Vanity. Oh…and nice to meet you…Holloway, was it? Have a drink on the house."

Gracefully, Vanity extracted herself from his grasp. "If you don't mind, Luther, I'd like to visit with Trance. We have a lot to talk about."

She locked eyes with Trance as if trying to see as deeply into him as he was trying to see into her.

"Ask Mr. Holloway to join us in the salon. Then I'll see you back to your house," Luther said.

She shook her head. "Some of these people will want refunds. The *captain* should sort that out," she said firmly.

Turning from Luther, Vanity slipped her arm through Trance's. "Will you join me for a drink? We have tea and coffee in our private suite."

"A whiskey will do," Trance said. "You'll find I'm not the zealot you left behind."

"Indeed not, Trance. You look wonderful. I hope you've prospered. Did you find what you wanted in Ohio?" She was guiding him toward the salon, on the promenade deck. Once inside, she released him and moved awkwardly toward a draped table.

"Yes, I did," Trance said, feeling the strain between them at once. He closed the door behind him, grateful she had rid them of Gant's unwelcome presence. "Have you found what you needed here, Vanity?"

"In some ways," she said thoughtfully, pouring two small whiskeys. She offered him one and lifted her own in a toast.

"To us," Trance said softly, growing warm again with longing.

"There is no *us*, Trance," Vanity whispered. "I gave that up. If you're here to reform me, you might as well leave as soon as the stageplank touches the dock. I'm done twisting myself around to suit others."

"I'm not here for that. I know it doesn't work. I went back to Ohio to become the man my parents wanted, and lived the part for three years. Then typhus carried them both away in the same night."

Her expression melted. "I'm so sorry!"

"I had tried to bend myself to suit them, yet I always knew it was pretense. I'm here to ask you to reconsider marrying that man."

She turned away and downed her whiskey. "Why didn't you come sooner?"

"I was waiting for you to send for me."

"And I didn't, did I? I was waiting for you to come to me."

"And now I have. Vanity, there's not enough time left for us to wait on each other. I need you now, Vanity. I love you more than ever. At least don't marry him until you've given me a chance to show you the man I am now...and will be for the rest of my days."

She turned, her face flushed. "Oh, Trance...! This is how you were when we first met! I thought I'd lost that part of you to your father!"

"You had," he said, watching her cross the space between them and come into his arms.

She was so soft, trembling as she twined her arms around his neck. She lifted her face, tears shining in her beautiful dark eyes. He lowered his head and brushed his lips across hers.

He had dreamed of this! He had wondered if he would still want her when at last she was in his arms. He did! He wanted her more intensely than ever in his life.

He cupped her cheeks, looking at her for a long moment, then watched in wonder as her eyes filled with tears.

He kissed each tear away, sliding his hands to her neck and then her shoulders. Her skin was like satin, as warm and smooth as he remembered. The black gown was in stark contrast to her pale skin. He wanted only to remove it, to see once again those lovely breasts, her slim waist, and inviting, gently curved hips.

He slid his hands around her bodice, feeling the rigidness of her stays underneath the slick satin. He pulled her close until her ripe bosom pressed against the front of his coat. "I want you, Vanity," he whispered. "But not here. I want to be alone with you."

She lifted her lips to his, kissing him openmouthed, sending his senses reeling. He forgot everything, wanting only to hold her, possess her, devour her. He was crazed with need, wanting to blot out the world so that it was just the two of them, alone forever!

Her hands were inside his coat, burning a trail along his sides, tugging to free the fabric from the waistband of his trousers.

Then she was kissing his cheeks, his chin, his neck, his throat. He was losing control, wanting to fall to his knees and drag her with him. He grasped her hips beneath the layers of black ruffles.

He tore his lips from hers, laughing softly. "This damned dress…"

The boat's whistle whooped, signaling their arrival at Sacramento's dock.

Vanity's eyes lit with excitement. "Come on!" She snatched up a heavy yellow-lined black peau de soie cloak and dragged him to the door. "My carriage will be waiting. I'll show you my house. It's a wonderful house! Mama would have loved it."

They were out the door and running along the gangway when Vanity stopped and stood rooted to the deck, looking over the railing at the stageplank. The first persons off the boat were Councilman Collins and his daughter.

Trance said nothing, but he watched Vanity's expression darken. He wanted nothing to spoil this first evening between them and so did not ask if she knew them. He seized her arm and spun her around, kissing her so hard he was sure he was hurting her.

But she returned his passion with an urgency of her own that made him wonder if he would be able to control himself during the carriage ride to her house.

Twenty-Two

Vanity could hardly believe Trance was real. She had never expected to see him again. She had tried to erase him from her mind and lock him from her heart, but there he was, smiling down at her with gentle, loving eyes.

In five years he'd become a calm man with eyes that sparkled with self-assurance.

"This is my house," she said when her carriage stopped on the quiet street.

It was tall and grand and painted white, with a wraparound porch and enough gingerbread trim to look like a landlocked riverboat.

"You're happy here, I hope," Trance said, climbing out and handing her down. "It's more than I could have given you."

Smiling, she ran her hand up his sleeve. He was wrong. He could have given her exactly what she needed. "This house is for my mother. I owe her so much. I try so hard to do things the way my mother would have wanted. I want to feel her sacrifice was worth it."

Trance smiled. "You've become a lovely woman, Vanity. May I come inside?"

"Of course!" she laughed. "Why do you think I brought you here?"

She hurried through the gate and up the stone walk, flanked by flowers, and up the wide sweep of steps to the front door.

She rang the bell. Almost at once her butler and bodyguard Bullo answered.

His towering bulk was made even more startling by his black livery. At the sight of Vanity, his fighter's face relaxed and he grinned crookedly. Then he saw Trance and scowled.

"It's all right, Bullo. Mr. Holloway is my dearest friend." She shrugged as Trance eyed the man. "A woman living alone needs protection."

She quickly glanced behind her before hurrying inside.

"It's magnificent," Trance said, gazing up at the crystal-drop-and-brass chandelier flooding the entrance hall with light. He peeked into her parlors, where no surface was left bare, no piece of furniture unadorned.

She had an impressive Chinese figurine collection and several European oils of nudes. The octagonal tables held small statues. The pretty flowered carpets were complemented by drapes tied back with thick tasseled cords.

"I have three of the sweetest Chinese maids in the city. I rescued them as they were being sold at auction to Chinatown brothels. My cook's from France. My dressmaker worked for some of the finest Virginia families. And my carriage men are all protégés of Quarter's, ex-slaves working toward trades of their own. Quarter's married now, you know, with a baby on the way…"

She hoped he didn't notice how she envied Quarter's good fortune. His wife Mathilda had been a house slave on an Alabama cotton plantation. They'd come together simply, marrying within a year. No vast differences plagued their love.

Trance lingered by the stairs.

"Would you like to see my upstairs rooms?" she asked, her heart pounding. "I keep several extra bedrooms for guests. Sandbar and Sharona stay over on holidays—you do know that I found my grandfather, don't you?" She refused to mention her connection to Howard Collins or Audrey.

"Quarter mentioned it."

She suddenly felt so awkward and unsure. A tingling awareness grew between them as they climbed the stairs. She pushed open each of her upstairs guest room doors, but they both knew only one room had any significance for them.

When she came to her own bedroom, she trembled with anticipation. All of a sudden she felt like a novice.

She led him into her personal sanctuary, with its white iron bed with the elaborate scrollwork and sumptuous comforter. Her bed linens were white silk, and frothy Valenciennes lace cascaded to the thick Wilton carpet.

The room was sweetly demure, the only place not done to please her mother's ghost. As she looked into Trance's eyes, she felt like a child. She wondered if she remembered how to make love!

She half expected him to crush her to his chest as he had that long-ago day when they first came together, but he stood looking at her as if memorizing her face.

"How long will you be in Sacramento?" she asked.

"As long as necessary."

"Then we have time…to get reacquainted," she whispered, hugging herself with delight. Still, she couldn't reach for him. She was engaged, she forced herself to remember. She was engaged…

When the silence between them grew unbearable, she whispered, "Do you want to be with me?"

"There's nothing I want more," he said.

Oh, to hear his voice so husky and seductive! She could not believe that this was real. She had left him so long ago. Only hours before she had waltzed onto the *Pacific Princess*'s stage believing she would soon marry Luther.

Trance opened his arms to her. Hesitantly, she moved closer until he was folding her against him with such exquisite tenderness that tears of joy sprang to her eyes.

His lips against hers were soft, his hands firm and comforting across her back.

Twice they had lost each other, she thought. This was their last chance, their only chance. That they still were in love was so clear to her she became afraid and pulled her lips free to press her cheek to his chest and ask herself if she dared risk being hurt a third time. If she married Luther she faced no risk of that.

Yet, in a breathless instant, she cast away years of restraint imprisoning her heart. From the first, their love had been difficult to harness, yet each precious moment with Trance had been all she could remember as being truly her own.

No stage, no thunderous applause, no expensive, brightly colored gown or exciting poker game compared to the wonder of being in Trance's arms.

She felt safe. She felt at home. She smiled into his eyes and whispered, "I still love you, Trance." The look of surprise and delight in his blue eyes was all she needed. She still belonged to him!

She offered herself for the last time, knowing Trance was all she had ever wanted. Her house, fame, and security were nothing compared to Trance's love. All she wanted was his touch, his caress, his warm eyes smiling down on her.

When his hands closed over the front of her gown, she drew her breath in sharply. She was starving for his touch! Desire exploded deep within her. She had forgotten his power to ignite her need. She had even thought her capacity to feel desire had diminished, but it flared now, made strong and keen by the long wait. She strained against his warm hands, wanting him to strip away the fabric keeping the warmth of his touch from her skin.

"Unhook me," she whispered, turning so that he could unfasten the hooks at her back. She struggled out of the dress and then turned for him to tug free the tiny ribbons on her lacy corset cover. Her petticoats fell in soft heaps around her ankles. She thought he would embrace her then, but he seemed occupied by her corset stays.

As he loosened the laces, she shook so violently she feared she would fall against him. Then she stepped from the heavy boned garment to stand naked before him.

She felt free of all restraint, free to stand naked while he was still fully dressed. She spread her hands beneath his lapels and pushed back his frock coat. She tugged at the tiny studs on his shirt and pulled it from the waistband of his snug trousers.

His chest was full and broad, his lightly furred skin pale, warm, and smooth, and almost quivering to her touch. They moved to the bed, where she sat down and started loosening his waistband.

He covered her eager fingers with his and whispered, "There's no hurry, darling Vanity."

She lay back and watched him settle on the bed beside her. Why was he waiting? she wondered, as he propped his head on his hand and gazed at her.

"How long I have dreamed of this!" he whispered, smoothing his warm palm over her breasts and then lightly teasing each nipple with his fingertips until they stood proud and aroused.

Her loins ached. She so longed to be filled with him and to experience the incredible pleasure she had known so very long ago only with him. But he was content to caress her breasts until she seized his hand and guided it lower. "Trance, don't tease me!"

"I've waited too long to hurry," he whispered, leaning close to kiss her playfully.

Then he cupped her mound, sending waves of aroused heat through her body. She grabbed at his shoulder, pulling him on top of her so that she could feel the soft hairs on his chest tickle her nipples. His hips were heavy between her legs.

She grew mindless with need, thinking that to have him now would keep him with her forever. She offered up all she possessed, her most tender recesses were bared to his exploring, arousing expert touch. Nothing was denied him!

"Oh, Trance, I love you so!" she whispered, panting against his neck. "Love me! Love me!"

Yet still he did not hurry but tortured her sweetly with the divinely gentle touch of his fingers.

"I've dreamed of this," he said, moving to lower his trousers. "I've yearned for you every night, every single night that we've been apart."

"I tried so hard to forget you," she said, her voice catching.

She was bewildered by his tenderness, but thrilled and touched by it, too. She feared he might think this their only night together. It was only the first of many, she hoped, pulling him close.

Yet again he pulled away to look at her lying beneath him, to gaze at her swollen breasts and then kiss them with a sweetness that inflamed her need.

Still he lingered, trailing his soft lips to her waist and belly, laying his cheek against her thighs and then thrilling her with moist kisses in a place where she could scarcely endure it without crying out.

Then suddenly, fiercely, he shifted, pushed down his trousers, revealing a desire so welcome and urgent she could only open completely to receive him. She was awestruck by the pleasure of it, rendered helpless to prevent her body from engulfing him with her own passion.

She was completely possessed, surrendered to his power, receiving him with little cries of long-denied delight, wanting the pulsing, throbbing moments to endure forever.

But her body could not stand it. A tingling sensation, like a silvery waterfall of stars, flooded her with instant, engulfing satisfaction.

She heard his cry mingled with her own and realized she was crushed in his embrace. He panted, gasped, shuddered, and almost wept. Long after he was spent he remained inside her, clutching her body against him as if it was his life, thrusting and thrusting as if he could not get enough.

"Vanity! Vanity…" He buried his face in her neck. "Dear Lord, how I love you! I've been empty without you. My life has been incomplete. Marry me, Vanity. Please!"

She lifted his wet face from her shoulder. The bedroom was too dim for her to see his eyes. She laughed softly. "Now who's in a hurry?"

"I can't bear to think of you marrying that man! He's not good enough for you. I'm not asking you to change. Simply marry me. This love between us can't be denied any longer!"

"I've been with no one else since you, Trance," she whispered, trying to blot Luther from her mind. "You were my first, my only. But we can't rush. We need time. You've changed. I've changed. Just hold me. Hold me!"

He stared down at her. Then slowly he pulled away and rolled onto his side. After a moment he sat up and moved to the edge of the bed. He swept back his darkened silver-blond hair. "To think that you saved yourself for—"

Alarmed by his reaction, she touched his arm. "I wasn't waiting," she interrupted. "I gave you up completely. I was waiting for a new love. None came."

She sat up then and reached for a dressing gown. She felt very vulnerable, very afraid, and very confused.

For a long time Trance was strangely silent. "You're right that we're strangers. I thought I could forget all that's happened since…Vanity, there's so much to tell you. I'm worried you won't understand. How can you, when I tell you…I told you I did all my parents asked of me…"

She nodded, feeling even more uneasy.

"I believed that was the right thing to do at the time. After all that had happened, my cooperation made them both so happy. They even became reconciled to Rowena's marriage. What I did was right…then." He seemed to be leading up to something. "I-I don't know how to tell you, Vanity, but I didn't wait for a new love."

Her heart shivered to a stop. Struggling to understand, she stammered, "I didn't expect you to…to stay away from women for the rest of your life…on my account," she said, though jealousy made her want to cry.

"Did you think I'd marry?" he asked softly.

She didn't know what to say. She felt numb, not wanting to believe he could have done that—not her Trance, husband to another!

A shadow of hurt moved through her. She stood slowly and crossed the room, facing the wall. He had tried harder than she to forget their love. "Do you love her, Trance?" she asked in a small, anguished voice.

"It's a disgrace to say so, but, no, I didn't. I only tried to, especially when she carried my child. She sacrificed her life to give me a son, Vanity. For a long time afterward I made myself believe I had loved her, but I didn't. I…" His words broke off.

She was crying softly, feeling the hot tears sear her face. It was all too much for one night. To see Ace Malone again and make a spectacle of herself…and in front of her father and half sister. To see Trance again and find herself in his arms—and now to learn he'd given of himself to another and had a child.

But the other was dead, she reminded herself. And Trance was there with her. Their lovemaking had been wonderful. More than wonderful.

It had been right.

"How long before you go back to your child?" she murmured, hoping he didn't know she was crying.

"I've brought him and his nanny along. They're at my hotel. I want you to meet my boy. He's three years old."

"You married quite soon after returning to Cold Crossing, then." Her voice was cool.

"As soon as my health returned, my parents introduced me to Sally. Two months later my father married us...in the parlor where I'd dreamed of marrying you. I tried not to think of that, but it was always just beneath my thoughts. I was determined to fulfill every promise I'd made to God and myself. It was the only way I knew to show my gratitude for my freedom. Can you understand, Vanity? Can you believe I'm here now because I want you...just as you are?"

"Did you make her happy? Were you good together?" The pain of her questions nearly made her double over.

"I believe she was happy with me. Intimately...she couldn't let go. With you, I knew real abandon. I couldn't forget. I tried. She couldn't enjoy it. For her it was a duty she feared and hated. I always felt like a... an animal. We finally stopped. If childbed fever hadn't taken her, we would not have had more children. To comfort myself and ease my guilt over her death, I've told myself it was better she died young than waste away as the wife of a man who didn't love her, but she deserved better than I gave. She deserved life!"

"Must you torment yourself?"

He brightened. "I'm asking that you give me one last chance. I've always believed that in spite of our differences we belonged together."

She looked up into his hope-filled face. She wanted to tell him she believed the same, but she was no longer sure. What compromises would they make to find happiness this time?

After a thoughtful silence, Trance crossed to where she stood and took her shoulders in his hands.

Quickly Vanity turned into his embrace, sobbing against his chest. "I'm sorry...for you...for your wife..." She lifted her face. "I love you so."

His mouth closed over hers. At once they were one, thinking no more of the past, too absorbed in each other to worry about the future. They were together, and that was all that mattered.

When they fell across the rumpled bed a second time, all the gentleness, all the leisurely savoring, was gone. Their love was explosive now, blazing between them, threatening to consume them. When it was over, they lay dazed and shaking, trying to prevent the world from intruding.

To keep it at bay, they turned to each other again. When at last they slept, they were twined together, dreaming of a true love where differences didn't matter.

She couldn't remember when the sky looked bluer. The clouds hung overhead in lazy puffs, and the breeze was sweetly cool.

She had never before noticed the loveliness of sunlight falling on her garden. That following morning, seated across from Trance on her terrace, she saw everything with new eyes.

In the distance came the whoop of a paddle-wheeler moving upriver. Beyond the stone garden wall the busy town bustled with life.

As they ate, she told him what she'd done since coming to Sacramento, of Sandbar and Sharona, of seeing Tenderfoot again and her mother's grave. She talked of the *Pacific Princess* and her weekly performances—and of Luther's proposal.

Trance just nodded.

She knew she had a glow about her. Happiness coursed through her now.

Vanity found Trance's new profession in railroading fascinating, particularly in the power his father-in-law's business would have over Sacramento's river trade.

But most of all she delighted in being a woman loved. She felt more beautiful than ever in her life. Though her hair tumbled untidily down her back, she didn't care. She was happy!

She felt as if she'd been given this day as a gift. That she would soon meet Trance's son by another woman no longer troubled her. If by some miracle she and Trance found their way to marriage, she hoped the boy would accept her.

Oh, yes, the sky was so very blue! She was a woman restored to love most precious!

Coming to California to reclaim Vanity had seemed a simple matter when Trance had set out. He had known through Quarter's letters that she'd done well for herself, but he hadn't realized just how well until he saw her magnificent boat and her fine house.

His pride was not so fragile that he couldn't accept that the woman he loved was wealthier than he, but he did wonder if he had anything to offer to equal the home and career she'd built.

That morning as they rode to Trance's hotel in Vanity's carriage—they'd made love again while dressing—he was reminded again of her comfortable means. Her carriage was surely one of the finest in town. She wore a lovely dove-gray hat and gown and looked so completely ladylike he was sure no one in Sacramento could best her. Certainly, she would be the most lovely creature ever to walk Cold Crossing's dusty lanes.

But he intended to make Sacramento his new home. As they pulled up to his hotel, he looked at Vanity as more than the object of his desire. Now he tried to imagine her as his son's mother.

Every person in the hotel lobby paused to stare admiringly as they entered. Trance's heart swelled. This splendid woman belonged to him!

Yet propriety wouldn't allow him to invite her to his suite to meet his boy. "I'll see if they're ready," he said, reluctant to leave Vanity alone in the lobby.

"I'll be fine...and waiting right here," she said. "Judge Williams is over there. He hasn't been to a performance since he realized I had no inten—" Vanity blushed. "Forgive me. I'll wait right here. Don't be long."

Three-year-old Jason and his nanny, Nell White, were waiting, dressed to go out, when Trance arrived. Trance swung his gleeful son into his arms. The child wore a blue sailor outfit with a hat sporting short ribbons.

"How's my boy?" Trance asked, laughing and hugging the blue-eyed lad with bowl-cut silky brown hair so like Sally's. Vanity would surely adore this smiling little imp! "How are you this afternoon, Mrs. White?"

"We've been waiting since breakfast," she said flatly.

He had already told Mrs. White that he'd come to California to find a former acquaintance he hoped to marry. She had seemed agreeable to the idea, being the matchmaking sort. A widower needed a good woman to make him happy and to mother his son, she often said.

To impress his choice, Mrs. White had donned an impeccable brown alpaca gown. She looked very presentable. She was a close friend of his late wife's mother—not to mention brave to come so far at his request—and Trance had always liked her.

"I trust your young lady was happy to see you again," Mrs. White said carefully.

Trance detected a hint of disapproval. Did she know he'd been out all night? He had hoped she only tapped at his door that morning and assumed he'd gone out early.

He had no intention of lying to the woman, but his nights were none of her business. He excused himself and went into his room to change his shirt while Jason gathered his tin soldiers into a box. Moments later they started for the lobby. Trance felt nervous.

Across the lobby, Vanity looked so entrancing. Trance was momentarily struck speechless. She looked nothing like the little heathen he'd fallen in love with so long ago. She was the most breathtaking lady he'd ever seen.

As Trance approached Vanity, Mrs. White drew Jason protectively to her side. She whispered in Trance's direction, "It's disgraceful the sort this hotel allows inside its doors. You should speak to the management. We should find better lodgings. Your boy shouldn't have to pass common harlots on his way to the street. The very idea!"

Thunderstruck, Trance whirled on the woman. She was referring to his beloved Vanity! Just as quickly, he looked back at Vanity, wondering if, indeed, he might be blinded by love.

Vanity's hair was done no differently from the style Sally's might have been, except the rich chestnut color did stand out in eye-catching splendor. Her gown was of the highest fashion but with a longer train and more pronounced bustle than seen in the Midwest. Her face was unpainted this morning, yet Mrs. White took her for a...a...

"What makes you think that young woman is improper?" Trance asked, reining his rising temper.

Mrs. White's cheeks colored. "It's not a Christian thing to say, but a person can just tell. Look how she holds herself. Look how she acknowledges the inviting glances from those strange men. A decent woman wouldn't...oh!" She covered her mouth as Vanity crossed to gaze out the window. "She struts like a peacock. The hussy! We should cover Jason's eyes!"

Unable to control his fury, Trance glared at Mrs. White, silencing her.

Vanity saw Trance then. Her lovely face lit up. She strolled across the lobby, smiling. Trance felt a rush of passion, confusion, and guilt about what Mrs. White had just said. And Jason, his blue eyes popping, had heard it all!

Vanity held out her gloved hands. Trance took them, gazing hungrily into her warm, eager face. He had never loved anyone but this beguiling creature! He wanted her as his wife.

Vanity dimpled. "Hello! This must be…" She turned her attention to Jason, who was edging from behind his nanny's skirts. "Hello, Jason. I'm delighted to make your acquaintance." She extended a gloved hand.

How could his son help but warm to her smile? Trance wondered. She crouched before him, her eyes drinking in his little face. She colored such an adorable shade of pink Trance wanted to kiss her.

"You're a very handsome young man," Vanity said. "Do you ride horseback? Have you been into the mountains yet?"

Jason smiled shyly, but said nothing. Finally he shook his head and hid behind Mrs. White again.

Smiling still, Vanity straightened and held out her hand to the nanny. "I'm honored to meet you, Mrs. White. Trance has told me how good you've been to Jason since his mother passed on. Did you enjoy your trip to California?"

Mrs. White regarded Vanity with distaste. She did not take Vanity's hand, but remained rigid, her silence eloquent.

Vanity let her hand fall.

"You may have the rest of the afternoon off, Mrs. White. Vanity and I will look after Jason," Trance said quietly.

Vanity's smile had wilted.

"That's a funny name," Jason piped up, his eyes dancing.

Vanity blinked. "T-that's my stage name. My real name's Mary Louise. Do you like riverboats, Jason? I've reserved a private dining room for us. Later, I'll teach you to fish with a cane pole."

Mrs. White's face drained of color. Aghast, she turned to stare at an advertisement posted near the hotel's entrance. Across the bold black-and-white picture of the *Pacific Princess* was the glaring headline reading SHOWS NIGHTLY! High-stepping dancing girls exposing petticoats had been drawn below the words FEATURING VANITY BLADE! SATURDAYS!

Mrs. White swept Trance with her horrified expression. "I will telegraph Jason's grandfather at once! This sort of business will not go on under my nose!"

"I should caution you—"

She kept her voice ominously low. "If your father-in-law thinks his grandson's future here may not be wholesome, he'll have no trouble getting custody. I'm shocked, Mr. Holloway! You—of all people! Sally must be turning in her grave!"

"Another word, Mrs. White, and I'll fire you."

"And who will look after the boy's daily needs, then, and his prayers, while you dally with…that sort?"

"Mrs. White, that's enough!"

"The scandal of it! Your parents must be turning in their graves, too! If Sally had known, she never would have married you! I'm appalled!"

Vanity stood, stunned, watching Trance, who was watching Mrs. White. Then she turned away.

Jason understood not a word. He knew only that his father was being scolded.

"Go now, Mrs. White!" Trance ordered. "You had best take care what tales you carry to Sally's father. You know nothing about Miss Blade. You've made a hasty judgment. I'll have your severance pay delivered to your new hotel. I'll include return fare to Ohio."

Torn by her anger and her sense of duty toward the boy, Mrs. White finally huffed away, muttering to herself and dabbing at her eyes with a linen handkerchief.

Trance didn't care who was watching. He took his son's hand. "Ready, Vanity, darling?"

Jason took her other hand and they walked out to the busy dusty street.

On the way to the riverfront, Vanity chatted steadily about her childhood on the river, enchanting Jason and warming Trance's heart with her grace and courage.

But when their eyes met, Trance saw the hurt. He wanted to comfort and reassure her, but Jason sat between them. Trance was forced to keep his distance and worry that Mrs. White had shattered the fragile new hope for happiness he and Vanity had found in each other's arms the night before.

Twenty-Three

They were the talk of Sacramento. John Travis Holloway and Vanity Blade could be seen all over town riding in her fine carriage, taking in the opera, going to the best places, and visiting the socially prominent not prejudiced against beauty, wealth, and fame—or railroads.

Every night for two weeks they were seen dining aboard the *Pacific Princess*, and when Vanity performed it was with a new vigor that thrilled her audience.

Rumors had it that Trance Holloway had dismissed his son's nanny for objecting to the beautiful entertainer. Now the boy was in the charge of a kindly Chinese maid from Miss Blade's own household.

Vanity Blade took on the soft look of a woman well bedded. She bubbled with laughter and sang songs onstage that made men fairly drool.

Trance Holloway could be said to possess a secret smile and a spring to his step, too. They were clearly in love, with an unmistakable glow about them.

Yet a storm brewed. Luther Gant could be seen each night scowling from the shadows of the *Pacific Princess*'s gangway, watching Vanity perform through the grand saloon's windows.

Luther had believed Vanity would never let a man into her life so quickly. She had certainly been expert at holding him at bay. As each day passed, and the wedding date drew nearer, Vanity spent every available moment with Holloway. Luther reckoned how to deal with his problem.

During her performance two weeks after Holloway's arrival, Luther waited for Vanity in her private salon, where she would come for her cloak and her nightly nip of bourbon.

Drumming his fingers on a side table, he waited in darkness while applause echoed across the dark river. Now that her Saturday night performance was over, the boat was nearly back at the landing. She had been avoiding him, he knew, but he needed only a few moments to reclaim her.

Vanity breezed in, still laughing from something Trance had said, and grabbed her velvet cloak—

Luther clutched a corner of it, holding tightly, anger just beneath the surface of his control. "Have you a minute for me, honey?" He kept his voice soft.

She gasped as he turned up the flame in the nearby oil lamp, her expression wary. "What are you doing here in the dark?" she asked crossly. Glancing out to see that Trance had gone on to wait for her at the stairs, Vanity closed the stateroom door. "Is something wrong?" Her cheeks flushed. She knew only too well that everything was wrong where Luther was concerned.

"We need to talk," Luther said.

"I suppose we do," she responded, crossing the cabin to a sideboard to pour herself a drink. "Everything's happening so fast. I suppose you're angry with me. Well, you needn't be. I don't have any idea what will come of all this."

That wasn't what he'd expected. Suddenly he knew how to proceed. "I thought we'd reached an understanding."

She sank to the bunk opposite his chair and twisted her hands. "I realize I'm—we're still engaged."

"Holloway's changed that," Luther said. He considered ordering a fatal accident for Mr. J. T. Holloway. "You don't appear interested in marrying me any longer," he said. "I scarcely need to point out your affair with Holloway is apparent to everyone. I feel like a cuckold, a laughingstock."

She was on her feet at once. "I knew this would happen if I let myself get...involved with...with any man! I don't belong to you...or anyone! I'm sorry I let you think I needed your...companionship." She gave him a look he found difficult to resist. "I love Trance with all my heart. I could be happy with him if it weren't for...that dear little boy. But I'm so afraid I won't make the right sort of mother. Already people are whispering the most awful things!"

"And they'll go on whispering," Luther said, surprised at her honesty and his angry reaction to it. He was puzzled, too, because she looked very peculiar, as if she had something weighty on her mind.

She looked at the tumbler in her hand and finally set it aside without drinking from it. "Shall we cancel the wedding?" she asked.

"No."

She blinked. "Do you want to go on captaining this boat?"

"Of course!" he said with alarm. He tried to appear reasonable. "If you need time…"

"I don't know what I need! I had my life in order, and now this! I want him, but if Trance and I marry, Trance has no idea how people may snub us. I don't care, of course. After all these years, I couldn't possibly. But he may find he cares someday, and surely his boy will. I have to think of that."

"You once said you and I were alike." Luther tried to sound hurt. If he could still get his hands on even a portion of her wealth, he wouldn't care if she slept with a saint or a demon.

Still, he had a certain desire for her charms and it rankled to think she'd given herself to a preacher's son when she could have Luther's expertise.

"I wish I knew what to do!" she exclaimed. She caught Luther's calculating eye and regained control. "You're the last person I should talk to about Trance."

Luther rose and stretched, hoping to remind her of his attractive physique. He considered himself more than enough man for her, and thought momentarily of showing her just how much, whether she was willing or not.

He decided against force. "Heaven's mighty far, Vanity. At least you know I have no illusions about you. If I marry you, I have no social standing to lose. You won't have to do anything to please me…well, nothing against the grain like you'd have to do for him.

"Get him out of your system, if you have to, but remember, if you marry him you'll boot-lick businessmen and their snotty little wives for the rest of your life. Imagine those miserable parties where you'll try to be hostess and where everyone will be waiting for you to say or do something improper. With me you don't have to worry."

Vanity gave him a sharp look, one he hadn't expected. "What have you wanted from me all these years, I wonder?"

"Perhaps only what he wants—your beautiful body. But you and I, Vanity, we'll never have to pretend. Life aboard this boat frees us from the hypocrites. I ask nothing of you. As my wife, you can go on singing whatever you like for as long as you like. You can dress as you please, gamble all you want, drink as much bourbon as you want. Haven't you already changed for him? Look at your gown. You could wear it to church. Be yourself, honey. Think with your head, not your…" He let his voice trail off, but she knew what he meant.

Vanity slapped him.

She was gone in a swirl of rustling satin, but Luther wasn't alarmed.

With that last bit of reasoning, he'd reached her. Who else would risk telling the beautiful, elusive Vanity Blade she was behaving like a bitch in heat?

> Forgive me, Trance. I'm not feeling well. I can't meet you for dinner this evening. Don't trouble yourself coming to my house. I'll be fine. Give Jason my love.

Puzzled, Trance stared at Vanity's hastily scribbled note. Not feeling well? He turned the note over, wondering why he found this message so peculiar. For the past two days she had seemed listless and detached. She had only picked at her meals. He had even caught her staring at him with unsettling intensity.

He folded her note and went to the window of his hotel suite. The darkened town winked with yellow lights. He began to unknot his cravat…

Not go to her house? He made a fist and walked to the bed. He wanted to see her! It wasn't like her just to send a note. Something must have happened.

If he wasn't with her, what would he do with himself for an entire evening? His life had merged completely with Vanity's. She was all he thought about. He wanted nothing more than to make love to her, or think of making love to her. The more they were together, the more he wanted her.

But the night before, she had seemed preoccupied. She had pleaded a headache and asked him to leave early. He'd found that suspicious, but hadn't said anything. She had claimed she was worried he spent too much time away from Jason, which was sadly true.

But the boy adored his new nursemaid, Poppy, and seemed content believing his papa had "business" keeping him away.

Trance reread the note. Why was it so brief, so curt, so lacking in intimacy? He was hungry for her touch, her warm, laughing eyes, her sweet and tender voice saying his name over and over. Was Luther refusing to set her free? She had said she was going to break the news to him right away. Or was the gossip wearing her down?

Had she tired of him?

A knot formed in his stomach, making the possibility of dinner alone repugnant. He wanted to go to her, to insist to know what was wrong, but finally he forced himself to unclench his fists.

She was ill, just as she said. She needed rest. Since his arrival, they had made love at least twice a day. The poor darling was probably exhausted.

He smiled to himself. He would keep his wits about him and go to her when she felt better. He was, after all, a grown man, no longer a headstrong youth.

He turned to the pile of invitations lying on the desk. He had answered not a one since his arrival, and that was no way to conduct his father-in-law's business. He had let his desire for Vanity keep him from his duties.

He didn't have an unlimited supply of money, and would soon have to account for his expenditures. Grinding his teeth in irritation, he knew he must do his best in that regard. If provided with grounds, his father-in-law would not hesitate to try to take custody of Jason. He had not been pleased when Trance announced his intention to take the man's only grandchild west permanently after one day's notice.

The uppermost engraved invitation was from the councilman he'd met that first night on Vanity's boat. The dinner Collins was giving happened to be that evening and was beginning in an hour. The man would likely have present just the sort of men who would prove helpful to Trance's business.

Glancing again at Vanity's bewildering note, Trance decided he should do something constructive. He reknotted his cravat, tucked it carefully beneath the lapels of his cutaway, and took up his brushed-silk hat.

Twenty-Four

"Mr. Holloway! We weren't expecting you, but come in. Do come in!"

Audrey Collins's flashing green eyes swept appreciatively over Trance's flattering cutaway and snug trousers. She linked arms with him and steered him out of the butler's range of hearing.

Her gown swept softly across the black-and-white-tiled vestibule. "I'm so pleased you've decided to join us!"

A pleasant aroma of venison and broiled elk steaks came from the dining room, where Trance could see a buffet table laden with an impressive array of food.

From the parlors came the sound of a sophisticated party—no harsh laughter and rattling poker chips. Somewhere a violin quartet played, giving the huge Italianate house an atmosphere of cultured refinement.

"Before I introduce you to everyone, let's slip away where we can get acquainted. Tell me everything you've been doing while in Sacramento." Audrey led him down the wide, high-ceilinged hall, away from the parlor doors. A massive black walnut clock struck the hour of nine.

Trance was taken aback by the house. Certainly nothing in Cold Crossing could compare. The Collins lumber mills must be bringing in a staggering fortune.

"I should have sent a message that I was coming after all," Trance said, smiling politely at Audrey as he followed her to a closed door. "I'm sorry I didn't reply sooner. I've been...busy."

"We know," she said. "In here, please. My father's study."

She had a commanding way about her that he didn't like. However, she looked so like Vanity he found himself staring, unconsciously comparing the two women.

Where Vanity moved with grace and carried herself naturally, her eyes friendly and twinkling, Audrey Collins moved with hauteur. She had the disdainful, bored attitude of one schooled to regard most of the world as her inferior.

278

"We're delighted to have you, Mr. Holloway. It doesn't matter what time our friends arrive," Audrey said, lifting her beautiful pale face so that her elaborate auburn curls slithered across her creamy bare shoulders. "We all need our little distractions, don't you know. I'd like to show you our house later on. Our friends back east think it's a bit ostentatious, but what else does one do with one's money in such a remote place? When I think of the life I might have led in Boston…But you don't want to hear about that, I'm sure." She drew him into the dimly lit study and closed the door.

He found it curious that she was willing to be alone in a room with him. Since Boston didn't offer the opportunities for making fortunes in lumber that California did, he doubted any life she might have led in Boston would have compared to this one.

At the heavy-legged sideboard, she poured dark Spanish sherry into two small cut-glass tumblers and then plucked a slim brown cheroot from the leather humidor. She lit it from the glass-globed lamp nearby.

Trance was surprised, and then realized she was deliberately provoking him. He turned his attention away from her to the glass-doored bookcases against the far wall.

The study was furnished with heavy pieces and was paneled, an intimidatingly masculine chamber crowded with leather-bound books and a formal arrangement of chairs and tables that reminded Trance of a headmaster's office. Feeling a stab of discomfort, he wished he hadn't come.

"Since that night we met on the *Pacific Princess*, Mr. Holloway, I've been anxious to talk with you. I convinced Father you would be an important man to have among our circle of friends. Railroads—shipping in general—and lumber go well together, don't you agree?"

Trance gave a slight nod. He felt like a small-town man vastly out of his element.

"Wasn't that Miss Blade simply too delightful? Father was scandalized that I wanted to hear her sing. One cannot take a step in this town without hearing talk of her. Father has no interest in Sacramento's seamy attractions, but I was ever so curious. I'd been warned she was a rowdy. Women like that are always brawling with no thought for consequences. I'm told she has a lover in every closet. You have a taste for scandalous women, so I'm told."

Trance drew his hand back from the offered glass. His first thought was to turn and leave. He didn't pretend courtesy. "Do you fancy yourself as that sort?" he asked, watching her puff on the cheroot.

"Oh, perhaps to a degree. I could never hope to reach her infamy, though. With my father's reputation to uphold, I mustn't be too naughty, but a certain amount keeps interest in the family high. I'm no fool, if you suspected I was like other wealthy daughters. I find my amusements."

"Is that why you invited me here—to amuse yourself?" He gave her the standard once-over she was expecting and watched her color rise.

"Oh, you are clever, Mr. Holloway! In a word, yes. I'm curious about a man who would dally so openly with a common woman when another has so much more to offer."

Trance realized what he loved most about Vanity was her lack of guile. This woman was playing with him. If she thought herself better than Vanity, she was a fool.

"What is it you're offering, Miss Collins?" he asked, taking the glass and sipping the nutty-tasting dark gold liquid.

"My name's Mrs. Whitney. At the moment I offer nothing, to you or any other. I'm a divorcée. I don't stay married to the wrong sort. I choose carefully, but if I make a mistake I'm not above defying convention to rectify it."

Trance managed to stifle his desire to laugh. "Should I be impressed?" he asked, feeling droll.

"Oh, but you should be, because what I have to offer the right man is more than social status, which we both know is necessary to the wife of a prosperous man. Fine breeding is necessary for a well-run home and children, even in this God-forsaken state." She strolled to the fireplace and gazed into the mirror above the black marble mantel.

Was she serious? he wondered, completely put off by her. He no longer found her beautiful.

"Men of social standing require decent women to hostess parties, to mother children, to do all those things the socially inferior know nothing about."

"Very interesting, Mrs. Whitney."

"If a man of rising status were to shackle himself with a common girl, certainly he'd be talked about. But, more importantly, he'd be shunned by those very people he needed most. Dalliance is one thing. An unfortunate marriage is quite another."

"Dalliance," he said, raising his head.

"Why, Mr. Holloway, such a foolish man's home might take on the look of a...a gambling palace. No decent, self-respecting businessman would bring his wife or friends there." She turned slowly, her gaze sweeping over the study's furnishings. *This* home was one of quality, her look seemed to say, while Vanity's was, well...

"It's common knowledge that men require a certain sort of woman to satisfy certain needs," Audrey lectured. "That's why your infatuation with Miss Blade is being tolerated with such amusement. A healthy, virile widower, a pretty singer of questionable morals—so *very* common."

Angrily, Trance put the goblet down and started for the door.

Audrey quickly blocked his exit. "Don't scowl so. Supposing, for the sake of our discussion, that a man found the best of both in one woman. He'd do marvelously well in business. He'd raise a respectable family. He'd surely enjoy all the benefits of his father-in-law's money—and he'd have no need for a mistress. No wisp of scandal would touch his children." She blew pungent tobacco smoke into his face. "You have a son, don't you, Mr. Holloway? Or may I call you John Travis?"

Trance could barely contain his anger but still said nothing.

Audrey reached up and patted his cheek. "Let's greet my father. Now, now, you're scowling again, Mr. Holloway. How is business going? Or have you even given it a thought?" Her voice was like silk. She moved toward the door, expecting him to follow.

He regarded her with contempt. "Send for a carriage. I'm not staying." He brushed past her into the hall.

For a moment she looked alarmed. Then she shrugged and nodded. "As you wish."

Moments later Trance found his hat and left. As he waited on the marble steps leading to the dusty street, he concentrated on keeping a tight rein on his rage. He'd let that miserable woman talk of Vanity as if she were a common whore! As if Audrey Collins Whitney had anything to offer a man!

He wondered what had possessed him to go out when Vanity was ill and needed him, whether she realized it or not.

The caleche that drew to a stop before him bore the Collins family crest on the door.

"I'll see you back to your hotel," Audrey said, coming up behind him. She patted his arm as she allowed the driver to hand her up.

Refusing to ride with her wasn't worth the effort, Trance thought. "The home of Miss Blade," he called to the driver.

"He has his instructions," Audrey countered, snuggling close and hooking her arm through his. "We'll take you to your hotel. The advantage of being well born, John Travis, is that I *know* how to behave but sometimes choose not to. That makes me exciting."

"In your opinion."

"Oh, in the opinion of many gentlemen interested in all I have to offer."

"Then you should have no trouble snaring one—or all—with your propositions. If you haven't already."

Vanity lifted her tear-stained face from her arms. She was a fool to stay away from Trance when she needed him most. What would he say when she told him?

He would want to marry her, of course. He already did. But she was not sure marriage was right for them, and she was not ready to risk it.

She needed no doctor to tell her that she was carrying Trance's child. Her body had already told her. She should have been delighted, and in a way she was. But she didn't want to marry Trance because she had no choice; she wanted their marriage to be a perfect union of hearts and minds.

If she was not the right woman for Trance, she must send him on his way. She had stayed away from Trance tonight to think.

Suddenly she sprang to her feet. Immediately sorry, she clutched her churning belly and hurried downstairs. Throwing a long cape over her dressing gown, she found her way through the darkened rooms to the butler's pantry, where she yanked the bell cord that would summon her driver. A clock on the wall struck ten.

Impatient now that she was thinking of telling Trance her secret, she dashed out the back door and across the pebbled walk to the carriage house. She *had* to see Trance. She had to see his face. Then she would know what to do.

She found Bullo with his head down on a crude table in the tidy tack room. In one fist was clutched one of her better bottles of whiskey.

"You're supposed to be guarding me!" she said angrily, shaking the huge man's shoulder. "Since when do you raid my cellar and help yourself to my whiskey? Don't I pay you well enough?"

He groaned and tried to raise his head.

"You shouldn't encourage him," she scolded the wizened gardener, who looked up at her with very red eyes. "This is what I get for having a soft heart, hiring old coots like you two. The house could burn down around your ears and you'd likely still be sitting here when it was over. Off to bed with both of you. I hope my driver's sober."

"We haven't been in the cellar, miss! We been finding these fine and rare potations sitting here on the table every night after supper. Ain't you the most understanding woman an ol' geezer could work for? Ain't you leaving this fine elixir so's we can sleep like babes?"

Mr. Haggerty worked himself to his feet, steadied himself, then took up his rake and hoe like sword and scepter. "I, mistress, am not a common thief."

"Oh, pooh! Good night."

Shaking her head, she hurried into the stable, where her driver was fumbling sleepily with the harnesses for her horses.

"As soon as you're ready, take me to the Federal Hotel."

He nodded, looking peeved.

She climbed into her phaeton, hoping she was doing the right thing.

Though it wasn't late, there was little traffic, but the ride to Trance's hotel seemed inordinately long. The night was cool and Vanity shivered again with the sensation that she was being watched.

She wished Bullo didn't have such a weakness for whiskey. Finding the bottles waiting, indeed! Such a story. She would have felt much safer if he'd been riding alongside her driver now.

The traffic in front of Trance's hotel increased as the crowd pouring out of the opera house nearby headed for the lines of waiting carriages and hacks.

For some minutes, Vanity's driver couldn't get close to the hotel, and Vanity didn't want to get out since she was wearing only a dressing gown and cape. She felt ill again and began to doubt her decision to talk to Trance when she still didn't know her own mind.

She rolled up the leather curtain and peered out, thinking to send a message to Trance's room with one of the doormen. Ahead were the dark, tall-hatted shapes of gentlemen and their ladies strolling along toward the Sierra House, a particularly fine restaurant and saloon where she and Trance had dined several afternoons.

The hotel was lit up as always, the yellow glare making her blink. It was then that she saw Trance alight from a fancy glass-doored caleche and start for the hotel's entrance without looking back. He was dressed as if he'd been to the opera.

He looked so marvelous striding toward the hotel's crowded doorway. She felt a rush of joy at seeing him and was about to call out to him when she saw a young woman in a pink silk gown get out of the carriage and dart after Trance, seizing his arm.

They looked as if they were exchanging heated words, but Vanity couldn't hear what was being said. Her heart twisted painfully. He had gone out, Vanity thought, trembling with hurt. And who was that with him?

When the young woman seized Trance's face and kissed him soundly to the delight of the opera crowd, Vanity fell back against the cushioned seat. Audrey Collins!

Yet how could that be? Why would he seek out her half sister? Afraid she would be ill, Vanity immediately abandoned her intention of seeing Trance.

Why *Audrey*? She represented all Vanity had tried to become, and all she could never hope to be. Audrey Collins and her mother were the reasons her father couldn't marry *her* mother. Worst of all, she was the one who might offer Trance a truly respectable marriage—and she could be a decent mother to his son!

She felt utterly alone. Disappointment and despair washed over her. Now was not the time to tell Trance she was pregnant. And it certainly was not the time to break off with Luther, who would surely suspect and ridicule her.

She would send a message to Trance saying she didn't wish to see him again. She would find some kind of reason…

Fighting back sobs, Vanity tapped for her driver. "I've changed my mind! Take me home!"

Early the following morning Vanity donned a gaudy red-and-black-striped gown more suitable for evening wear, and had her driver take her out to the wharves.

Making her way carefully up the stageplank to the *Pacific Princess* and Luther's cabin, Vanity paused at his door. Unmistakable waves of morning sickness rolled through her body. Then, feeling heavy and dull with resolution, she tapped.

Moments later Luther flung the door wide. "Goddammit! If you'd just let a man sleep—" His jaw dropped as he regarded her. "What are you doing here at this time of day? Are you all right? You look like hell!"

"I'm glad to see you, too," she murmured, grateful for his honesty.

Though Luther was in his drawers, he stepped out into the passageway, surveying Vanity's bright gown and ashen face.

"You look awful."

"I thought you might like to know that I've gotten Trance out of my system," she said flatly.

"And about time. The wedding date is less than a week away!" He glanced back at his door, then eased it closed.

"I've decided I want to go upriver afterward, as far away as possible. I need quiet."

"Now wait a minute! I've got you booked onstage every night next week! I've made a lot of plans, and they don't include getting grounded in upriver shallows!"

"If you want to marry me, we'll be going to the mountains for as long as I say!" Vanity snapped.

"Forgive me, pet. I didn't realize you were here because you and Holloway had a lovers' spat. Has he pricked your pride? We'll go anywhere—" Luther had started to slip his arm around her trembling shoulder.

"Go to hell!"

"Ah, we sound married already. It warms my heart."

Vanity wondered if it was necessary to marry Luther after all. She had had the physical release she needed with Trance. Perhaps she should just go away and live by herself.

Luther apparently read her second thoughts. "We'll talk everything out after the wedding. You just make sure that wedding gown of yours is the best to be had in California."

She dragged herself to the main deck, yearning for a whiskey. She didn't glance back to see Luther's expression. Marrying him would give him control of her money, which was all he truly cared about, after all. She would have a name for her child. Did she need one that much?

Thursday evening the talkative Chinese dressmaker and her mincing, solicitous assistants came and went three times for the final fittings of a most impressive gown of cream peau de soie with a deep flounce of Valenciennes lace and an ivory veil so long it caught on the corners of every table in the chamber.

Madame Chong, as she was known, was still upset that Miss Blade intended no trousseau or going away outfits for her honeymoon.

"Just the gown," Vanity said, looking down at the orange blossoms along the flounce. "Only the gown."

During the week she had driven by the *Pacific Princess* only once to see Luther, and he was so busy supervising the draping of red and white bunting all over the boat's railings and posts that Vanity had gone home.

Vanity sent the note to Trance, explaining that their differences made it impossible for her to see him any longer. She refused all visitors, returned all messages unread, and stayed in her house brooding.

She would marry Luther for the sake of her child's name, but already she was considering leaving him on their wedding night. She hoped he wanted her wealth enough to comply.

She ate alone in her room that night, scarcely tasting the food, only grateful that it stayed down. She went to bed early, not thinking to check the rest of her house. She left that to Bullo.

She lay awake thinking, until her head pounded with confusion. She had to think of Trance's future and that of his son. She had to think of her own baby. Her own needs came last, yet thinking she would never see Trance again broke her heart. This time there would be no good-byes. For all she knew, he might have left town.

She slept fitfully and dreamed of searching for something in the desert, searching until she was frantic and confused. She awoke to the unmistakable thud of boots on the first floor.

Taking a paraffin lamp, she ventured down the staircase. "Bullo? Is that you down there?" Was the man into her liquor stores again? She'd have to fire him!

Though she found lamps burning throughout the downstairs rooms, and the aroma of sweet cigar smoke lingering in the air, she found no one about.

In the dining room she found the drawers in her walnut sideboard open, empty of her fine English silverware.

Someone snickered from behind her. "I've heard you're getting married. Congratulations are in order," came a deep, vaguely familiar voice.

Whirling, Vanity looked at the dark corners behind her chairs and potted ferns. If only she'd thought to bring her pistol! "Take what you want and leave," she said, trying to sound bold and calm.

The chuckle got louder. "What an intriguing prospect."

Angrily, she advanced, holding the lamp high, and then she saw him, a disheveled, bearded man standing in the far corner beyond the tall walnut china closet. "How did you get in? Where's my man?"

"Drunk once again, I'll wager," he drawled, moving from the shadows and noticeably dragging one foot. "The fool gets drunk just about this time every evening. I know, I've been watching. He likes corn whiskey best. You have plenty in that third cellar."

So that was how Bullo was getting her whiskey! It was waiting for him on the table in the tack room each evening, just as he had said. Vanity shivered to think a common thief would take such pains. "You have what you came for. Now go!"

"Do show me a bit of courtesy, darlin' Vanity. Would you be so good as to help fill my bag?" He lifted a dirty haversack and then dropped it to the floor, where it landed with a thud. "Show me where you keep your cash and jewels. Your bedchamber, perhaps?"

Vanity edged toward the door. Why would a thief use her name like that? Then his impudent drawl hit home!

She broke for the door, only to hear him following, the soft scrape of his dragging leg raising the nap on her fine carpets. She heard an equally soft cocking of a pistol hammer and whirled, flattening herself against the parlor door.

He aimed the pistol at her abdomen.

"This can't be," she whispered, watching him limp into the lamplight. A shudder of horror went through her, and her legs turned to jelly. "You're dead! I shot you myself!"

He grinned crookedly with that same dullness in his dark eyes that she remembered from so long ago. His black hair was lank and unkempt, the once thin moustache grown long over his lip, a heavy beard obscuring his sharp jaw. An ugly scar puckered the entire left side of his face.

His dark, dirty clothes were ill fitting, and he gave off an odor making her think he hadn't washed in years. His right hand hung awkwardly, partially shielding his crotch. Of all the changes in Jules Pearson's appearance, she found that most striking.

He laughed, shaking his head as if he found her amazingly stupid. "Pearsons don't die so easily," he said.

She had to place the lamp on the table or drop it. "Jules..." she said, almost breathlessly. She was holding onto herself to keep from fainting. "Go away from me. I'm not your wife! I never was. No one knows I married you that night. I won't let you hold me to it!"

His eyebrows arched. "You did murder that night, Vanity, but the man you killed wasn't me. That was my brother. I'm Jock, and I know you almost as well as Jules did. At least, I intended to." He grinned. In five years, his teeth had gone bad. "We have some unfinished business, you and I. I've come for money, too, to get new clothes and all the rest. I knew you'd help with that. I think they still hang murderesses in Mississippi."

Vanity stumbled backward into the parlor. "Your *brother*?"

He waved the pistol. "It was easy! Two men posing as one slip into an elegant home, only one goes out. Then while he plays poker at a nearby public place, the one who hid in the cellar takes whatever strikes his fancy." He made a *poof* sound with his lips, kissing his fingertips. "No one could ever prove Jules Pearson had committed a crime, because 'I' always had a perfect alibi, and a half dozen witnesses. In all your years on the river, you never heard of Ghost?"

"I can't...I won't help you! Take whatever you find here, but then you must go! I'm...I'm ill. Pregnant. You have no hold over me."

His face lit up. "But I do! If Luther Gant doesn't mind marrying a murderess, I know other ways to make you do all I ask—and more. I've spent the last five years in prison planning this, thanks to you. You *owe* me!"

"How could I be responsible for that?"

He crossed the room quickly, his entire right side showing signs of impairment, but he seized her with undiminished strength and poked the muzzle of his pistol into her belly. "The Ghost needs two men who look exactly alike. The first bit of work I tried alone failed."

The muzzle slid down, pressing painfully through the soft silkiness of her dressing gown. "If you don't value yourself, or your precious cargo, perhaps you'll value a certain small boy seen on lonely walks along the river with a rather negligent Chinese nanny. If trial, prison, and hanging don't frighten you, perhaps you'll think about that small boy falling into the deep, dark river." He laughed, his breath foul against her cheek.

Trembling, Vanity stiffened. "Come upstairs."

"Now I do like the sound of that," he said.

Her skin crawling, she mounted the stairs, her mind momentarily blank.

In her upstairs drawing room, Vanity needed three attempts to work the combination on her iron safe. When she pulled open the thick door, Jock pushed her aside and riffled her papers, quickly finding bundles of cash, which he stuffed into his grimy shirt.

"Now go," she said. "But if anything happens to—"

"I need far more than this. I need income! You have a way with cards—and men. You could keep me very nicely, Vanity. Who can say I'm not Jules Pearson? No Pearsons remain in Louisiana. No one will ever know what you did, and that small boy will be safe forevermore." His eyes moved up and down her body. "For now, I need a doctor."

Closing her eyes, Vanity felt bile sting her throat. He had the whore's disease! That was why he looked so horrid. "I have stocks, some money in banks, but most of my capital is tied up in the *Pacific Princess*."

He smiled. "I intend to live there."

"But what about Luther?"

"Your captain?" He grinned. "Fire him. Shoot him. I'm not particular. Just get rid of him. I'm taking his place. We might even marry, making the bond between us public."

Vanity crossed the room and opened the drawer of her desk. It was empty.

"Is this what you're looking for?" Jock asked, tugging her pistol from the waistband of his trousers. Again he aimed at her belly. "I'll give you until tomorrow. You'll find me waiting—somewhere."

Twenty-Five

Vanity waited for Luther within the protection of her phaeton. Sending a deck hand to fetch him from the *Pacific Princess*'s offices, she resisted sipping courage from a silver decanter tucked in the carriage's dash.

He kept her waiting several minutes, affording her unwanted time to question her course of action. When at last he jerked open the carriage door and scowled at her, she was shaking.

"They said you—" His expression changed from mild irritation and curiosity to alarm. "You look like hell, Vanity!" He climbed in beside her, the peck he gave her cheek reeking of whiskey and cigar smoke.

Her stomach turned over. "Luther, I'm terribly sorry, but I'm ill. I won't be able to marry you tomorrow night. If you'll excuse me, I must go now."

Luther caught her arm before she could signal her driver. "Wait a minute! Don't I deserve more of an explanation than that? If you're ill we can marry Sunday or next week. I've put a lot of effort into this, Vanity. What have you got, a touch of ague? Or…" His eyes suddenly narrowed and his tips tightened into a suspicious smile. "All right. What's really going on?"

"Nothing," she said lamely. "I-I just can't marry you."

His eyes turned to flint. "Not at all?"

"No. The wedding's off. And…I don't need you as my captain any longer. I want you off the *Pacific Princess* by this afternoon. I'm going away." She handed him an envelope filled with cash.

Visions of the peaceful, undemanding heights of Tenderfoot beckoned. All she wanted was to get away from this madness!

Finally she lifted her gaze and was stunned to see to what degree animosity had distorted Luther's ordinarily attractive features.

His lips curled back. "You teasing bitch! If you think I'm settling for some kind of cheap payoff when I've held out four years for the whole pot, you've got another thing coming! I'll have your jackassed lover run out of town on one of his own goddamned rails!" He threw the envelope into her lap.

Vanity protested feebly, but her stomach was in control. For a tense moment she could do nothing but hold herself very still until she was reasonably certain she would not vomit.

"Trance has nothing to do with my decision. If you're smart, you'll accept my offer. I-I must go!" She clapped her hand over her mouth and shoved him roughly against the door.

Eyes wide, Luther scrambled from the carriage.

"Take me home!" Vanity called sharply to her driver, flinging the envelope after Luther.

The small carriage clattered away, leaving Luther eating dust. Greenbacks fluttered across the wharf.

He slammed a fist into his palm. "I'll bet it all the bitch is storked!"

Only moments ago he had been putting the finishing touches on a wedding celebration promising to draw attention from a hundred miles around, and net him a fortune. He had bluffed his way into Vanity's life, and guided her patiently toward the life they would lead together. Now that the preparations were done, and the boat stood ready to receive its bride, its cabins and staterooms completely booked, the wines ordered, the chefs on the alert, and the preacher summoned, not to mention the photographer and newspaper reporters, he found all his plans thwarted by one damnable man from Ohio.

Storming aboard the boat, Luther took the stairs two at a time and thundered through the grand saloon wanting some unsuspecting underling to cross his path. He would break heads! Seeing the makeshift altar on the stage, he seized a vase of flowers from the nearest table and hurled it.

He'd hired a dozen extra stewards, had the stateroom on the Texas deck stripped and refitted as a bridal suite. Fine white silk sheets were already turned down on the nuptial bed.

He'd seen to every detail, right down to the most costly champagne to be served until dawn to every passenger aboard! No gambler—of cards or anything else—had ever netted a finer prize than the lovely, elusive Vanity Blade!

Knocking aside several tables, Luther cut a path of destruction through the grand saloon, then stopped outside at the railing, where he continued to fume.

By God, if she wouldn't marry him, and fired him as an afterthought, he'd spread her precious secret from one end of Sacramento to the other!

Within the hour, Holloway would have to flee town, if only to keep the laughter from reaching his son. Finding herself the object of scandal and ridicule, Vanity would have no choice but to seek refuge on the *Pacific Princess,* and in Luther's arms.

He swung around, wild to save that which he had worked so long and hard to achieve. If he moved quickly, she might still be his.

Without stopping for his hat, Luther left the boat at a trot. He knew just where to find Mr. J. T. Holloway. After marching all those blocks, he'd be in exactly the right temper to drive the man from California— with his fists!

Though it was not yet dusk, Trance threw on his frock coat and headed for the comforting dimness of the Federal's saloon. He hadn't been back in Sacramento more than an hour and already his resolve to confront Vanity and demand an explanation was sinking in the mire of his confusion.

He'd taken Jason to Spring Hill, where his sister, Rowena, had settled with her husband after their trek west. She had three little ones of her own now, and had been overjoyed to see Trance for the first time since he'd gone away to war, nearly nine years ago.

They'd had a happy reunion, but he cut short his plans to stay; he couldn't avoid Vanity another moment. Leaving Jason to get better acquainted with his cousins, Trance returned to Sacramento to learn why Vanity had spurned him.

Seated at a rear table with a full bottle of Old Mill Kentucky bourbon, he drank steadily until his courage was restored. Sober, Trance couldn't bear hearing her say she'd stopped loving him, or that he was too dull for her way of life, or that she didn't want to try being Jason's stepmother. Drunk, he would be able to stand anything she had to say.

Every message he'd sent to Vanity since she'd written to say she didn't want to see him again had been returned unopened. Twice he'd driven by, only to be forcibly rebuffed by that monster of a butler she kept in ridiculous black livery.

So long as he couldn't talk to her, he felt helpless. Feeling helpless made him angry, and the last person he wanted to feel angry toward was his love.

The hotel's long narrow saloon was a dignified chamber with a long carved bar on one side. He found comfort in the murky shadows.

Feeling the scalding warmth of the bourbon travel through him, he readied himself to do battle with the woman he'd loved all his life. Mumbling to himself, he was about to stand when he heard someone shout his name. A stocky man wearing red sleeve garters stood in the entrance.

"Outside, Holloway! We have to talk!"

Trance sat back down.

Jerked upright, barely feeling his feet touch the floor, Trance stared, blinking, into the blazing eyes of the man who was now clutching his shirt.

"You'll come outside, bastard!" the man shouted, sending a fine spray of spittle across Trance's nose and lips.

Trance beat the man's hands away with his fists. "Who the hell are you?" His tongue felt so thick he could hardly understand himself.

Sidestepping the infuriated intruder, Trance swayed out of punching range. He grabbed his bottle from the table and raised it to his lips. If Vanity thought he'd leave on this lout's account…

The man dashed the bottle to the floor, shattering it. "I'm the *Pacific Princess*'s captain, and I'm marrying Vanity Blade tomorrow night at eight o'clock. I don't care what you said to make her change her mind…I'm here to make you do whatever is necessary to make her change it back! She's mine, and you're leaving town right now." He swung his fist.

"Not marrying…" Trance ducked, blocking the blow with his forearm. The words penetrated Trance's stupor like an axe blade. He straightened, feeling reason return. "Not marrying you?" He threw back his head and crowed with laughter. He had known she wouldn't!

"Everything is arranged, and you're not interfering!" Luther seized Trance's sleeve, preparing to drag him from the saloon.

With an iron fist, Trance again dashed the man's hand away. Then his knuckles crashed into Luther's jaw.

Luther sprawled against a table. From the rear of the saloon came the burly bouncer with his club in hand. Trance straightened his coat and marched from the darkened, smoky sanctuary.

He was halfway across the sedate lobby, on his way to grab Vanity by the hair if necessary, when Luther leaped on his back. They pitched forward and hit the floor, scattering heavy chairs.

Trance lost touch with where he was or why he was fighting. He'd fought for his rights as a man for most of his life. It was as if he was back in a dusty alley, punching, kicking, and biting, knowing he would be punished for it, and knowing he could do nothing less.

Even drunk, he was a powerful adversary. Amid shouts and screams, crashing urns, and tables, Trance found his feet again and again, delivering blow after blow until he knew nothing but the power of his fists.

His hands were wrapped tightly around someone's throat. His face throbbed with pain, and his stinging lips were swollen, his tongue cut where he'd bitten it. Dull pain burned in his abdomen and pulsed in his rib cage, but he ignored it.

Someone seized Trance from behind. He was dragged back, arms pinned, while several other gentlemen fell on Luther, preventing him from leaping to his feet.

Trance was pulled to the lobby door and flung into the street, landing so hard the wind was knocked out of him. Luther sprawled some distance away, but somehow scrambled to his feet and leaped on Trance.

They fought onto the steps of the opera house, drawing a crowd so thick no one could break through to stop them.

After several minutes, Trance felt himself losing strength. His arms changed to dead weights. Every time he dragged himself to his feet again, the pain in his chest worsened.

When he fell and saw stars, Luther kicked him again. Knowing several ribs were cracked, Trance still found his feet and fought on, even though his fists were bloody now and his face pulp.

Landing blow after bone-shuddering blow, Trance saw Luther still climb to his feet, but he was taking longer to straighten up. His punches only grazed Trance's head.

Trance finally landed one to Luther's jaw that reverberated to his shoulder. The man's head snapped to one side and he crumpled in the middle of the street.

Staggering backward, Trance's legs buckled. Panting, he dropped to one knee, thinking he could not feel more pain. He was a single raw nerve, and yet fresh pain struck when he thought of Vanity.

The twisting agony in his heart became unyielding. He clutched at his chest as if having an attack, and waited for Luther to drag himself to a standing position and attack again.

But Luther lay still.

A hotel doorman pushed through the crowd and plucked at Luther's limp wrist. A doctor stepped from the crush of opera patrons, crouched beside the inert body, and placed two fingers against Luther Gant's throat.

"He's still alive. Someone carry him over to my office. He's not going anywhere for days." The man crossed to where Trance balanced precariously. "Need help, friend?"

Trance took the man's hand and stood. He tried to draw a breath and winced. Pressing the heel of his hand into his side, he stumbled away, shaking off the doctor's entreaties to be tended.

The admiring crowd parted before him. He wiped blood from his eyes, looked up, and realized he was walking away from the direction of Vanity's house.

Turning, and keeping his chin high, he made his way through the crowds into the dusk, aiming his battered body toward his agony's source and solace.

Vanity seated herself in Sandbar and Sharona's small front room. Sharona offered tea, but Vanity felt too ill to drink it. She waited to speak while her grandfather scraped burned tobacco from the bowl of his corncob pipe and then refilled it, sucking until the sweet aroma of Square Deal tobacco wafted through the air.

"I couldn't go away without seeing you," Vanity said at last, her voice cracking.

Sharona sipped her tea, her expression thoughtful. "We wondered why we hadn't been invited to your wedding. I thought perhaps it was because of me."

Startled, Vanity covered her mouth. She shook her head. "I let Luther make all the arrangements...Oh, I've been in such a muddle! That's why I came—to tell you I'm not marrying Luther after all. I've fired him, in fact, and I imagine he'll be gone from town before long. I hope he is, for his sake."

"Can you tell us what happened?" Sharona asked carefully.

Vanity shook her head. After a moment, two hot tears slid down her cheeks and she nodded. "I think I'm carrying a baby." Quickly she lifted her eyes to catch her grandfather's reaction.

His face drained, and his eyes filled with pain. Sharona was quick to take his hand and squeeze it. "No, I'm all right, dear." He searched Vanity's face, his sorrow evident. "More than twenty-five years ago I would have jumped to my feet and ordered you from my sight. This is my chance to say how sorry I am that this has happened to you. You're welcome to come live with us."

Vanity shook her head. "I have to go away. I don't want to, but I have to. And I couldn't go without saying good-bye, and to be sure you knew I'll come back—if I can."

She stood and went to her grandfather, bending over his head and hugging his shoulders. "Thank you for understanding." She caught Sharona's sympathetic gaze as she pulled away. Impulsively, she reached for Sharona's hand.

"If we can do anything for you..." Sharona said. "Trance will understand."

"Oh, you mustn't tell him! He's gone from Sacramento, after all. I-I had one of my maids check his hotel yesterday. I'll write...I must go!"

She was out the door, rushing along the dusty, darkening street before Sharona and her grandfather could even rise from their chairs.

Vanity was back at her house in good time. She had been to the bank before stopping at her grandfather's house. In her bedchamber, she removed bundles of cash from her reticule and stacked them with all her valuables in a small flowered carpetbag.

She felt strangely calm. Leaving the carpetbag, she gathered the paper-wrapped wedding gown, which had been delivered that morning, and carried it down to the entry. She had just laid it across the banister in preparation for taking it to a pawnshop when she heard scuffling on the verandah.

Peeking through the glass curtains over the window in the partially opened front door, she saw Bullo getting ready to slug Trance.

She flung the door wide. "Don't! Bullo, what are you thinking? Oh, my God! Trance!" Then she stopped herself from running into Trance's arms.

"I didn't hit him, Mistth Blade! I was justh doing what you told me to do! I've been keeping everybody away, justh like you thaid." Looking frightened, Bullo backed away, wringing huge, hairy hands.

"Never mind. I'll handle this."

Trance staggered across the veranda.

"What's happened to you?" she whispered.

His voice was accusing. "I want to know why you've refused to see me!"

"I'm going away. I don't want—"

"Going away? Why?" he demanded, seizing her shoulders. "Tell me why!"

She struggled to be free of his grip. If he pressed her, she might not be able to stop herself from saying she carried his baby, that she was fighting the only way she knew to save the life of his son.

He spoke softly. "I thought you loved me."

Crying inside, Vanity nevertheless appeared in control. Jules...Jock was out there, somewhere, watching, waiting. She threw back her head, her eyes blazing. "I don't have to explain myself to you, or anyone. I'll soon be gone, so you'll be free to court anyone you like. I'm sure you'll find my half sister far better suited to you than me. She's had all the advantages I've missed."

His eyes widened. "Councilman Collins is your father?"

She didn't have time to bother with unimportant details. "Trance, you're only prolonging something painful for us both. Think of Jason..."

"Audrey means nothing—"

"Trance! Think of Jason! Are you sure he's safe?"

He frowned.

Vanity turned away and stepped inside, fearing he would grab her and shake the truth from her. As she eased the door closed between them, an unexpected welling of disappointment filled her heart. She *wanted* him to force her to explain! She wanted—needed—his help!

She heard nothing, no footsteps across the veranda, no turning of the knob, no gentle voice coaxing her.

Step by step, she pulled herself up the stairs to her bedroom. How could she go on without Trance? How could she bear his child alone? How could she think to cooperate with Jock in any way? Her child's future would be ruined if he was raised near that man.

Pausing, she heard Trance's footsteps moving down the walk, out into the street, away...away...forever.

With effort, she surveyed her haven, now a reminder that she shared her life with no one who truly cared about her.

On the floor lay the bulging carpetbag. Jock might make her sell her house, her clothes, the carriage. She would be left with nothing to show for all that she had accomplished in her life. She would have nothing to give her child but shame.

She stood numb in the middle of her frilly bedchamber, staring at the bed where she and Trance had made such beautiful love. Of all the things she possessed, his love had been the most intangible. She could not live in it, wear it, ride around inside it, or stuff it into a carpetbag to give away. Yet it had been a soft, warm treasure.

There was no explanation for their love. It wasn't logical. It might not even be good for either of them. But it existed, making all they did more precious.

Without Trance she would endure the same pitiable existence as her mother. Without her, Trance would drift into the twilight of his life a lonely man.

She went to a small box she kept beneath some old clothes in the bureau. The contents had nearly been forgotten in a safety deposit box in her Albany hotel. She had sent for the things less than a year ago.

She plucked a scrap of kelly-green satin from the box. It was wrapped around the scuffed, rusting jackknife she had snatched from Trance so long ago. Beneath those things was Maxx's copper penny.

Without Trance, none of her possessions or accomplishments had any worth, not even these. She had committed a murder. She was now rejecting the man she loved in order to yield to a vile man with no worth whatsoever.

Lifting her eyes, she saw a rigid woman staring at her from the looking glass over her dressing table. The woman's dark eyes were large and pained, no longer beautiful, but dull and haunted. Though her face was still attractive, it was less so now, made somehow older and weary by the empty future she envisioned ahead of her.

This stranger in the looking glass wore an enviable gown, and she was surrounded by expensive furnishings in a lovely room in a large, impressive house.

This woman held title to a renowned riverboat, and had captured the hearts of gentlemen too numerous to mention. With a smile, she could have had any one of those men, but so long as she allowed Jock to blackmail her, she was his prisoner, just as Trance had been one in the bawdy house cellar.

Somehow in her quest to fulfill her dead mother's dreams, she had stumbled into a life that surely would have been her mother's worst nightmare.

Vanity felt very cold. Staring at herself, she looked beyond the gown, beyond the trappings, far, far beyond the accomplishments that she enumerated whenever she felt dissatisfied.

"Who *are* you?" she whispered to the stranger she saw there.

She always felt the need to fulfill what her mother had dreamed of for her. She had gone onstage. She had sung her bawdy songs, and danced her gay dances, wearing bright colors while ignoring the crude surroundings of the saloon, imagining the glittering world about which her mother had fantasized.

She had gone to find Maxx, and there she had lived the life of an indulged adolescent. She had gone to Du Barry Vale but had learned that well-born young ladies could live a life as tawdry as anything found in a saloon.

She'd gone to Cold Crossing hoping to be a dutiful wife, to Albany to become a burlesque queen, to Natchez again, still searching for all she had lost. And finally to California.

So much pretense. So much confusion. And now Jock and her guilt were keeping her from the one person she wanted, keeping her from her own true self!

If she paid Jock again, she would be as good as dead.

She looked deeply into her eyes and realized with horror that from the time she was five years old, she had been performing. From mountain saloon, to riverboat cabin, to school, church, and stage she had performed. Only during those precious private moments with Trance had she been herself!

"Who am I?" she cried, hearing her voice echo.

She whirled, seeing everything clearly for the first time. She had this house as a monument to her mother's dreams. She danced across a stage and sang suggestive songs because that was the life her *mother* had wanted, and that was the life *she* had lost to a drunkard's stray bullet.

Vanity had even taken her mother's name. For so long she'd felt an abiding, unnamed guilt, casting herself in any role in the hope of feeling worthy of the life her mother had given her at the cost of her own dreams.

In living her mother's life, Vanity had lost her own dreams, and now, if she let Jock control her, she would go on performing until she died.

She would lie and hurt the only man she'd ever loved. She would likely end her days whoring to keep Jock in cash. And what of her child?

Would her child feel guilt over being born? Would she herself eventually lose herself somewhere, dreaming away her last days, thrusting onto her child the dreams she was unable to fulfill? Would her child continue the legacy of pretense?

Crossing her arms over her heaving, swollen breasts, she screamed out, "No!"

She would no longer live dreams that were not her own. She would go away, but not to hide. She would go away to begin again, to find the woman she was, to rebuild her life. If she had to be five years old again, she would do whatever was necessary to seize control of her own destiny!

The first step was to free herself from Jock.

Suddenly feeling weak, she sank onto a chair. Possibilities swirled in her mind. She pressed her temples. She had so little time to think, to decide.

Then she rose, knowing no argument, no gentle reasoning, no amount of begging or weeping would make Jock set her free. There was only one way to rid herself of this venomous man.

She went to her bed stand, but found the drawer empty of her pocket pistol. Then she remembered that Jock had taken it.

She undressed quickly and then pulled on a plain cotton calico gown she wore when assisting her gardener. Lifting the limp skirt, she hurried out to the stairway leading to the attic.

There she found the old trunk she'd taken east after her mother had died. In it were her mother's musty, fading gowns. She didn't pause to feel remorse or grief. She loved her mother, but she was a performer no more.

At the bottom of the pile of brittle satins was the old Colt five-shot pistol she had once toyed with in the cabin in Tenderfoot. Laughing, she quickly silenced herself with a hand to her lips, and remembered prancing about in her mother's finery and brandishing the pistol at imaginary ravishers. She slid the small, short-barreled weapon from its oiled cloth.

She cleaned it, taking her time and formulating her plan. Then she went down the attic stairs, picked up the carpetbag, and walked down the staircase to the big front door. She would return to this house a free woman—or a dead one.

The night air felt cool on her face. She strode down the street, knowing that if Jock was watching from the shadows and saw her with the carpetbag, he would follow.

Twenty-Six

In an alley between two saloons, Vanity leaned against the wall, listening to her pounding heart. Lanternlight poured across a wooden walkway. Her ears began to ring, and she crumpled in a heap, oblivious to approaching footsteps.

As she regained consciousness, she saw a pistol glinting inches from her face. Jock's grinning face was behind it. Her scream ripped the darkness.

A savage hand seized her and yanked her up.

She struggled, trying to tug her pistol from her skirt pocket. A stinging blow to her wrist sent the old weapon thudding softly into the dust at her feet.

Jock slammed her against the wall. "Scream again, and I'll gut you!"

"I've brought money," she said in a small voice.

"Then let's go!" he hissed.

She clawed his face, bit whatever was nearest her mouth, and released the flesh between her teeth only when he tried to rip her hair from her head.

"Let's go!" He dragged her into the deserted street and shoved her ahead of him.

After washing the blood from his face and changing his torn shirt, Trance was detained from leaving his hotel. No longer among the Federal's favored guests, he was asked to pay all damages for the fight in the lobby.

After promising to do so he pushed aside the stuffy manager and barged out the doors, collaring the first black man he saw. "Can you help me find 'Lija Quarter?" He jabbed a twenty-dollar greenback in the startled doorman's face.

After being given hasty directions to the far side of town, Trance set out at a march. His body still throbbed as he saw Quarter approaching along a dusty lane across town twenty minutes later. If anyone would know why Vanity wanted to go away, Quarter would.

Wearily, Trance paused, watching Quarter stop at his porch and recognize him.

"Mr. Trance?" Quarter wore a tailored brown frock coat. His keen dark eyes took in Trance's condition as quickly as he hastened back to the gate and seized Trance's hand. "Old friend! I've been hoping you'd drop by, but, Sweet Susie! Look at you! You got a real nose for trouble, you do. Come inside where we can talk." Quarter drew Trance into the warmth of his house behind the unpainted picket fence.

Startled at the sight of their battered guest, Quarter's wife rose from a table covered with a blue-checked cloth. She went immediately for medicinal whiskey and a soothing salve to dab on Trance's bruises.

Trance refused a chair. "No time for that," he said, waving away Mathilda's ministrations.

As quickly as he could, Trance described his suspicions that Vanity was in serious trouble. He concluded with his battle with Luther Gant in the street.

"And when I went to her house just now, she said she was going away. Do you know what's wrong with her?" Trance asked.

"Sit yourself down half a minute," Quarter said, forcing a whiskey on him. Then he sat, frowning.

At length Quarter mused, "I haven't seen Vanity since I heard she was marrying Gant. Now you say she's not marrying him?" He shook his head. "It don't sit right, does it?"

Mathilda interrupted. "Mr. Holloway, you say Miss Vanity welcomed you when you first saw her?"

Trance winced, remembering. "Yes. She welcomed me the very first night."

"Two weeks ago?" Mathilda asked, her pretty eyes darkening with embarrassment.

"Almost three."

She bent and whispered to Quarter.

Quarter's eyes went wide. "Could she be sure?"

Mathilda shrugged, avoiding Trance's gaze. "A woman knows such things."

Quarter heaved a troubled sigh.

"Did you know Audrey Collins was Vanity's half sister?" Trance asked.

Quarter sighed again, rubbing his eyes. "Sweet Susie! Yes, I knew. She told me right after she found her father. It hurt her bad the sort he turned out to be. Offered her money, you know. Uh-uh-uh," he said, shaking his head.

"While you men sit here talking yourselves to death, Miss Vanity might be on her way out of town. If I was you, I'd ask her right out what I said, 'Lija. Go to her house. If she ain't there, you'd best trot on over to the *Princess*. If I was getting out of town, I wouldn't wait on two fools like you!"

"Yes'm," Quarter said, winking as he nudged Trance to his feet.

Without deck hands swarming the docks, Sacramento's riverfront was eerily quiet. Trance stopped running every so often to dig his fist into his cracked ribs. Quarter was nearly a block ahead and stopped, turning back to shout and wave. Trance tried to hurry.

Coming into view of the river, Trance saw why Quarter had waved so frantically. Though no running lanterns were lit, and no whistle whooped to announce her departure, the *Pacific Princess* had a full head of steam. Pitch-black smoke rolled from her stacks, giving an acrid smell to the night air.

Sparks showered from the stacks. The paddles began beating the water, tearing the boat from her moorings. The stageplank swung from side to side as the boat edged away and straightened in the current.

Quarter dashed all the way to the edge of the dock, looking as if he decided at the last instant not to leap the distance between the dock and the bobbing stageplank twenty feet out.

"Is anybody aboard?" Trance panted, staggering up behind Quarter and groaning as he drove his fist deeper into his side.

"Somebody has to be, to keep up them boilers! Sweet Susie! I don't like the looks of this!"

Quarter clutched Trance's sleeve. "We can take a couple of horses down to the next bend. I know a man with a skiff...We can row out to meet her. My belly says this isn't right."

He pointed, and Trance shuddered when he saw a pale, skirted figure running along the promenade gangway, a dark shadow chasing close behind.

• • •

With the steady beat of the *Pacific Princess*'s engines, Vanity felt the moments of her life ticking away. It had been an easy matter to clear the decks, for few passengers had been booked for the evening.

With the captain nowhere to be found, and preparations for the wedding complete, the stewards and deck hands had been idling about. Without a second thought, they'd accepted an evening off, granted by the boat's beautiful owner.

Now the only crew aboard were a few stokers and the graveyard-shift pilot. Running silent, with white bunting scalloping between the posts, the *Pacific Princess* looked like a death ship drifting toward Satan's shore.

Grinning, Jock turned to Vanity. "Can this boat pilot itself?"

"You know as well as I that it can't."

"Then we're going to tie up at the first place that suits me so I can throw your pilot off."

She bounded away along the narrow gangway, hoping to take refuge in her salon, where Luther had always kept a big-handled Colt army revolver.

"Not so fast!" Jock snapped, catching her in spite of his limp. He swung her around.

Raking his face with her fingernails, Vanity broke free and tore through the dreadful silence of the grand saloon. Gaining the advantage, she emerged at the stern and dashed along the gangway and down the stairs, heading for the boiler room.

As she burst through the doors into the suffocating heat, she fell into the path of a startled, grimy youth toting a huge cut of timber toward the roaring flames in the boiler's gaping mouth.

Without explanation, she snatched up the racing wedge and jammed it into the spring mechanism of the steam-pressure valve. Protecting her hand with her skirt, she flung the boiler's door closed and latched it.

The stokers watched her with horrified expressions. With the racing wedge in place, if the boiler overheated, no steam would be vented off. The boiler would explode!

"If you value your lives, slip overboard as soon as you can. And get help!"

She was about to escape the stifling room when Jock burst in behind her and brandished her mother's Colt pistol at the stokers. Then he dragged her out, laughing as she struggled. "Where might a man tidy up on this tub?" he asked, stopping in the shadows to apply his mouth to hers.

"Luther had a..." She wrenched her face away, spat, then wiped her lips clean. Would she have to submit to keep him aboard long enough for the boilers to blow?

"Show me," he growled, pushing her away.

She led the way down to Luther's cabin, half hoping to find Luther there, but she hadn't seen him since she broke their engagement.

Gripping her arm painfully, Jock pulled her into the cramped cabin and struck a match to the wick in Luther's bunkside lantern.

"Very nice, indeed," he murmured, surveying Luther's washstand and shaving equipment.

"You're breaking my arm!"

"And where did you keep yourself when you were aboard your boat? The Texas deck, like always? Was that where you were planning to spend your honeymoon?"

She shook her head violently, sickened to think of what lay ahead. If she was lucky, she'd be blown to fiery bits. If she was not...

"Yes, the Texas deck!" she gasped when he twisted her arm.

Abandoning the shaving equipment, they made their way up to the Texas deck, below the pilothouse. Before Jock could force Vanity into the stateroom, she tried to knee him, knowing he might beat her savagely for the attempt.

But her timing was off and Jock seemed to think she had just stumbled.

"I must speak to my pilot!" she said. "He'll need to know we're stopping..."

Jock's eyes flashed. "I'll take care of him when the time comes. Get inside!"

Opening the door, he shoved her in and together they gaped at the opulence inside. An elaborate white iron bed with ice-white lace draperies, covers, and skirt had been installed amid blood-red fringed and plush trimmings.

Luther had had the paneling stained and freshly varnished a dark reddish-brown and had replaced the carpet with a new Turkish one in black and the darkest of reds.

All around the stateroom stood vases and vases of red roses. The windows were draped in emperor-red damask, festooned with black tassels and kept closed so that not a hint of daylight would penetrate.

Vanity shuddered.

"Ready yourself, sweets," Jock said, smiling approvingly at Luther Gant's taste. He slipped the key from the door and went out, locking her in.

She dared not sit on the hideous bed. Luther had made their bridal chamber a mockery of innocence and lust. She scarcely wanted to cross the ugly carpet, but she darted to the row of windows, hoping to climb out.

Luther had had them all latched from the outside! Surely, he'd not found one of her crew to do such a thing.

Vanity listened to the frantic beat of the paddle wheels being driven by a boiler with its safety valves wedged shut. Her boat had already reached racing speed, and might be hurtling toward a tricky bend in the river. She could hear her pilot bellowing oaths down the speaking tube to the boiler room. It would be a race to see if the side-wheeler ripped into a snag or blasted apart in flames.

Her heart hammering, she wondered if she had the courage to endure what she'd set into motion. Or perhaps the stokers had disobeyed her insane order. Perhaps they would remove the wedge from the valve and steam peacefully into San Francisco's bay, leaving her locked in with her dead husband's repulsive brother.

Crying out with frustration, Vanity finally tossed aside the lace curtains draped around the bed and fell onto the mattress. She could do nothing but wait.

The moments ticked by maddeningly until she was sure the beat of the paddles sounded queer, as if her boat was shuddering under the strain of red-line steam pressure, that at any moment the boilers would explode, ripping the boat to pieces. Explosions aboard riverboats were common, but would one explode on cue, saving her?

She spread her hands across her belly, thinking gently of Trance on her veranda and the look of disbelief on his face as she turned away.

Now he would never know how much she truly loved him. But even if she never lived to build her own dreams, she knew he would have been the foundation of her life. When the flames came, she would carry her love for him in her heart.

Ominously, the key turned in the lock. To keep herself from screaming, she clutched two fistfuls of coverlet and watched Jock come into the stateroom dragging his right foot.

With his disease-hollowed eyes and crooked, evil smile, he looked sinister in one of Luther's cutaways. He looked much as he had aboard the *J. J. Pearson* the night she tried to win it from him—or his brother. She now could not tell which man to fit into each of her memories.

Though his hair was overlong and tinged with gray now, he had washed and shaved. His skin had a gray tinge, and the right side of his face drooped. A puckered scar covered his left temple, looking as if the skull beneath it had actually been crushed.

As he advanced into the stateroom, she went rigid. He worked at the cork of a large bottle of champagne until it shot across the room, gushing foam onto the blood-red carpet.

"I do believe your intended thought of everything," Jock said, as he lifted the bottle to his lips and swallowed several times. Foamy liquid spilled from the corners of his mouth and ran down his ruffled shirtfront.

"I know you won't hurt me," Vanity said, surprising even herself as she watched his eyes. "You can't make it without your brother. You *need* me!"

She kept herself very still, watching his every move, wondering if there would be a moment when she might escape him. But he was not as stupid or distracted as she hoped. He kept himself squarely between the door and bed where she sat. Nodding his head, he grinned at her, the thoughts mirrored in his ugly dark eyes naked to her.

"Need you? You're nothing but a meal ticket," he said, surveying her body with leisurely impudence. He seemed inordinately interested in the way she clutched the coverlet. "Have you found a knife?" he asked, lunging and seizing her wrists. He shook them. "A pistol, then?"

He jerked her to her feet, felt the sides of her skirt where she'd previously hidden a pistol. Tearing the covers from the bed, he found nothing.

Satisfied, he flung her backward onto the bed and jumped on top of her, laughing sourly, his lips still wet with champagne. "I'll show you how much I need you!"

She fought his hands until she thought she would go mad with revulsion. "No one's tending the boilers!" she shouted when she freed her mouth, unable to stand more. "The boat's going to blow!"

Laughing, Jock shook his head. "I don't believe you. What loyal crew would let that happen with a beautiful woman aboard?"

"The crew's gone!"

Jock clucked in sympathy. "Shall we just take a look to be sure?"

She had to hold her breath to keep from sighing with relief when he climbed off her and yanked her to her feet. As they stumbled out onto the gangway, Jock clutching her around the middle and fondling her freely, she could hear the high, unmistakable laboring of the engines, and the frantic thrashing of the paddles. She had never felt a riverboat speed through the water like this. "Did you—"

She had no chance to ask if Jock had spoken to her pilot, for the old man was bearing down on them now from the stairs leading to the pilothouse, cussing and shaking his fists. When he saw Vanity clasped to Jock's chest and saw Jock raise and aim the old Colt pistol, he ducked just in time.

The bullet shattered a pane of glass behind him.

Releasing Vanity, Jock went for the pilot. She didn't wait to see if the old man could hold his own. She ran.

Her first thought was to leap from the railing, but her chances of survival would be better if she could jump from a lower deck.

She heard scuffling on the narrow gangway near the pilothouse, then heard a scream of terror as her pilot was flung over the railing. Seconds later she heard a splash. At least in his fall he had cleared the boiler deck.

She slipped down the stairs to the saloon deck and dashed for the stern, where she might leap safely into the river. The throb of the engines was deadly now. At any moment...

From the murky dark shore came the faint but unmistakable shout of her name. She twisted, thinking she must be imagining it.

"Vanity! Van-i-ty! Signal if you hear-r-r!"

Her heart lifted. Was there even the slightest chance she might escape? To signal, she'd have to return to the pilothouse.

She could hear nothing to indicate where Jock might be now. The roar of the unvented boilers was deafening. She slipped back up to the Texas deck and made her way carefully to the narrow stairs leading to the pilothouse.

With Jock nowhere to be seen, she began hoping he had been thrown overboard instead. Once inside the pilothouse, she seized the big wheel and gave a mighty stomp to one of the lower handholds, throwing the wheel into a fast turn.

Instantly the boat responded, turning savagely toward the shore. She jerked the whistle cord once, splitting the darkness with one jarring whoop.

She didn't know who was waiting onshore to help her, but she had this one last chance. She lunged for the pilot's bench, where her two pilots kept a few personal belongings. She knew Sandbar kept a silver-mounted flintlock pistol handy.

Though the heavy weapon felt comforting in her shaking hands, she had no idea how to load or fire it.

"Just what are you doing?" Jock hissed, looming in the doorway, his face twisted with fury.

"Someone's got to pilot this boat!" she snapped, swinging, hoping to knock him senseless with the pistol butt.

Avoiding her swing, he seized her. She struggled clear and dashed out the door, nearly throwing herself over the railing, where she would surely break a leg falling to the promenade deck.

Though slowed by his limp, Jock caught her and wrestled her down the narrow steps. With strength she never knew she had, she fought him. Every step toward the bridal chamber door was hard-won for Jock, who yelped when she kicked or bit, and nearly broke her arm when she landed one last desperate knee jab to his groin.

"Bitch! I ought to kill you!" he growled in agony. As he was about to strike her and send her tumbling backward into the bridal chamber, the boat shuddered.

Their eyes locked.

With the slightest release of pressure on his hold about her shoulders, Vanity whirled, then struck out with the pistol butt. It found a soft target and produced a grunt of pain. She wasted no time but dashed along the promenade gangway toward the stern. Jock stumbled after her, holding his face. There came a deafening roar and the boat was split in half.

Running with the last of her strength, Vanity felt the blast against her back. The dark nothingness ahead of her flared to red-and-white glare. All was chaos, her mind, her senses, her legs still pumping but now in midair.

The *Pacific Princess*'s boilers shot into the air like gigantic cannons, raining flame and live steam over the boat. An agonized shriek echoed across the river.

Then Vanity was wet, sinking, flailing against water and a strong current. She struggled to breathe and thrashed through blackness, knowing she must reach the river's surface or drown.

With a lung-tearing gasp, Vanity broke to the surface. Just as quickly she was dragged under again, her arms and legs too weak to resist the river's strength.

Summoning the last of her strength, she surfaced and swam a few awkward strokes in what she hoped was the direction of the shore, concentrating only on keeping her head above water. Finally, drifting with the current, helpless but alive, she twisted around in the water to see the *Pacific Princess* in flames.

Everywhere else there was darkness and silence. She relaxed into the insistent current, knowing she would float, if only for a while.

Then she heard her name called loudly. She swam a few more strokes, gulped river water, then sank. The shout seemed to have been coming from the water.

Splashing to the surface one last time, she saw a lantern hanging from the bow of a skiff. Two men reached for her.

Weeping for joy, Vanity went under. Quarter seized her wrist. Trance heaved her on board. She lay there, dazed, gazing up into his battered, anguished face. "How did you find me?"

Quarter smoothed back her hair. "Don't talk now, Vanity. Sweet Susie's pearls! You are one lucky woman! I never saw a boat blow like that one. What in heaven's name were you doing?"

She couldn't answer. She lifted her arms to Trance and savored the feel of him as he drew her close and held her. Against his chest she heard his pounding heart.

Twenty-Seven

As quickly as possible, Quarter rowed Vanity and Trance to shore. Save for their feeble lanternlight, all was oppressively dark. The light from the flaming, slowly sinking riverboat grew dimmer with each moment.

Trance carried Vanity from the skiff and laid her gently in some tall grass away from the chilly river breeze. She looked so pale, so fragile. As Quarter ran to a clearing nearby where fuel wood was stacked, Trance pulled off his coat and laid it over Vanity's motionless form.

Dropping to his knees beside her, he said a quick, fervent prayer of thanks and then lay against her, hoping to lend her some of his warmth.

Vanity murmured something. Trance stroked her face. "You're safe now. No one's going to hurt you anymore."

She curled against him, and it thrilled him to think that though she was unconscious, she turned to him in her need.

As the *Pacific Princess* went under, Trance closed his eyes. He knew nothing but that he had Vanity back, and this time he would not let her go.

At dawn Vanity awoke to see Trance's blue eyes opened wide and fixed on her face. At once her blood tingled. For ten blessed seconds she knew only that she was with her love, and she basked in his loving gaze.

But then memory returned. Jock...her baby...the explosion in the boilers...

Trance smiled down at her and adjusted his coat higher around her neck. "Feeling better?"

Nearby was a crackling campfire, throwing welcome warmth onto them.

She nodded. "Where are we?"

"A few miles south of Sacramento." He pointed to the serene

surface of the river.

"I don't want to think about my boat. I-I don't care about losing it. I'm glad it's gone."

"What happened?"

She shook her head. "It's not important now—" She tried to sit up. "My pilot!" she said. "He was thrown overboard. Did you see him?"

"No. I wish you'd tell me what you were doing, where you were going—and who was chasing you."

They heard footsteps coming through the dew-damp grasses and looked up to see Quarter emerge from the mists, his dark face grave.

"I reckon you both should see this," he said softly, looking very unlike himself.

"What is it?" Trance asked, climbing to his feet and surveying the tall grasses along the riverbank.

Shaking and weak, Vanity got to her feet, too. Her dress hung in clammy folds around her legs. "Not my pilot?" she asked again, thinking Quarter had found the man drowned on the shore.

Quarter shook his head. "He's all right. I've found someone else."

Vanity's blood ran cold.

They picked their way along the shore to a copse of cottonwoods leaning out over the shallows. Propped against a tree trunk lay a man in a dark cutaway coat. What had been long, lank greasy hair the night before was now a singed stubble. His face and hands were a hideous black. He was breathing with difficulty, his body rigid and twitching with pain.

Gasping, Vanity twisted away. At once she was struggling against Trance's hold, wanting only to run. "Let me go!" she wept, pushing at Trance as he struggled to hold her.

"Who is that?" Trance asked.

Vanity couldn't control her sobs. "Let me go!"

Quarter put his hands on her shoulders, trying to calm her. "Don't fret yourself, Vanity. In the blast he inhaled live steam. His lungs are burned. He hasn't got long. You can't blame yourself. I've done all I can for him, and I...stayed beside him all night, though I can't say why. He's been raving...He would've killed you, Vanity. You've got to believe that he would have."

"Who is that?" Trance demanded.

Vanity wailed, pushing at Trance and finally breaking his hold. She started away, sickened to think of what she'd been forced to do to another human being in order to save herself. And her baby. And Jason.

Quarter's voice was soft and low. "That's my other half brother,

Jock. I swear, I thought I'd killed him five years ago in Natchez. Look at his head. That's where I hit him. He was the meanest, cruelest human being I ever knew. He made my life hell from the day he found out we shared the same daddy." He shook his head. "Jules was the smarter of the two. Jock could never let that rest. He made up for it in plain meanness."

Slowly, Vanity turned. "Jules and Jock were your *brothers*? Oh, my God!"

Quarter nodded. "My father was none other than Gifford Pearson himself, cane planter. My mother was one of his slaves."

"And that's why you stayed with him all those years?" Trance asked.

Quarter nodded, his eyes liquid pools. "They tormented my mother, came close to killing her twice. They swore they'd have her whipped and hanged if I ever revealed my boss man was two men. I did everything they told me to do. When it comes to the thieving, I'm as guilty as they were. I sold all they stole. We did it for years."

Jock laughed harshly. "We...were going to...share you that night, Vanity."

"What does he mean?" Trance asked.

Vanity shuddered. "The night you and I found each other in Natchez Under the Hill, I had just been forced at gunpoint to marry Jules Pearson. A-a while later...I shot him to death...rather than..." She winced and shuddered again. There, she'd confessed, and her guilt and shame melted away.

She finally met Trance's look of astonishment.

"That's why I had to leave for California so quickly, Trance. I might've...I still could be..." A sob caught in her throat. "I'm sorry. I couldn't tell you."

Jock laughed, his burned hands in the air, his body tensing, his blackened face reflecting intense pain. Then abruptly he seized up, arched back...

Vanity twisted away, stumbling to escape the sound of his dying. She was several yards away when Trance rushed to her side and supported her as she crumpled.

"Don't listen. Don't even think about it. It's over! You'll be all right. I'm here, Vanity, if that means anything to you."

She fell against Trance's chest as he crouched beside her. "Take me home, please!"

· · ·

Vanity was startled when she awoke to discover that in spite of all that had happened, she had been able to sleep soundly.

Lying in her own bed, remembering how just a few days ago Jock had invaded her home and her life, she felt as if she was a stranger in someone else's house. The room she had enjoyed for so long was no longer her own.

She slipped from the soft bed and went to throw open the drapes. By the long shadows on the garden, she knew it to be late afternoon. She pulled on a dressing gown and went into the hall, all the while thinking how quiet her house was, and how alien everything seemed. It was as if she'd been gone a long while, and had come back to a changed place.

But she was the one who had changed. She made her way down the stairs, surprised to find how weak she was. She startled one of her Chinese maids laying the table for the evening meal, and when Bullo stood up from the kitchen table, looking worried and contrite, she patted his arm.

"I'm all right. You mustn't worry. I'll provide for you all...if I have anything left." Then she went back through the dining room to the terrace, where she found Quarter and Trance seated and talking.

Trance rose at once and came to her. "You're supposed to be resting!"

She shook her head and smiled. "I want to leave as soon as possible... Trance, don't look so upset. I'll explain, if I can. Quarter, thank you," she said, going into her friend's arms when he stood. "Am I foolish to want to go back to Tenderfoot, if only for a few weeks? I'm so tired and confused. I need time to think."

"After what-all you've been through, a few days away couldn't hurt," Quarter said. "Trance can go with you."

"Would you mind terribly leaving us alone a few minutes?" Vanity asked, smiling apologetically.

Quarter gave Trance a wink, then stepped away toward the dining room doors, nodding his good-byes. "You won't be leaving without telling your friends, will you?"

"Thankfully, that foolishness is over." Vanity sighed, taking the chair Trance held for her.

When they were alone, Vanity tried gathering her thoughts. "Do we need to go through everything, Trance?"

"You agreed to leave town with Jock Pearson when he started blackmailing you about killing Jules in Natchez."

Wearily, she nodded. "It was a stupid thing to do. I'm sorry."

"I guess you had no choice. I won't scold you for not telling someone, least of all me. I've been stupid a few times in my life, too." He shot her a meaningful look.

Smiling weakly, Vanity sighed. "Now that my boat is gone, I'm glad. All my cash was in a carpetbag on it. It was blown to bits in the explosion. All I have left is this house. It should bring a fair price."

"You had insurance, surely."

"It won't pay off when they find the racing wedge was in the valve. I'll tell them it was. Trance, that's not important now. I'm done with it all. I don't know what I'll do with myself after I've rested in Tenderfoot, but I am selling everything I have left, and I'm leaving Sacramento for good. I don't know where I belong. I don't have any idea who I am or what I want to do with the rest of my life. I've been such a complete fool."

"Do you love me, Vanity?"

"Oh, Trance…" She leaned toward him. "Yes, I always have, and I believe it's enough, but…" She felt a rush of disquiet go through her stomach. The damnable morning sickness was upon her again. "This time I want to be very, vary careful. I don't want to make a hasty decision. In the past I've acted so rashly, leaving Tenderfoot, going away to school, going to Cold Crossing, and then Albany…I've never thought anything out. I've just reacted, and Trance, I've been living my life for others. Who knows what I'll want when I finally begin living for myself?"

His eyes held a strange shine. "You're going to learn about yourself as I did after Sally died."

"That's another thing. I can't love you alone now. I must love both you and Jason. He's such a dear little boy. I would not hurt him for anything. Let me go my own way for just a while longer, until I know who I am and what I want. That will give you time to reconsider. Audrey Collins, or someone like her, wouldn't bring scandal to your son."

"I have no interest in her!"

"But I want you to be absolutely sure. I'll go to Tenderfoot. You can meet me there. If you don't, I'll know you realized I was not what you truly wanted. If I'm not waiting…"

"I don't think I can stand to let you go again!" he said.

"But your work! Your future!"

He laughed, running his long fingers through his pale hair. "I have no work, Vanity. I've been a puppet, just like you. I went to work for my father-in-law because it was expected of me, but my heart's not in it. My heart's not in any sort of work that I can think of."

"But what about your dream of going to sea?" she asked, thinking they were like lost children. "I don't want to keep you from that, if it's what you really want."

Trance leaned back in his chair, clasping his hands behind his head. "I dreamed of going to sea because my father didn't want me to go. The only thing I have ever really wanted has been you. I want to marry you and love you all the rest of my days. I'll work hard at anything, if I can be with you. Vanity, we can find our future together. Marry me!"

"I want to give up my mother's name," she said. "I want to be called Mary again."

"Do you want to call me John Travis? Trance is a rebellious boy's name."

Vanity covered her eyes with trembling fingertips. Then she swept her fingers back through her chestnut waves. "I'm afraid to make another mistake. I'm afraid I'll try to be someone I'm not all over again. I imagine a little house with a fence and chickens in the yard, and I ask myself: Is this my dream or someone else's?"

"All we can do is try," Trance whispered.

He rose, crossed the space separating them, and crouched before her, taking her chilled fingers into his warm hands. He pulled her fingertips to his lips and kissed them, his blue eyes warm with hope.

His pale hair fell across his forehead. She brushed it back and then curved her palm along his cheek. He was so very dear. They had suffered so much already. With a single word she could nurture his hope, or shatter it.

"I still feel a very strong need to go to Tenderfoot, if only for a few days. I need to be near my mother. Do as I ask, and join me if you still want me. And bring Jason. Trust me, Trance. I need to do this."

He leaned close and brushed her lips lightly with his. "You look more beautiful to me this minute than you have ever looked before."

"And I love you more than I have ever loved you," she said.

Trance straightened. He was wearing the shirt he'd changed into the night before. "I've left Jason with my sister. It'll take two to three days to fetch him back. I'll see you in Tenderfoot no later than a week from today." He moved toward the dining room doors where the white-lace sheers billowed in the afternoon breeze. He looked suddenly uneasy, as if he was afraid to leave her, afraid that this time when they were so close to being together at last that he would somehow lose her.

He kept himself very straight and gave her a little smile. She felt warmth flood her heart. He was so very dear.

"A week," she whispered.

He nodded once, then strode out, leaving Vanity alone on the terrace. Her hands spread protectively across her belly. She closed her eyes and tried with all her heart to know what she wanted from the future.

Epilogue

A chill wind whispered through the pine tops. The smell of snow was in the air, and the silence of the mountains was so soothing Mary Louise thought she would like to stay in the mountains forever.

Quarter had driven her to Tenderfoot in a hired buckboard wagon with three trunks packed with the few things she had decided to take with her into her new life. They had found her mother's old cabin too dilapidated for habitation, but the man at the Broken Rock had suggested a small house high on the mountainside, and there Mary unloaded and laid out her bedroll.

Now she could look out over the scattered rooftops, remembering her childhood and the serenity she had once known. The echoes from the past were many and pleasant in her mind, the ghosts crossing in front of her gaze capable of drawing tears.

It was now the afternoon of the seventh day. From the moment she awoke to the refreshing morning chill and the slant of clean sunshine coming in the crude window of the little house, she had begun waiting for Trance—John Travis—to join her. It was the biggest gamble of her life.

She had gathered firewood for her campfire and boiled coffee. She had walked down to the saloon to make sure the man there knew she was waiting for company. She'd bought a few things to make stew, and had been simmering it over the fire all afternoon.

From the moment she had arrived, she had not doubted she would be waiting there for John Travis—forever.

Now as the shadows of the mountains crawled across the pines, swallowing the valley and river below in a blue dusk, Mary Louise began to wonder if John Travis would be joining her after all. Would he even be able to find a riverboat that would stop at Tenderfoot Landing?

From the front door she could see the curve of the river below. The echoes and ghosts of the past had been fading all afternoon, leaving her to hear only the rush of the wind and to see the sun-bleached land of her birthplace.

She had known from the moment Quarter drove away, leaving her to her thoughts, that she couldn't live like a hermit. She needed something to do, and her first thought had been to make a new dress.

The dress cloth she'd found in Tenderfoot's remaining dry-goods store was just the pale blue she wanted. She was well along with it and now thinking of sewing little baby dresses. She'd been overtaken by maternal instinct, and laughed at herself.

She knew now she was not likely to learn who she was in a few afternoons alone in the mountains. What she wanted would take a lifetime. And that lifetime should be lived with one she loved, someone who would share the joy of discovery.

She was holding up the new skirt to her waist and realizing she must think of the coming months that would bring change to her shape when she heard the whoop of a stern-wheeler as it came around the bend and edged in toward the overgrown landing.

Every old-timer left in the town shambled from his sunny spot to greet the visitors. Mary Louise felt a welling of happiness at the sight. It was a dear old town. Perhaps her mother hadn't been so wrong after all to finish her life in such a place.

The riverboat *Linnea* lowered her stageplank to the rotting wharf. A man and small boy stood at the white railing, searching the crowd. When they hurried down the stageplank and started toward town, they were lost to sight beyond some boulders and trees.

Mary Louise wanted ever so much to race down the hill to meet them, but since morning she had imagined waiting there at the house, stirring the stew as if her husband and son were coming home after a visit to town. She wanted to know how it felt to be a wife waiting at home.

When many minutes passed and they didn't appear at the curve in the nearly overgrown two-wheel track leading toward the house, she went to the fence, impatient, worried.

Then they appeared, John Travis with his hat off and his wool coat flapping open. Jason rode upon his shoulders, his fingers laced in his father's blond hair and his shoe heels thudding against his father's broad chest.

Mary Louise clapped her hands over her mouth, wanting to hold back her tears of joy. Her eyes brimmed, blurring her vision as John Travis caught sight of her and swung Jason down. Then he and Jason were running, waving, laughing, calling out to her, "Hello! Hello!"

Mary pulled up her skirts and ran, too, forgetting the stew, forgetting the picture she'd wanted to make standing in front of the wind-scoured house.

When John Travis caught her up in his arms and swung her around, she felt giddy and laughed like a child.

"Whatever is cooking, it smells good!" he said, his eyes on her face, taking in her smile and the happiness in her eyes.

They talked of the river trip up from Sacramento, and the amazingly fast sale of her house to a physician from New Jersey. They ate supper on speckled-blue tinware she'd bought at the dry-goods store, and she complained of the price she'd paid.

"We had to stop in Elizabethtown on the way," John Travis said, finishing the soda biscuits and then nodding when Jason wanted to explore. "There's a store for sale there. Stock and all. The idea appealed to me, Van—Mary. It wouldn't have to be forever, but it would be something to try. There's so much we haven't tried yet. Marry me, please! I love you so."

She laughed, and finally moved close to sit in the circle of his arms. "You've had to ask so many times."

Jason darted from the rear of the house. "I heard something in the weeds!" he said excitedly, huddling down between them.

For a beautiful moment the air around them became very still. Mary looked down on the glossy brown head of Trance's—John Travis's—son. The boy was clinging to her leg through her skirts, just as if she was his mother! When he lifted his face and seemed reassured, she smiled at him. "Did you like the store your papa saw in Elizabethtown?" she asked.

"It had a birdcage with a real canary in it! And licorice whips this-s-s long!" He stretched his arms from side to side. Then he darted away to investigate the house.

"He seems at ease with me," Mary whispered, her heart filled with joy.

John Travis turned her face and kissed her, his lips warm and urgent. "I love you," he said. "I want you!"

"I might make a good mother after all."

"The very best," he said, kissing her again.

Mary Louise took a deep breath, her heart suddenly hammering. "Would you like two sons, or a son and daughter?" Her lips trembled as she spoke.

In the distance came a coyote howl that sent Jason pounding back to the safety of Mary's skirts. He looked up at her, his pale face reflecting fright. "I'm not scared!" he said. "Am I, Papa?" he asked, turning to John Travis.

John Travis ruffled his son's hair. "Find us some more firewood. We're staying the night here, and we have to keep your new mama very warm because we love her very much. Then tomorrow we're going to buy a store in Elizabethtown."

Jason whooped with delight and was gone in seconds, scrambling about, gathering twigs and branches, then throwing them into the campfire.

"Vanity—Mary, I want to say something wonderful. I just don't know what. I love you. I don't want anything to happen to you. God, a baby of our own! When will you stop keeping things from me?"

She clung to him and laughed. "I never will again. Hold me, John Travis. I love you."

"We'll never get away from the people we tried to be, you know. It's already a part of us. But we can try new things together. As long as I have you, I know I'll be all I've ever wanted to be. Happy."

"It won't be perfect, or easy," Mary said.

He looked into her eyes, love making him strong and gentle. "But it'll be good, Vanity." And then he was kissing her in that sweet and wonderful way with the enduring love that had sustained them through so much.

There on the steep side of the mountain, with a jumble of dark shacks around them and the leaping warmth of the campfire before them to keep them safe, they welcomed the night with Jason snug between them.

In time there would be a small house and a plain bedroom with a wide spring bed to receive them. There they would make love, and Mary Louise Mackenzie Holloway would bring forth her first child.

John Travis would be there beside her, and Jason would be visiting a neighbor. Always there would be bread to bake and friends to receive, and reading lessons to give, and around them a small town growing.

Perhaps they would travel back to the places they had once been, and perhaps they would remember the people they had once tried to be.

But when the days were all done, nothing would matter but Vanity and Trance in their wide bed, twined together, searching, growing, learning, and loving into the unknown future they would share as Mary Louise and John Travis.

Together they would find their true selves, through love. They would make each other proud.

CACTUS ROSE

In the heat of the southwest, desire is the kindling for two lost souls—and the flame of passion threatens to consume them both.

Rosie Saladay needs to get married—fast. The young widow needs help to protect her late husband's ranch, but no decent woman can live alone with a hired hand. With the wealthy Wesley Morris making a play for her land, Rosie needs a husband or she risks losing everything. So she hangs a sign at the local saloon: "Husband wanted. Apply inside. No conjugal rights."

Delmar Grant is a sucker for a damsel in distress, and even with Rosie's restrictions on "boots under her bed" stated firmly in black and white, something about the lovely widow's plea leaves him unable to turn away her proposal of marriage.

Though neither planned on falling in love, passion ignites between the unlikely couple. But their buried secrets—and enemies with both greed and a grudge—threaten to tear them apart. They'll discover this marriage of convenience may cost them more than they could have ever bargained for.

ANGEL

When her mother dies, fourteen-year-old Angel has no one to turn to but Dalt, a gruff-spoken mountain man with an unsettling leer and a dark past. Angel follows Dalt to the boomtowns of the Colorado territory, where she is thrust into the hardscrabble world of dancehalls, mining camps, and saloons.

From gold mines to gambling palaces, *Angel* tells the story of a girl navigating her way through life, as an orphan, a pioneer, and ultimately a miner's wife and respected madam...a story bound up with the tale of the one man in all the West who dared to love her.

AUTUMN BLAZE

Firemaker is a wild, golden-haired beauty who was taken from her home as a baby and raised by a Comanche tribe. Carter Machesney is the handsome Texas Ranger charged with finding her, and reacquainting her with the life she never really knew.

Though they speak in different tongues, the instant flare of passion between Firemaker and Carter is a language both can speak, and their love is one that bridges both worlds.

HURRICANE SWEEP

Hurricane Sweep spans three generations of women—three generations of strife, heartbreak, and determination.

Florie is a delicate Southern belle who must flee north to escape her family's cruelty, only to endure the torment of both harsh winters and a sadistic husband. Loraine, Florie's beautiful and impulsive daughter, bares her body to the wrong man, yet hides her heart from the right one. And Jolie, Florie's pampered granddaughter, finds herself in the center of the whirlwind of her family's secrets.

Each woman is caught in a bitter struggle between power and pride, searching for a love great enough to obliterate generations of buried dreams and broken hearts.

KISS OF GOLD

From England to an isolated Colorado mining town, Daisie Browning yearns to find her lost father—the last thing she expects to find is love. Until, stranded, robbed, and beset by swindlers, she reluctantly accepts the help of the handsome and rakish Tyler Reede, all the while resisting his advances.

But soon Daisie finds herself drawn to Tyler, and she'll discover that almost everything she's been looking for can be found in his passionate embrace.

SNOWS OF CRAGGMOOR

When Merri Glenden's aunt died, she took many deep, dark secrets to the grave. But the one thing Aunt Coral couldn't keep hidden was the existence of Merri's living relatives, including a cousin who shares Merri's name. Determined to connect with a family she never knew but has always craved, Merri travels to Colorado to seek out her kin.

Upon her arrival at the foreboding Craggmoor—the mansion built by her mining tycoon great-grandfather—Merri finds herself surrounded by antagonistic strangers rather than the welcoming relations she'd hoped for.

Soon she discovers there is no one in the old house whom she can trust...no one but the handsome Garth Favor, who vows to help her unveil her family's secrets once and for all, no matter the cost.

SUMMERSEA

Betz Witherspoon isn't looking forward to the long, hot summer ahead. Stuck at a high-class resort with her feisty young charge, Betz only decides enduring her precocious heiress's mischief might be worth it when she meets the handsome and mysterious Adam Teague.

Stealing away to the resort's most secluded spots, the summer's heat pales against the blaze of passion between Betz and Adam. But Betz finds her scorching romance beginning to fizzle as puzzling events threaten the future of her charge. To survive the season, Betz will have to trust the enigmatic Adam...and her own heart.

SWEET WHISPERS

Seeking a new start, Sadie Evans settles in Warren Bluffs with hopes of leaving her past behind. She finds her fresh start in the small town, in her new home and new job, but also in the safe and passionate embrace of handsome deputy sheriff, Jim Warren.

But just when it seems as if Sadie's wish for a new life has been granted, secrets she meant to keep buried forever return to haunt her. Once again, she's scorned by the very town she has come to love—so Sadie must pin her hopes on Jim Warren's heart turning out to be the only home she'll ever need.

TIMBERHILL

When Carolyn Adams Clure returns to her family estate, Timberhill, she's there to face her nightmares, solve the mystery of her parents' dark past, and clear her father's name once and for all. Almost upon arrival, however, she is swept up into a maelstrom of fear, intrigue, and, most alarmingly, love.

In a horrifying but intriguing development for Carolyn, cult-like events begin to unfold in her midst and, before long, she finds both her life and her heart at stake.

9 781682 300916